Off the Record

Off the Record

JOE JOYCE

HEINEMANN : LONDON

William Heinemann Ltd
Michelin House, 81 Fulham Road, London SW3 6RB
LONDON   MELBOURNE   AUCKLAND

First published in Great Britain 1989
Copyright © 1989 by Joe Joyce

British Library Cataloguing-in-Publication Data

Joyce, Joe, *1947*–
    Off the record.
    I. Title
    823'.914 [F]

ISBN 0 434 37068 1

Photoset and printed in Great Britain
by Redwood Burn Limited, Trowbridge, Wiltshire

For Catherine and Joanna

Prologue

Tears swelled up in his eyes and the wind whipped them away and replaced them again. He blinked and he saw the waves chop across the bay and splay onto the sloped butt of the pier beneath him. Clouds tinged a raw red by the unseen sun hurled towards him like accusations.

His mind was as numb as the cold stone of the pier wall beneath his arms. He was aware only that the night was over, the time for thinking gone. Long gone.

He blinked again and he saw the gun lying on the granite wall and felt it warm the palm of his outstretched hand. You've got to do it, his mind said calmly from a distance, from somewhere out by his hand. There's no other way.

His hand raised and steadied the gun into the wind and he looked down the short barrel. It blotted out a small arc of the raging sea and he concentrated on the sector of black calm in the hope that it would offer an answer. That the gun could still the turmoil in his mind and block out the elements. But the wind whistled over its sight and pushed at his face, taunting.

Another sound snagged at the edge of his hearing. He blinked as though to clear his ears as well and he heard it again, a harsh snapping that came and went on some tide of its own. Instinctively, he swung from the pier wall and a large black dog was thundering towards him, its jaws working in rhythm with its legs.

The long jaws came closer and the barking grew louder and subdued the wind and the waves. He looked at the pointed nose and red eyes and he choked on a sudden panic. The bastard, he thought and he jerked the trigger. Again and again and again.

The animal wavered and its barking turned into an anguished croak. Its front legs folded and its chest and head cracked onto the ground and skidded along the concrete. A spot of white fur on its shoulder grew dark and matted and blood spat in large globules from its slack jaws with every used breath. It splashed on the concrete.

The fucker, he sobbed aloud in horror.

A wave of nausea broke from his stomach and he almost gagged on vomit. It subsided and a surge of hot self-pity took its place. Now look what he's made me do, he thought angrily. Hasn't he done enough already? Why won't he leave me alone?

He swallowed and glanced around suddenly in another instinctive gesture of self-preservation. The enclosed water of the harbour rose and fell gently and the wind ruffled its surface with barely touching brush-strokes. The pier was empty. Far away, a cluster of cars chased each other, unheeded and unheeding, and the city crouched low under the hills.

His attention swivelled back reluctantly to the dying dog and he felt sick again at the sight of its struggling chest and trembling legs. The wind dropped suddenly, gathering its breath, and he heard the dog whimper. Please die, he pleaded. Please.

Tears swelled up in his eyes and hung there, unable to break. His body shuddered like the dying dog's and he gripped the gun tighter and turned away.

He'll pay for this, he thought. For all of it.

One

The train built up a semblance of speed and bucked and rattled as it shot across the level crossing and the bay opened out beside him. Hard grey sand rippled away to the distant sea, a thin blue line that merged with the hard blue of the sky. Off to the right the spires of Dun Laoghaire rose like burned pines from a plain.

Seamus Ryle blinked at the harsh light and the sudden open spaces after the narrow city streets. This is a waste of time, he thought, but what the hell: it was better than sitting in the deserted newsroom or struggling over the damn feature. The sun was out and a breath of fresh air was just what he needed.

Ryle had ignored the phone until its insistence broke through his lethargy. The caller had the querulous accent of a true Dubliner and asked if he was the editor. Ryle grunted a half-lie of assent: there was no one around to challenge his claim.

'D'you want a story?' the man asked in a conspiratorial tone and then raised his voice to a satisfied note. 'There's a maniac running amok with a gun out here.'

'Where?'

'In Dun Laoghaire. He's shot a dog. Stone dead.'

'He's shot a dog,' Ryle repeated.

'That's what I said.' The man sounded querulous again. 'He riddled the dog on the pier and God knows who he'll do next.'

'Is he still there? With the smoking gun?' Ryle smiled, unable to resist the cliched image.

'No, he's gone into hiding. There's a big search on, guards everywhere.'

'Okay, we'll look into it,' Ryle said without enthusiasm. What would they come up with next, the great public who had nothing better to do than pester newspapers at this unearthly hour of the morning? 'Thanks for calling.'

'By the way,' the man said, 'I hear you pay for tip-offs.'

'Give me your name and address,' Ryle sighed. He'd be lucky, he thought while he jotted down the details.

Ryle hung up, strode over to the radio and yawned and stretched his long body while he waited for the news headlines. His narrow face was pale but held the hint of an interested smile that made him look younger that his thirty-four years. He had an air of plausibility that still worked on strangers and he was wearing a short leather jacket, faded blue jeans and desert boots.

A man had been shot dead in Belfast by someone who put a ladder up to his bedroom window, smashed the glass and fired at him in bed; he had not been named yet. The Labour Court was starting talks on a dairy strike; the government had been accused of doing nothing to stop the spiralling cost of living; a train had crashed in France and the weather would be bright and cold with frost later. There was no mention of a gunman running amok in Dun Laoghaire.

Ryle rolled a sheet of paper into his typewriter and listed the news items. He wondered idly if the latest victim in Belfast had been asleep when he was shot or if he had woken up when his bedroom window exploded, struggling to consciousness when he was hit. A shot dog was hardly news compared to that. Yet it might turn out to be an off-beat story or even a genuine hard-nosed story if there really was a gunman at large. Anyway, he hadn't had a walk on Dun Laoghaire pier for months.

He fed another sheet of paper into the typewriter and tapped out a note for the news editor. 'Gone to Dun Laoghaire to check tip-off about a sniper.' Ryle rocked his chair back on its legs and cupped his hands behind his ginger head.

The news room had the seedy air of a night-club thrown open to the morning after's daylight. Old press releases, newspaper cuttings and political speeches were piled on desks, neatly preserved by cleaners in the mistaken belief that yesterday's news was still valuable. But the attempt at tidiness only showed up the seediness. A splinter of weak sunshine reached through the valley of the buildings behind and lit on a scuffed desk top, making the dust dance.

Why not, Ryle thought and let his chair fall forward. He added another line to his memo: 'otherwise, all quiet'.

The ancient train coasted into the station as though exhausted by its efforts. Ryle zipped up his parka and walked past the big bolted gates of the car ferry terminal and the self-satisfied façades of the yacht clubs and the pier stretched before him like a beckoning finger. It was deserted but for a distant figure approaching the lighthouse at its tip. There was no sign of policemen, dead dogs or snipers.

He wasn't surprised, he didn't seriously expect anything much to come of this. The journey was more a token of his revolt against the boring jobs he'd been give recently. If the news editor genuinely wanted him to show initiative he could hardly complain. He set off along the upper level, washed clean by recent rain, and wrapped his coat closer as he emerged from the shelter of a high wall and the wind hurled in from the east across Scotsman's Bay and snatched at his breath. Halfway down the pier he met the figure he had seen near the lighthouse coming back. Ryle had almost passed him when he realised he was a harbour policeman.

'Yes,' the policeman nodded in reply to his query. 'It was a Doberman, something like that.'

'What happened?'

'I don't know,' the policeman shrugged, 'I've just come on duty. Someone shot him back there.' The policeman pointed back towards the head of the pier and Ryle turned and walked with him.

'What was it all about?'

'No idea. The guards are looking into it. They'd be able to tell you more.'

They walked in silence until the policeman waved his hand. 'It was somewhere along here,' he said. Ryle looked at the wet ground but there was nothing to be seen. In front of them the wind set the perspex sheets of a shelter's roof chattering like a mechanical aviary.

'Where's the dog gone?'

'To the dump, I suppose. The corporation took it away.'

Ryle strolled on to the town centre and found the alleyway to the garda station. He explained what he wanted to a jovial, middle-aged garda.

'Well now,' the garda smiled, 'isn't there enough news in the country without you worrying about dead dogs?'

'It might be a sort of man-bites-dog story,' Ryle smiled back. 'It's not news if a dog bites a man but it is if a man bites a dog.'

'It'd be even bigger news if the dog shot the man,' the garda laughed.

'You're right. But who shot the dog?'

'We don't know.'

'But you're looking for the gunman?'

'Inquiries are continuing.'

'Did anyone see it?'

'The woman who reported it. She owned the dog.'

'She was there?'

'Yes.'

'Where would I find her?'

The garda looked at him speculatively for a moment, then went away and consulted something on a desk. He returned to the hatch and said, 'Ethel Barnes. Miss,' and added an address. Ryle rooted in an inside pocket, found an envelope and noted them.

'If you want any official comment you'd better get on to the press office,' the garda warned at the sight of his pen.

'Sure,' Ryle replied. 'And they'll probably laugh at me too.'

The street was close by, a terraced cul-de-sac of once comfortable Victorian houses broken up into offices and bedsitters. The number was near the top of the road and Ryle opened the gate and climbed the steps to the front door. There were two bells with name tags but neither said Barnes and neither answered his rings. Ryle went back down the steps and around to the basement door underneath.

He heard nothing as he pushed the bell and was about to turn away when the door was opened noiselessly by a woman wearing a heavy tweed coat. She was tall, almost his own height of just over six feet, and had grey hair tied tightly in a bun.

'Miss Barnes?'

She nodded. She could be anything between fifty and seventy, Ryle reckoned while he explained who he was. 'It won't take long,' he concluded, 'I won't delay you.'

'I'm not going anywhere.' She stood back to let him enter and waved a hand behind her and said, 'back, David'. She led him into a room that was heavy with heat and dark furniture which cluttered the corners and walls and cramped the space. An electric heater was on full in the middle of the floor. A terrier sniffed around Ryle's legs and clambered onto a bean bag while Ryle took the armchair Miss Barnes indicated.

Ethel Barnes sat down on a faded couch, wrapped her coat around her and held it tight with folded arms. 'It all happened so suddenly.' She paused and glanced at Ryle then away again. 'That's what people always say, isn't it?'

'What happened?' he prompted.

'I was taking the dogs for their morning walk down the pier. Little David' – she looked at the dozing terrier – 'and Goliath. That was a joke, you know, his name. We had David first and when we got Goliath he seemed so big, well, we called him Goliath.'

'He was a Doberman?'

'Partially. Of mixed parentage, I would have said.' She paused. 'He looked somewhat fierce, I suppose. Perhaps that's why . . . '

'How did it happen?'

'He was standing by the pier wall and he just shot Goliath when he stopped beside him. I suppose he had been there all the time but I didn't notice him until . . . it happened.'

'Can you describe him?'

'Not very well.' She gestured vaguely. 'About average height, dark hair. He was leaning on the pier wall. It's quite high along there and he was resting his arms on the top of the wall.'

'Did you see the gun?'

She nodded. 'It was a little thing really. A revolver, I suppose. I think he had it in his hand before, before he fired. I mean he was holding it before Goliath stopped.'

'Had you ever seen the man before?'

She shook her head. 'Goliath and David were racing up and down, full of energy, barking. They were being playful but he may have thought Goliath was going to attack him. That's why we got him, you know, as a guard dog. All the burglaries . . . '

She stopped and stared into the distance. Ryle began to wonder if her languid appearance and speech was as normal as he had assumed. 'Did he say anything?' he persisted.

'No. He just turned from the wall and shot Goliath.'

'How many shots did he fire?'

'I don't know. I didn't hear anything. At least I don't remember. I just saw Goliath fall, stagger and fall, and he stopped barking.' She turned her gaze back to Ryle but did not seem to see him. 'I may have screamed and I ran. I don't know. The next thing I remember I was crossing the road and a car braked to avoid me. The driver shouted abuse – I must have run out in front of him but I don't remember.'

'It must have been a very frightening experience,' Ryle said. She folded her arms tighter and stared at the electric heater and shivered. Ryle was perspiring.

'What did the police say?'

'They were polite but not too interested. They have so much else to concern them, I suppose. Much more important matters than the death of a dog.' Her voice wavered. 'Poor Goliath.'

Ryle said nothing and, after a moment, the woman began talking again, talking about her life and her family and its slumped fortunes. She stared into the unreal flickers of the plastic coals on the heater and he watched her with growing trepidation. Shit, he thought, she's flipped, she's in shock.

She calmly chronicled the descent of her family from life in an eight-bedroom house with servants in Ballsbridge to her own lonely existence in the basement, the servants' quarters of what had once been the family's summer home, while the upstairs was rented out in flats. Totally oblivious to Ryle's presence, she went on about the amount of maintenance work the house required and how its cost swallowed up almost all the rent she received from the tenants upstairs.

'Maybe you should see your doctor,' Ryle offered tentatively when she paused. 'It must have been a very frightening experience.'

'Yes,' she said quietly, still staring at the dull red glow rotating on top of the heater.

'Would you like me to call him for you?'

'Her.'

'Her.'

'No, thank you.' She pulled her gaze away from the fire and stood up. 'I shall be all right.'

She showed him to the door. 'I'm sorry I could not help you any more,' she said formally, without meaning.

'Sorry for intruding,' he said. 'Thanks for your help.' She shut the door while he was wondering if he should say something more.

Ryle climbed back to the street and walked down to the railings where the road ended abruptly, pointing out over the pier like another level that someone had thought better of building. A container ship was heading out to sea, looking ridiculously top-heavy with its stacks of outsize boxes. Across the bay the brown hill of Howth squatted like a huge mud pile left to sink slowly into the water. After the basement gloom his eyes ached from the brightness and the wind turned the perspiration on his back into its own sleety cold. He shivered.

Fuck it, he thought, you're not a social worker. Just get the story. But what was the story? Some lunatic had shot a dog because it annoyed him with its barking. Not much of a story, unless it was the start of a campaign by an anti-dog group. The fantasy took hold of his imagination: hit squads in balaclava masks ambushing dogs, releasing long rhetorical statements about freeing the population from the tyranny of turds.

He grimaced into the wind and a memory of childhood walks along the pier, a Sunday afternoon ritual, came to him. It was always crowded and the sun always seemed to shine. Although his father would always say – part of the ritual – that it was about to rain if you could see Howth clearly. And add that if you couldn't see it then it must be raining already.

He remembered, more recently, a leaden hot evening with Breda pushing the pram along the pier, trying to outpace her anger, while a motor boat tut-tutted across the harbour and the halyards of the moored yachts tolled a dirge on their metal masts.

It's going to rain, he decided. Or snow. His mind's eye went back to the elderly woman in her heavy coat shivering in her

9

overheated room. She didn't want the pointless sympathy of some news hack, he thought. Nobody ever did: haven't you learned anything in the past fifteen years? He looked at his watch and turned back to the town centre in search of a telephone.

The third one worked and he kept the door ajar to relieve the stench of urine. Harry Stacy, the news editor, answered on the first ring. 'What's all this shit about snipers?' he roared. 'Nobody's heard anything about it.'

'The story hasn't quite worked out.'

'Tell me,' Stacy suggested with theatrical patience. Ryle told him what had happened without embellishment. 'A dog,' the news editor groaned. 'You've spent three hours chasing a dog killer?'

'It might have made a story.'

'And you keep moaning that I never give you any decent stories. How the hell can I when you go skiving off like this?'

'It was a tip-off. It was worth . . . '

'Bullshit. Get back here. No, wait.' Stacy turned away to ask somebody something. 'Go down to the central criminal court. The jury's just gone out in a murder trial. I want a full story, not two paragraphs of a verdict. The background, the whole tale.'

'But I don't know anything about the case.'

'Find out. That's what you're paid for. Not for chasing off after harebrained stories.' Ryle began to argue but Stacy cut him short. 'If you're lucky you'll have plenty of time. The jury'll stay out till midnight.' The news editor hung up.

Ryle cursed. You can't win arguments with news editors or God, he muttered sourly and cursed himself for not bringing his car as he went in search of a bus.

The news room was back in its element, alive with light and sound and purpose. Typewriters clacked in uneven bursts; people hurried about in shirt sleeves; a television blared out a news bulletin and nobody took any notice. The atmosphere crackled with the extra buzz of an out of the ordinary story.

Ryle did not notice. The long hours of drink and boredom waiting for the jury to make up its mind had dulled his senses and left him irritable. It had been a long day and all a waste of time.

Stacy stood behind the news desk shuffling through a sheaf of copy paper and talking on the phone at the same time. Short and tubby, he constantly twitched away a lock of greying hair that fell over his right eye. He had been the paper's hotshot reporter in his day and was now its successful news editor. No longer required to prove anything to anyone, he simply enjoyed his job. His expression hardened when he saw Ryle approach.

'Congratulations,' he snapped, 'you've done it again.'

'The jury's only just come back,' Ryle said defensively. 'They took eight hours to decide they couldn't agree.'

'You missed the story.' Stacy waved him away for a moment and listened to the phone. Ryle waited dully, not knowing what he was talking about. 'Do a par about a retrial,' Stacy said.

'What about the background? Don't you want it?'

'Nobody wants background without a guilty verdict,' Stacy said slowly and put down the phone. 'Anyway,' he smiled an unfriendly smile, 'everything's been overtaken by the real story. The one you missed.'

Ryle stared at him and the news editor waited while his accusation sank in. A sickly dread settled on Ryle. 'What story?' he muttered at last.

The news editor put his hand on his hips and glared at him. 'The body that was floating in Dun Laoghaire harbour. While you were ambling about looking for dead dogs.'

'What?' Ryle's surprise was like a complimentary pat on the head to Stacy. 'Shot?'

The news editor shook his head. 'No, the dog didn't do it.' Someone behind Ryle sniggered loudly. 'But do you know whose body it was?'

'You're going to tell me,' Ryle said sourly.

'Maurice F. Clark.' Stacy paused. 'You do know who Maurice F. Clark is?'

Ryle nodded absently. Clark was a politician, a member of the governing party. Still only a backbencher, he had been marked out as one who was going far, a possible future party leader and Taoiseach. He had been in the Dáil a mere three years but his carefully cultivated concerns and his style put him head and shoulders above his colleagues. His clean-cut good looks and his age helped: he was thirty-five.

'He's been shot?'

Stacy shook his head impatiently. 'Have you been drinking all day?' Ryle began to protest but the news editor silenced him with a look. 'We think he drowned,' he added. 'The real question is how – and why?'

'Why?'

'That's what I want to know,' Stacy growled. 'And you're not helping me find out.'

'You want me to go back out there?' Ryle offered, feeling like he was already struggling with a hangover.

'For what? To see if Dun Laoghaire harbour is still there?'

'There might be a connection. With the dog.'

Stacy looked at him closely and shrugged. 'Two pars on the murder retrial. We're tight for space.'

Ryle was about to argue but Stacy snapped 'Now' and picked up a phone. Ryle sat down at his desk, pulled over a typewriter and looked into its innards. So much for the New Year's resolutions, he thought. But how was I to know?

He rattled off three paragraphs with scarcely a pause, dropped the story on the news desk and went over to the basket where copies of earlier reports were kept. None of the stories on Clark's death were there and he saw them in front of Stacy. Ryle drifted over to a group gathering around the television set as the hyped-up title sequence of a current affairs programme began.

'It could happen to a bishop,' a colleague sympathised.

Ryle nodded. But it's the last thing I need right now, he told himself, if I'm ever to get out of this rut.

Clark's features filled the screen, an identikit of the youthful successful politician with his well-groomed brown hair, direct gaze and resolute chin. The titles swivelled and danced over his picture and the presenter declared that the finding of his dead body had sent a shock through the political system. But it was soon apparent that the programme knew nothing more than the bare details of the discovery. Behind the sonorous script, however, was the unmentioned but identifiable hint of an unspecified political scandal.

Ryle wandered back to the news desk and leafed through the library cuttings on Clark: none had had time to yellow with age. There were details of his previous occupation as a lecturer in politics, picture captions from his election victory, and a generalised interview in which he denied that his knowledge of the theory put him above his colleagues in the practice of the art. But it did: at least, his style of calm confidence and gentle self-denigration did. He had been pacing himself perfectly, Ryle thought as he flicked through the file, not too pushy but building up an uncontentious public profile and getting all the right kind of mentions.

'Well?' the news editor tipped back his chair, propped the back of his head in his hands and looked at Ryle.

Ryle shrugged. 'I missed the story.'

'We should have a talk one of these days.'

Ryle nodded glumly.

'Where are you living now?' Ryle looked surprised and Stacy added, 'I rang your number this morning and got a frosty answer. From a woman who didn't seem too happy to be reminded of you.'

'In a flat.'

'You'd better give me the new number.'

Ryle walked around the desk to a typewritten list pinned to the wall, took out his pen and wrote a new phone number opposite his name. His pen hovered over the old number but he left it untouched.

Stacy watched him. 'Your wife, was it?'

Ryle turned back to face him. 'There might be a connection with the dog,' he said.

Stacy accepted the change of subject with a barely perceptible raising of his eyes. 'It wasn't his, was it?'

'No.'

'Any connection with the owner?'

'Doubt it. And she said she didn't recognise the killer.'

'Go on home,' Stacy grunted and added without conviction, 'We'll take a look at it again tomorrow.'

Outside, it was freezing hard and the city looked crisp. A stream of ice lined the gutters and spread treacherous traps onto the footpaths. A perfectly rounded moon glared coldly down side streets as Ryle walked to his bus stop and joined a short straggle of restless people.

January is a wonderful month, he thought bitterly as he watched his breath balloon before him.

Two

Crises made Mike Erlanger calm and he was totally at ease as he pulled the heavy door behind him and stepped down to the gravel driveway. He glanced back at the bedroom window where Becky stood wrapped in the duvet and smiled up to her. She winked and pushed a hand out between the folds of the quilt and waggled her fingers. Used to New England winters, she was defeated by the seeping damp of the Irish climate which forced her to huddle in one room of the large old house surrounded by heaters and listening to the equally defeated gurgling of the central heating.

Erlanger had on a dark pin-stripe suit and no overcoat.

The engine fired instantly and he let the car crunch slowly down the driveway. He stopped to open the gate, tapped the metal plaque which warned 'Beware of the dog' in a semi-superstitious gesture and grunted 'bow wow'. If there ever had been a dog, it wasn't there now and wasn't listed on the landlord's detailed inventory. Otherwise, it would undoubtedly have added another few pounds to the already exorbitant rent, he thought.

He drove through, checked the road and turned inland over the shoulder of Killiney Hill and headed for Dublin. On the radio an announcer said it was eight o'clock and time for the news. The main item was the death of Maurice Clark: the results of an autopsy were expected to be known today, the news reader said, before going back over the discovery of Clark's body the previous evening.

Erlanger listened for every nuance. He had learned of Clark's death in a headline an hour earlier, had quickly shrugged off his initial surprise and begun to tease out all the possible implications. The news was already a well-established fact in his mind, obliterating almost all memories of Clark as an individual. Erlanger never wasted time on unalterable facts.

Traffic was still light in the semi-darkness and he drove quickly, his attention focused on the radio. A political commentator gave a professional rundown of the consequences for the Government, already unpopular for its economic restrictions and, with the new year, beginning to feel the first stirrings of pressure for a general election. The Dáil was about to resume after its Christmas break and the prospect of a by-election promised to fuel political nervousness.

The bulletin moved on to other stories from Northern Ireland and Erlanger turned it off as he drove down the ramp into an underground car park and circled over to his space. He took a briefcase from behind his seat and climbed the steps to the street to buy the newspapers.

Becky was still standing by the bedroom window, cocooned in the duvet and watching the sun rise and dilute a bank of grey fog to off-white, when a dirty blue Avenger wound slowly up the drive. She stepped out of sight and watched as two men got out and rang the door bell.

When she opened the door they showed no surprise at her state of dress and the older of the two asked for Michael J. Erlanger, pronouncing each syllable of the surname separately.

'He's not here,' she said. 'I'm Mrs Erlanger. Can I help you?'

'Police,' he said, holding up a small plastic card. 'A routine matter. Your husband might be able to help us.'

The man looked like he had been up all night and a faint smell of stale whiskey off his breath made her feel slightly nauseous.

'You've just missed him. He's gone to work.'

The man nodded.

'I can give you his phone number,' she volunteered.

'It's all right,' the detective said. 'We can contact him again.'

She watched them go then climbed up the elegant stairs, got back into bed and picked up the phone. Erlanger was opening the main door to his office when the phone on his desk began to ring.

'They've been,' Becky told him. 'Two sleazy-looking characters. In plain clothes.'

'They say anything?'

'Wanted to talk to you. That's all. They'll be there in twenty minutes if they've gone directly.'

Erlanger hung up, straightened himself up to his full six foot two inches and turned around slowly, his eyes raking over everything in the room as methodically as a prospective buyer. His gaze stopped at a filing cabinet whose wooden veneer matched the room's panelling. He looked at it speculatively and then shook his head – there was nothing in there.

He walked out to his secretary's office and looked around again. Her desk was empty but for a hooded electric typewriter and a telephone. In a corner, two comfortable chairs were placed on either side of a coffee table carrying a scattering of Irish and American business magazines. Nearby, a copper-coloured model of a drilling rig stood in a perspex case on top of a pedestal.

Erlanger walked back to his desk, sat down and pulled out a large diary from a drawer. It opened at today's date and he noted that he had two appointments, one for lunch with the junior Minister for Justice. He smiled at the prospect of the cops seeing him lunching with one of their masters: who would be most embarrassed, he wondered, if they turned up at the restaurant to talk to him?

He leafed back through the book, back to the start of the year, and then took out the previous year's diary, methodically reading each entry. He had gone back to early December before he found the name Maurice Clark. Shelbourne Hotel 4 pm, the entry said. Erlanger remembered them sitting in a corner of the club-like hotel lounge among the crowds of resting shoppers and the usual reclining businessmen about town. He had been businesslike, smothering his success in a tough man-of-the-world exterior. Clark had been transparent, aggressive at first but he had capitulated quickly and accepted reality. After a while, he no longer bothered to hide his dejection.

Erlanger stared at the entry, wondering about the set of imponderables created by the new situation. Precautions always paid off, he thought, it was always worth putting your defences in place. Unless his cautious pre-planning was about to rebound on him. It was to early to tell.

He continued to turn back the pages while he waited.

*   *   *

Jim Whelan put down the phone and shuffled back along the hall to the kitchen. His wife looked up and he shook his head once and slumped onto a stool at the breakfast counter.

'Nobody knows anything.' He jammed his hands into the pockets of his dressing gown and stared through the window. A patch of limp grass led down to a line of skeletal shrubs but he didn't see the back garden. Maura Whelan clattered dishes into the sink and let water gush over them.

He turned suddenly to glance at his watch. 'The news,' he said, 'we've missed it.'

'There was nothing new,' she said. 'It was the same as the last one.'

He shook his head in bewilderment. 'It's incredible,' he sighed.

'Are you finished?' She took hold of a plate and he shifted his stare to the remains of his breakfast and nodded.

'I was supposed to see him in Leinster House today.'

'What about?' She slid the dishes into the sink.

'Nothing in particular.' He shrugged. 'He said the other night he'd see me there today. That he wouldn't be around yesterday. He was taking the day off. God.'

She stopped in mid-action and glanced around at him with suds drooping from her wrists. His thinning hair stood up in an erratic point, his eyes were raw with tiredness and his fattening jowls were shaded with brown stubble. He was slouched into a flabby oval ball shape, running directly from angular youth to middle-aged sedentary seed. He looked like the opening sequence of a television advertisement for an invigorating breakfast cereal. Bloody politics, she thought.

'Were you talking to him?' he looked back at her.

'Me?'

'At the party?'

'You know I didn't talk to Maurice.' She turned back to the sink and pulled out the stopper. The water ran away in a frenzied gurgle.

'I don't know why you never liked him.'

'I didn't dislike him,' she said with a hint of defensiveness. 'I never thought it was fair, that's all. The way he was promoted above other people who had better claims on advancement than he had.'

'He wasn't promoted,' he said automatically.

'He was about to be. Leapfrogged over others.'

'Me, you mean.' He raised his chin in an exasperated gesture. They'd been through all this before.

'Yes, you,' Maura said, drying her hands vigorously and warming to her theme. 'You've put in the work, endless hours of it for six, seven years. At everyone's beck and call, all hours of the day and night. All for the party.'

'And for us. For myself,' he amended quickly.

'And he comes along out of nowhere,' she ignored him, 'the golden-haired boy, and pushes you into the background. Blocks off your and everyone else's chances.'

'It isn't like that.'

'That's what it looks like,' she said, more snappishly than she meant to sound.

'He was my best friend.'

'He wasn't much of a friend until he got into politics himself,' she snorted. 'I don't remember him doing anything to get you elected. But he latched onto you pretty quickly once he got in himself. He was using you. Picking your brains, relying on your experience, taking anything he could get. He was a sly opportunist.'

She stopped suddenly and saw the surprise and hurt in his eyes. Damn, she thought, but she could not shake off an irrational suspicion that Clark's death was another of his publicity generating stunts. Nor her continuing irritation at seeing her husband play second fiddle to Clark. 'I'm sorry.' She turned away and bent down to load dried plates into a cupboard. 'I can't change how I feel just because he's dead.'

Whelan turned away too and looked out the window. Small birds took off in a frantic flurry from a raised table in the next door garden and he watched them scatter from an invisible threat into a clump of stunted trees. He yawned.

He was more exhausted mentally than physically after a restless night trying to make sense of the staggering news. He had wandered shocked around the sleeping house for hours but it didn't make any sense, couldn't make any sense.

'He seemed fine at the party,' he said.

Maura slammed the door of the cupboard, irritable now at her own irritation. She faced him with her hands on her hips, her upset sharpening her pointed features. 'Are you going to mope around here all day?'

He looked at her in surprise, confused by her aggression.

'I'm sorry he's dead, too,' she said. 'I didn't like him much but I didn't want him dead either. Okay?' She turned away. 'Life goes on.'

'My best friend's been murdered,' he said.

'Murdered?' She turned back. 'What do you mean murdered?'

'Killed,' he said vaguely.

'Why?' She stared at him.

'I don't know. I can't think of a single reason.'

She stared at him for a moment, then sighed and left the room. Yes, he thought and repeated to himself the word that had muddled his mind all night. Murdered.

Inspector William Devane knocked curtly on the door and walked in without waiting for an answer. The Chief Superintendent was seated by the window, a file open on his desk. He squinted over his glasses and nodded towards the only other chair. Devane took a packet of Sweet Afton from the pocket of his raincoat and lit a cigarette.

The Chief Superintendent grimaced with distaste as the smoke eddied across the desk but continued reading. Devane looked out the window at the patch of grass, still crusted with the night's frost, beneath the high walls of Dublin Castle. He had a lugubrious face that sagged down into heavy jowls and always looked rumpled – passers-by seeing him coming out of a police station would assume, if they noticed him at all, that he was a back-street car-dealer who had been helping with inquiries into something shady. He felt tired and he waited without curiosity for what he knew was coming.

The Chief Superintendent folded his reading glasses and put them to one side. 'Right,' he said, joining his hands on the buff-coloured file. 'This is the sort of case we need like a hole in the head. Trouble, trouble and more trouble.'

'That's our business.' Devane gave a fleeting smile that looked more like a grimace at a sudden stomach upset.

'Yes, well, I don't need to tell you about its sensitivity. There's a lot of interest, inside the force and – ' he paused ' – elsewhere. We need to keep it as tight as possible. A short, sharp and conclusive investigation.'

Devane nodded automatically and looked around for an ashtray. There was none in sight and he flicked the ash into a metal bin. His superior did not appear to notice.

'Some politicians are already unhappy about your methods,' the Chief said. 'They don't like you calling round to their homes to question them. Makes them feel like criminals, apparently.'

Devane searched his face for any trace of humour but, as usual, found none. 'Has to be done,' he shrugged. 'We have to talk to everyone who met Clark the night before he died. It just so happens that that includes a lot of his political friends. Nearly half the Dáil by the looks of it.'

'I know. But they don't like you calling at their houses at all hours. They'd prefer you to talk to them in their offices.'

'I thought that'd make them more uneasy. Having me wandering around Leinster House.'

'Apparently not. Anyhow there's hardly any need to talk to everyone who knew him.' The Chief made a placatory gesture and looked directly at Devane. 'But I'm not telling you how to run the investigation, just passing on information. What have you got?'

'Nothing conclusive yet. Clark seems to have drowned. No signs of violence or a struggle. But he was armed and shot the dog, probably just before he died. Which gives us an approximate time of death.'

'Witnesses?'

'Only the dog's owner.'

Devane shook his head. 'The mailboat should have been leaving about that time but its schedule was disrupted by the storms last week and it wasn't in Dun Laoghaire at all.'

The Chief Superintendent sat back and looked out the window for a moment. 'What do you think?' he asked. 'Any evidence of foul play?' Devane shook his head.

'If he wanted to kill himself why would he choose drowning?' the Chief mused. 'He could have shot himself. Would have been preferable. Quicker.' Devane said nothing and the Chief continued. 'Which leaves an accident. He could have fallen in. What do you think?'

'It's possible. My mind is open.'

'Surely more probable than possible. No sign of foul play. Suicide? How can you ever prove that one way or the other in a case like this? The evidence, such as it is, would seem to point to an accident.'

'There are other factors,' Devane suggested mildly.

'Like what?'

'The gun. He didn't have a firearms certificate.'

The Chief snorted. 'Well, there's not much we can do about that now.'

'And he had some strange friends. For a man in his position.'

'Who?'

'He was very close to some revolutionary types.'

The Chief Superintendent gave him a cold-eyed stare. 'I don't see that your job, our job, is to investigate his political beliefs. Our job is to find out the circumstances of his death and to do it as efficiently as possible. In a case like this, a prominent person, a lot of public interest, our responsibility is to find out what happened quickly. We have a duty to resolve the mystery and stop rumour and speculation getting out of hand.'

'And to determine if a crime was committed,' Devane added evenly. He made a mental note that the Chief hadn't asked him about Clark's unlikely friends – a lot of people had been doing a lot of talking in the last few hours, he decided.

'Yes, of course. But there is no evidence of a crime.'

'No. But there are suspicious circumstances.'

'I wouldn't necessarily describe his, ah, associates as suspicious, however strange they might be.'

So he knows all about that, Devane noted with interest, he's been well briefed. People had been very busy. 'We don't want to jump to conclusions, especially not the wrong conclusions, and leave ourselves open to charges of a cover-up later.'

'There is no question of a cover-up.' The Chief Superintendent's irritation showed as he shuffled in his chair. 'You have a completely free hand to do your job and I would resent any suggestion to the contrary.'

'I'm not suggesting that. Just that we want to find out the truth.'

'Of course. That's why I gave you the job. I want a thorough investigation and I want it done with all possible speed. But I don't think it's necessary to go down all sorts of irrelevant and blind alleys.'

The two men stared at each other across the desk, each knowing what the other was thinking. The Chief had his orders, not the kind that would ever be written down or stated explicitly, least of all to relatively low-ranking officers. Devane was letting his superior know that he knew he wasn't part of that club.

They had known each other for two decades, had worked together on numerous cases. Devane had been the Chief Superintendent's sergeant when he was a detective inspector: they had been constant companions and good friends for several years. But the Chief's rapid promotion had broken up their partnership; a wary mutual respect replaced their former friendship.

'Okay, Bill,' the Chief harked back to their old relationship and prepared to assess his subordinate's intentions. 'What's eating you?'

Devane sighed. He had accurately predicted to his own assistant that the reason for his summons to the Chief's office was for him to be told to get a quick and preferably safe result. That was why they had been given the job; the powers that be had balked at letting the Special Branch thunder all over the case, creating a suspicion of political intrigue by their very involvement. Devane had no doubt that the Chief had been subjected to a similar interview with his superiors earlier. And the Commissioner had probably been hauled in front of the Minister before that – although the Commissioner was so attuned to the whims of the Minister that they need not have talked at all. Devane's assistant had looked shocked at his cynicism.

23

'The whole thing stinks,' Devane said, tiring of the fencing. He lit another cigarette. 'What you say is strictly true but everything tells me this is a can of worms.'

'Your notorious intuition.' The Chief smiled bleakly. He stood up, tugged down his uniform tunic, squared his shoulders and looked out the window. He was in his late fifties but still prided himself on his fitness, his ability to handle himself physically. His face was a picture of square health, marked by a crooked nose and topped by short grey stubble. He always wore a uniform by choice.

'There's more to it than that.'

'Such as?' The Chief perched himself on the low windowsill, demonstrating that this was no longer a formal discussion.

'The gun. It wasn't just illegal because Clark didn't have a cert. The serial number was filed off.' He paused. 'And it was probably part of an IRA shipment from America.'

The Chief cursed under his breath and stared at the Inspector as if he had developed an unsightly disease. He pursed his lips and rubbed a hand over his eyes.

'There's no proof yet,' Devane continued. 'I took it up to Ballistics as soon as I got it. One of the lads there took one look at it and said immediately, "Ah, another Thirty-eight Special from Boston." A National Guard armoury was raided there about eighteen months ago and twenty-five rifles and revolvers taken. Several have turned up here and in the North in the last few months.'

The Chief put his hands in his trouser pockets and raised one leg after the other to prop them against the side of his desk. 'What do you make of that?'

Devane gave a short laugh. 'I think we need to know why a Government backbencher was toting an IRA gun, and using it, just before he was found dead. Don't you?'

'Who else knows about this?'

Devane gave him another of his sickly smiles and shook his head at the Chief's transparency before replying. Subtlety was not his strong point, he thought; he was a good old-style cop who much preferred to deal with straight, honest-to-God crime than with the complexities of politically motivated activities. 'A

24

couple of my lads. And Ballistics can put two and two together if they bother to look at the label on the bag.'

'Maybe you're right. And it is a can of worms.' The Chief let his legs drop to the floor and confirmed Devane's view of him. 'These damn cases are always the same. It's enough to have to deal with all the routine hoods as well as the super-patriots. But these cases . . . ' He shook his head. 'Politicians hanging over your shoulder, the media blundering about and every bar fly in the country claiming he knows the real story. And the whole thing becomes a shambles. This bloody country is obsessed with conspiracies.'

'Which doesn't mean they don't exist.'

'Yes . . . But we shouldn't waste time looking for them if they don't exist.'

'I'm not.'

'Well what are you looking for?'

'Ballistics are checking the records to see if the bullets match any others we've come across recently.'

'You're trying to prove Clark was an IRA gunman,' the Chief said tetchily, as if the idea were a personal slight.

Devane shrugged. 'I'm going through all the routines. We've sent copies of the ballistics to Belfast to see if the RUC have any matches.'

'Jesus Christ, Bill.' The Chief sounded like he'd been kicked in the stomach and sat down at his desk again to regain control. 'That wasn't very bright.'

'I didn't tell them where the bullets or the gun came from. As far as they're concerned it's a weapon we picked up in a search.'

'You should have checked with me first.'

'And you'd have said no,' Devane said as a matter of fact.

'I gave you this case because I know you're a good policeman,' the Chief said. 'And that you'd do your duty . . . ' He let the thought hang in the air for a moment and shook his head. 'What if you find the gun was used in some other crime, an IRA assassination or something?' He squeezed his eyes shut and winced inwardly at the potential consequences. A Southern politician linked to a Northern murder. Holy Christ.

'That's not our problem,' Devane said, smarting from the

implication that he would do his duty. He knew the Chief hadn't meant that as it was normally meant. 'I'm only following the leads. Wherever they take me.'

The Chief looked at him but his mind was on other people. 'Well, keep me informed from now on,' he said at last. 'About everything. Every development and every move. Before you make it.'

Devane stood up and headed for the door.

'By the way,' the Chief halted him, 'I hear some defence counsel is giving you a hard time in the Special Criminal Court.'

'He's got nothing better to fire at me than sarcasm. And sarcasm has as much influence on that bench as the Pope on the Kremlin.'

'Some of those lawyers are out to get you,' the Chief said. 'You should be careful.'

Devane wondered if that was a threat or if he was just being paranoid. 'He'll have to try harder than that,' he replied.

The Chief Superintendent watched the door swing shut behind him and tried to collect his thoughts. Devane left the building and walked up Dublin Castle's internal roadway to his own office with his hands in his pockets and his coat flapping behind him. He regretted telling the Chief about the gun; it would certainly increase the pressure on him from above. Although it might stop the demands for a quick result for a day or so while they worried like hell about its implications.

He imagined the Chief Superintendent already on the phone, calling the Commissioner's office to tell them the wonderful news that one of their political masters might have been an IRA killer. And the Commissioner passing the word to the Department of Justice. But would the Department then tell the Minister, he wondered and flashed a wicked smile to a uniformed garda standing by the gateway.

Devane turned into the detective unit and slouched up the stairs to his own office, thinking about his next move. This case had all the signs of a can of particularly juicy worms. He could feel them wriggling already.

Three

Seamus Ryle kicked the blankets from underneath one side of the mattress and tossed himself against the other side. He rolled onto the floor on top of the bedclothes, scrambled to his feet and dressed with his teeth clamped shut against the cold. Two strides took him to the other side of the bedsitter where he plugged in an electric heater and a kettle in almost one movement.

The bedsitter had appeared well-designed, like a large shipboard cabin, the first time he saw it. Neat and compact, it had seemed to fulfil all his requirements. But the longer he stayed there the more depressing it became. Daylight came in fitfully and he was always conscious that it was below ground level. Still, he was rarely there during the day and it was only temporary anyway.

He shaved quickly in the sink beside the kettle and poured boiling water over instant coffee. He unknotted the top of a plastic bag of sliced bread and furry green eyes of mould glared back at him. He rolled up the bag, squashed it into the overflowing bin and sipped impatiently at the hot coffee.

There had to be a connection between Clark and the dog; it was too much of a coincidence. If he hadn't been so dense in the office the night before it would have been clear, as clear as it had become after a couple more drinks had straightened out his brain. Either Clark had been shot and the guards were trying to keep it quiet or he had shot the dog. A politician had been murdered or he had been running amok with a gun when he died. Either way, it was a hell of a story. Just what he needed to repair relations with Stacy. As long as no one else had made the connections, of course.

He checked the time and emptied half the cup into the sink, pulled on his coat and left. His car was the only one left outside and he clawed impatiently at the crust of frost on its windscreen. At the end of the road he stopped at a newsagent and bought all the daily newspapers. If any of the others have it, he thought, I'm really in deep shit. He drove on to Dun Laoghaire before looking at them.

Outside Ethel Barnes' house he looked through the papers quickly and thoroughly, first the others then his own. There was no mention of the dog and the relief felt like a satisfying breakfast. So far so good. He glanced at the papers again to see which had the clearest head and shoulders picture of Clark, placed it on top of his pile and went to the basement door.

'Hello,' she said. She looked quite cheerful and pulled the door wide as if she had been expecting him. The terrier pranced about his feet and he walked into the over-furnished room.

'Would you like a cup of tea?' she asked and he nodded gratefully. 'I'm sorry I didn't offer you anything yesterday.'

'About yesterday,' he shifted in the chair. 'I hope you didn't . . .'

'You were right,' she said matter-of-factly. 'I was upset, more so than I realised. I'm much better now, thank you.'

He glanced through the papers more slowly and folded the picture of Clark into a portrait for her return.

'I haven't seen the newspapers yet,' she said as she put down a tray on a low table. 'I don't think I said it to you yesterday, but I meant to, that I would prefer it if my name were not quoted. If that were possible.'

'You needn't worry. There's no mention of you in our paper.'

She poured a cup of tea and held a milk jug over it awaiting his assent. 'One cannot be too careful nowadays although I'm sure it would not matter.'

Ryle took the cup in one hand and offered the photograph of Clark to her with the other. 'Is that the man who shot your dog?'

She sat down and held the folded newspaper upright with both hands. 'I wouldn't have thought so.' She shook her head and paused, still scrutinising the picture. 'I don't have a clear picture of him, just an impression. He was more haggard-looking, gaunter. This man looks too ... successful, self-satisfied.'

Ryle swallowed his disappointment with a sip of tea as she put the newspaper down beside the tray and looked at him inquiringly.

'Did you know him?' he asked, nodding at Clark's picture.
'No.'

'Never come across him?'

'Not that I'm aware of. I saw his picture on the television last night and I wondered if he could be the man. But I can't say.'

'Could it have been him?' Ryle asked forlornly. The story he had already visualised in banner headlines was fading into an empty space, leaving more than a blank page in his mind. 'Is it possible?'

'I would have thought not.' She bent forward to look at the picture again. 'But the police appear certain it was him.'

Ryle wasn't sure he had heard her correctly. He leaned forward, a gesture she mistook for a request for more tea, and he had to contain the surge of excitement that swept through his brain while she refilled the cup. 'They were here again?' he asked, leaning back again.

'Yes. They called last night, fairly late. I wasn't going to open the door but they kept ringing. I suppose they heard the television or something. They showed me pictures of Mr Clark but I told them the same as I have told you . . . I could not say it was him.'

'Were they disappointed?'

'Oh no. They seemed quite certain that Mr Clark shot Goliath.'

'Did they say why they were so certain?'

'The older man, who did all the talking, just said it as a fact, that Mr Clark had shot Goliath. He wanted to know if I could recognise him. If he had said anything to me. Or if I had any idea why he had done it.'

'Do you?'

She shook her head. 'None at all. Then he wanted to know if I had seen anybody else on the pier and what the man, Mr Clark, had done after he shot Goliath.'

'Did you see anyone else?'

'No. I have no memory of anyone or anything else. You don't get many people out that early this time of year. I don't . . . I didn't notice anyone. And I didn't see what the man did afterwards. There was a car that nearly struck me, my fault, when I ran across the road after the shooting and they wanted to know if I could describe it or its driver. I couldn't, I'm afraid.'

'Did they say anything else?'

'I think they were very disappointed. The detective said that I was probably the last person to see Mr Clark alive. They hoped I could give them some kind of lead. But there was nothing more I could tell them.'

Ryle was elated. He'd been right, the headlines were back on his mental page, bigger and bolder than before. He'd got a story to more than make up for yesterday's fiasco and wipe the smirks off Stacy's face. Just for the satisfaction of hearing it again, he took Ethel Barnes back over what she had told him. He asked if he could quote her but she said she would prefer to be left out of it altogether.

'You are probably disappointed with me too,' she said as she showed him out.

'Far from it,' he replied. 'I'm glad that you're feeling better. And don't worry, I won't drag you into it.'

He left his car where it was and walked the short distance to the garda station. Inside, he knocked at the glass hatch of the public office. It was opened by the policeman to whom he had spoken the previous day. This is my lucky day, thought Ryle: he didn't know the garda's name and had been trying to think of a way of describing him that wouldn't cause him trouble.

'Still chasing dogs?' the garda asked. He did not look so jovial today.

'Not quite.'

'I didn't think so.'

'Is the detective dealing with it in?'

'It's in a different league now. The boys from the castle have taken over.'

'Are they here?'

'No.'

'Is there anyone here?'

'The people you want are in headquarters – the garda press office.'

'Who was dealing with it when it was only a dog?'

'They're very helpful in the press office. Love to hear from lads like you. Just sitting around waiting for your calls.'

'Off the record, are there any developments?'

'I know nothing about it. It's out of our hands and, honestly, I can't talk to you any more.'

'Okay.' Ryle admitted defeat.

'And, by the way,' the policeman added, 'we never talked about it before either. Right?'

Another light flashed on the telephone console and Mike Erlanger said 'hold on' into the receiver. He punched two buttons to hold one call and take the other from his secretary.

'Mr Erlanger.' He knew from her formality that there was someone with her and from the shade of unease in her voice who they were. 'There are two gentlemen here to see you. Detectives.'

'Be with them in a moment.' He punched the buttons in reverse order to take back his first call. 'Harvey,' he said. 'You don't worry about all that. You just make out a comprehensive geological report and I'll handle the public relations.'

'I don't think you appreciate how serious this could be,' Harvey said. 'Our situation here could become untenable.'

'I know, I know.'

'The environmentalists are really stirring them up. They're beginning to think they'll all glow in the dark. They're looking at me strangely, like I was already glowing, for chrissakes.'

'Harvey.' Erlanger suppressed a laugh. 'I told you, I'll handle it. I'll come down to the meeting and I'll take care of it. What's more important now is that we keep the drilling on target and that you get that report to me as soon as possible.'

'I hope you do appreciate the situation here, Mike.'

'I do, Harvey, I do. Everything is under control. And I've got to go now, there's two cops waiting to talk with me.'

'What?' Harvey shrieked.

Erlanger put down the receiver. That'll freak him altogether, he thought gleefully. Still, the kid worried too much; what had someone his age to worry about? Especially when Uncle Mike is here to take care of everything. He grinned sardonically, stood up and took off his jacket. He shoved a wooden hanger into the armholes and smoothed the fabric.

Did I worry that much at his age, he wondered. He tried to remember but nothing specific sprang to mind. But I never knew what the hell was going on then either. It was only with age that you realised that it was mostly nothing much. Or that nothing mattered much. He hung the jacket on the back of the door, loosened his tie and opened the door briskly.

'Gentlemen,' he said to the detectives who stood large and looming in the middle of the reception area, 'please come in.'

The head waiter guided Erlanger through a forest of large potted plants that looked too rubbery to be real but probably were. At least they should be, Erlanger had often thought, given the prices that they charged. He sat at his regular table and told the waiter who today's guest was.

Erlanger joined his hands on the table and glanced around with an amiable half-smile: the archetypal successful American businessman. He heard Tommy Lyster, the junior Minister for Justice, before he saw him, booming greetings to several acquaintances as he rolled and glad-handed his way among the tables. Erlanger watched a couple of other diners smirking at Lyster's progress and caught the eye of someone he knew. The man raised his eyebrows in a laugh: Erlanger broadened his smile.

Lyster cannoned around a potted plant and stretched out a heavy hand to Erlanger. Everything about him was heavy, from his thick navy suit to his weathered red face. 'My apologies first,' he breathed heavily as he squeezed his bulk awkwardly behind the table, for not being able to accept your gracious invitation to your wonderful party the other night.'

'Not at all.' Erlanger waved his comment away.

'It was a constituency matter. A golden jubilee of a wedding, good friends of mine, and I couldn't miss it. Besides,' he chuckled and dropped his voice as if he were about to impart a secret, 'they have relations everywhere. You can't swing a cat in my constituency without hitting one of them.'

'This is more civilised,' Erlanger said. 'The party turned into something of a mob scene, I'm afraid.'

'That's not what I heard at all. I'm told it was a great night, a great night.'

32

The head waiter hovered over them and they both ordered French onion soup. Lyster chose roast beef, well done, and Erlanger asked for the black sole and bottles of red and white wine.

'Maurice Clark's death must have come as a great shock,' Erlanger said as they sipped at the onion soup.

'Terrible.'

'He looked fine at my place. Though I was only speaking with him for a few moments. It really was too crowded, despite what you've heard.'

'It's shaken the party, I can tell you,' Lyster said mournfully. 'He was an up and coming lad, in his prime. Very sad, tragic.'

'I've just had a couple of your officers to see me about it.'

Lyster's eyes shot up from his soup. 'Officers?'

'Detectives.'

'They didn't cause you any upset, did they?' Lyster asked solicitously.

'Not at all,' Erlanger laughed away Lyster's concern uncertainly. What if I said they had, he wondered. 'It was just routine. Inquiring if I had noticed anything unusual about Maurice at the party.'

'Well, I hardly think that was necessary,' Lyster said. 'To trouble decent people like yourself.'

'It was no trouble. They were only doing their job.' Erlanger paused while a waiter delivered the main course. 'Does anyone know what happened?'

'Oh it was an accident, I'm sure.' The Minister tackled the plate of beef as though it was of more interest than his dead colleague.

'No signs of violence or anything like that?' Erlanger probed gently.

'Oh no, nothing like that. An accident, I'd say. He probably went for a stroll on the pier, slipped in.'

'That's what the police think, is it?'

Lyster dragged his attention away from his plate, wondering about his persistence, and not intending to admit that he had no idea what the police thought. The reports that came into the Department's Security section from garda headquarters were never left lying around for him to see.

In his mid-fifties, Lyster had risen as high as he would ever go in politics and he knew it. He cared nothing about the policy issues or administrative tasks of his ministry, spending most of his energies on his constituency and on elaborate conspiracies to enrage his Minister, who tried, with occasional success, to ignore him. Lyster knew he had been appointed for no better reason than as a reward for three decades of party loyalty. But he was enjoying to the full the greater opportunities his reward had provided for indulging his one true passion: scheming.

'Inquiries are continuing,' he said. 'But I'm sure they'll find it was an accident.'

Erlanger tried to read in his round face what his reply meant. He was still coming to grips with the intricate undertones of Irish speech, particularly that of politicians. Was the Minister just giving his own opinion or telling him what the outcome of the inquiry would be, no matter what?

Lyster was still watching him closely, scenting a faint whiff of a conspiracy. Erlanger decided not to pursue Lyster's meaning but rather to explain his curiosity.

'I feel a certain responsibility for it,' he said with a subtle air of troubled sincerity. 'I mean, he seems to have died just after my party or within a couple of hours of leaving my home. It doesn't do a man any good to find his guests turning up in the sea next day. You know what I mean?'

Lyster nodded soberly. 'The drink.'

Erlanger had not meant anything in particular but he said nothing.

'I wouldn't worry about it,' Lyster continued with a touch of disapproval. 'Maurice was a very abstemious man. I doubt if he ever got drunk in his life. Between ourselves, too cautious about his image.'

'I was only talking with him a couple of minutes and he certainly wasn't drunk then. He seemed in fine form.'

'He probably slipped on a patch of ice. Went for a breath of fresh air and slipped or tripped over something and fell in,' Lyster repeated with the tone of someone giving a final verdict. Clark and his death did not really concern him. Unless there was more to it than met the eye. 'It was a tragedy, a tragic accident.'

Erlanger looked consoled and the conversation slipped safely into the weather. Erlanger admitted that the only thing he really missed, living in Ireland, was the winter skiing in America. He turned on all his charms and regaled Lyster with exaggerated stories of social life on the slopes.

As they waited for coffee, Lyster got around to what he considered to be the main point of the lunch. 'By the way,' he asked casually, 'how's the prospecting?'

'Coming along, slow but sure.' Erlanger smiled knowingly.

'Have you hit anything yet?'

'It's not that simple,' Erlanger laughed, 'not like the oil wells in the movies. But it looks promising, very promising.'

That's no secret.' Lyster made it sound like a criticism. 'Your shares are doing nicely.' The 25p shares in Erlanger's company, Atlantis Mining, had built up steadily on the unlisted stock market to 70p each.

'There's no hard news, I assure you. Prospects look good but there's nothing definite.'

'Will they hit the pound, do you think?'

'Probably.' Erlanger looked glum. 'To be honest, I'm not wildly enthusiastic about that. It's nice to have people demonstrate their faith in you with their money but speculators could damage us more than they'd help us at present. I'm not concerned with short-term gains. If everything works out, there'll be lots for everybody.' He paused and smiled brightly at Lyster. 'You won't have to ask me then if the shares will reach a pound.'

'It's always nice to be in at the beginning, though.'

'Yeah, it can be exciting.' Erlanger beamed at him.

Over coffee, Erlanger looked serious again and said there was something he wanted to mention to the Minister. It might not be his place to do so but he was going to anyway, and for the best of motives. Lyster sharpened his senses without moving a muscle.

'It seems to me,' Erlanger began, 'that your police force is under a lot of pressure. Nothing it can't handle, of course. But there are all these bank robberies and the IRA and so on.'

'True,' Lyster nodded.

'Intelligence is obviously essential for the police to keep on top of the situation. And it occurred to me that, if it was of use to you, I could put you in touch with somebody who might be able to help in that area.' Erlanger paused to sip his coffee. 'A friend of mine runs a company in Illinois that manufactures surveillance equipment. Specialises in supplying law enforcement agencies.'

'Bugs and things?'

Erlanger nodded. 'Perhaps you're well equipped in that area already – I don't want to know. It just occurred to me that he might be a useful contact, if you needed any hardware of that type.'

Lyster appeared to give the idea deep thought for a moment. 'Are you sort of an agent for him?'

'No, not at all,' Erlanger laughed. 'Not in any formal sense. I'm not on a commission or trying to sell you anything. But I do admit to having an interest in law and order in Ireland. I mean, nobody wants to mine uranium of all things in an area where there is political instability. Not that there are any worries about Ireland on that score.'

'No, there aren't. We're good friends of America here, practically the fifty-first state.'

'I know that. But you might just bear it in mind. I'd be happy to help out if I could be of use.'

Lyster swallowed the remains of his coffee and changed the subject.

Ryle was about to hang up the phone when Peter Grifford answered breezily. 'The Nineteenth Hole,' he said. 'Ah, the dead have arisen,' he added after Ryle identified himself. 'I thought you had retired or something.'

'That's your line,' Ryle laughed. Grifford, a detective sergeant, delighted in telling everybody that he was approaching retirement, including bewildered suspects who usually took the information as an obscure threat. 'How long is it now?'

'Fourteen months, twelve days. And counting. Very good of you to call and inquire after all this time.'

'Actually . . . ' Ryle began.

36

'You mean you haven't organised the presentation?' Grifford groaned with mock indignation. 'A small token of the grateful media's appreciation of a remarkable career in the service of the nation.'

'I'm writing it down. Meanwhile, I'm grappling with a dead dog and a dead politician.'

'Interesting combination. How do you tell one from the other?'

'The politician is the one who fired the shots.'

Grifford whistled. 'You've come a long way. Very well informed these days.'

'Am I?' Ryle sought confirmation that Ethel Barnes' information was correct. Grifford was attached to a city centre police station and seemed to spend his time meandering aimlessly around the streets, in search of nothing more than his pension. But he always seemed to know what was going on although Ryle never knew how or why he was so well informed.

'Of course. What else do you know?'

'Bugger all. I don't even know how that's known.'

'Elementary. He left his prints all over the gun which matched the bullets from the dog. Text book deductions.'

'But where was the gun?'

'Lying on the pier. Conveniently.'

'And how did he die?'

'Drowned.'

'Any signs of violence on the body?'

'Not that I've heard.'

'What's it all about?'

'Haven't a clue.' Grifford sighed. 'And, if you don't mind, I've got work to do. Do you have any idea how much is involved in organising a golf tournament?'

Ryle thanked him and rubbed his hands with satisfaction. That was it: the story stood up. Stacy had listened to it earlier with a sceptical silence and insisted on corroboration from a second source. Ryle leaned back in his chair and waited impatiently for the news editor to emerge from the editor's office.

'I've got it confirmed,' Ryle told him, enthusiastically. 'And the autopsy result. He drowned.'

'On the record?'

'No,' Ryle laughed. 'A contact.'

'What are they saying on the record?'

'Nothing.'

'Did you put your story to them?'

'Yes,' Ryle lied impatiently. He had merely asked the garda press office a lot of detailed questions to which they offered the stock non-answers. He had no intention of telling them something they probably had not been told by their own investigators.

'And?' Stacy added.

'Inquiries are continuing. They won't say anything about anything.'

'Well done,' Stacy muttered, sitting down at his desk and dropping a sheaf of papers in front of him. Ryle stared over his shoulder at the list of news stories. Clark's death was the top item: there would be a story about the political implications and an exclusive about him shooting a dog.

'What did the editor say?' Ryle asked, making no secret of his eagerness.

'It goes inside.'

'What?' Ryle stepped back to stare down at him. 'That's ridiculous.'

'That's his decision.'

'It's a great story and it's exclusive. Clark running around with a gun in his hand before he died and we can prove it.'

'I know the story,' Stacy retorted.

'And what are we leading with?' Ryle stabbed at the news list. 'The political implications? We had all that today. That's not a story.'

'Where is your story?' Stacy demanded coldly.

'Ah, come on . . . '

'Don't go off at half-cock on me again,' Stacy warned and got up. 'Did I say I disagree with you? You just write the story.'

'Why did he decide that?'

The news editor shrugged. 'Respect for the dead. Don't kick a man when he's down. Or drowned.'

Ryle laughed derisively but Stacy cut him short with a threatening glare. 'You just write the story. Don't screw it up. And leave the rest to me.'

Ryle went back to his desk and pulled over his typewriter. 'Do it straight,' Stacy shouted to him. 'No hysterics.'

Ryle nodded back and let his instant outrage cool. He shifted his attention to the blank page and tapped out a catchline. It was nice to be able to throw a fit of pique now and again, he thought. But it's ridiculous to put it inside; it's a hell of a good story, the best story this paper's had in months. He looked up and saw Stacy watching and nodded again and forced himself to concentrate on a single paragraph.

He hunched over and read it twice before releasing it from the machine. 'Mr Maurice Clark was armed with a revolver and shot dead a dog shortly before he himself was drowned in Dun Laoghaire harbour, gardai investigating his death have discovered.'

That's pretty straight, Ryle smirked happily, even bland. But you don't need to hype the big ones: it really is one hell of a story. One to rattle a few breakfast teacups in the morning.

Four

The congregation slumped to its knees and Jim Whelan bowed his forehead against his interlocked fingers. He was in the midst of a solid block of sombre politicians behind the Taoiseach and his ministers who jammed the front rows, shoulder to shoulder. In the aisle to Whelan's left, Clark's coffin stood on a wooden trestle, festooned with mass cards. The atmosphere was rich with solemnity and the soothing scent of incense.

Whelan tried to concentrate on the service but his thoughts kept coming back to the same conclusion. All right, he admitted irritably to himself, Maurice's death is an opportunity, even a heaven-sent opportunity. He glanced superstitiously at the altar as though his presumption might bring instant retribution.

He had listened intently to the priest's eulogy for Clark, to the clichés about his untimely loss and the predictable religious messages about redemption and the mysteries of God's ways. He had agreed with every word of praise of Clark but nonetheless his mind kept returning to what Clark's death meant for his own career.

His wife was wrong or, at least, not altogether right. Clark *had* been using him but that wasn't a one-way street. It was something that Whelan, as well as Clark, had chosen deliberately. A mutual arrangement in both their interests. He had been using Clark too, hanging onto his coat tails in the expectation that he would be dragged along on his predicted path.

Whelan automatically joined in the muttered responses to the celebrant and everyone stood up.

All his political energies had gone into fortifying his constituency base and that was secure, more or less. As secure as it would ever be, given that he had not inherited the seat from his father nor had any other divine rights to it. It was time to realise his true ambitions: he had no intention of becoming a perennial backbencher, mere voting fodder, always reliable and relied upon, and never considered for government office. Whelan wanted to be at the centre of power.

He had failed so far to make his mark on the party's leaders. His association with Clark had helped but Clark was gone now, leaving him without a patron. Yet creating a vacancy and an opportunity.

It's all right to think like that, he told himself with a vague feeling of guilt, but not right now. Not at Maurice's funeral, for God's sake. But his mind went on working out the possibilities, dreaming about the prospects.

The service ended and the Taoiseach lead the mourners past Clark's widow. Camera shutters stuttered in the cavernous silence as he bent down to shake her hand and whisper something. Whelan sidled into the long line of people waiting their turn. First things first, he thought, I've got to sort out the little constituency problem. Clear the decks.

Seamus Ryle stood on the steps and watched the flood of people fan out into the cold sunlight and eddy among the cars into everchanging groups, chatting discreetly and being seen. A fleet of official black Mercedes was drawn up near the steps, looking small and squat compared to the two stretched limousines of the undertakers. Appropriate, Ryle thought; the correct status is being observed. State power overshadowed by death.

A reporter from a rival paper took up position beside him and they formed an obtrusive little group, their casual jackets contrasting with the dark overcoats of everyone around them. 'The entire Cabinet's here,' the reporter said, jotting another name in his notebook. 'And the shadow cabinet, I reckon.'

'And every other politician,' Ryle added, trying to spot someone he could talk to. He had to keep up the momentum, keep the story running. Now that he had got it off the ground and lifted himself out of the mire.

A knot of people created a moving power centre around the Taoiseach as he progressed slowly through the crush. He stopped to have a word with the Leader of the Opposition and photographers zoomed in on them like hunters on prey and squeezed their shutter buttons in a barrage of clicks that carried through the still air.

'Detectives mingled with the mourners.' The reporter beside him muttered an old newspaper cliché about the funerals of murder victims. 'Don't suppose I could get away with that line.'

Ryle giggled with him and glanced at the plainclothes police drivers now standing by the ministerial cars and the Special Branch men standing out bulkily in the Taoiseach's entourage.

'I doubt if they'd find any guilty looks among this shower,' he said. 'The politicians are much more expert at mingling with mourners than they are.'

Ryle saw Jim Whelan and was about to leave his vantage point when he spotted Sergeant Peter Grifford standing at the outer edge of the crowd. He was wearing a well-cut camel-hair coat and a matching brown hat and soft leather gloves. He looked almost as out of place as Ryle in his green parka, more like a successful horse-breeder than the usual rumpled detectives. Ryle wondered what he was doing at the funeral and threaded his way towards him.

'Didn't know you had friends in high places,' Ryle greeted him .

'It's my age,' Grifford said sonorously. 'Spend all my time going to funerals. Great social occasions.'

'Certainly the social funeral of the year.' Ryle recognised the heads of several nationalised companies grouped in a conservative cartel. 'Many thanks for your help last night.'

Grifford gave no indication that he had heard. They watched silently while Maurice Clark's widow, her arm held by another woman, emerged from the church and disappeared into the crowd. She was shrouded in black and her face was a pale sliver, unrecognisable at this distance.

'D'you know her?' Ryle asked.

Grifford shook his head. 'And I don't think she'll want to make your acquaintance either.'

'Why not? I've never had any dealings with her.'

Grifford gave him a sideways look but realised that Ryle was not trying to be smart. He was about to say something when a short, harassed-looking man came towards him purposefully and asked if he could have a word. Grifford nodded, raised his eyebrows discreetly to Ryle and moved away. Ryle watched them in surprise. Very interesting, he thought. The man was one of the Taoiseach's advisers.

They disappeared from his sight and he shrugged and wandered through the crowd, looking for Whelan.

'Happy New Year,' he said when he found him.

'Some start to it, isn't it?' Whelan said glumly.

'You knew him well?'

'He was my closest friend in politics.'

Ryle decided it wasn't the time to tease out exactly what that meant. 'Can I buy you a pint later?' he asked and Whelan nodded absently. 'You'll be in Leinster House?'

Whelan nodded again. 'After four. I'll be free.'

Tommy Lyster, the junior Justice Minister, walked up to them with a look of funereal satisfaction on his face, as though he found solace in mortality. 'Well, James,' he declared to Whelan. 'Hear you're in the wars again.'

Whelan cast a warning glance towards Ryle and introduced the reporter to the Minister. They shook hands perfunctorily.

'As I was about to say,' Lyster said to Whelan. 'A fine body of men, the media.' He turned his attention to Ryle, narrowed his eyes and nodded. 'Yes,' he decided, 'you're the fella that had that scurrilous article in the paper this morning. Live and let live is my motto and I've nothing against the media, but in all my years in politics I've never read anything so disgraceful.'

'What?' Ryle mumbled.

'Typical of the worst excesses of the gutter press, which I never associated with your paper until now. Upsetting a poor young widow with sly innuendos. And on the morning of her husband's funeral. The worst kind of cheap sensationalism to sell papers.'

'Are you saying my story was wrong?'

'I'm saying you might at least have the decency to let the dead rest in peace. Especially on the day of the funeral. Instead of rubbing salt in the wound of the distraught family's grief.'

'Don't you want to know why he died?'

'It was an accident. A sad, tragic, terrible accident.'

Whelan looked from one to the other like a bewildered spectator trying to follow an unfamiliar sport.

'Can I quote you on that?'

'No, you can't,' Lyster raised his voice and lowered it quickly as some people nearby looked his way. 'Don't try your dirty little tricks on me. You've done enough damage for one day.'

Lyster turned on his heel and marched off into the crowd, cutting a narrow track through the clusters of people. Ryle muttered a curse and watched him go. Whelan gave him a halfhearted punch in the shoulder with a flash of exuberance from another age. 'What was all that about?' he asked.

'What did he mean? About you being in the wars?' Ryle turned back to him.

'Just a little constituency wrangle,' Whelan shrugged. 'Nothing to get excited about. What have you got in today's paper?'

'A story about your friend's death.'

'Saying what?'

'I'll fill you in on the whole story later.'

'That's what you want to talk to me about? Maurice?'

Ryle nodded. 'I assumed you'd want to know why he died.'

Whelan paused and looked away. Do I, he asked himself guiltily, do I really care? 'Yes, I do,' he said with more than enough conviction to encourage Ryle. 'But why don't we meet in Buswell's instead of at the Dáil?'

The tricolour sagged at half mast over Leinster House, a spot of dim colour above the grey parliament building, in the early afternoon gloom. Inside, the formalities of Maurice Clark's death had been noted in brief tributes and a minute of silence. Then the heightened mood of the first day of term had reasserted itself, loaded with the promise and the prospect of uncertainty.

In the members' bar the atmosphere was of cosy familiarity, edged with the undercurrents of unending political manoeuvring. Jim Whelan worried at a glass of whiskey and watched Tommy Lyster hunch over the phone at the other end of the counter. He wasn't too keen on this. Lyster was not the ideal person to confide in, but at least he knew how to deal with these kinds of problems. Lyster took out an envelope, wrote on the back of it and put down the receiver.

'Problems?' Whelan asked conversationally when the Junior Minister rejoined him.

'Where would we be without them?' Lyster guffawed and took a large swig from his whiskey. 'The local paper looking for a quote on something. On anything. It's their deadline day and they have a hole in the front page.'

Whelan joined in his laughter.

'Never trust the media, James,' Lyster added knowingly. 'A shower of coffin-dancers. That's the only thing they like. Especially before you're dead. Apart from that fella you were talking to this morning. He doesn't know when to stop dancing.'

Whelan nodded absently. He had just read Ryle's report and didn't know what to make of it. But he didn't want to get into that now. 'I'd like your advice on a little local matter in my area,' he said.

'Ah, the planning scandal.' Lyster licked his lips in anticipation.

Whelan cursed silently. The whole thing was out. 'What have you heard?'

'Oh, nothing much. Just that some scandal over planning permission is about to hit the papers. And you're up to your tonsils in it.'

'It's not like that.'

'It never is,' Lyster shook with silent mirth. 'But you know what the T's like about these things.'

'That's why I'd like your advice,' Whelan said deferentially and called for another round of drinks. 'One of the evening papers is on my back. And I haven't done anything wrong.'

Lyster poured some water into his new whiskey and waited to be told.

Whelan gulped some whiskey. 'My constituency chairman asked me to get some land re-zoned. Gave me a lot of good reasons about development and jobs and the rest of it. So I put down a re-zoning motion for the council and all the local residents' groups went wild about having an industrial estate in their back gardens.'

'They're always creating a fuss about these things,' Lyster said dismissively.

'What he neglected to tell me was that his brother owns the land. And that he's being investigated by the fraud squad over an insurance swindle involving some buildings already on it,' Whelan sighed. 'Arson.'

'Are you involved?'

'No. Of course not. But you see how it can be made to look in print. Linking me into political skulduggery, which is one thing, but financial fraud as well.'

Lyster pursed his lips. 'Withdraw the motion.'

'That's the problem. I can't. He's very influential in the constituency. And I've never been his first choice as candidate.' Whelan paused. 'He says he'll make sure I'm never selected again if I back out now.'

'Tell him to go to hell.'

'Wouldn't I love to. But he carries a lot of clout locally. And it's become a matter of family pride with him.'

'Face him down,' Lyster advised. 'Tell him to fuck off. And withdraw the motion.'

'It's not that simple.'

'It is,' Lyster insisted. 'You're the Dáil deputy. You control the constituency.'

'But I don't,' Whelan moaned. 'Not that securely. He's run the party there since the flood and I've always had to handle him with kid gloves. A lot of people think he's past it and that's the problem, too. He's trying to reassert his control.'

'I'll have a word with him,' Lyster said confidently. 'Who is he anyway?'

Whelan gave a name and Lyster nodded as if something had suddenly become clear. The man's family had been deeply involved in the party since its foundation. 'I'll still have a word with him,' Lyster offered.

'Thanks,' Whelan said, 'but I think I'd better handle this myself.'

46

'Don't waste any time, then,' Lyster said with a touch of disappointment. 'You know how the Taoiseach hates this sort of stuff in the papers.'

Whelan nodded glumly. He knew only too well. Not to mention the fact that it could scupper all his other plans. He had to get out from under this, and quickly.

'Listen.' Lyster leaned towards him. 'You lay it on the line. He's causing the party trouble. And the party comes before any individual or family. No matter what their record. So you tell him to fuck off. It's as simple as that.'

Darkness was falling as Seamus Ryle hurried along Molesworth Street, late. Ahead of him the large iron gates of Leinster House stood open and the building itself was a series of lighted windows stacked upon each other. He turned into Buswell's Hotel and stood at the door of the bar. It was packed with politicians and their friends, big countrymen who watched everyone and everything with undisguised interest. There was no sign of Jim Whelan.

Two women left a corner table and Ryle took their places and settled down to wait, hoping that Whelan hadn't been and gone. He had his back to the bar but he could see everything in the wall of mirrors before him.

He could never understand why politicians preferred to meet journalists in Buswell's when they weren't sure they should be talking to them. They were as likely to be seen there by their colleagues as in the Leinster House bar. He must ask Whelan. But Whelan had other things on his mind when he arrived, flustered.

'That place is a mad house.' He sat down and quickly scanned the other occupants of the bar. 'You forget what it's like when you get away from it even for a few weeks.'

'What's up?'

'Crazy stories. Mostly your fault, of course. You've set off all sorts of mad rumours about Maurice. Election fever. You name it.'

'Is there any chance of an election?'

'Are you mad? Who wants an election in the dead of winter?

No, that's only Opposition play-acting. They'd get the fright of their lives if one was sprung on them.'

'What are they saying about Maurice?'

'Utter nonsense, head-banger stuff.' Whelan looked around again. 'Let me get you a drink.' He shot off to the bar as though his re-election depended on it. Another hour in the members' bar after leaving Lyster had exposed him to the full extent of the gossip and to a barrage of questions. He had left in a state of confused agitation.

'Tell me about the rumours,' Ryle persisted when Whelan returned, balancing two glasses of whiskey and a jug of water.

'It's all bullshit,' Whelan said impatiently.

'I know. I'm only curious.'

Whelan sighed heavily and poured some water into his whiskey. 'The usual. An irate husband did it after he caught him on the job. He really died in a minister's car driven by a drunken minister which may or may not have killed someone else as well in a hit-and-run accident. He was shot by a drugs dealer in a row over money. Think up one yourself.'

'Might it have been an irate husband?'

'Ah Jesus, Ryle.' Whelan moaned and threw his hands in the air. 'There you go. That's the trouble with these rumours: people start speculating and adding two and two and making forty. I told you it's all bullshit.'

'Did the Taoiseach tell the party meeting anything about it?'

'There was no discussion. Just a minute's silence and then the meeting was adjourned. No one said anything. You're the only one who seems to know anything,' he added pointedly.

'Well, he wasn't shot, but he was armed,' Ryle said. 'That's about all I know.'

'But what was he doing there? Shooting a dog?' Whelan gave him a bewildered look.

Ryle shrugged. 'I haven't a clue. Did you know he had a gun?' Whelan shook his head. 'Any reason why he might have had one?'

'No. Of course not.'

'Any threats to his life?'

'No. Listen.' Whelan leaned forward and tapped the edge of

a cardboard beer mat on the mottled marble table. 'I know you think we're all gangsters and shysters, but even if we were Maurice wouldn't have been like that. You know what I mean?'

'Sure.' Ryle grinned. 'He wasn't a gangster like the rest of you.'

Whelan ignored the taunt. There were dark rings under his eyes and he had the grey pallor of somebody who spent too much time indoors. 'He was the straightest person I've ever known, in or out of politics. I used to say to him in fact that he had to be prepared to bend things a little if he wanted to get on.'

'How do you mean?'

'Small things.' Whelan gestured impatiently. 'Constituents asking him to do something about social welfare payments or whatever. He would look into their cases in detail and then tell them they weren't entitled to anything.'

'What's wrong with that?'

'Nothing.' Whelan threw the beer mat onto the table and sat back. A skelp of loud laughter broke from a group of men at the bar. 'Nothing at all. But there's ways of doing these things. You can't just tell people bluntly they're not entitled to something and thank you very much for calling. They probably know that already if they're calling on you. But they want to hear you say you'll do what you can, see you go through the motions. Voters are like God – they love a trier.'

'How was he so successful as a politician then?'

'He was one of the lucky ones, above the mundane stuff to a certain extent. To the extent that anyone can be in this system. And you guys liked him so the party bosses liked him because it's nice to have a bit of integrity to show off.'

'Jesus,' Ryle muttered in surprise. He had never heard Whelan talk like this before. 'You're becoming more cynical than me. Has this got something to do with your constituency problem?'

Whelan shook his head. 'I thought you wanted to talk about Maurice.' He sighed and went on: 'He should never have been in politics. He should have stayed an academic and I always told him so.' He let out a short laugh. 'He used to say I was displaying my ignorance about academic politics.'

'When was the last time you saw him?'

'The night before he died. At a party.' He told Ryle about the party at Mike Erlanger's house. Ryle asked him who Erlanger was and jotted down his name. 'He was at the funeral this morning,' Whelan added.

Ryle questioned him about the party but Whelan said he hadn't talked much to Clark; he thought Clark had left earlier than he had. He had no memory of seeing him when he himself was leaving at about four.

'Was his wife with him?'

Whelan nodded.

'So she would've been the last person to see him alive,' Ryle said.

Whelan looked around the bar as if he were seeing it for the first time and said nothing. Then he leaned forward and picked up the beer mat again and examined its edges for a moment. He looked up at Ryle, earnestly. 'You're not going to write any of this stuff, are you?'

'What stuff?' Ryle shrugged, being deliberately dense.

'His personal life. Who he left with.'

Ryle hastened to reassure him, knowing he was about to hear something interesting. 'We're not that kind of paper,' he declared with an air of disdain, thinking, Maybe an irate husband is not such a ludicrous story. 'I'm only interested in how and why he died.'

Whelan nodded absently and drained his glass. Ryle suggested another drink, afraid Whelan might dash away now that he was on the point of telling him something.

'Things were not the best between them,' Whelan said when Ryle had set down two more whiskeys. 'Their marriage was heading for a break-up. I don't know the ins and outs of it – Maurice didn't talk about it, not to me at any rate. But it was obvious that things were not going well.'

Ryle poured some water into his new drink and sipped it as cautiously as if he were tasting the information. 'So what happened at the party?' he asked finally.

'Maurice and Yvonne had some kind of argument and they didn't leave together. All I'm saying is that you can't assume she was the last person to see him alive.'

50

'Who did he leave with?'

'By himself, I suppose. I don't know. I didn't see him go.'

There goes the irate husband theory again, Ryle thought ruefully. 'Who did she, Yvonne, leave with?'

Whelan looked at him uneasily. 'You're not going to print any of this, okay? Right?' He insisted.

'I'm not going to race away and do a story saying Clark's marriage was breaking up,' Ryle replied. 'Relax.'

'I'm only marking your card. For your own information so you don't get the wrong end of the stick if you come across a garbled version of it.'

'I'm interested in how and why he died, nothing else,' Ryle repeated.

'So am I. That's why I'm telling you this.' Whelan paused. 'She left with a man called Burke. An accountant.'

'Why?'

'What do you mean "why"? Because they had an argument.'

'Yes, but who's Burke? Why did she leave with him?'

'An accountant,' Whelan repeated as if that explained everything.

Ryle suddenly saw the light. 'Is she having an affair with him?'

'I don't know.' Whelan looked around nervously and lowered his voice. A family group at the next table was concentrating on their other neighbours. 'Yes, I suppose so. I mean they've been seen together a lot. She didn't just ask him for a lift home. Because he was the only one there, like.'

'Did Maurice know about it?'

'It's not one of the great secrets of our time,' Whelan snapped as if Ryle was being slow-witted. 'Have you ever met her? She's a very tough lady, very ambitious. She drove Maurice into politics. For her own sake, not for his. She was really the politician, not him. He spent a lot of time trying to live up to her ambitions.'

'Do you think her affair had anything to do with his death?'

'Oh no, I don't.' Whelan said with horror. 'Genuinely, I don't. And for God's sake don't rush off and write any of this. Don't even repeat it.' He searched Ryle's face earnestly.

'Cross my heart,' Ryle said.

Whelan nodded uncertainly. 'This is only deep background. Like I said, I'm only marking your card. It has nothing to do with his death.'

It could have everything to do with his death, Ryle thought. It sounded like the perfect explanation for suicide. Or the ideal motive for murder. Across the table, Whelan sank back into his chair and looked into his drink with a pained mixture of misery and guilt on his face.

Five

The few people in Grafton Street moved sluggishly through the wintry morning like the walking wounded after the horrors of Christmas shopping and the January sales. Ryle jammed his hands into the pockets of his parka and lowered his head against the biting wind that whipped down the narrow street between the bright-windowed shops with their distant prospects of summer. He was still smiling faintly to himself at the memory of the news editor's greeting.

'Hey, Scoop.' Stacy had looked up from the news list he was typing and called him over. 'What's today's instalment?'

'Don't know yet,' Ryle shrugged off his coat.

'There will be a story, won't there?'

'Don't know that yet either.'

Stacy gave him a narrow-eyed stare. 'You're not resting on your laurels are you? One story does not a happy news editor make.'

'No.' Ryle sounded affronted. 'I've got a lot more stuff. Bits and pieces. But I don't know where it's going yet.'

'Why aren't you finding out?'

'I'm going to.'

'Nobody in here's going to tell you.'

Ryle nodded sagely and slipped his arms back into his coat. Who was he to look a gift horse in the mouth? He could do with a leisurely breakfast. And a chance to get out before Stacy remembered yesterday's lapse when he had written nothing, not even an account of Maurice Clark's funeral. He and Whelan had got into a long and philosophical drunken discussion that had seen them to another hotel where politicians from country constituencies were staying. He had made several attempts to find out what Whelan's problems were but without success. Whelan had only ended up stalking off annoyed. It had been a long night.

He had only a vague idea of what he should do next but he had to keep the story moving. Or get thrown back into the daily drudgery. He was under no illusions that Stacy would let him coast for too long. Still, it was nice to bask in a decent story for a change. 'Hey, Scoop.' It's pathetic to be so eager for praise, he thought. But it's a lot nicer than being in everybody's shithouse.

'Stick 'em up,' a voice croaked in his ear and something prodded him in the back. Ryle swung around.

'Jesus,' he swore. 'You fellas watch too much television.'

'On-the-job training.' Sergeant Peter Grifford grimaced at him. 'You look like a man who needs some coffee. And yes, thank you, I'll have one too.'

'You've been reading my mind,' said Ryle happily. It was wonderful the way things could fall into place when a story was running right. Grifford was just the man he needed.

They had met several years earlier on a balmy summer evening with the sweet smell of new-mown hay and the flowers in the unkempt hedges unperturbed by a gaping crater and the mangled metal of a bombed car in a country lane. Ryle was in a media group shifting restlessly behind a police cordon and waiting for someone to give them details, any details, of what had happened. The ambulances had been and gone, taking the scraps of two bodies away, and the scene had settled into the routine aftermath of sudden violence.

Grifford came through the cordon and Ryle buttonholed him for something to do rather than with any real expectation of getting information. To his surprise, Grifford asked for a lift back into the city. Ryle hesitated, nervous that he would miss something by leaving the area. They're not going to tell you anything, Grifford said and on the journey into Dublin he gave him a full account of what had happened.

After that, Ryle had called Grifford regularly and had always got straight answers to his questions. Sometimes they had no contact for months and yet the relationship, professionally friendly but otherwise distant, would resume whenever there was a story of interest to both. Ryle wondered occasionally why Grifford did it. Unlike most policemen he never asked for anything in return.

54

They went into the hot, coffee-laden atmosphere of Bewleys and Grifford selected a red banquette with suspect springs. He took off his overcoat and folded it carefully over a chair. A group of waitresses stood in animated conversation beside the service counter, ignoring the few customers.

'Tourists love this place.' Grifford watched the women. 'You know why? Because they're the only ones who can wait long enough to be served. Apart from leisured gentlemen like us.'

He straightened his waistcoat, picked up a spoon and began to pile brown sugar grains into a peak.

'So, what moves?' Ryle asked. 'I was surprised to see you at the funeral yesterday.'

'The wheels of God grind slowly.' Grifford concentrated on the sugar bowl. He glanced sideways at Ryle. 'You mean, what was I, a humble policeman, doing there?'

Ryle nodded, a little embarrassed at the direct question he himself had wanted to ask. 'The same as I'm doing here,' Grifford said. 'Tailing you.'

Ryle laughed lightly and raised his hand as a waitress turned in their general direction. She came and took their orders.

'What have I done?' Ryle smiled.

'Oh no, you're above suspicion. In so far as anyone ever is, of course. It's what you're going to do.' Grifford paused and settled back into his seat. 'We, that is the Garda Siochana, have decided that you will do our work for us and lead us to Maurice Clark's killer. Being the incompetent and lazy lot that you undoubtedly think we are, we have decided to rely on your invaluable investigative skills to solve this mystery for us. And save the taxpayer a fortune in overtime. My orders are to follow along and when you say "book him, Dano" I'll hop out of the bushes, slap the cuffs on and read him his rights.'

'When are you going to shave your head and start calling yourself Kojak?'

'No need to be flippant.' Grifford turned businesslike. 'So what have you discovered? Save me the trouble of rooting through your rubbish bin.'

'Nothing. Except what you've told me.'

Grifford shook his head sorrowfully. 'I thought you never revealed your sources.'

'Only to remind the absent-minded ones.'

'Can't be too careful, you know. Even the tables have ears, especially the ones with marbles.' He tapped the pitted marble table top and grimaced again.

'I can't keep up with you this early,' Ryle groaned. 'Give it to me simply. What's going on?'

Grifford sipped his coffee noisily. 'Follow the money or the motive, they say, and they will lead you to your man. Or woman,' he said. 'Which are you pursuing?'

'The motive, I suppose. Is there money involved?'

'There's always money involved.'

'And there might be a woman, too.' Grifford looked curious and Ryle told him about Clark's widow's affair.

'Interesting.' Grifford did not sound very interested. 'But there's another angle worth following, isn't there? The gun. An illegally held gun. Where do you get a gun without a permit?'

'I don't know.' Ryle shrugged to cover the mental kick he gave himself. Dumb shit – concentrating on Clark's marital problems and you missed the most obvious question. 'From criminals,' he added, trying to sound knowledgeable. 'Isn't there a pub where you're supposed to be able to buy them? Or even rent them?'

'You could get it from a small-time hood or you could steal it.' Grifford paused. 'Or you could belong to an organisation that gives it to you.'

Ryle twisted around to look at him and a spring snapped in the seat. 'What are you trying to say?'

'Thinking aloud. Looking at the options. There were three, I said. One . . . '

'What organisation?'

'Well, you can consider the options there too. Process of elimination. I don't think the party issues its members with guns. Not these days, anyway. Clark was a charitable man, into good works and that sort of thing. But he'd hardly have got a gun from the Vincent de Paul either. I don't think they arm their volunteers to distribute food parcels.'

'You're saying Clark was in the IRA?' Ryle did not try to conceal his astonishment.

Grifford sighed at his enthusiasm. 'All I'm saying is follow the gun. Along with the woman and the money.' Grifford dabbed at his mouth with a paper handkerchief and got up. 'Thank you for the coffee.'

'Hang on,' Ryle protested. 'You can't just walk out and leave me with a bombshell like that.'

Grifford gave him a sympathetic glance and put out a hand to restrain him as Ryle began to haul himself out of the seat. 'Let me go first. Wouldn't do to be seen coming out with the man I'm tailing.'

Ryle sank back, resigned. Grifford pulled on his overcoat and turned back to him. 'One word of friendly advice,' he said. 'You shouldn't get as drunk as you did last night. You probably don't even remember the most interesting thing you were told.'

Grifford winked and walked out. Ryle stared after him for a few minutes. He's playing games with me, he thought, his mind boggling at the story Grifford had dangled before him. Clark in the IRA was an incredible story. But it was ridiculous. So why's he tipping me off, then? Did the guards really think that? The idea was crazy. Still, it's a crazy country and anything's possible.

He tried to stop himself glancing at the doorways across the street when he emerged from the restaurant but he couldn't. He looked furtively up and down the street, feeling foolish. There was no sign of Grifford. This is ridiculous, he told himself angrily. He couldn't have been in the IRA. Not Clark. There was nothing in his background to even hint at it. Or was there? There were a few other politicians of whom you could believe it. But not Clark. Surely not?

Ryle crossed the road at a pedestrian crossing and walked towards the arched entrance to Stephen's Green. A line of Hare Krishna disciples trailed mutely across the park entrance, their shaven heads grey with the cold. Ryle let them pass and strolled around the squat stone in memory of Parnell and over towards the pond.

Forget the violence for the moment, he thought; get back to the sex. The ice on the pond had been broken to let the ducks into the water. Ryle watched a portly lapwing waddle carefully across towards the fractured edge of the ice and wondered how he was going to approach the widow's lover. Full-frontally, he decided, there was no other way of breaking the ice.

The young woman at the reception desk played a telephone switchboard with one hand as though it was a large calculator and raised her head to ask if she could help him. Ryle asked for James Burke, gave his name, said it was personal and no, he did not have an appointment. He took a seat and listened to her sing-song telephone voice endlessly repeating and mixing the same selection of phrases as he waited.

A short, dapper man in his late thirties came down a curving stairway and approached Ryle with an inquisitive and busi-nesslike air. He wore a sober grey suit, his brown hair was receding and a neatly trimmed beard edged his pink face. 'Mr Ryle?' he asked in a mildly impatient tone that carried an unmistakable hint that this had better be important.

Ryle stood up and towered over him to explain who he worked for and that he would like to talk to him about a personal matter. 'Is there somewhere we could have a private word?'

'In connection with what?' Burke's eyes narrowed with suspicion.

'Maurice Clark.'

Burke's assurance crumbled into a startled snort, half fear and half outrage. 'I know nothing. I have nothing to say.'

'I don't want to quote you. Or involve you in this in any way.'

'Then go away.' Burke lowered his voice and glanced nervously at the receptionist.

'But I am trying to find out certain things and I think you might be able to help me. Off the record.'

'Who sent you here? I have nothing to say to you. No comment.'

'There are a couple of things about the night of Clark's death . . .' Ryle let the sentence dwindle into a sinister silence. 'And I don't really want to bother his widow. At the moment.'

'I have told the police everything there is to say on the matter. I have no comment to make.'

'They interviewed you? About the party in Killiney?'

Burke began to walk away, as if suddenly realising he was free of physical restraints. Ryle strode with him, aware of the weakness of his position and deciding to go for broke.

'About the fact that you took her home from the party? While Clark went off to his death. Or did you in fact take her home?' Burke stopped and started to say something but it came out as a strangled cough. Ryle tried to press his advantage. 'I don't want to write any of that. If I can find out some other things . . . '

Burke glared at him and said, 'Over here,' leading him across the lobby to a small interview room. Ryle followed, his unease at making such crude threats easily smothered by his elation. That's how you get scoops, he told himself: the foot in the door, the foot on someone's neck.

Burke positioned himself behind a high-backed chair as if it might afford him some protection. Ryle stood across a light-coloured wooden table from him, almost against the wall.

'I resent your insinuation,' Burke said peevishly. 'Yes, I took her home. After he had gone off and abandoned her. And I know nothing about his death.'

Ryle tried to remember precisely what it was he wanted to know but it eluded him for a moment. 'Did Clark ever threaten you?' he asked.

'Threaten me?' Burke sounded surprised. The words came out jerkily and he kept his eyes fixed on Ryle's chest.

'With violence.' Ryle resisted an urge to bend his knees and bring his eyes down to Burke's level.

'No.'

'He knew about you and Yvonne.'

'Yes,' Burke said, almost defiantly.

'What did he think about that?'

'I thought you weren't interested in that. I thought you only had matters of great public importance on your mind,' Burke said sarcastically. 'Isn't that what you call it? No. Matters of national interest.'

Ryle took the point. 'Clark and his wife had an argument at the party the night he died,' he said. 'Do you know what it was about?'

'Not in detail.'

'Roughly?'

'Roughly, it was over his relationship with that gangster Erlanger.' Burke paused, surprised by his own vehemence. Take it easy, he instructed himself. 'They spent quite a while talking privately in an upstairs room. He and Erlanger that is. He was upset afterwards. Yvonne asked him what had happened and he wouldn't tell her. They got into one of their rows and he eventually walked off and left her there. He abandoned her.'

'Why d'you say Erlanger's a gangster?'

Burke shifted position uneasily. 'A figure of speech,' he said. 'We are talking privately, aren't we?'

Ryle nodded. 'What's, ah, Mrs Clark got against Erlanger?'

'Nothing per se. She thinks he is, was, manipulating Maurice.'

'How?'

'I don't know exactly. Neither does Yvonne. Maurice owed him a lot of money.'

'Money?' Ryle said with a note of surprise that made Burke glance up at him quickly. He looked away again, realising too late that Ryle knew nothing of what had been going on. But he didn't really care. He wanted to say what had to be said, had wanted to for days except that he had had no one to tell.

'Maurice Clark,' Burke continued, 'was a politician on the make. In all the worst possible senses. Prepared to do anything to succeed. Didn't give a tinker's curse about who or what he trampled on along the way.'

Burke let go of the chair and walked over to the window. 'What you people have written about him makes me want to fucking puke,' he said to the glass, his sudden passion emphasised by an uncharacteristic adjective. He turned back to face Ryle who could no longer see his face clearly against the daylight outside. 'He was out to make money, set himself up for his political career. He was in a hurry and that's how he came to owe Erlanger, and a lot of others, money. You know what Erlanger's game is?'

Ryle shook his head to indicate his ignorance.

Burke gestured disdain. 'Uranium mining. He's got a company on the unlisted securities market which has attracted a lot of speculation. Maurice got shares in it in a private placing and was hoping to make a killing out of them. Something seems to have gone wrong with his plans but I don't know what. Never paid for the shares, I suspect, and Erlanger was putting pressure on him.'

'To do what?'

'I don't know. Pay him back, I presume.'

'How much was involved?'

'I've no idea. That's what most of the arguments between Maurice and Yvonne were about. He wouldn't tell her what he was doing. At one stage she found out by accident that he had re-mortgaged their house without her knowledge. And he wouldn't tell her why or for what.'

Burke walked back from the window and took up position behind the chair again. 'While I'm at it.' He stared at Ryle with contempt and a destructive determination to go on talking. 'I presume you know that Maurice was no saint either.'

Ryle looked back at him, trying to keep up with the flood of information and innuendo that was swamping his mind. 'How do you mean?' he said.

'I thought it must be her who put you on to me. To further the revolution, I presumed.'

'Who?' Ryle asked, bewildered.

'Obviously it was the politicians, then.' Burke nodded to himself with satisfaction. 'His friends in Leinster House. Lovely people. It shouldn't surprise me. Do you know what some of them are doing? Accusing Yvonne of being responsible for his death, more or less.'

'How?' Ryle asked lamely. Jesus, he thought, what've I dug up here?

'The fact that you're here indicates that you know how,' Burke snapped. 'She pushed him too hard or something. That's a laugh. And the fact that she was having an affair. But they didn't tell you about *his* affair, did they? No, that's different, of course. Typical of those macho troglodytes. They'd consider it a terrible crime for his wife to have an affair but perfectly all right for him. One of the boys.' He gave a harsh laugh and added, with the force of an incontrovertible piece of evidence, 'For him, in fact, to continue a previous relationship throughout his marriage to Yvonne.'

'With whom?'

'With one of his students.' Burke gave him a look of sour triumph. 'Does that make it even more interesting, more vital to the national interest?'

'Who is she?'

Burke gave a sickly laugh. 'Oh, no, I'm not going to play their game. Go back to his political friends. I'm sure they will be delighted to tell you.' Burke gave another short laugh. 'And talk to Maurice's bank manager, while you're at it. See what he thinks of your paper's estimation of the loss the country has suffered.'

Burke straightened the chair he had used as a shield and headed for the door. 'One more thing,' Ryle said quickly. 'Did Clark have strong feelings about the North, about uniting Ireland?'

Burke looked at him properly for the first time, as if he had suddenly realised a playground bully was no threat after all. He gave an amused snort. 'Haven't you been listening to anything I said? He cared about nothing, nothing at all. Only about his own material and political advancement.'

He walked out, letting the door slam behind him.

Ryle replaced the receiver and went down the narrow corridor to the press entrance into the Dáil chamber. He slipped onto a chair inside the door and surveyed the somnolent scene beneath him. An Opposition member was on his feet, castigating the Minister responsible for public works for not merely failing but failing utterly to live up to his promises to drain a river in his constituency. His voice rose with foreboding as he declared that the farmers would sweep the governing party away at the next election as surely as the floods washed away their livelihoods every winter.

He stopped as though surprised at the symmetry of his own image. The Minister straightened himself in the Taoiseach's chair, his reveries interrupted by the sudden silence. The back-bencher launched into another subject and the Minister let his head rest on the triangled tips of his fingers, returning to sleep or to his thoughts.

Ryle looked along the press bench to a reporter who raised her eyes to the darkened skylight at the chamber's dome. He sidled over to her and asked if she had seen Jim Whelan. She shook her head.

'Five minutes,' the chairman told the speaker who looked up at the clock with the desperation of a punch-drunk boxer facing the final round, shuffled his notes and staggered into another bout of grievances.

Ryle wandered slowly down the corridors whose width and elegance switched from the old and gracious to the modern and practical as the former stately home of Leinster House had been adapted and expanded into a functional parliament building.

'It's deadly dull,' a colleague from his own paper groaned in the bar. 'You wouldn't believe how quickly the excitement of a new term sinks into boring routine.'

'Was there some excitement earlier?'

The reporter shook his head. 'I meant relatively speaking.' He had not seen Whelan either and Ryle retraced his steps to the press gallery and called Whelan's office again. He had not returned.

Ryle gave up for the moment and left the building. The afternoon was dull and tired as though the day was weary of its unequal battle with the long winter nights. He hurried back to the warmth of the news room as if his speed alone would maintain the momentum of his investigations.

'What's the story?' Stacy demanded.

'I don't know yet,' Ryle admitted, hooking his jacket over his shoulder and sitting on the edge of the news desk. 'But there's a hell of a lot of angles to this.'

He was eager to tell the news editor all he had learned but Stacy was called away to a phone. Ryle went to his own desk, pulled over a typewriter and stared into the middle distance of the news room, idly watching the sub-editors at the other end going through the rituals of people arriving for work.

He began typing a densely packed jumble of notes, mostly phrases and snatches of information, everything he could remember from his conversations since Clark's body was discovered. It was a boring chore but it had to be done. Especially with a story like this that seemed to be taking off in half a dozen different directions. And it might help to sort out his thoughts.

Clark appeared to have led a double life, if one took the accounts of his political friend Whelan and of his – competitor, Ryle supposed – at face value. But he did not take either entirely at face value: Whelan was a politician first and foremost and Burke was . . . what was he, Ryle wondered? A bit of a weirdo, maybe. Both were peddling a line but one did not often come up against such total contradictions.

Even more intriguing than all the sexual goings-on were Grifford's hints about Clark's connections with the IRA. It seemed impossible: Clark's party was totally opposed to the IRA and under periodic pressure from civil liberties groups because of its efforts to suppress subversion. One could not square membership of the party with membership of the IRA. Unless Clark had been a plant, Ryle decided. But a plant in which? It would have to be in the party. Ryle scratched his head. Or would it?

He suddenly realised that Grifford had given him a story he could write immediately. The gun had been illegally held. He had been so wrapped up in the mass of hints and speculation that he had relegated the information to the back of his mind. He smiled with satisfaction: that was a grand story to be going on with. Clark was toting an illegal gun and shooting dogs. While, he added wryly, pursuing or being pursued by women or financiers. Or Provos. Or all three. Jesus. Whatever else he was, Mr Clark seemed to have been one hell of a busy man.

But what had Grifford meant about last night when . . . Ryle remembered Whelan, dialled his number and got him.

'You were holding out on me yesterday,' Ryle greeted him.

'What?'

'Maurice Clark's mistress. Who is she?'

Whelan closed his eyes and said nothing. God damn it, he thought, what am I getting into now? He opened his eyes and glanced at his secretary who was clacking slowly on her electric typewriter.

'What do you mean?' he stalled.

'You know very well what I mean,' Ryle blustered, imagining Whelan's discomfort. 'I know all about it. Except for her name.'

'I can't go into that at the moment.'

'I'll meet you later.'

'I've a constituency meeting.'

'To do with the problem you don't want to talk about?'

'I'll be home about midnight.' Whelan hung up with a sigh. He's not going to put any of that in the paper, he assured himself uncertainly. They never do. Not in this country, thank God.

Ryle went over to Stacy and told him Clark had had an illegal gun. Stacy nodded, typed in the information and went on to the next item on his list. Ryle watched him for a moment, expecting some comment, but the news editor ignored him.

He picked up his telephone and dialled the detective unit at a city centre garda station and asked for Grifford. The sergeant wasn't there; neither was he at home. Ryle thought about phoning a couple of pubs but decided it would be a waste of time. He had been with Grifford once when he was paged by a barman: Grifford ignored the summons and explained to Ryle's inquiring look that he did not expose himself so easily to anyone who might want to identify him.

Ryle checked his watch; it was just after five thirty. He pulled over a telephone directory, found Erlanger's office number and dialled it. A recorded message answered and he listened to it but hung up before the tone. He considered phoning Erlanger at home but changed his mind. It would be better to appear on his doorstep: it was always too easy for people to slam down telephones. Especially gangsters.

'Remember that conversation,' Ryle said when he found Grifford at home an hour later. 'About the weapon. I presume your speculation was based on fact.'

'Naturally.'

'And that our friend was not licensed?'

'Correct,' Grifford said. 'Why didn't you listen the first time?'

'Just want to be sure. And the other stuff, about his organisation?'

'Can't talk to you now,' Grifford said. 'My rashers are going cold.'

The story ended up a mishmash of his earlier report and random bits of new information. Hanging on the fact that Clark had an unlicensed gun, it went back over the night or morning of Clark's death, identifying the missing hours between his departure from the party and the killing of the dog. It did not mention Clark's domestic or financial troubles.

Ryle was on the last page when his extension rang.

'Seamus?' a woman's voice said, then added with pointed formality, 'This is Breda.'

'Hello.' Ryle was surprised and a little wary. 'How are you?'

'Fine,' she said distantly.

'I've been meaning to call you but it's been very busy here.'

'Yes,' she said without interest. 'I called to tell you something you should know.'

'What?' Ryle said urgently, his stomach tightening, fearing the worst. 'Is it Lorraine?'

'No.'

'How is she?' He relaxed.

'Fine.'

'She doing anything new?'

'There's nothing to stop you coming to see her,' Breda said coldly, 'if you're so interested.'

'I know,' he sighed. But it wasn't that simple. 'It's just very busy at the moment.'

'Of course,' she said with a tone of deliberate patience.

'I think we should have a talk.'

'Is there any point?' she asked.

'There are some things I need from there.'

'All right.'

'This evening? I'm nearly finished now.'

'No.'

'Tomorrow evening?'

'All right,' she said and added quickly, before he could distract her again, 'Two men called here looking for you. Said they wanted to check if you were still living here. Or where you're living now.'

'Who were they?' Ryle asked.

'They said they were policemen.'

Ryle muttered a curse. What the hell was going on?

The cleaners were finished and packing their equipment into a closet off the corridor. James Burke sat at his desk and listened to their idle gossip and the clanging of metal on metal as the dismantled the vacuum cleaner. He had pretended to be busy when they came into his office, studying papers as they emptied a bin, dusted the furniture and swept the floor. He had gone through the same pretence earlier when a colleague had invited him for an after-work drink.

Ryle's visit had brought all his most terrible nightmares out into the open light of day. He had hardly slept since he had heard of Clark's death. Then the police had come and asked him some polite questions and gone away, apparently satisfied. But Ryle's arrival confirmed his worst fears: he was being dragged into the forefront of a murder investigation. The prime suspect.

If only he could talk to Yvonne. But she had warned him to keep away, not even to call her. Not now, she said in their only conversation since Clark's death, it's not politic. She had put down the phone and left him with a sick sense of isolation.

The voices of the cleaners faded down the corridor and were cut off by the finality of a banging door. In the silence, he picked up the telephone and listened to its hum.

He had to do it, he told himself. He had to do something. Or be left as the patsy. He had no illusions any more about politics and the way politicians operated. Their world fascinated him, a world without qualms, scruples, morals or even convictions. That was part of what attracted him to Yvonne, seeing into this strange world through her scabrous humour and feeling that he knew what was really going on. That and the sex they had together. He'd never experienced anything like it before. He shook the memory away nervously.

Clark's death had changed everything. He'd learned enough about politics to know they'd want a scapegoat. And, he had realised after Yvonne's curt call, he was the ideal scapegoat. If only he could talk to her.

He punched out Mike Erlanger's number with the top of his pen as if it would insulate him against what he had to do. Erlanger answered on the second ring with his surname. 'How're you doing?' Erlanger sounded expansive.

'It's about Maurice Clark,' Burke said. 'Rather, it's about Yvonne.'

'How is she?' Erlanger closed his eyes and gave a mental sigh. Here we go, he thought. He'd been waiting for this but hadn't expected Burke to be her emissary.

'She's standing up to it well, all things considered. But you could help her enormously.'

'Anything I can do . . . ' Erlanger let his voice drop off with resignation and thought impatiently, get on with.

'Yes. You could take some of the pressure off her. By admitting that you are more responsible for his death than she is.'

Erlanger's eyes snapped open. Maybe this wasn't what he had feared at all. Or maybe Burke, in his usual way, was cocking up a simple blackmail demand. His silence made Burke think for a relieved moment that he had gone away. 'I don't know what you mean,' Erlanger said finally. His voice was even, no longer friendly but not hostile either. 'If she's got something to say to me . . . '

'No, no,' Burke said nervously. 'I don't want her involved in anything. But there are people accusing her of causing Maurice's death . . . '

'Of killing him?' Erlanger said with relief which translated into surprise in Burke's ear.

'Indirectly. But on that score you have more to answer for than she has. And I think you should do something about it.'

'About what?' Erlanger asked with a cautious hint of exasperation. 'I still don't know what you're talking about.'

'The pressures you put on Maurice, the debt you got him into, the shady deals . . . '

'Hold it,' Erlanger broke in again but Burke ignored the interruption.

' . . . the sort of things that broke up their marriage.'

Erlanger let out a peal of relieved laughter. 'You think I broke up their marriage. You think that.' His voice rose with incredulity. 'I've been told that you Irish sometimes live in a make-believe world but this is the best I've come across yet. You're the one balling Clark's wife and you're saying that I broke up their marriage?'

Burke dragged his pen hard along the side of the square he had doodled. It broke through the paper and dug into the sheets underneath. 'I know what your game is. You're just out to make money.'

'Hey, you're right.' Erlanger laughed again, satisfied now that his fears are not been realised. Not yet, at any rate. 'I'm a businessman and I'm out to make money. You're absolutely right. That's what businessmen are for. What the hell do they teach you in accountancy school here?'

'You know exactly what I mean.' Burke tried to control his confused anger.

'Look.' Erlanger sounded patient. 'You keep telling me I know but I don't know. As far as I can make out, you're trying to blame me in some way for Clark's death. But I can assure you, it had nothing to do with me. And I had nothing to do with it. Ask the police. They'll tell you.'

'Yvonne is being blamed for everything,' Burke moaned. 'The politicians are trying to pin everything on her. They've even set the media after her. They're trying to break her down and someone's got to protect her.'

'I'm happy to do anything I can to help her,' Erlanger lied. The bitch could stew in hell for all he cared but caution on the telephone was second nature to him. 'What I don't understand is what you think I should do. Or why. But let's leave the why out of it for a minute.'

'I want you to admit that you had involved Maurice in a financial web that was putting enormous strain on him. And that might have had some bearing on his death. Assuming he killed himself.'

'There's a lot of "ifs" there.' Erlanger paused as if considering the proposition. 'Look, you're not thinking too straight at

69

the moment. You must be under a lot of strain yourself. You've got to be high up the suspect list after all. The oldest motive in the book and all that.'

Burke winced at his chief fear being voiced so casually. He pushed it to the back of his mind and asked limply, 'You're not going to help?'

'I've offered to help in any way I can,' Erlanger said slowly. 'But I'm not going to claim to have had something to do with a matter I had nothing to do with. Sure, Clark and I had some business dealings but that's all they were. Business. All up front and above board.'

There was silence, then Erlanger sighed and Burke heard the click as he put down his receiver. Burke listened to the open line, empty of sound, for a moment. Then he hung up and rested his head in his hands. He was sweating and he squeezed his eyelids shut until they hurt.

That had gone all wrong. But Erlanger wouldn't get away that easily. He was responsible in some way for Maurice Clark's death. I know it, Burke told himself, I know it. And I'm not going to be the fall guy.

Six

Detective Garda Casey pushed through the glass-panelled door and merged into the cluster of policemen grouped inside. The courtroom was drowsy with overused heat and its elaborate tiers gave the impression of a miniature theatre where a long-running play had gone stale through repetition of parts played too often. Two men were perched in the dock between prison warders, looking uninterested. A scattering of people higher up in the public gallery were outnumbered by uniformed policemen.

An unused jury box masked the witness stand and the three judges but he could hear Inspector Bill Devane replying in a tired voice as a defending barrister tried to railroad him into an indiscretion.

'Come now, Inspector,' the barrister chided with the weary patience of a man who knows the ways of the world. 'Isn't it the simple truth of the matter that you had decided before you ever met my clients that they were guilty?'

'No, Your Honour.'

'On the basis, perhaps, of paid information from an informer?'

'No, Your Honour.'

'And that you approached them with the single-minded intention of extracting confessions?'

'No, your honour.'

'And that you had already convicted them in your own mind?'

'No, Your Honour.'

'That you had once again set yourself up as judge and jury?' The barrister oozed disdain.

'I would never do that, your honour.' A subdued titter of knowing laughter barely ruffled the atmosphere. One of the judges pointed out that it was after four o'clock and asked the barrister if he had many more questions.

'Yes, my lord.' He glared threateningly at Devane. 'Perhaps we should continue in the morning.'

'Very well,' the presiding judge grumbled and the courtroom shuffled to its feet. The two men in the dock waved to some people in the public gallery before they disappeared down the stairs to the cells.

Casey waited while Devane recovered his raincoat and lit a cigarette in the corridor. 'The Chief wants to see you,' he said. 'Urgently.'

Devane raised his eyes inquiringly and squinted through the smoke. 'He didn't say why,' Casey said and added, pleased with his unofficial knowledge, 'but he's got an answer from Belfast.'

Devane knew that already but he merely grunted and followed him to an unmarked car.

'Will they be convicted?' Casey asked as he waited for a uniformed garda to swing back a crowd barrier and let their car out of the cordoned-off street.

'They confessed, didn't they?'

Casey took the implied rebuke silently and concentrated on driving. Devane could be a difficult man to work with, impatient, stubborn and moody at times. He found the Inspector's absolute certainty once he had made up his mind unnerving. That barrister was right, he thought, he really does think he's the judge and jury.

'What about James Burke?' Devane brought him back to the Clark case.

'The general impression is that he's straight, a respectable type. Not the kind of person to get involved in anything criminal.'

Devane restrained himself from saying that that didn't mean much. He had no time for theories that some people were preordained to commit crime by social deprivation, the shape of their skulls or anything else. No one was a criminal type until they committed a crime.

Burke had been having an affair with Clark's wife. Which indicated to Devane a capacity for subterfuge. Although everybody seemed to know about it, including Clark. So he was an incompetent plotter. The kind who might resort to violence if challenged?

'We've finished the interviews with the politicians,' Casey said. 'All those who were on the Erlangers' guest list. The lads are going back through the statements again.'

Devane nodded. 'And the, ah, other woman?' He smiled fleetingly at the phrase.

'We're waiting for instructions about her.'

The Chief Superintendent was furious. He tossed Ryle's newspaper to Devane and stamped around the room twice as if trying to tether him to his chair with an invisible rope. Devane read the report about Clark having an unlicensed gun and looked up at the Chief as though unable to understand its significance.

'That's the second leak,' the Chief said accusingly.

'It didn't come from me.'

'It's coming from somebody.'

Devane shrugged. 'I don't have time to worry about that.'

'Well, it's only a minor problem.' The Chief sighed into his chair with an air of defeat. 'Compared with our other one.' He picked up a sheet of paper, waved it in the air as if he was trying to cool it and let it flutter back to the desk. 'I told you. You shouldn't have done it.'

'At least we know for sure now. It was an IRA gun.'

'And what do we tell the RUC? What do I tell the Commissioner?'

'We tell them we need the gun as a possible exhibit here and we can't release it out of our jurisdiction.' What you tell the Commissioner is your problem, he thought. 'Anyhow,' he added aloud, 'they haven't got anyone for that shooting. All they said was that Ballistics matched the gun we sent them with a couple of bullets fired at a checkpoint in Armagh.' Devane paused. 'No one was hurt.'

The Chief glared as if Devane were deliberately provoking him. He started to say something but checked himself.

'I mean,' Devane added in a conciliatory tone, 'they're not likely to pursue the request very hard. They don't even have anybody in mind for it.'

The Chief straightened up and leaned on his desk, taking charge. 'So where does this leave everything?'

'It means Clark had a gun used by the IRA . . . '

'Do the RUC say it was the IRA?' the Chief demanded irritably.

'No. Who else would it have been?'

The Chief dismissed the question with a wave of his hand.

'We have to follow that lead a bit more,'Devane said. 'Find out how Clark came to have it.'

'And how do you propose to do that?'

'Dig around a bit,' Devane said vaguely. 'Find out more about his associates, who would have given it to him. And why.'

The Chief put his face in his hands and stroked his eyes with the tips of his fingers.

'I'd like to ask the Special Branch and C3 for their files on Clark. If any,' Devane added.

The Chief rested his jaw in one palm. 'You're determined to stir this one up, aren't you? Go blundering about all over the place.'

'C3 know about it already,' Devane admitted. C3, the police Intelligence section, was the channel through which they communicated with the RUC in Belfast. 'They're hounding me for details.'

'What did you tell them?'

'To ask you.' Devane ignored the Chief's impatient sigh. 'I thought we'd offer them a trade. We give them all we've got on the gun and they give us a look at their file on Clark. If any.'

The Chief thought better of what he had been going to say. 'I doubt if they have one,' he offered calmly. 'Keeping files on politicians . . . ' He shook his head.

'Clark might crop up in someone else's file.'

'I'll see what I can do,' the Chief said. 'But no more wild initiatives without telling me beforehand. Understood?'

Devane nodded absently. 'There is the question of the woman,' he said, 'Clark's mistress.'

The Chief gave him a look that said there was no limit to his patience and Devane was wasting his time trying to test it.

'She's the most obvious link. Involved with some so-called revolutionaries.'

The Chief sighed. 'We're not concerned with Clark's political beliefs or his personal life. I told you that before, didn't I?' Devane wondered what the hell else they were supposed to be concerned with but let the remark pass. It was certainly a new definition of policing not to be concerned with people's hidden lives.

'All right,' the Chief added, 'I'll think about it. But I don't want anything heavy-handed. Subtlety's the key word. There's a lot of nervous people about.'

That sounded like a quote, Devane decided, today's motto from on high. He nodded and stood up.

'Just for your information,' the Chief added mildly, 'the word from the Department is that they would like a final report by Tuesday. In case the Minister has to answer questions in the Dáil.'

Devane calculated quickly: that gave him another four days, more or less.

Seamus Ryle stopped as a horde of small children swept across the schoolyard with coats, scarves and bags flying and broke like a wave around him. Another year, he thought, and Lorraine will be one of them, passing another landmark. Where will I be then? The children's yells were absorbed into the line of waiting mothers and he continued on towards a corner door. He climbed the stairs inside, stepping around a couple of tiny stragglers who were studiously plopping down from step to step.

The classroom door was wide open and a woman was kneeling before a low cupboard, replacing a pile of books. She was in her late twenties and had tight curls of brown hair spread in a wide halo around her face. She was wearing a long black dress with a faded floral pattern and high-heeled black boots.

He tapped at the door and said 'Miss Gantly?' as she straightened up. She nodded and her face hardened and her hands moved slowly onto her hips as he told her who he was.

'Fuck off,' she said in a south Dublin suburban drawl, separating the words to reinforce the message. Involuntarily, she glanced past Ryle but the corridor was empty.

Ryle was taken aback. 'But you haven't heard what I was going to say.'

'I know what you're going to say. I heard from your friends.'

'My friends?' Ryle's heart sank. 'The other papers have been here?'

'Cut the bullshit,' she said derisively.

They looked at each other for a moment, she hostile, he confused. Then with relief he grasped the reason for her attitude. 'You don't believe I'm a journalist,' he said and rummaged in an inside pocket. She watched with a bitter smirk while he sorted through a handful of letters, bits of paper and a cheque book. 'I can't find my press card,' he said at last. 'Nobody ever asks to see those things.'

'Really?' She sounded triumphant. 'Why don't you just fuck off then? And tell your bosses I won't be intimidated.'

'Who's intimidating you?'

She laughed without humour.

'I'm not trying to intimidate you,' Ryle said desperately. 'I'm only looking for your help.'

She held her hostile stance in silence. Ryle pulled a notebook from his pocket, printed his name and the newspaper's phone number and tore out the page. He held it out to her but she ignored it; he left it on the cupboard.

'Check it against the phone book if you like, and give me a call there,' he pleaded. 'That'll prove I am who I say I am.' She still said nothing. 'Okay?' He shrugged and left her standing with her hands on her hips, like an irate matron seeing off a malingering schoolboy.

What the hell did Clark ever see in her, he wondered when he was back in his car. She was no beauty. She was big, fat and had a lousy manner. No, he amended his description as his anger at her abrupt dismissal of him cooled, she was plump, even homely. A handful, in every sense of the word. It was difficult to visualise her as Clark's lover. But then, he had come to realise, he really knew next to nothing about Clark in spite of all the square feet of newsprint written about him.

And what did she mean about intimidation?

Another idea occurred to him and he flipped through his notebook in search of an address. He looked up a map and found that Clark's widow lived close by. He thought about it for

76

a moment but decided he wasn't up to that today: confronting bereaved relatives was a journalistic art he had never mastered. Especially not in these kinds of murky circumstances.

He drove fast towards the city along the Stillorgan dual carriageway, not thinking of anything in particular, not going anywhere in particular. A maudlin song about a grey-haired mother hummed from the radio and his attention picked up when it gave way to the news headlines in Irish. He understood just enough to be able to decipher the main stories: a bus strike was threatened and another bank had been robbed. The rest was foreign.

The traffic bunched up in Donnybrook and crawled like a slow snake, pulling itself forward in a series of contractions and expansions. He wondered what he was going to say to Breda tonight. He had to have something worked out or they'd sink into the usual tetchy monosyllables, hovering on the edge of an unspecified argument. It was a simple question, really. To go or to stay. Rather, to go back or to make the final break.

He was agonising over why it was so difficult to make up his mind when he noticed he was outside Mike Erlanger's office building. In a sudden spurt of decisiveness, he indicated left and drove onto the footpath to get the car off the no-parking lines.

'He's not here,' Erlanger's secretary said. 'Can I help you or take a message?'

Ryle debated for a moment and decided he would leave his name and number. 'Is it about the meeting?' she asked as she jotted down the details.

'The meeting?'

'The meeting about the exploration. That's where Mr Erlanger's gone. He left early to get there on time.'

Ryle looked bemused and she told him there was to be a public meeting that night in the village near the site of their exploratory drilling. Erlanger and some environmentalists were to address it. 'I'm sure your paper has been told,' she said. 'One of the other papers called to see if Mr Erlanger had a prepared speech.'

Ryle thanked her, ran back to his car and cursed the traffic as he drove to his office. He had something to do, another angle to pursue.

Stacy was deep in discussion with the deputy editor at the other end of the newsroom and Ryle rummaged about the news desk until he found the notice about the meeting. It had come from an environmental group and he scanned through a lengthy tract about the dangers of uranium mining and nuclear weapons until he got to the details of where and when the meeting was taking place. From a map on the wall he calculated the rough distance from Dublin to the River Shannon. There was plenty of time to get there.

'Is anyone marked for this?' Ryle held out the invitation to Stacy as he returned to his desk.

The news editor glanced at it and shook his head. 'If you're volunteering to do stories you can do the bus strike talks.'

'This is to do with the Clark story,' Ryle pleaded. 'A witness I've been trying to find is going to be there. It's important.'

Stacy took the invitation and studied it. 'Okay,' he nodded, 'but cover the meeting as well.'

Ryle switched off the engine and stretched himself in the sudden silence. Convoys of trucks and buses leaving Dublin on the winding road towards the west had delayed him and made the drive tiring. He stepped out into the freezing air and walked across the gravelled car park to a narrow door marked by a drooping bulb.

There was nobody in the small lobby and Ryle followed a corridor into the hall itself. It was small and narrow with a line of windows on one side sealed with heavy shutters. Rows of collapsible wooden chairs faced a stage where faded curtains were drawn back to reveal a bare table with five chairs behind it. A man in a heavy overcoat was squatting beside a bottled gas heater at the side of the stage. Ryle noticed a similar heater at each corner of the hall: a smell of gas was more discernible than any feeling of heat.

He went back outside to wait, glad of his heavy sweater, his leather jacket and his parka. Cars began to arrive and people straggled into the hall, no one hurrying into the meeting, which was supposed to have begun twenty minutes earlier. He went back into the building, declared his credentials and was brought to a room off the hall and introduced to a man called Jonathan in his late twenties. He was dressed in tweeds and looked like an earnest environmentalist. Why did these people always look like their caricatures, Ryle wondered.

Jonathan assumed, as earnest protestors always did, that Ryle had travelled from Dublin because of his personal, as well as his paper's, concern over uranium mining. Ireland had to be protected from the evils of the nuclear industry, he declared as if he were already addressing the meeting.

Ryle was not listening. Mike Erlanger had come in with two other men and he recognised him immediately: everything about him proclaimed what he was, from his well-cut conservative suit to his slightly tanned face and his well-groomed salt and pepper hair. He had the bearing of a man used to being the centre of attention, which he was now, and who took it as his natural due.

Another caricature, Ryle thought. Of a businessman, though, not a gangster as James Burke had described him. The confrontation between two such predictable-looking protagonists was hardly going to break new ground in the nuclear debate, Ryle decided. Not that he cared a lot about the nuclear debate at the moment. He merely wanted the opportunity for a lengthy chat with Erlanger on neutral ground.

One of the men with Erlanger greeted Jonathan by name and introduced himself to Ryle. 'I'm chairing the meeting,' he said. 'Would you like to meet Mr Erlanger and his associate?'

Erlanger gave them a firm handshake and chatted easily with Jonathan as Ryle tried to figure out a way of having a private talk with him. He was still waiting for an opening when the chairman began to herd the others towards the stage. Ryle seized his last chance and halted Erlanger with a hand on his arm.

'Could I have a word with you later?'

'Sure.' Erlanger gave him a broad smile and passed by.

Ryle went back to the body of the hall and found a seat beside a clear passageway. The steady noise subsided into coughs and the scraping of chairs as the speakers took their places. The chairman announced Jonathan as someone known to them all, almost one of their own. Ryle detected a barb: Jonathan obviously lived locally but was not quite a local. Ryle balanced a notebook on his knee and forced himself to concentrate on the speech, waiting for a news angle.

Jonathan ran through the dangers of digging uranium out of the earth, from the radon gas which inevitably accompanied it to the tailings which would be left on the surface to blight the landscape and threaten the countryside with radioactivity for centuries, even millenniums, to come. Half the Irish midlands could be threatened: if the radioactive waste were to seep into the nearby River Shannon it would spread the length of the river, half the length of the country, carrying dangerous waste to population centres like Limerick.

Nobody seemed unduly worried about the prospect of poisoning Limerick but Ryle noted the comment: it would serve as a story if nothing better emerged. Jonathan ended his speech with an impassioned appeal to the local population not to allow illusory promises of jobs and wealth to mean the introduction into Ireland of the most dangerous and uncertain industry known to man. Especially, he added, when Ireland 'benefited' neither from nuclear weapons nor nuclear power.

Ryle wrote rapidly as Jonathan concluded. There was applause throughout the hall, polite rather than heartfelt.

'I am here,' Erlanger began quietly, 'primarily to answer your questions and I assume you'll have an opportunity in a few minutes to put anything you wish to me.' He looked at the chairman who nodded. 'Coming here tonight, I wasn't sure what I should say to you by way of introduction. Talking it over with my wife Becky on the way, she suggested that I tell you why I am here, why I am in Ireland.' He paused. 'Apart from my Irish grandmother, that is.' A mixed murmur of laughter and appreciation spread through the hall. Erlanger used the pause to extract a slim book from his briefcase and held it up in his right hand like a witness about to swear an oath.

'This.' He waved the booklet gently as the hall fell silent. 'This is a little book that I doubt any of you have seen. To me and my family, however, it has been something akin to a bible – if one can say that without any desire to cause offence or to blaspheme – for the past thirty years. It is called, not very imaginatively, "Prospecting for Uranium" and it was published by the United States Atomic Energy Commission. And, I can safely say, its appearance all of thirty years ago changed the lives of my family.

'My dad was selling insurance and we, my father, mother and myself, lived in a small city in Colorado at the time. It was just after the war which the first atomic bombs ended and the United States, or that part of it, was swept with uranium fever. Everyone was looking for it, for this wonderful new material that was the hope of the future. It was, I guess, something like the Klondike gold rush in the eighteen-nineties. The last of the prospecting frontiers when one man with a shovel and pick could just go out there and strike it rich.

'My dad gave up selling insurance and became a "rock hound", as they called them, setting off with his pick and shovel in search of uranium. Actually, it wasn't quite like the Klondike: he set off in his automobile and armed with a geiger counter which was the basic tool of all prospectors. He never hit the big one, though some did, but he found enough to make a better living than we ever had out of insurance. And he had caught the prospecting bug which, I guess, he passed on to me.

'It was inevitable, to cut a long story short, that the days of the lone prospectors, the lone men with their geiger counters, would come to an end and that the big conglomerates would buy them out and take over. My dad ended up working for one of them in the famous Elliot Lake mines in northern Ontario, Canada, one of the biggest uranium mines in the world. That was where I had my first mining experiences, just at the end of the old days when it was still like something out of the movies. Conditions were primitive; we lived in a near wilderness, a shanty town of tents. It was easy to imagine yourself back in the Klondike or even the Wild West.

'That all began to change just after I got there. Organisation and civilisation were moving into uranium. Another era was ending. And that wasn't a bad thing either. New standards were imposed, including safety standards which had not been in the forefront of anyone's mind in the heady days of the "rock hounds", sudden fortunes and the excitement of never knowing what was over the next ridge.' Erlanger paused. 'That is why I am in Ireland today and with you folks tonight. Uranium prospecting and mining are in my blood; I'm a "rock hound" too at heart even if the trappings of the business have changed and I've got to wear a business suit.' He smiled.

'My dad's retired now and lives in Florida. He's still hale and hearty and as deeply interested in the business as ever; he has never shaken off that bug. He remains my most valued adviser. I'm only sorry he's not here tonight to enthral you with the stories that filled my boyhood. Unfortunately, his gift for story-telling wasn't passed on to me with his love of mining. But I know that he wishes us luck in the hope that, together, all of us will succeed in our search.'

He sat down to prolonged applause. He's as smooth as he looks, Ryle thought, he's told them what they wanted to hear. He had taken no notes – there had been nothing newsworthy. The chairman rose to his feet and waited for the applause to splutter and die before inviting questions. There was an uneven hush, accentuated by coughs, until a wizened-looking man in the third row asked what were the chances of uranium being found in the area.

'Very promising,' Erlanger said. 'I don't want to go into all the technical details at the present time but it's fair to say promising, very promising. Lots of factors will have to come into play before a final decision to mine is taken, of course. Those factors look good, too,' he added.

He paused as if deciding whether to say more, to take them into his confidence. 'Take the price of uranium, for instance. Ore in the ground is only worth what someone is prepared to pay you to dig it out. And things look good on that score. Uranium's gone up from six dollars fifty a pound in the summer of nineteen-seventy-three to about forty dollars a pound now. Summer seventy-three, as you all know, was just before the Yom Kippur war and the oil crisis. I don't know how you folks fared, having to queue for hours for gas – petrol – because of some Arab sheik but I can tell you Americans were damn angry about it. A lot of people want to make sure that nothing like that ever happens again to us or to our friends. And uranium in our own hands and those of our friends is one way of doing just that.' Several people nodded.

A young woman, making her question sound like an accusation, inquired which multi-national mining company was behind Erlanger. None, Erlanger told her: Atlantis was an independent and entirely Irish company. He had no plans to raise money outside Ireland, he told another questioner, but that would depend ultimately on how much he could raise within Ireland if they were to develop the mine to its full potential.

Ryle made a mental note of the subtle change in Erlanger's answers: he was now talking about 'full potentials' and assuming the uranium was there to be mined. He checked his watch and debated whether to file his story now or later. The best prospect of a news story lay in the question and answer session but if he waited for all of that and cornered Erlanger afterwards he'd miss the bloody deadline. Or be forced to cut short his talk with Erlanger. He didn't want to do either. But his main interest, he reminded himself, was in the Maurice Clark story and he wanted a long chat with Erlanger. Better clear the decks now.

He tiptoed down the hall and sidled through a knot of large men blocking the doorway. A questioner was asking how many workers the mine would need as he went out of earshot. A man at the outer door directed him to a public telephone a couple of hundred yards away and Ryle set off to walk towards it.

Once out of the pool of light around the hall he was aware of the darkness and the country night sounds. The clear sky glistened with an incredible number of icy stars and stretched concavely over him from horizon to horizon like an upturned colander. A shooting star streaked across a short segment of space near the horizon and died.

Ryle concentrated on the first two paragraphs of his report while he waited for the telephone operator to answer and to be put through to the paper's reverse charge number. He was well into the story, dictating from his notes to a copytaker, when he remembered that he had been supposed to call on Breda several hours earlier. Shit, he muttered and apologised to the copytaker.

He finished the story and hung up without talking to the news desk. He checked his watch again; it was just after ten-thirty. He'd better phone Breda and explain now in case it was too late to call when he got another opportunity.

'Mrs Ryle's not here,' a babysitter said and took a message.

Ryle cursed his own memory and walked rapidly back towards the hall. How could he have forgotten? When he had been thinking of what to say and all? His lapse was going to make things even more difficult with Breda and he wondered where she was. He was speculating about why that should bother him when he heard car doors banging and engines stuttering. Both sides of the narrow door to the hall were open and people were flooding out.

He broke into a run but the press of people blocked his progress. He muttered apologies to surprised faces as he shoved and dodged his way back inside. Erlanger was gone from the stage where Jonathan was kneeling to talk down to someone. Ryle glanced around but could see no sign of Erlanger or his associate among the few clusters of people still chatting around the hall. He pushed his way through an uneven line of chairs and glanced into the room where he had met Erlanger earlier. It was empty.

'Where's Erlanger?' he asked Jonathan who was about to straighten up from his conversation.

'Gone. They left immediately the meeting ended. By the back door.' He made their departure sound like an admission of guilt.

'Where've they gone?'

'No idea.' Jonathan squatted down on the stage again. 'What did you think? Of the meeting?'

Ryle, unheeding, glanced around again and contemplated trying outside, then dismissed the thought: Erlanger was gone. 'Shit,' he said.

'What I love about the Irish . . . ' Erlanger accepted a glass of whiskey from Harvey and settled back into the deep couch, '. . . is their greed. It's not like the greed back home, all flinty-eyed and hard, figuring the angles and the percentages. Here, it's a sort of innocent greed that smiles out at you from their eyes, kind of naive and trusting. I find it touching. I like it.'

Becky sipped her drink in the fireside armchair and smiled. 'You can drop the folksy act, Mike,' she said. 'The meeting's over.'

'No act. An honest opinion that's struck me before. It came back to me tonight, looking out at all those faces and seeing the little lodes of greed twinkling at the edges of their eyes. Like little smiles. When Irish eyes are smiling.' He began to croon.

'Get off the podium,' Becky laughed. 'Return to earth.'

'What do you say, Harv?' Erlanger winked at her. 'Doesn't it give you a little thrill too? Like seeing the metals glinting in the rocks, eh?'

Harvey swallowed a large gulp of whiskey and topped up his glass again before turning from the drinks cabinet. He caught sight of his mournful face and prematurely thinning hair reflected in the blackness of the picture window. Outside, the river was discernible only by the sheen of the stars on the water's slow-moving blackness. But the window threw back a bright reflection of the room, himself and the back of Erlanger's head and the leaping flames from the fire. He sat down opposite Becky.

'It went fine,' he admitted. 'I think you out-gunned them.'

'Told you, didn't I? Nothing to worry about. Only paper tigers, these guys.'

'They'd been stirring things up, handing out leaflets around the site about the dangers of radon gas.' Harvey sounded apologetic.

'Sure.' Erlanger stretched out an expansive arm. 'And they'll go on doing it. But we called their bluff tonight. This was their big shot and they found out that they're going to lose. The people are with us.'

Harvey nodded. 'They're a pain in the ass though.'

'We can live with that,' Erlanger said with an air of finality. 'Have you got that drilling report for me?'

Harvey reached an arm over to a shelf, took down a folder and stretched over to him with it. Erlanger put down his drink and leafed through the half-dozen loose sheets. He settled on the last page and read it through while Becky and Harvey exchanged small talk about his adjustment to rural life.

'It's so peaceful here,' she suggested, playing the role of the executive wife.

'Dull,' Harvey whined. 'Nothing ever happens.'

'Perfect,' Erlanger interrupted. 'Well done. Just what we need.' He looked at Becky and began to haul himself out of the couch. 'I guess we should be getting back.'

'What was happening with the police?' Harvey asked in a rush as though it had been playing on his mind.

Erlanger stopped and looked at him in confusion.

'You said they called on you.'

'Oh, that,' Erlanger replied easily. 'Routine. Just checking on the movements of Maurice Clark before he was found dead the other day.'

'That's all?'

'That's all. You weren't talking to him at the party, were you?'

'No,' Harvey said quickly. 'I don't think so. I didn't recognise him from the pictures.'

'Have they been to see you?'

'Who? The police?' Harvey sounded edgy. 'No.'

'They probably will. I gave them the full guest list.'

'Why would they want to see me?'

'Routine.' Erlanger shrugged. 'It's nothing to do with us.' He held out Becky's coat and said to her, 'Unless they find it was your chicken surprise that killed him.'

The barman let out another bellow of 'Ah, now lads, it's gone the time' but continued to belie his instructions by starting another pint of Guinness to add to the line of half-filled glasses on the counter. Most of the lights were out but the pub was still crowded; nobody gave any sign of leaving. The barman topped up some of the glasses and placed two in front of Ryle and Jonathan.

'You might as well,' Jonathan was saying.

'But what's there to see?' Ryle persisted.

'Actually not a lot. But you might as well have a look now that you're here.'

'I've got to drive back to Dublin.'

'You're better off waiting a little then. Until the drunks have got home. This is the most dangerous hour of the day on the roads, you know.'

Ryle looked at him sharply but saw no trace of irony in his face. He's pissed, Ryle thought. And I will be soon if I don't watch it. He had accepted Jonathan's invitation to have a drink on the off chance that Erlanger might also have gone to the local pub. Ryle had long since given up watching the door in the hope that he would arrive. The whole journey had been a waste of time. He felt too lazy to move from the convivial warmth and opted instead to listen to Jonathan reliving the meeting with the freeze-frame certainty of a sports commentator.

'He didn't answer a single point, not one.'

Ryle nodded. They had been over all this already.

'Not a single one,' Jonathan repeated as if he were analysing the performance of a biased referee.

'He didn't have to,' Ryle heard himself say. 'He did a soft-sell and you went for reason. That was your mistake. You can't beat wishful thinking with facts.'

'No, no. You're wrong. These things have to be decided by reason, by facts.'

'Maybe they should be but they never are.'

'What should I have done? Descended to his level, spun them fairy tales?'

'Horror stories.' Ryle warmed to his theme. 'Lambs with two heads, calves with no legs. Their unborn children deformed, freaks of the most horrific kind. Even their own mothers won't want to look at them.'

'You can't scare people like that,' Jonathan protested.

'Why not? It's what you believe, isn't it?'

'Well, yes, there is a definite risk of genetic problems. That's well-documented; difficult to quantify though. There's certainly an increase in congenital problems and of cancers associated with . . . '

'Better still,' Ryle interrupted. 'Tell them they'll all die roaring. Nobody gives a fiddler's about posterity anyhow.'

When they left the pub Ryle insisted on driving and Jonathan guided him through a maze of roads that became narrower and narrower. 'Slow down,' he instructed after they had travelled a while along a single-lane road that looked as though it had been recently tarred. 'There's a gateway just ahead on the left. You can park there.'

Ryle steered the car to a halt and flicked off the lights. It occurred to him as he got out that Jonathan was a frequent visitor here, returning regularly to the focal point of an obsession. Ryle grabbed the top bar of a gate which Jonathan was scaling and felt the dry cold of the metal sink through the warmth of his hands. He swung his legs over the top and jumped down quickly.

They walked across grass grazed low on the frozen earth and headed for a gap in the boundary hedge of skeletal bushes. They climbed an earthen bank, jumped down to another field and walked alongside a small grove of evergreen trees on their right. An open gateway led into another field where the grass was long but lay dead and broken under a layer of frost. It crunched gently under their feet, the sound combining with their breathing to break the total silence.

'I do think your approach is wrong,' Jonathan said suddenly, his breath spurting into clouds before his face. 'One mustn't lower oneself to their level. Common sense and reason *will* win out in the end.'

'Is that it?' Ryle pointed to a simple triangle rising out of the lower end of the field. Vehicle tracks led across to it.

'That's it.'

'Doesn't look like much,' Ryle said as they approached a covered mound of machinery.

'It doesn't, does it?' Jonathan stood back as Ryle circled around the small drilling rig. 'Not much at all for something which could have such devastating consequences.'

A dog began to bark nearby as Ryle tried to pull up a corner of the heavy tarpaulin. It was weighed down by stones and the heavy frost had turned it rigid. The dog's barking took on a more frenzied edge and Jonathan moved over to where he could see the outline of a single-storey farmhouse through the bushes at the end of the field.

There was a sudden blaze of light as a door opened and a figure stood in the doorway. In between the barks they could hear a man's voice but not his words.

'I think perhaps we should leave,' Jonathan suggested quietly. Ryle stood beside him, looking through the hedge at the yellow-lit doorway a few hundred yards away. The dog stopped barking suddenly and the man's voice carried clearly through the brittle air. 'Go get him,' it ordered.

Together they turned and began to walk quickly back the way they had come. The dog was barking excitedly again and the noise was coming closer. Ryle looked over his shoulder and thought he saw a black shadow leap through the bushes. The barking came closer still and they could hear the man's voice following, urging it on. They began to run.

'Into the trees,' Jonathan gasped. They turned towards the grove, at a run now. The crack of a shotgun snapped viciously and hung in a sudden silence. They ran faster. Ryle's foot broke through a thin crust of frost and squelched into mud. He pulled it free in mid stride and reached the wire fence by the trees. They climbed over, Jonathan grasping a spiked barb in his hurry.

Ryle glanced back. He could make out the figure of the man by the drilling rig. The dog was running around it in circles, no longer in pursuit. 'It's all right,' Ryle gasped and they stopped.

The shotgun exploded again and pellets peppered the branches above them. Ryle cursed and they ran blindly through the trees, branches whipping their bodies, out into the next field and over the gate to the car.

Ryle started the engine immediately and reversed blindly into the road. He straightened the car and drove off, one hand rubbing furiously at the clouded windscreen. Jonathan sucked at his cut palm. 'There you are,' he panted as though proving a point, 'that's the nuclear industry for you.'

Seven

Ryle read through the long telex message from the Irish Farmers' Association a second time but his mind wandered again. His head drummed dully, his eyes ached in the garish artificial light and his brain felt like coarse sand. He had got home very late, woken up late and hurried into the news room late to find a pile of routine stories waiting for him. He hadn't had the energy to argue with Stacy but it hadn't improved his mood.

He began the press release again but his brain would not keep pace with his eyes and he gave up in the middle of the third paragraph. He wandered over to the coffee machine and waited while a financial reporter cursed and banged it as a dribble of muddy liquid flowed down the waste pipe where a plastic cup should have sat. The reporter reached in and tugged a cup into place before inserting more coins and pressing the button for white with sugar.

'I see you've been moving the markets,' he said as he took the full cup. Ryle stared at him blankly. 'Atlantis shares shot up to over a pound this morning. They say it's your story that the uranium find is viable.'

Ryle grunted and took another coffee back to his desk. He might have moved the markets, whatever that meant, but he hadn't moved the Clark story: all he'd got last night was a muddy shoe and a sour hangover. He settled his cup on the sheet of telex paper and dialled a number.

'Hi,' Erlanger said enthusiastically. 'That was an excellent report you did. I looked for you afterwards but you'd gone.'

'I was hoping to talk to you about something else,' Ryle said.

'Yeah? If I can help I will.'

'Maurice Clark. I gather he was in your house the night before he died.'

Erlanger agreed. 'We decided to have a mid-January party instead of a pre-Christmas one. People need more cheering up this time of year than before Christmas, we reckoned.'

'How was he then?'

'Fine, I think.' Erlanger paused as if he was thinking. 'There were a lot of people there.'

'You were talking to him?'

'I guess so. I was the host. I had a few words with everybody.'

'I've heard you and he had a long discussion,' Ryle said.

'That's not correct,' Erlanger replied. 'Sure I must have talked with him and I did discuss business matters with some people. But I don't recollect having that kind of talk with Maurice.'

'Did you have business dealings with him?'

'That's not something I should comment on,' Erlanger said, 'But I guess in the circumstances I can confirm it. As background. He had some shares in my company. Like a lot of people.' He chuckled.

'How many shares?'

'I can't say offhand. And I shouldn't get into that. I'm breaking my rules by telling you anything at all but I'm trying to be as helpful as I can.'

'Okay,' Ryle said, trying to shake off his mental torpor and remember what else he wanted to know from him.

'Besides,' Erlanger added, 'There are other ways you can get access to that information. It's a matter of record.'

'Right,' Ryle covered his uncertainty. 'Thanks for your help.'

'Any time.' Erlanger hung up.

Ryle sat back, wondering without enthusiasm about registers of shareholders and files in the Companies' Office. Another avenue had turned into a cul de sac. He shouldn't have phoned, should have waited to talk to Erlanger in person as he had originally intended. It was always better.

He sipped the tired metal taste of the cold coffee and stared into the middle distance. Another reporter caught his eye and shook his head in sympathy. It's the air in this place, he told himself, it's a hazard to health. He leaned forward to pull off his sweater but that didn't feel any better. He should phone Breda, he reminded himself. The thought deepened his gloom and he sighed and turned back to the farmers' complaints. But the obscurities of farm prices were beyond him and he took it over to the news desk.

'I can't make head or tail of this stuff,' he moaned. Stacy gave him a withering look and glanced through the press release. 'And anyway, I thought I was still on the Clark story.'

Stacy stretched out a languid hand and impaled the message on a spike. 'Happy?' he asked with a benefactor's smile.

'As a pig in shit,' Ryle grunted and perched himself on the news desk. Stacy seemed unusually becalmed and Ryle told him about the previous night's meeting and why he'd wanted to talk to Erlanger. 'I missed him because of having to file that story,' he moaned.

Stacy shrugged.

'And I was shot at.'

Stacy suddenly gave him his full attention and Ryle re-counted his visit to the mining site. Stacy's concern dissolved into a dry laugh. 'I thought it was something serious,' he said.

'Have you ever been shot at?' Ryle retorted, hurt by his flippancy. The episode had been farcical but it had still un-settled him.

Stacy sprang to his feet and hitched his trousers over his expanding stomach. 'Let's have a cup of coffee,' he suggested.

The two men strode down the main corridor of Leinster House between the portraits of dead patriots, silent and purposeful. They swung around a pillar in the entrance hall and Jim Whelan stopped before the revolving door and stuck out his hand.

'You won't mind if I don't see you out to the gate,' he said. The rain was falling steadily outside into a myriad of tiny individual pools that rippled beneath the lights.

The other man took his time tucking his scarf inside the lapels of his coat. He settled his tweed hat firmly and finally took Whelan's hand and gave it a perfunctory shake. He didn't meet his eyes.

'Thanks very much for coming in,' Whelan said gravely. 'I appreciate it.'

The man muttered something, pushed his way through the door and went out into the wet. Whelan returned the way he had come, letting his face relax into a sly smile as soon as he was out of sight. It had gone perfectly, couldn't have been better if he had planned it all. There'd be no more problems from that quarter.

He bestowed a neck-wrenching wink on a passing member of the Opposition and stopped momentarily at the foot of the stairs. A celebratory drink was in order, he thought. No, that would have to be later: he had work to do. He climbed the stairs.

Inviting his constituency trouble-maker to lunch in Leinster House had been a stroke of genius. He'd had him on his own ground. And luck had smiled on him, too. They'd been on their way into the restaurant when they met the Taoiseach who appeared to be cruising the near-deserted corridors for someone to talk to. He stopped and Whelan introduced his constituency chairman.

'I hope you're taking good care of our deputy out there,' the Taoiseach had said. 'We'd hate to have anything happen to him.'

It couldn't have been better if he had briefed the Taoiseach himself, Whelan thought. After that, it had been a piece of cake. He'd gone through the more-in-sorrow-than-in-anger routine . . . Assured his chairman that he Whelan was not a man to go back on his word but that he had no choice . . . For the greater good of the party . . . He had to drop his re-zoning motion.

The chairman had put up no resistance. The Taoiseach's casual words had done the trick, Whelan reckoned. Had set the right tone, given the impression that Whelan was on the inside track, that the powers-that-be backed him, were concerned about him. Maybe they weren't all that casual, he thought suddenly as he laboured up the last tier of steps. But the pinprick of uncertainty disappeared just as quickly. So what if the Taoiseach had been quite deliberate and not just making small talk? The message was still the same. For both of them.

He turned into the corridor and headed jauntily towards his office. He felt like a successful dieter, trim, energetic; it was as if he'd discovered a lost world. Everything was possible now. He'd find a way of stepping into Maurice Clark's shoes.

*   *   *

Ryle watched the barman reach for an electric kettle and pull out a large, caterer's tin of instant coffee. His stomach balked at the prospect of more acrid coffee: to hell with it, he decided. 'I'll change that to a pint,' he said. Stacy indicated two pints to the barman.

'Is this story going anywhere?' the news editor demanded without preliminaries. They sat on stools at the bar, the only customers. Some of the lights were on, managing to make the inside more gloomy than the twilight outside.

'There are a couple of good angles,' Ryle replied warily.

'You've written what? One, two pieces in four, five days. You're not working for a magazine.' Stacy gulped his Guinness and wiped the froth off his lips.

'With stories like this,' he went on, 'you've got to hit them hard and fast. Preferably in the first few hours. Or day at the most. While everyone's reeling with the shock. Before all the barriers go up and they get their answers off pat.' He raised his drink again. 'I don't think you're going to get anywhere if you haven't cracked it by now.'

'It's not that kind of story,' Ryle countered feebly. 'It's more complicated. There are so many angles to it.'

Stacy shrugged and told him to run through everything he knew. Why did I let myself walk into this right now, Ryle wondered, but he did as he was told, trying to inject more excitement and enthusiasm into the narrative than he felt.

'You can forget the sex angles for starters,' Stacy said when Ryle finished. 'There's no way any of that's going into the paper.'

'Even if it was the reason for his death?' Ryle shot back, seeing an opportunity to divert the discussion from the direction he feared it was facing.

'You know how the editor feels about this whole story,' Stacy said. 'He doesn't like it. He thinks the man's dead and should be left to rest in peace. The story, he thinks, is in the political consequences, the by-election and all that.'

'What if he was murdered?' Ryle channelled his disgust at himself, at the story, at the world into the question. 'Would he not consider that to be a story?'

'Yes. If he was. But we don't know that, do we?'

'It's a possibility. Even a probability.' Ryle felt the alcohol begin to clear his head.

'We're not the guards,' Stacy sighed. 'You're not a guard. Our job is to report what's happening.'

'How can we report what's happening if we don't find out what's happening?'

Stacy did not answer him directly. 'You know very well we don't have the time or the bodies to chase everything that looks interesting. We've got to concentrate on what will make a story. We've got a paper to get out today and every day.'

'It'd be a hell of a mistake to drop it now,' Ryle persevered. 'There's obviously a whole lot more to this than meets the eye. The stories about the dog and the gun have proved that already.'

'And have you noticed the wild rush among the other papers to lift those stories?' Stacy asked sarcastically. Ryle's reports had not been followed up in detail by any other papers nor had they prompted any public comments. 'I'm not knocking them. But you have no clear idea where this story is going. Even what the story is.'

'But I can't know until I find out. Can I?'

Stacy summoned the barman with a nod and paid for the drinks.

'Do you believe Clark had IRA connections?' he asked while he waited for his change.

Ryle shrugged. 'At this stage I'll believe anything about him.'

'It seems unlikely. To put it mildly.'

'It seemed unlikely that he'd go round shooting dogs, too,' Ryle said bitterly. The alcohol had livened up his brain but the discussion wasn't improving his mood. Just when he had got his teeth into a decent story, it looked like it was going to be snatched away from him again. And after all the time and effort he had put into it.

'Look,' Stacy said quietly. 'I'm just pointing out the realities. You know them as well as I do.'

Ryle stared through a line of bottles at his fractured reflection in a mottled advertising mirror. His ginger hair looked dark in the half-light and his pale face was pitted with the mirror's blemishes. If it were a portrait, he thought, the artist would have to be complimented on his perception.

Stacy caught his eye in the mirror. 'I'm not trying to discourage you,' he said. 'Far from it. It's good to see you taking the initiative again. It's been a while, you know.'

Ryle nodded into the mirror. 'So what are you telling me?'

'I know you've got a lot of personal problems,' Stacy said. 'And if I can help . . . '

Ryle shifted impatiently on his stool and looked away quickly. Stacy stopped, noting his instant reaction. 'All I'm saying,' he added after a moment, 'is that you need to write more stories about this. Otherwise, I can't afford to give you the time.'

The barman slapped the change down on the counter and they strolled in silence back to the office. The evening was still young and the streets were filling with people leaving work and heading home.

'Features were looking for you earlier,' Stacy said as they went into the building. Ryle cursed. 'Are you doing something for them?'

'A series on young people and religion,' Ryle said gloomily.

'That your idea?' Stacy sounded incredulous.

'It was your idea,' Ryle snorted. 'You volunteered me to them.'

'But that was ages ago. Before Christmas. You haven't done it yet?'

'I've done some interviews,' Ryle said defensively and the dread of having to finish the articles clouded in on him like a sea fog rolling in over the land. That was all he needed right now.

Stacy headed for the news desk where his deputy was flapping his arms at somebody and looking as though he had been pulled backwards through a hedge. Ryle sat down at his desk and picked up the phone. He'd got one reprieve and he'd better try and negotiate another one with Breda. There was no point putting it off. He had begun dialling her number when a colleague dropped a handwritten note in front of him.

'Phone Miss Gantly', it said. Breda's phone was ringing in his ear and he put it down hurriedly. Suddenly, he felt much better.

A shower of hailstones drummed on the car and Ryle slowed down as he reached Ranelagh, peering through the bouncing ice at street names. It was early evening but there was no one on the streets. Passing cars threw swathes of water onto the footpaths and blinded the drivers behind in a murky wash. Shop windows glowed through the gloom, staying open late in the transient suburb of flatland.

He missed the turning, reversed into an archway and drove back to the cul de sac of terraced houses. The hailstones hopped on the hood of his parka as he hurried up the road and pushed open a rickety iron gate that scraped reluctantly off the ground. He huddled into the doorway and glanced at the untended lawn, the size of a hearth rug.

He waited, not knowing what to expect. She had been brusque on the phone, giving him a time and directions and making no reference to what she wanted to talk about. He hadn't mentioned it either, content in the knowledge that she had called him and was presumably prepared to talk. The hailstones stopped abruptly and Rosie Gantly opened the door.

She led him silently through a short communal hallway and into the living room of her flat. The room was dark apart from a flood of light from another doorway which illuminated three posters on the opposite wall. A stylised drawing of Che Guevara was pinned beside silhouettes of people with raised fists and a slogan in Spanish. The third was a Sinn Fein poster depicting Britain as a visored soldier with raised truncheon beating down on Ireland's bowed head.

She led him into a small, functional kitchen, pointed at a chair and poured two glasses of red wine. Her curly hair was tight and damp and she was wearing shapeless trousers and a large sweater. Her face was scrubbed clean and her feet were bare. She sat down across the narrow table from him and sipped at her wine. She still said nothing.

Ryle broke the silence by going into his usual routine. The

reporter's equivalent of the policeman's caution, he thought as he recited that nothing she said would be attributed to her, he was just trying to find out how and why Clark had died.

'I don't want any more hassle,' she said without looking at him. 'So I want to be left out of it.'

Ryle repeated his assurances and asked who was harassing her.

'The party,' she said. 'A couple of heavies came around to warn me off.'

'Off what?'

She shrugged. 'Not to go to Maurice's funeral, cause any trouble. That sort of thing. Things would be made very difficult for me unless I kept quiet.'

'Who were they?'

'I don't know. Two guys who obviously modelled themselves on B-movie gangsters. Heavy with threats and innuendos: important people wouldn't like it; did my employers know about my political activities? That sort of stuff.' She shrugged it away as if it was an everyday occurrence, a routine matter of no importance.

'What did they want you to keep quiet about?'

'My relationship with Maurice, I suppose. They didn't spell it out. It was all corner-of-the-mouth stuff.'

'Did you go to the funeral?'

'No. Not because of them, though.' She glanced at him as if he might contradict her. 'I couldn't stomach all that hypocrisy, the sanctimonious shit from everyone who killed him.'

'Who killed him?'

'The whole lot of them. His so-called political friends, the viper.' She saw his next question coming. 'That's his wife, the lovely Yvonne. My name for her. She was always pushing him to get ahead, be successful, be a VIP. That was her favourite phrase. "But, Maurice, I only want you to be a VIP, I'm only trying to help." Viper.' She gave a short laugh. 'She's one of those women who give us all a bad name. Trying to live her life, achieve her ambitions, through a man.'

She poured herself some more wine and topped up Ryle's barely touched glass. He watched her closely, mildly surprised at her overt bitterness. She appeared detached, almost shy, and totally different from the first impression he had had of her at the school. She seemed curiously vulnerable, no longer the tough person who had confronted him with sarcasm and defiance.

'I saw her on TV,' she went on, 'playing the grieving widow and loving every minute of it. All the lackeys fawning around. I suppose that's what they were afraid of, that I'd turn up and upset the show. I never had any intention, I don't go in for that particular sick ritual. Maurice is dead. Goodbye, Maurice. End of story.'

'As simple as that,' Ryle said. He couldn't work her out. She wasn't as he had expected but then he didn't know what he had expected.

She shook her head vigorously and looked at him for the first time. Her eyes were a soft brown and he was conscious of the scent of some kind of bath oil. 'Anyway, what is it you want? To write about me, reveal the secret life of an establishment politician now that he's safely dead? There's lots of living ones you could write that about too. But the bourgeois press is not going to do that or tell the truth about the Viper and the rest of them, is it?'

Her demeanour contradicted the aggression of her words and she drank a large mouthful of wine. Maybe she just wants a shoulder to cry on, Ryle thought. Maybe she's drunk. Maybe she's just upset. She returned his stare, her eyes unyielding. 'Well, is it?' she demanded.

He shook his head, remembering Stacy's statement of reality. He knew he wasn't going to write about those things but he was becoming increasingly curious about Clark's life as well as his death. 'How did you meet him?'

She tucked her right foot under her left thigh and took a moment to reply. 'In college,' she sighed as if she had made a decision to tell all. 'He was my tutor on politics for a year. We got on well and began going out together, which made him nervous. He was afraid he'd be accused of favouritism or using his position or something. So we couldn't be seen together and we'd meet far away from the usual student haunts. It was always a hole-and-corner affair, I suppose.'

She drank again and continued. 'It sort of petered out when I left. We were just good friends really. I went to London for a couple of years and when I came back Maurice was a politician, married and the hope of the future.

'Then we ran into each other one day in Grafton Street. We only talked for a few minutes but the change in him was amazing. He'd always been a relaxed sort of person but he was really edgy and jumpy. I gave him my phone number and was surprised when he called me. He came round and poured out all his troubles and it became a regular thing. He'd call around a couple of times a week for a chat and some sanity, as he used to say.'

She twisted her glass by the stem and watched the dregs float about. 'And then, well, our old relationship started up again.' She grasped the wine bottle by the neck, refilled the glass and offered it to Ryle. He shook his head.

'I presume you didn't agree about politics,' he prompted. He wondered again what Clark had seen in her and what she had seen in Clark.

'Never,' she said. 'He was one of these infuriating people who's all moderation and reasonableness. Maurice the moderate. He could never see how corrupt the system is. He liked to think of himself as a pragmatist, doing what he could to help people. And he'd get angry when I pointed out that he was only tinkering with capitalism to make it more palatable and stave off the revolution.'

'But you obviously liked him a lot.' He was thinking aloud, trying to answer his own unspoken questions. Her left-wing rhetoric seemed at odds with her whole demeanour, like an inappropriate overlay of paint on beautiful wood.

'Yes,' she said as if she was admitting to a shortcoming. 'God preserve us from decent people, but he was a genuinely nice guy. A real warm human being' – she smiled faintly – 'a lamb really. He appealed to some of my better, or worst, instincts. The kind that made me want to mother him, calm him down and comfort him and tell him that everything was going to be all right.' She paused. 'But that's my problem and we're talking about him, aren't we?'

Ryle nodded and decided to get down to business. All he really needed to know was how and why Clark died, to complement the when and where of his death. Interesting as it might be, he didn't need to know what Rosie and he had seen in each other.

'You mentioned his problems. Was he under any kind of threat?'

'If you mean was anyone threatening to kill him or something like that, no, not that I know of.' She talked as if she had already given the question some thought. 'He wasn't that kind of person, the kind that anyone would want to kill. But he was under all kinds of political threats from his so-called party friends and the Viper and those sorts of people.

'He used to come from Leinster House and constituency meetings and tell me about all the petty manoeuvres and back-stabbing. To be honest, I only half listened but he found it relaxing to talk. He was on the defensive all the time, trying to protect himself politically from his friends, his own party. And the Viper was at him constantly. She got him into it in the first place. Her family has always been big in the party. And she had a much better stomach for all that shit than he had. She revels in it, actually.'

'How about financial pressures?'

'They were heavy too. He never told me the details, probably because he knew I would disapprove. But I know he had some get-rich-quick schemes going which were a little shady.' She gave a fleeting smile and a barely perceptible shake of her head at some memory. 'He wasn't much of a politician when it came down to it. He wasn't nearly cynical enough.'

'Shady in what way?' Ryle smelled a possible story.

She shrugged. 'He didn't want anyone to know the details. In case they'd damage him politically. I presumed they were the usual corrupt property deals or something like that. But he never told me.'

'But they had gone wrong.'

'I don't know,' she said vaguely and Ryle decided she was lying. 'All I know is that whatever his schemes were, they hadn't improved his financial problems. They seemed to be getting worse. But he never told me.'

Maybe she's not lying, he thought. What was he doing here anyway? This was all very interesting but wasn't getting him anywhere. Why did she agree to see him? What the hell had he expected? 'When was the last time you saw him?' he asked aloud.

She looked him straight in the eye and held his return gaze in silence for several seconds. 'The day he died.' She broke her stare – now we're getting somewhere, Ryle thought, maybe she has something to tell me. 'What time did he die exactly?' she asked.

'About eight in the morning,' Ryle replied, calming his excitement. Maybe she wanted to know for some personal reason rather than to help reconstruct Clark's last movements. She probably had nobody to talk to about it, he realised, nobody with whom she could mull over the usual details of unexpected death. Maybe all she wanted was a shoulder to grieve on. 'The body was found in the harbour about six or eight hours later.'

She nodded. 'I saw him about four that morning. He called here.'

Ryle tried to hide his growing excitement. She could have been the last person to talk to Clark. 'That was after the party in Erlanger's house.' He made it a simple statement.

She nodded again, vaguely. 'I knew he was going to a party and I wasn't expecting him. He was very edgy and depressed and only stayed a short time.'

'Did he say what was wrong?'

'Not really. Something about being trapped and that someone was moving in on him. I didn't know what he was talking about then and I don't know now. He wasn't very coherent and I wasn't very alert. He woke me up.'

'Someone was pursuing him?' Ryle let his excitement run free and she glanced at him wearily.

'Not in the sense that someone was literally chasing him,' she said with a patient air, like a preoccupied adult explaining something to a child. 'It was a more abstract kind of thing. Like a problem that had got out of hand.'

'I've been told that he had a row with his wife at the party.' Ryle reined himself in.

She shook her head dismissively. 'That was nothing out of the ordinary.'

'I've heard as well that he had a long discussion with Erlanger.' He spelled out who Erlanger was but she shook her head again.

'I don't know,' she said. 'He wasn't making a lot of sense, not to me.'

'Did he say where he was going when he left?'

'No. He was only here about twenty minutes. Gone by half four. I only woke up properly after he had left.'

'Was he armed?' Ryle asked intently. 'Did he have a gun on him?'

'I don't think so.' She sounded bemused at the sudden change in his line of questioning. 'Not that I noticed.'

'Did he ever carry a gun?'

'No.'

'You're sure?'

'Certain.' To his surprise she coloured slightly and turned away. 'He had a file with some papers. The last night. That's all.' She paused and then looked back at him. 'He left it behind.'

Ryle searched her eyes silently for a moment, trying to read the answer to his next question. 'Is it ... ' he began and stopped, suddenly apprehensive that he would say the wrong thing. 'What was it about?'

'Neutrality.'

Ryle's expression fluctuated from amazement to disappointment. He didn't know what he had expected but this wasn't it, this was an anti-climax.

'Government policy on neutrality,' she added. 'A proposal to have Ireland join NATO.'

'Jesus Christ,' Ryle muttered. 'What's that got to do with anything?'

'A hell of a lot,' she said icily. 'Don't you realise what it means?'

'Joining NATO? Sure. It'd be one big controversial decision.' But it's politics, he thought. When he had been hoping for something sinister, more dramatic. Something that would explain what Clark was doing with a gun on Dun Laoghaire pier at dawn.

She stood up and looked down at him with a hint of disgust, once more the person who had dismissed him at their first meeting. 'Can you only see things as cheap fucking headlines?' Passion and a touch of anger flushed her cheeks. 'It means American bases in Ireland. A new army of occupation. We lose the little independence we've got. And we get nuked when the American warmongers push the button.'

Ryle nodded several times. 'Yes, I know, I know. But what does it have to do with his death?'

She flounced out of the room and Ryle watched her disappear with dismay. I've blown it, he thought, just when it was getting interesting. She really does believe the rhetoric.

An old, rounded fridge shuddered into silence in the corner behind him and he glanced around the kitchen. It was basic and impersonal, equipped by a landlord from auction rooms. Rosie was right about the significance of joining NATO, he conceded and cursed his own reaction. But the document was probably only a speech or something. Interesting but not earth-shattering.

She came back with a cheap brown cardboard folder and tossed it on the table. Ryle straightened it and flicked through the contents while she poured herself some more wine. She didn't offer him any.

There were less than twenty pages, some of them fudged photocopies stapled together of documents headed with the words National Security Council. Others were written answers to Dáil questions and extracts from speeches. Ryle leafed back to the first two loose sheets which looked clean and new. The heading on the first caught his eye like a flashing beacon. 'Strictly Confidential', it said, and he read underneath 'Report to Taoiseach from Backbench Committee on Foreign Affairs'.

His earlier excitement rekindled like a hot flame springing from ashes as he read. This was more than merely interesting. This could be dynamite. He tried to slow his eyes down to absorb the information. This *was* dynamite.

'You were right,' Ryle admitted. 'This is important.'

'You can take it with you,' Rosie said, 'on two conditions. That you publicise it and that you don't say where you got it.'

Ryle nodded his agreement and traced the title with his finger. 'Do you know anything about this committee?'

'Maurice was the chairperson. That's all.' She reached over and turned the first page. 'That's his signature.'

Ryle examined the handwriting above Clark's typed name and the word chairman. The signature was written in upright and clear letters, childlike in its clarity.

'You're sure?' He looked at her uncertainly and she nodded. 'Did he tell you anything about it?'

'Not about this. He'd talked about the committee before and what was going on there but he never mentioned this.'

Ryle turned back to the first page and re-read the opening paragraph. 'Did he ever tell you he had talked to the Taoiseach about neutrality?'

'No,' she said with certainty. 'I would have remembered that. We talked about neutrality a long time ago and I would have thought that Maurice supported it.'

'So what do you make of this?'

'He had changed his mind. Had it changed for him probably. The government obviously wants to sell out and join NATO and had involved him in preparing the ground.'

Ryle nodded vaguely, careful not to question her political assumptions any more although he did not necessarily share them. They didn't matter: there was a hell of a story here whatever way you looked at it. 'How did he come to leave this here? Did he just forget it?'

'That's what I thought at first,' she replied carefully. 'I only noticed it after he left and I didn't read it until later. I couldn't believe that he would have agreed to anything like that. Then, after his death, I began to wonder if he hadn't left it deliberately. That's why I called you.'

That made sense, Ryle thought. 'Do you think it had something to do with his death?'

'Yes.'

'You think he was killed, murdered, because of this?'

'It wouldn't surprise me.'

Ryle shook his head, a gesture of disbelief and amazement. She could well be right, he thought. Clark was running scared from something the night he died. He was carrying this powder keg with him. And leaving it here. In his safe house.

'Maybe he was refusing to go along with them,' Rosie offered, seeing in Ryle's face the connections and speculations that his brain was producing, 'threatening to expose what they're up to.'

'But he signed it,' Ryle protested. 'This *is* his signature?'

'Look, I don't know what happened.' She felt tired; she'd been over and over all this in her own mind. 'All I know is that it's all part of a conspiracy to get us into NATO and I want it publicised. The Irish people have a right to know what's being done behind their backs. I think that's what Maurice thought, too. I think that's why he was killed. And I think that's why he left it with me.'

Eight

Ryle waited at the express checkout, impatient to be done with his haphazard attempt at a weekly shop and to get back to the story. Not that he had got away from it for a waking moment. His mind was racing with endless possibilities but there was not a lot he could actually do about them right now. The news room was effectively closed down on Saturday; besides he needed to plan his next move carefully.

The only thing he knew for certain was that he had a humdinger of a story. On its face value alone, it was a shock-horror political story about the government trying to ditch neutrality. But the connection with Clark's death made it a lot more than that. His first inclination had been to rush out and talk it over with everyone he could think of. But it had to be handled properly. The last thing he wanted was to screw it up by blundering about.

He edged forward and piled the tins onto the conveyor belt while the woman ahead of him rooted methodically through her purse. Cash registers beeped electronically and merged with the mechanised muzak.

Clark had been in a bad way, under pressure from somebody or something. Though Rosie had been insistent that he was not actually being pursued when she last saw him. That was not the impression I got, she had said irritably when he had pushed her about Clark's subsequent movements. He was under some kind of general pressure, she repeated.

And the pressure, Ryle decided, had to do with the contents of the document. They had to be connected. And they were in turn somehow connected with his death. That, if nothing else, seemed obvious. Rosie was probably right: he had left it with her deliberately. But why? Because he wanted to hide it from somebody, didn't want to have it with him for some reason? He wondered once again where Clark had been going after he left

Rosie and who he could have been meeting at that hour of the night. At five o'clock in the morning, for God's sake? The answer to that question would probably solve the whole mystery.

Ryle stuffed his groceries into a plastic bag and tossed it into the back of the car. He went out into the sullen afternoon in search of a newsagent, bought the papers and collected a fistful of change for the pay phone outside his bedsitter. This is ridiculous, he told himself, I'm sitting on top of a shit-hot story and I have to pursue it through a public phone.

He drove to his bedsitter and forced himself to ignore Clark's folder, propped up on the fake wooden mantelpiece over the electric heater. He glanced through the papers but nothing held his attention. Shit, he said aloud, he had to talk to somebody about it. He went out into the hallway and shoved a couple of coins into the pay phone. He dialled Stacy's home number, rehearsing what he was going to tell him. So much for the news editor's lecture the previous day about the story having gone dead, he thought happily. This will soften his bark.

Stacy's phone rang out unanswered.

Ryle found a large plastic bag and began a half-hearted attempt to tidy up the bedsitter. He gathered up scraps of stale food and used containers and covered them up with old newspapers. He could go into the office, he thought, get the keys of the library from the security man and rummage through the cuttings files on neutrality. But he probably wouldn't be able to find anything there without help. And, anyway, Clark's folder contained a more comprehensive summary of official policy on neutrality than was likely to be in the library.

It was not a subject that came up for public debate very often, one of those rare policies that had acquired a near-mystical status and popularity, a sort of symbol of national self-confidence. All to do with the Second World War when Ireland had asserted its new independence, resisting pressure from Britain and the United States to become involved.

He remembered his father's coarse uniform tunic from those days, and his hilarious stories about the exploits of the part-time soldiers and the endless rumours and scares about a German invasion. And his mother and her friends worrying about the glimmer man, the inspector who went around checking that they were not using the rationed gas supply when they shouldn't have been. His earliest memories seemed to have been dominated by talk of The Emergency, as everyone called the war, and he had grown up feeling deprived at having been left out of something that seemed to have been such fun.

Staying out of the shooting war had been a popular decision that copper-bottomed the policy of neutrality. Any politician who dared suggest it might be wrong did so at his peril. Few of any consequence did and Ireland stayed out of NATO.

Ryle knotted the top of the garbage bag, hoisted it into his arms and took it outside. He paused at the phone on his way back and thought about phoning Breda. Later, he decided.

He took Clark's folder off the mantelpiece, settled down in his one armchair and started to read through it again, from the back. The last document was a smudgy photocopy of the United States National Security Council's analysis of Ireland's refusal to join NATO, setting out official American policy towards Ireland's position as a neutral country and its consequences in a war with the Soviet Union. Ireland's membership of NATO would be logical and desirable and it could make a valuable contribution in terms of air and naval bases, Ryle read. But the United States saw no military necessity to press for such facilities and adopted a position of being ready to welcome Ireland into NATO. Besides, the report added, the denial of Irish territory to enemy forces was already covered by NATO commitments.

He read through the other documents which set out the tortured positions of Irish officialdom as they nervously narrowed the definition of neutrality in response to one expediency or another. It ended up meaning that Ireland did not take part in any military alliances. Neutral in arms but not neutral in politics or ideology.

Then he looked through the most recent pages, the ones signed by Maurice Clark, setting out why it was time to change that policy, why Ireland should come off the fence, join NATO and become fully involved in the defence of the West. Ryle worked through his arguments, from economic to political to moral, and back to the opening paragraph, the paragraph that had grabbed his attention when he had first seen it, the paragraph that meant that this was not just the inconsequential musings of a backbencher.

He put the file down on the newly cleared table and ran his fingers through his hair. You've got to handle this one right, he ordered himself. For maximum impact.

Breda opened the door. Lorraine stood behind her and stared at him with the utterly expressionless look of the undecided child. Can she have forgotten me already, Ryle asked himself forlornly as he greeted her. The child clutched Breda's skirt uncertainly, looking like a miniature version of her mother. The resemblance was unmistakable even through the pudgy remnants of baby fat: she had the same light blue eyes and elegantly proportioned face topped by lightly toasted hair. She climbed into Breda's arms and he followed them into the living room.

A coal fire blazed, the television was on and toys were strewn about the floor. Ryle took off his coat and offered the child a roll of sweets while Breda turned down the sound on a hysterical game show where somebody was on the point of winning a revolving car.

'Do you want something to eat?' Breda inquired, letting her eyes sweep over him, automatically disapproving of his scruffiness, his over-worn leather jacket and crumpled jeans. She had tried for a time to take him in hand, to impose her own dress sense on his total disinterest in clothes. The leather jacket had been one of her purchases but was now battered and shapeless through too much wear and carelessness.

'No, thanks,' he lied. 'I've eaten.'

They exchanged formal inquiries, like diplomats from hostile powers thrown together at a public reception, while Lorraine gradually warmed to him. He settled down with her on the floor as she showed him some toys and Breda left them alone.

He watched over the child with a corner of his mind as she manipulated jigsaw pieces with her chubby fingers but his thoughts were still on the story. He prompted her to pick the even-sided pieces, thinking how easy it was to fill in the gaps once you knew the framework. That was the problem: he hadn't a clue what the overall framework was. He was collecting more and more pieces but he still had no idea how they fitted together.

A picture of jungle animals, cosy-looking in their cartoon caricatures, took shape and Lorraine slotted in the last piece of a lion's head and broke it all up and began again. Ryle yawned in the warmth and the child prevented him from dozing off with her demands for attention until Breda returned to announce bedtime. Lorraine clung to him briefly and he savoured his temporary role as her saviour.

He felt the soft firmness of her cheek on his face after she was gone and he slumped on the couch, watching television and waiting for Breda to come back. We should have our talk, he thought, but not now. I can't concentrate on anything right now.

The room felt familiar but strange, like something he had encountered in a dream. Its warmth and the family trappings were seductive, all the more so when he thought of what awaited him in the bedsitter. But memories of the skirmishes and half-battles they had fought here diluted its attractions. It wasn't that simple, he thought, it's not just a question of a cosy place to live.

'She seems very well,' he said when Breda sat down on the armchair. She nodded and stared at the mumbling television. She was wearing a tight-waisted polka-dot skirt and a Shetland sweater and her features were sharpened a shade too much by tiredness. Still beautiful, he thought objectively as he studied her profile. But she, too, seemed familiar but strange.

'I'm sorry about the other night,' he said.

'It's all right.' She sounded uninterested.

'There's a big story breaking.'

'Yes.' She turned the word into both a question and a statement of the obvious.

He chose to take it as a question and told her all he had been doing and what he had found out. She made polite noises occasionally but he did not really notice. He knew he was talking for his own benefit, because he had to tell somebody, even an uninterested audience.

'You're enjoying yourself, then,' she said with a hint of unconscious acrimony when he had finished.

He nodded his agreement to the television and fell silent. Yes, I am enjoying myself, he thought, haven't enjoyed myself so much for a long time. But it was no use trying to explain to her the thrill of unfolding a good story, the fulfilment of digging out things that somebody in authority mightn't want you to know. And the satisfaction of being fully occupied, even pre-occupied again. He knew it was all a silly game to her: cops and robbers for grown-up boys, nothing to do with real life. That was one of their problems, maybe even their main problem.

'Tell me about the guards who called,' he said after a while. 'Did they give their names?'

She shook her head. 'They said it was just a routine check about your car registration or something.'

Car registration, he thought derisively. That was a feeble excuse for whatever they were at. He asked her to describe them and to go through everything they had said but her answers told him nothing more. Just that somebody was checking up on him.

'Did you give them the new address?'

'I told them they could find you at the paper. You were always there.' She looked at him as though she was challenging him to deny the truth of her statement. Or, perhaps, giving him an opening to discuss their relationship. He merely nodded.

As he left, she handed him a plastic bag. 'The things you wanted,' she said. She closed the door as soon as he went out. It was cold and dark and rain fell straight down through the pale street lighting.

Ryle stood by the weeping window of a bare Chinese takeaway and looked out through the narrow tracks left by the condensation streaming down the inside of the pane. The rain hammered down and it seemed as if the world was being drowned in swirls of water.

Behind him, two drunks conversed in mumbled sniggers and a teenage girl waited in self-conscious silence. As always, he felt relieved to get away from Breda's, a sense of release at being freed from a rut. Yet he also felt a nagging and illogical resentment at being excluded from their lives. He suddenly noticed dispassionately that he now thought of it as her home, no longer his. But that didn't necessarily mean anything.

A diminutive woman gave him his order and he dashed through the downpour to his car and drove home. Home, he thought with an edge of bitterness as he entered the dank bedsitter; this isn't it either.

He set the food down on the table beside Clark's file and ate from the aluminium containers, dropping forkfuls of boiled rice on top of the balls of sweet and sour prawns. When he finished he made a cup of instant coffee, turned his radio on and flicked along the dial until he found some faintly martial music. He opened the folder again and slumped back in the armchair to stare at the first paragraph of the page on top of the file. He knew it by heart by now.

'Further to our recent conversations,' it read, 'this committee has considered all aspects of the policy on neutrality and has concluded that it should be revised for the following reasons.'

That meant that Clark had been discussing NATO membership with the Taoiseach. That, in itself, was no inside-page story or mere historical footnote. But the story was much more complex and explosive. This slender file with its bland mixture of political and diplomatic language was the reason behind Clark's death. He had been running scared because of it. He may well have been armed because of it. And armed by the IRA.

Ryle stared at the inanimate papers but they could tell him nothing more. They brought together a tantalising cocktail which had to explain everything. Unless, he sighed suddenly, Clark was killed by something else altogether. Such as jealousy.

Nine

The city's churches all seemed to be spilling out their Sunday congregations as Ryle drove through streets scoured clean by two days of rain. His impatience at yesterday's inactivity was gone and he felt as refreshed as the new day. He was back in action and knew what he was going to do.

The news room had an appropriately reverential stillness about it as if it, too, recognised the Sabbath. A radio rumbled quietly in a corner and a lone reporter read a Sunday supplement with his feet up on a desk. Ryle asked him where Stacy was.

'Gone to lunch.'

Ryle switched on the photocopier and waited for its red light to stop blinking. He copied everything in the file Rosie had given him and then fixed a blank sheet of paper over the page with Clark's signature. He blanked out the text and copied the handwritten signature.

He put the original into a drawer in his desk, typed a note for Stacy and left with the photocopies. Driving northwards out of the city, he listened to two politicians haggling on the radio about the state of the nation and an Opposition move to force an early by-election in Clark's constituency. An outrageous piece of political cynicism and opportunism, the government supporter fumed. What are you afraid of, his opponent taunted, if everything is as rosy as you say?

Ryle watched a plane float into the airport and drove on to a village where the signs of encroaching suburbia were marked by competing hoardings offering unique housing opportunities. On the radio, the politicians were followed by a pundit explaining that the Opposition move was designed to force a general election earlier than the government wished. It had little prospect of success, he opined.

Ryle switched it off as the programme moved on to the

week's routine violence in Northern Ireland and another set of politicians proclaiming well-practised positions.

Jim Whelan showed no surprise at his arrival. 'Would you like a spot of lunch?' he asked. Ryle declined and Whelan showed him into a living room. 'Be with you in a few minutes,' he added. 'The papers are all there but you've probably seen them already.'

Ryle sank into a button-back armchair and looked about. He had been here once before, he remembered, during an election campaign. Three, four years ago. That was the way with newspapers; you moved in and lived on top of somebody while a story ran and then you disappeared until the next one. Whelan didn't seem to mind, though. Maybe that was the way in politics too.

The room was well-furnished in a conventional way, lived-in but not worn: a three-piece suite in a dark-brown velvety material, a coffee table, a large television, laddered shelves in an alcove, a shallow sideboard and a couple of muted prints on the walls. A formal photograph of four children, descending in height from left to right like one side of a demographic pyramid, stood on the top shelf. Ryle could hear their exuberant voices, interspersed with adult mumbles, from another room.

Breda would love this, he thought, the family lunch followed by the Sunday drive in the mountains. That was all she wanted really, simple family things that filled him with an obscure dread. She was a traditionalist at heart. Which was one of their problems, a rare one these days. He hadn't realised it until it was too late, until after Lorraine was born and Breda had abandoned her public relations job with alacrity. All she had really wanted to be was a housewife. Which would have been okay with him if she hadn't wanted him to play the traditional husband and father. He had been taken in by appearances, he supposed, assuming from her looks that Breda was a careerist, sharing some of his own footloose attitudes. Just like Rosie, a homely-looking school teacher who was anything but. Ryle shook his head in an unconscious gesture of wonder at how easy it was to misinterpret people. Particularly women.

Breda would have been happier if he worked from nine to

five, Monday to Friday, pottered about the garden and washed the car on Saturdays and went for a drive on Sundays. Doing the things a family was supposed to do, the ordinary, orderly things which made him twitchy and uneasy. He much preferred the unsocial hours and the barely controlled hysteria and uncertainties of journalism with its ever-beckoning prospect of something exciting, that tomorrow holds something other than today's boredom. The prospect of a good story.

Whelan elbowed open the door and carried in a tray of coffee cups and biscuits and set it down on top of the newspapers on the coffee table. 'How's the family?' he asked as if he could read Ryle's thoughts, but he was only exercising his avuncular politician's style. 'How many children is it now?'

'Just the one.'

'I see the Opposition are trying to stir it up.' Whelan proffered milk and sugar, the social formalities over. 'Working themselves into a lather over an election.'

'Might they succeed?' Ryle sat up on the edge of his chair and took a biscuit.

'Not a chance. Even if they won the by-election the figures are against them.' Whelan sat down. 'So, what's up?'

'I want you to take a look at something.' Ryle juggled his papers and held out the photocopy with nothing but Clark's name on it. 'Is that Maurice Clark's signature?'

Whelan examined it closely. 'What's it from?' he inquired.

'I'll show you in a minute. Is it his signature?'

Whelan looked at it again and nodded after a moment. 'It looks like it.'

Ryle smiled at him. 'Jesus, Jim, is it or isn't it? This isn't a court. Can't you give me a straight answer?'

'It is.' Whelan did not return the smile. 'But I hope I won't have to swear I never said that.'

'You won't have to,' Ryle reassured him easily, content that he had got what he wanted. 'But you're sure it is?'

Whelan shifted uneasily. 'Put it like this. If it's on something non-controversial, I'd have no hesitation. But I presume it's something controversial or you wouldn't be asking.' He paused. 'What have you got?'

Ryle handed him the copies of the two typed pages recommending membership of NATO. Whelan read them with a perplexed look but his face relaxed slowly as his fears dissolved. 'It's a heap of shit.' He tossed them back onto the table with relief.

'You just said the signature was authentic,' Ryle protested.

'Yes, I said it looks authentic. But the rest of it's shit. It's a forgery.'

'How do you know?'

Whelan looked around the room as if he did not know where to start. 'The whole thing is ludicrous.' His gaze settled back on Ryle. 'Maurice didn't believe any of that. The committee never discussed it. The Taoiseach never talked to us about it. It has to be a forgery.'

'You never discussed neutrality at all?'

'No, never. I'm the secretary and I've been at all the meetings and I'm positive it's never been discussed.'

'Were there any plans to discuss it?'

'No. Absolutely not. I drew up the agenda for the next meeting. I'll show it to you if you want. There's nothing like that on it.' Whelan sat back, satisfied there was nothing for him or the party to worry about. 'And another thing . . . ' he leant forward again and picked up the first page, ' . . . the committee reports to the Minister for Foreign Affairs, not the Taoiseach as it says here. It's definitely a forgery.'

'But Maurice might have had talks without you knowing about it,' Ryle suggested.

'No way.' Whelan shook his head emphatically. 'He'd have told me. We worked very closely together on the committee. As well as being friends.'

'Then why was he carrying a forged document around with him? The day he died?'

'Was he? Says who? Look, you've been sold a pup.' Whelan became solemn as a thought struck him. 'I hope you haven't paid any money for this.'

Ryle weighed up Whelan's certainty, hanging on to the one fact he had wanted from him. It is Clark's signature, he told himself, that's all I needed to know. The gist of the story stood up. The fact that the committee hadn't discussed neutrality was secondary. It might even improve the story, deepen the mystery, if Clark hadn't informed his backbench colleagues or his best friend of what he was up to.

The door opened and Maura came in with a coffee pot. 'You know each other,' Whelan said vaguely and they both nodded yes but without conviction. Ryle got to his feet and towered over her as she refilled his cup. She was of an age where the years were beginning to make her look older than her husband.

Ryle slid back into the armchair as she left and changed the subject. 'Did you see Maurice leave Erlanger's party?'

'Why?' Whelan eyed him suspiciously, determined not to fall for any more reporter's tricks.

'I want to know if he left alone.'

'What are you getting at now?'

'He didn't leave with Rosie Gantly, did he?' Ryle tried to make the question sound matter-of-fact, almost innocent.

'She wasn't there. Christ.' Whelan shivered at the thought. 'What are you up to now? All the private stuff about Maurice was off the record. Way off the record. Strictly for your own information.'

'Sure,' Ryle nodded. 'I'm just trying to check out some things.'

Whelan squirmed uneasily. 'Seriously. You're not going to do anything about her, are you?'

'No, I'm not,' Ryle said, surprised at Whelan's nervousness. 'Even if I did the paper wouldn't print it. And I'm not.'

Whelan nodded without looking convinced. He sagged back into his chair.

'All I'm trying to find out,' Ryle added reasonably, 'is whether he had these papers with him when he left the party. Whoever he left with might know.'

'I don't remember.' Whelan shook his head with impatience. 'But you're definitely barking up the wrong tree. I told you I'd help you any way I can to find out what happened to Maurice and that's why I'm being as helpful as I can. But this is a forgery. It has to be.'

'What does the committee think of neutrality?' Ryle persisted.

'We've never discussed it. But I've no doubt everyone thinks the same as I do, the same as Maurice did. It's sacrosanct. Nobody in the committee, in the party or in the government would contemplate this.' He waved towards the document. 'Not for a second. I'm absolutely positive of that.'

Ryle leaned forward and recovered the two pages and put them with the others.

'What's more,' Whelan added, 'I'd seriously reconsider my position in the party if there was any question of us going into NATO. And I wouldn't be the only one.'

'But it is his signature?'

'It looks like it, yes.' Whelan sighed. 'I'm not going back on what I said. But I'm telling you as a friend that you've been given a bum steer. A forgery, in fact.'

Thanks very much, Ryle thought. But that's not what I wanted to know. Another story almost spoiled by checking out the facts. Although everything was far from spoiled. The neutrality issue as such was not what concerned him anyhow.

'Have you sorted out your other problem yet?' Ryle asked as they stood at the door.

'Give over, will you,' Whelan said good-naturedly. 'You guys are worse than a dog with a bone. It was only a storm in a teacup. Nothing to interest a serious paper.'

Ryle pulled out the flimsy sheets of carbon paper and tidied the typed pages into two piles. He tipped the heavy typewriter onto its end, put the top copy of the story in its place and read carefully from start to finish.

'Mr Maurice Clark had a controversial document urging the Government to join NATO in his possession several hours before he met his death in mysterious circumstances in Dun Laoghaire habour last week,' it began. He had toned it down and changed the emphasis in deference to Whelan's emphatic denial, opting for a safe recital of seemingly verifiable facts rather than a dramatic political interpretation.

The story went on to quote at length from the two-page

document with Clark's signature, cited sources on his committee denying they ever discussed neutrality and ended with brief summaries of official policy and how Clark had died after shooting the dog.

He corrected his typing errors on both copies, folded them in half and dropped them on the news desk in front of Stacy.

'That's it as it stands at the moment,' he said as Stacy picked up the top copy eagerly. 'But I want to talk to somebody about some bits of it. I think you should hold it till I get back.'

It was beginning to get dark again as Ryle drove to Rosie Gantly's house and parked at the end of her road. She greeted him warmly, like a casual friend; like Whelan, she showed no surprise at his unannounced visit. He sat at her kitchen table again and refused her offer of coffee. While she made herself a cup he told her broadly what should be going into the next morning's paper.

'Are you sure Maurice never mentioned discussing this with the Taoiseach or anyone else?' he asked.

'Certain.' She sat down opposite him. 'I would remember if he had.'

'Other members of the committee deny they ever talked about neutrality.'

'They would, wouldn't they?' She smiled slightly, appearing more relaxed and less distant than she had been the last time he was there.

'Did he ever have these particular documents with him before that last night?'

'No. Not that I know of. He often carried a briefcase.' She smiled faintly at a memory. 'But he didn't open it up and produce secret files for me to read. Not normally.'

'Did he say anything specifically about them before he left? The night he left them?'

'No. He didn't mention the file at all.' She leaned back and looked at him. 'I told you it was only after he left that I noticed it.'

Ryle asked her to go back over everything Clark had said and everything that had happened that night. She asked why and he told her he had to have it all clear in his own mind. She sipped her coffee and said nothing. 'Look,' he added, 'I'm sticking my neck way out with this story. One of Clark's friends, one of his other friends, is emphatic that it's a forgery.'

'Is that what you think?'

'I don't know,' Ryle admitted. 'I'm writing a straightforward story saying he had this document on him shortly before he died and this is what it says.'

'I didn't forge it if that's what you're trying to ask me.' A note of challenge gave an edge to her voice and she waited for Ryle to respond. He nodded and she relaxed again. 'Maurice left it here like I told you. I didn't even know he had left it or what it was until after he had gone.'

'I really need to know everything that happened.' He pleaded with his eyes.

Rosie studied his face for a moment and sipped her coffee. Then she said, 'He must have been at the door for quite a while before he woke me and it was another while before I got up and let him in. I was very disoriented . . . had gone to bed late, with a lot of drink and . . . well, I was angry and told him to fuck off.'

Ryle nodded sympathetically and waited for her to continue.

'It wasn't immediately obvious to me that he was in a bad way. I was in a bad way myself. I was very angry insofar as I could feel anything. The fucking bell had kept on ringing, he'd kept his finger on it and didn't let go till I opened the door.

'He walked in and I gave out to him, what the fuck did he think he was at, that sort of thing. I don't know what he said at first, if he said anything. I wasn't listening, too caught up in my own fury. I ranted at him that I wasn't one of his political groupies and he couldn't treat me like this. Then he said "I wanted to talk to you" and that sent me into another rage.'

She paused and gulped down some coffee. She stared at the worn wood of the table, no longer looking at him. 'I told him to get out, that I wasn't talking to anyone at that hour of the night. I just walked back to the door and opened it and he came out after a moment. He stopped beside me, put his hand on my face and said something like "I'm trapped" or "They've got me trapped" and "They're moving in on me". Maybe not those exact words but something like that.'

She paused again and Ryle waited but she did not go on. 'That was all?' he asked quietly, mainly to break the silence. 'Just that?'

'I knocked his hand away and told him to fuck off,' she said bleakly. 'That was it.'

She got up quickly and flicked on the electric kettle and stood with her back to him. Neither said anything as the water rumbled to the boil. Ryle watched her back and wondered if she was crying. Everything she had said was imbued with self-criticism and guilt at the way she had treated Clark. She obviously loved him, he thought and wondered again at what she had seen in him. What Clark saw in her did not seem so much of a mystery to him any more.

Rosie made herself another cup of coffee and sat down again. Her eyes were dry.

'I'm sorry to go on about this,' Ryle began but she cut short his apology with a wave of her hand. 'Are you sure that was when he left the documents here?'

'Certain.'

'Could someone else have left them?'

'No. They weren't here before he came and they were here immediately after he left.'

'You said you'd been drinking . . . '

'I don't get so drunk that I don't know what's going on,' she said ruefully, as if she regretted an inhibiting disability. 'Nobody else left the file here.'

Ryle said again that he was sorry he'd had to go over it all again and Rosie said it was okay. On his way out he stopped for a moment in the living room. 'Are you in Sinn Fein?' He nodded at the party poster calling for victory to the IRA.

'No.' She halted beside him. 'Some of their policies are okay but they're reactionaries at heart.'

'Did Maurice feel the same way about them?'

She looked at him curiously. 'At heart Maurice was a reactionary too,' she replied enigmatically. 'What are you implying?'

'Just wondering how he felt about the IRA, Sinn Fein?'

'Like everyone else here. All behind them a few years ago

when Catholics were getting shot and beaten up in the North. But he changed his mind when they fought back, went on the offensive.' She stared at the poster for a moment. 'We love victims, don't we? The Irish people love the underdog as long as he's having the shit kicked out of him but they get upset when he bites back. Spoils the ballads, I suppose.'

She flashed an impish smile at him. 'You've got a point,' he said, although he wasn't too sure he knew what it was.

She turned and pointed at another poster. 'I'm not a member of the Tupamaros either,' she laughed lightly, 'in case you're interested. Or worried.'

As he walked to his car Ryle felt relieved. He had got the reassurance he wanted from Rosie; he was happy that she was telling the truth. He ran his mind's eye over the story he had written, visualising it page by page and deciding that it was all right, nothing needed to be changed. He was concentrating so deeply on it that he had reached his car before he noticed the man lounging against the passenger door. Ryle stopped abruptly.

'Aren't you the fast mover,' Sergeant Peter Grifford drawled sardonically. 'And the poor man hardly cold in his grave.'

Ryle stalked around to the driver's door, his mind beginning to race. Grifford waited with his hand on the door handle. Ryle hesitated a moment before leaning over and unlocking it. He started the engine and swung the car into a tight turn as Grifford slammed his door shut.

'Nature abhors a vacuum,' Grifford continued without concern, 'isn't that what they say? I suppose it'd be worse if it was the official widow. Might cause an official scandal.'

Ryle pulled into the pavement, braked hard and shut off the engine. 'What the fuck are you up to?' He glowered at Grifford.

'So how is Red Rosie?' Grifford smiled back pleasantly. 'Looking for a shoulder to cry on?'

'Leave her alone,' Ryle heard himself say and felt surprised at his own vehemence.

Grifford nodded to himself. 'So that is the way it is.'

Ryle tried to contain his anger and work out what was going

on. But all he could think of was the problems that would follow if the gardai moved in on Rosie. She would think he had tipped them off, had set her up. She could screw up the story, deny everything. And refuse to talk to him again. His upset, he admitted too, was fuelled by the fact that he liked her. He only hoped she had not seen Grifford getting into his car.

'What are you playing at now?' Ryle repeated his question.

'Following you, of course. Like I told you. Waiting for you to lead me to Clark's killer.' Grifford leaned towards him and lowered his voice. 'Did Rosie do it? A crime of passion? Should I slap the cuffs on her now?'

Ryle sighed and started the car. 'I'd like that.' Grifford sat back again. 'We don't have half enough passionate crime in this country. Our criminal motives are much more boring and materialistic. Or revolutionary. For money or for Ireland. Or because of the drink, Your Worship.' Grifford looked quizzically at Ryle. 'Was that the motive? She is a revolutionary, you know.'

Ryle drove fast and gave a derisive snort. 'That's the trouble with you lads. You put meaningless labels on people and you believe them and then you jump to conclusions.'

'I don't think Rosie would like to hear you disparage her revolutionary activities like that. "Meaningless".' Grifford shook his head sadly.

'How would you describe them?' Ryle tried to regain the initiative.

'Dangerous,' Grifford said. 'Seditious. Trouble-makers, determined to subvert democracy and clap the likes of you in irons.'

Ryle laughed again with derision.

'And how would you describe her?' Grifford smiled. 'A warm and wonderful human being. Who only lives for her aged mother and charitable works. Loves stray animals and rescues seagulls from oil spills. Wouldn't hurt a hair on anyone's head.'

'That sounds about right,' Ryle shot back sardonically. Inwardly he thought that wasn't all that unlikely. Rosie was a warm human being with a sense of humour. Which was rare among self-proclaimed revolutionaries.

Grifford nodded sagely. 'Just like every terrorist who's ever been shot in the back on the job.'

Ryle accelerated towards an orange light and sped through the red at an intersection. A car starting to come across his path braked and the driver pounded his horn in a staccato of shocks. Ryle grinned with malevolence but Grifford paid no attention.

'You should be more worried about them than me,' the sergeant smiled at him. 'Policemen are always in demand after the revolution, especially low-level types like me. And when they close down your paper and tell me to lock you up, I'll do it. Happily. We only carry out orders. Ours not to reason why.'

'I don't think Rosie's much of a revolutionary threat.'

'Maybe, maybe not. At least we do her and her ilk the courtesy of taking them as seriously as they take themselves. And she associates with some unsavoury types.'

'Like Clark,' Ryle snorted.

'Like bank robbers.'

'Who?'

Grifford shrugged. 'Some of her group could assist with inquiries into a couple of armed robberies over the last year. If they had a mind to.'

'Why don't you charge them?'

'Lack of evidence,' Grifford said, and they continued a sparring conversation until Ryle parked close to his office.

'Thanks for the lift,' Grifford said as they got out.

'Any time,' Ryle replied. 'I hope you left your car in Ranelagh.'

Grifford raised a hand to the passing traffic and an unmarked car pulled out of the stream and waited for him further down the road, its yellow indicator flashing. Shit, Ryle thought, they really are following me.

'Should I arrest her now then?' Grifford asked.

'Why don't you?' Ryle replied flippantly. 'Charge her with sedition.'

Grifford seemed to give the idea serious consideration. 'That's a charge that seems to have gone out of fashion these days. Unfortunately.'

'It might earn you promotion,' Ryle retorted. 'Or speed up your retirement.'

The news room had reached its peak of activity for a slack Sunday. Ryle went straight to the news desk and told Stacy that the story stood as he had written it.

'Great story,' Stacy said with rare enthusiasm. 'You were right. There's more angles to this than to a bookies' convention.'

'I didn't expect the sex angle to lead into this kind of political controversy,' Ryle admitted.

'Give me a copy of the documents. We might use a picture inside.'

'Inside?' Ryle bristled.

'It's going on the front page,' Stacy reassured him. 'Lead story. With a carry-over inside. And a few minor changes. The editor doesn't like references to mysteries so I've changed your "mysterious circumstances" to "unexplained circumstances".'

Ryle shrugged and went to his desk. The story was coming together at last even if he still did not know where it was leading or what the framework was. Yet Whelan's certainty and Grifford's sudden reappearance worried him. He considered going back and warning Rosie that he had been followed to her house. But what good would that do? Anyway they obviously knew about her affair with Clark. So why hadn't they been to her? Or had they? He'd forgotten to ask her.

It was time to sort out what the guards were up to, Ryle decided. Before he started pursuing the really big story. He leafed through a telephone directory, fired by the kick of having made a major breakthrough and also by a vague apprehension. Suppose Whelan was right and it was a forgery. And now it's the lead story. He dismissed the thought and ran his finger down the list of names, concentrating on addresses rather than numbers.

Inspector Bill Devane walked slowly down the darkened hallway and peered through the spy hole at the man who had knocked. He didn't recognise him. He went into the front room, breathing heavily, and peered through a gap in the curtains at the cul de sac outside. A car was parked beside his gateway and he glanced at its exhaust pipe. The engine was not running and there was nobody in it. He went to open the door.

Suddenly unsure of his reception, Ryle identified himself and asked if he could talk to the Inspector for a few minutes. Devane pointed to the front room and turned on the overhead light. They stood in the centre of the floor, facing each other and managing to crowd the room with their presence.

'Why am I being followed?' Ryle demanded.

'Who's following you?' Devane asked with polite disinterest.

'One of your men.' Ryle paused. 'Sergeant Peter Grifford.'

'Grifford,' Devane grunted. 'He's not one of my men.'

'You're in charge of the Maurice Clark case and he's following me because of that.'

'Is he?' Devane concealed his sudden interest.

Ryle nodded.

'What've you got to hide?'

'Me? Nothing.' Ryle found Devane disconcerting. The Inspector's heavy face was weary with suspicion and he had not taken his blank stare off Ryle for a moment. He was several inches shorter than Ryle but he somehow managed to make him feel like a guilty boy. Ryle fought against the urge to shift his own eyes and held Devane's gaze.

'Grifford's in one of the central city stations, isn't he?' Devane said at last as though they were exchanging social pleasantries about a slight mutual acquaintance. 'He's not in CDU.'

Ryle nodded. He knew Devane was a member of the Central Detective Unit but he was unsure about its relationship with detectives attached to local police stations. 'He says he's following me because of the Clark case. And you're in charge of that,' Ryle repeated doggedly.

'He told you that?' Devane's voice carried a hint of amusement but his face remained stony. 'It can't be very serious then, can it?'

'It's annoying,' Ryle said lamely.

'Did he follow you here?'

'No. I don't think so.' Ryle felt like a fool.

'Why is he following you?'

'That's what I want to know.'

'You should ask him.'

'He said it's because of the Clark case.' Ryle said, now feeling a complete fool.

An awkward silence settled on the room. 'Whiskey?' Devane asked suddenly and went to a sideboard without waiting for an answer. He took out a bottle, poured two drinks and handed one to Ryle. 'Sit down,' he muttered and left the room. Ryle sat and sipped the neat whiskey and overcame a sudden urge to get up and leave. What if Devane has gone to call the police, he thought wildly. Calm down, for God's sake.

Devane brought back a jug of water in one hand and a packet of Sweet Afton cigarettes in the other. He poured some water into Ryle's glass, sat down and lit a cigarette.

'If you have any information about Mr Clark's death you are obliged to tell me,' he said formally.

'I don't know anything you don't know already,' Ryle replied cautiously. His confidence was returning as the whiskey put them on a more even footing.

'Nothing more than what you've written?'

Devane was letting him off the hook, Ryle thought with relief. He decided to try and retrieve something from this impetuous visit. 'I've heard that the gun Clark had came from the IRA.'

'Did it?'

'I don't know. I just heard that.'

'What else have you heard?' Devane asked in a monotone that matched his impassive policeman's look of interminable patience.

Ryle sipped his drink to give himself a moment to think. 'Things. One of which is going into tomorrow's paper.'

Devane waited politely.

'I'll tell you about it in a moment,' Ryle offered a trade. 'To finish with the IRA connection first. Is it true?'

'I can't discuss an on-going investigation.'

'Would I be wrong if I wrote that Clark's gun had come from the IRA?'

Devane switched his attention to his drink. 'Can you prove it?'

'Can I put it another way? Would I be wrong to say that he had an illegal gun?'

'I thought you'd already written that. Somebody did.'

128

Ryle nodded. 'I wrote that he did not have a permit for the gun. Which is not exactly the same thing as an IRA gun.'

Devane grunted. 'The only guidance I could give you would be to look at where the weapon originated.'

'Where did it come from?' Ryle asked eagerly.

'I told you I can't discuss an official investigation.'

They sipped their drinks in silence while Ryle racked his tired brain to come up with another way to broach the question. Devane was obviously prepared to tell him something if he could find the key that would unlock his answers. 'Would I be very wrong if I said it had come from the North?'

Devane said nothing, gave no indication that he had heard the question.

'That it had been used by the IRA in the North?' Ryle added, hoping that Devane was playing the game he thought he was playing and had not gone deaf temporarily.

Devane did not respond.

'That it had killed someone in the North?' Ryle pressed on, looking for a response, any response, rather than believing anything he was saying might be true.

'You would have to prove that,' Devane said to Ryle's delight: he *was* playing the game. And he had confirmed Grifford's tip-off. Clark really had had an IRA gun.

'Prove which?' he asked, to get the message clear.

'That it had killed someone.'

Ryle paused to consider whether he should pursue the issue any further but decided not to push his luck. Devane had told him enough by saying nothing. He had established the first part of the real story for him. All he had to do now was find out why Clark had an IRA gun. The possibilities were mind-boggling.

'I've a story in tomorrow's paper about a document Clark had shortly before he died.' He gave Devane a brief résumé. The Inspector seemed unimpressed.

'Where did you get these documents?' he asked at last, as if politeness required some show of interest on his part.

Ryle ignored the question, taking pleasure in using Devane's own technique. 'Does that angle mean anything to you, attach itself to any of your loose ends?'

'It's politics,' Devane shrugged, unconsciously echoing Ryle's first response when Rosie had given him the file. 'I'm only concerned with crime or possible crime.'

'You don't think it might have something to do with his death?'

'Bodies are pulled out of Dun Laoghaire harbour all the time and get only a cursory examination,' Devane said. 'This one's different only because of his identity.'

'And because of the gun?' Ryle prompted.

'And the gun,' Devane agreed. 'But he wasn't shot and there's no reason to suspect foul play.'

'No signs of violence?'

Devane shook his head.

'But you haven't ruled it out or you'd have finished your inquiries by now, wouldn't you?'

'Maybe I'm just slow,' Devane pursed his lips.

'But what was he doing with an IRA gun?' Ryle probed gently.

'I've already told you, I can't discuss details of an investigation,' Devane said sharply.

Ryle backed off, thanked him for the drink and Devane showed him out. 'Give my regards to Grifford,' he said, 'I haven't seen him for years.' He watched as Ryle drove up to the turning circle at the end of the road and swung the car around in an ebullient circle. Now we're motoring, Ryle said aloud, as he rubbed away the condensation on the windscreen.

Devane closed the door before the car passed again and picked up his phone. He heard the car engine fade as he told his assistant to collect first editions of all the morning newspapers and bring them round. 'It's going to be a bitch of a week,' he sighed.

Ten

Tommy Lyster hauled himself out of his official black Mercedes, stretched unhurriedly and glanced over the wedge of traffic at the bare trees in St Stephen's Green. It was unlikely that any of his rural constituents were among the motorists on their way to work but, he thought, you never know. Someone might recognise him and be impressed by his early arrival. They were not to know that the absence of the Justice Minister, rather than dedication to his job, had brought him to Dublin so early. Lyster made a point of being around when his boss was not.

As soon as he waddled up the steps of the Department of Justice he knew his instinct was right. Something was up.

His pasty-faced private secretary swung the door open and said in a nervous burst: 'Good morning, Minister, the Secretary would like to see you right away.'

Lyster gave no indication that he had heard or that he had noticed the tension in the young man's voice. 'If that's convenient,' his secretary mumbled without conviction. No one in his world dawdled over a summons from the Department's permanent head.

Lyster stepped into the waiting lift and let him jab the button. 'Have a good weekend?' he beamed.

'Yes, Minister. Thank you.'

'Chasing women, I suppose.' Lyster delighted in unsettling him and was rewarded with a polite cough and a slight blush. His secretary was not yet accustomed to Lyster's use of idle banter as a sort of personal piped music. His predecessor, distracted by his need to take every ministerial utterance earnestly, had sought a transfer.

'We used to prefer nurses in my day,' Lyster chuckled. 'Great crack, nurses. And always good cooks too. You could do worse than a nurse.'

The lift stopped and the private secretary led Lyster to his office. 'I'll tell the Secretary you're ready to see him,' he sighed with relief. Lyster settled into his chair and nodded. He looked out at the grey sky hanging over the city like an uneasy sleep and congratulated himself on his decision to get in early. It always paid to be on the ball, especially when that gobshite was away. He waited with satisfaction for the Secretary to arrive. The phone rang instead.

'Good morning, Minister,' the permanent Secretary said calmly. 'The Taoiseach's office is on the line. He has called several times already.'

Lyster straightened up and gripped the receiver tighter as the connection clicked in his ear and a voice said 'yes'. Lyster broke his round face into a grin. 'Hello, Taoiseach.' The voice replied, 'Putting you through now.'

'Where've you been?' the Taoiseach demanded.

'I had to come up from the constituency, Taoiseach,' Lyster blustered. 'We left about half past . . .'

'What the hell's going on over there, Tommy? Have you read the papers?'

'Oh, yes, Taoiseach.' Lyster had scanned the columns of death notices and cast a cursory eye over the sports pages.

'Bring me a full report. In person. In an hour.' The Taoiseach hung up.

Lyster was still holding the dead phone a moment later when the Secretary entered with a weak knock.

'What the hell's going on over here?' Lyster echoed, banging down the phone.

'You've seen the papers, Minister?' the Secretary said.

'Only the death notices.' Lyster suppressed a belch.

The Secretary picked up one of the papers stacked neatly on a coffee table and pointed a thin finger at Ryle's story. Lyster read the first few paragraphs and looked up at the Secretary. 'Is this true?' he demanded.

'I have no idea,' the Secretary sniffed. He knew the junior Minister for what he was and treated him with a distant, off-hand civility. 'It's a matter for Foreign Affairs or the Government, I would have thought.'

Lyster narrowed his eyes but controlled his tongue. 'Don't the guards know whether or not young Clark had these so-called documents on him before he died?'

'I am not aware of any official reports to that effect, Minister.'

'Well, would you find out?' Lyster puffed up his chest with the authority of the Taoiseach's summons. 'I want a full report on it immediately. A full comprehensive report.'

Jim Whelan let the newspaper crumple onto the floor and cursed loudly. 'It's that bitch,' he exclaimed. 'It's her doing.'

'Jim.' Maura stretched his name into a rising warning. She turned back to fastening the boy's overcoat and told him to say goodbye to his father. Whelan ruffled the child's hair distractedly and his wife sighed and smoothed it again and led him out of the kitchen.

Whelan buttered some toast, swallowed a mouthful of tea and forced his indignation to recede. There was no point in getting mad. There was nothing to get mad about. He wasn't even sure why he was getting so mad. Except that he felt a sneaking guilt that this was all his fault, because he had put Ryle onto Rosie. But he'd have found her anyway, he assured himself, with or without my help.

Maura came back, gathered the newspaper off the floor and straightened out the pages. She sat down opposite him and began to read. 'What does it mean?' she asked.

'Mean?' he almost shouted. 'It doesn't mean anything. It's just a bit of shit-stirring.'

'Maybe it's true.'

'Don't be ridiculous. Of course it's not true. I told you that yesterday.'

'Yes, and you told that reporter friend of yours too.'

Whelan sighed. He knew what she was getting at but she just didn't understand the way politics operated. In fact, he thought impatiently, she deliberately refused to understand. She insisted on seeing every political development as a personal slight against him. Which was touching in a way but also very tiring.

'Why did he write it if it isn't true?' she asked innocently.

'Because that bitch put him up to it.' He took the paper from her and scanned down the column. '"Mr Clark told friends shortly before his death ..."' he read aloud. 'That's her. I know it.'

'I don't see why you wasted your time talking to that reporter, then.'

'That's not the point,' he said irritably. 'The point is, what do I do about it?' Maurice would have been able to handle it, he thought, turn it effortlessly to his advantage. And I have to do the same. If I'm going to step into his shoes, I've got to take over his role. And now's the time to do it.

'I don't see why you have to do anything about it. It's got nothing to do with you.'

'I have a responsibility to set the record straight,' he said automatically and suddenly realised how he could use the situation. 'As the Number Two on the Foreign Affairs Committee,' he added, already drafting a statement, 'it is incumbent on me to set out the true facts.'

'I think you'd be better off steering clear of the whole thing,' she shrugged, aware that he wasn't talking to her any more. She took the paper back and began leafing through the other pages.

Whelan got out a battered address book. He knew exactly what Maurice would have done and how he could do it, too. It was another God-sent opportunity.

The banging grew more insistent and began to dominate the dream. Ryle woke suddenly and stumbled out of bed with part of his mind still cocooned in sleep. He was wearing only a shirt and he shivered as he stumbled to the door, opened it a fraction and peered out.

The girl from the bedsitter next door barely suppressed a smile at the sight of his ghostly face. 'Phone call,' she said. 'He said to wake you up, it's urgent.'

Ryle grabbed his parka from a chair, gripped it around himself and shuffled out to the hall. He lifted the receiver off the payphone.

'Get your radio on,' Stacy snapped and hung up.

Ryle hobbled back to his room like an invalid following the incomprehensible orders of an authoritarian nurse. He turned on the radio and recognised Whelan's voice immediately.

'No question or doubt about it.' Whelan was in full flight, aloft on a rising current of righteous indignation. 'It's a forgery. On a par with the Casement diaries. A despicable attempt by some unscrupulous group or individual to denigrate a dead man and this Government. As I said, we never discussed neutrality in that committee or any other committee and if we ever did it would have been in order to find ways of strengthening our traditional policy. The Irish people can rest assured that we will never lead them into NATO or have any hand, act or part in abandoning neutrality under any circumstances.'

Whelan paused for breath and the interviewer thanked him quickly and announced a break for ads. Bullshit. Ryle yawned and curled up in the chair. He was dozing off when the phone rang again.

'They want you to go on the programme,' Stacy said.

'I can't make it out there in time,' Ryle croaked.

'They'll do it by phone.' Stacy broke off to talk to somebody else. Ryle leaned against the wall and another jaw-stretching yawn made his eyes water. He shifted his bare feet on the worn linoleum but moved them back again as the iced damp seeped into him.

Stacy came back on the line. 'There's a couple of detectives here looking for you.'

'For me?' But Stacy was gone again, immersed in an agitated conversation with several other people. The girl next door came out, dressed in a fake-fur coat, and locked her door. She looked down at his naked legs and gave him a smile and a silent whistle as she passed. Ryle laughed out loud.

'Glad you think it's so fucking funny,' Stacy snarled. 'The programme producer says its too late to take you now but they want a quick comment on Whelan.'

'He's a prick.'

'I told him we stand by our story,' Stacy said with exaggerated patience. 'We do stand by the story, don't we?'

'Yeah, we stand by the story.' Ryle shifted his weight and felt the slithery cold of the floor. He yawned and shivered.

'Whelan says he proved to you that it wasn't true.'

'He says what?' Ryle finally jolted himself awake.

'On the radio. He said you showed him the document yesterday and he proved to you that it was a forgery.'

'Jesus. He really is a prick.'

Stacy broke off to talk to someone again. Ryle shivered but he didn't notice the cold any more. Whelan had some nerve, he thought, with a mixture of admiration and indignation. But if he's trying to shaft me like that then I'm under no obligation to keep his identification of Clark's signature secret. He waited impatiently for Stacy's attention to return.

But the news editor gave him no chance to talk. 'The cops are in with the editor,' he snapped. 'Get in here fast.'

Twenty minutes later Ryle shouldered open the door into the news room and almost bumped into Inspector Devane and another detective. Devane gave no indication that he recognised him and Ryle held the door open to let them out. And good riddance, he thought sourly. That was one problem out of the way.

Stacy was engrossed in a phone conversation and Ryle made straight for the coffee machine. Another reporter slapped him on the shoulder and told him what a great story he had written. 'Hasn't been so much activity around here so early in the day for years,' he grinned delightedly.

Ryle sat down at his desk and sipped the coffee. Two handwritten notes told him that James Burke and Jonathan had phoned, but he didn't feel like returning their calls. The last thing he needed was another lecture from Jonathan about the evils of uranium mining and Burke was not high on his current list of priorities.

'They've left,' Stacy said needlessly as he sauntered over to Ryle's desk and pulled up a chair. Ryle nodded. 'The editor gave them a copy of the document. And they told him where you got it.'

'Shit.' Ryle looked at him in surprise. 'Why'd he do that?'

Stacy ignored him. 'Not exactly an impeccable source. In the editor's opinion. He doesn't like it. She's got an obvious axe to grind.'

'The story's all right,' Ryle retorted. 'Giving the cops that stuff is not. It could cause a lot of problems.'

'How well do you know her?' Stacy insisted.

'I believe her.'

'We can't stand four-square behind this story just on her say-so.' Stacy raised a palm to stop Ryle's objection. 'The editor feels.'

Ryle restrained himself and threw down his ace card. 'I didn't write it just on her say-so. Whelan identified Clark's signature. He said it was authentic.'

'That's not what he said on the radio.'

'Well that's what the fucker told me. He's only questioning it because he doesn't want to believe the rest of the document. And he's been sent out to do a snow job on it.'

Stacy said nothing and Ryle ran through his conversation with Whelan. 'Are you sure you're not splitting hairs?' Stacy asked. 'Being too subtle?'

Ryle shook his head.

'Okay. That helps.' Stacy stood up.

'Why did the editor give them the document?' Ryle demanded again.

'Because we're a law-abiding newspaper,' Stacy sighed. 'Ever ready to assist the proper authorities in the endless search for truth and justice.'

Ryle scoffed but somebody summoned the news editor and Stacy cut short his objections with a shrug. Ryle got another coffee and leafed through the morning's paper, not really paying any attention to what he saw. Around him the news room was settling back into its normal mid-morning torpor with phones ringing unanswered and people chatting unhurriedly. He wandered over to the radio in a corner as the news headlines came on: Whelan's denial of his story was the third item. As he went back towards his desk he saw the features editor heading towards him from the far end of the room. Shit, he groaned quietly, not now.

Stacy called him and he sped eagerly over to the news desk and took the phone held out to him. 'Fleet Street,' said Stacy.

'Seamus. Great story, mate,' an English voice said with the instant familiarity of someone who needs something in a hurry. 'Could you explain one or two points? Put you down for a credit.'

'Sure.' Ryle was aware of the features editor hovering behind him. 'No problem.'

'Why does neutrality cause such a flap with the Irish?'

Ryle squeezed his eyes and tried to unravel the issue into some kind of quick and coherent explanation. He was unable to sum it up in a pithy sentence and he rambled around the subject for a minute, still conscious of the features editor waiting by his shoulder.

'But what's the reasoning behind it?' the reporter persisted. 'I mean, it doesn't seem to make a lot of sense.'

'Partition,' Ryle said authoritatively. When in doubt, be certain, he thought, and warmed to the theme. 'Joining NATO would have meant an agreement to accept national boundaries as they were. As they are. And to recognise the British presence in Northern Ireland.'

'Right. It's the Brits again,' the English reporter said, grasping a familiar theme and trying to display his understanding of Irish affairs.

'That was in the Fifties,' Ryle added. The bloody features editor showed no sign of moving. 'There hasn't been a lot about it since then.'

'Well, we're all in the Common Market together now, aren't we?'

'That's one of the arguments for change in this document.' He launched into a leisurely summary of the main details of Clark's document, hoping to bore the features editor rather then enlighten the Fleet Street reporter.

'Sounds reasonable. No such thing as isolationism in the nuclear age. The fallout won't respect national frontiers.'

'Yeah, he touched on that point.'

'And this murdered backbencher, what'shisname, was promoting NATO membership?'

'He hadn't said anything about it before his death. Which is why it's a story now. And we're not sure yet that he was murdered.' Ryle smiled grimly as the features editor was dragged away in an earnest conversation by the deputy editor.

'Has the IRA said anything?' The English reporter pulled him back sharply.

'How do you mean?' Ryle stalled, afraid someone else had got the story about the gun.

'Where they stand on neutrality? Might they have knocked him off for his pro-NATO stance?'

Ryle did a mental double-take. That was another angle that hadn't occurred to him. At least, not as explicitly as that. The IRA was the angle he wanted to pursue. Why Clark had one of its guns. And the extent of his involvement with the Provos. But suppose they'd bumped off Clark for his views and Rosie was in league with them. Jesus. His brain felt feverish.

'Not at all. They haven't said anything.' He tried to sound bored at the very idea.

'Any official government comment?'

'Not yet.' Ryle did not mention Whelan and the English reporter gave him his number to call if there were any developments. He put down the phone and stood thinking for a moment.

'Today's story,' Stacy interrupted him. 'What's the follow-up?'

Ryle shook off his brainstorm. When in doubt, be decisive, he told himself again. He had to win some more time and, above all, keep clear of the ritual reaction stories. 'I'm following up Clark's gun and the fact that it came from the IRA,' he declared. 'And had been used in the North.'

'Hold on,' Stacy raised a hand. 'We can't just ignore today's story. We are still standing by it, aren't we?'

Ryle shrugged impatiently. 'But I've got nothing more on neutrality. It's all in today's paper.'

The news editor began itemising a list on his fingers. 'We're lifting Whelan off the radio. A couple of other backbenchers are looking for your blood. The Opposition is putting down a special Dáil question. And there might be something from the diplomatic circuit.'

'I don't want to get bogged down in any of that,' Ryle pleaded. 'I've got to stick to Clark's trail. That's what's producing the real stories.'

Stacy reached over his desk and held out a sheet of blue notepaper. 'And this has just come in.' Ryle took it and perched on the side of the desk. 'Maybe we should start a new column, Stacy added. 'Denials of Seamus Ryle stories.'

It was a letter to the editor from Clark's widow, written in a tone of hurt dignity and an unexpected legalistic turn of phrase. She hadn't written it herself, Ryle decided, as he read the accusation that he and the newspaper were deliberately trying to vilify a dead man who could have no recourse to the law to disprove the outrageous slanders on his reputation.

'Shit.' Ryle handed him back the letter.

'Maybe they're protesting too much.' Stacy shrugged. 'I told the editor your theory about the gun. I hope it doesn't come from the same source.'

Ryle shook his head. 'Two cops.'

'Who?'

Ryle hesitated and Stacy insisted he needed to know. 'You're beginning to keep the editor awake at night,' he added.

'The one in charge of the investigation,' Ryle admitted.

'The one who was just in here?' Stacy sounded impressed. Ryle nodded. 'Can you quote him?'

'No.'

'Or give any details?'

Ryle shook his head. 'The gun had been used in the North. But I've no idea why Clark had it and that's the story I want to chase. It could turn out to be a really big one.'

Stacy nodded agreement and turned cautious as the possible implications sank in. 'We want to be very sure of our ground before we accuse Clark of something like that. Even if he's dead and can't sue.' He stood up and flashed a wan smile. 'And it would be nice if we could quote somebody once in a while on this story. Other than their denials.'

The Chief Superintendent straightened the photocopies on his desk with the nails of his index fingers as if the sheets might be contagious. He read the opening paragraphs and took off his reading glasses and folded them with an air of finality. He looked up at Inspector Devane with a puzzled frown. 'Why are you giving me these?' he asked innocently.

'I thought you wanted them,' Devane scowled.

'Me? No.'

'You wanted to see the reason for all the fuss,' Devane said, making it sound like an accusation. He stood at the other side of the desk, wearing his raincoat and sounding slightly breathless, as though he had hurried back from Ryle's office with the document. He was in a foul mood.

The Chief flicked his fingers dismissively over the papers. 'This is politics.'

'It's had me running round like a blue-arsed fly all morning,' Devane growled. 'And had you in a major panic a couple of hours ago.'

The Chief leaned back in his chair so he could look up at Devane without stretching his neck. 'The point at issue,' he said evenly, 'was whether or not Maurice Clark had these with him immediately before he died. And whether or not they had any bearing on his death.'

'Do they?' Devane demanded.

The Chief stared back at him and took his time before ignoring his question. 'What does the reporter say? Does he confirm the source?'

'They won't confirm or deny anything,' Devane retorted impatiently. 'How do you know the source?'

The Chief shrugged and propped his hands behind his head.

'Jesus Christ!' Devane exploded. 'How am I supposed to conduct an investigation when I don't know what's going on? Am I just a fucking messenger boy? Running around town collecting bits of paper which were supposed to be tablets of stone but now turn out to be of no interest to anyone.'

'What is this?' The Chief made a feeble attempt to sound hurt. 'Are you trying to give me the third degree or something?'

'The source,' Devane insisted. 'How do you know it was Clark's mistress?'

'Sit down,' the Chief said. Devane remained standing and jammed his hands aggressively into his pockets, determined now to bring everything into the open. The Chief sighed. 'Peter Grifford told me,' he said.

'Of course.' Devane nodded several times. 'That explains everything.' So Ryle was right. It wasn't just the usual reporter's paranoia that everyone was interested in their activities. Grifford was involved.

'And may I ask how many others are working on this case behind my back?' Devane made no attempt to hide his feelings.

'Nobody.' The Chief sounded surprised. 'You're in charge of it, full stop.'

'What's Grifford doing then?'

'What's he doing? Nothing.'

'Providing information.'

'Grifford,' the Chief shrugged impatiently, 'is a piss artist. As you well know. You wouldn't want to pay much attention to what he says.'

'So why's he telling you the source of this stuff? And following this reporter. If he's not involved.'

'Who says he's following the reporter?'

'The reporter,' Devane snapped.

The Chief got to his feet and straightened his back as if he was about to go on parade. He turned away and looked out of the window. 'Grifford called me this morning to tell me the source of the article. Said he just wanted to mark our cards. You know how he goes on. He didn't say where he got the information and I didn't ask.' He turned back to face Devane. 'I presume he's just acting the bollocks as usual, pretending to be involved in something that's none of his business.'

Devane shook his head decisively and told him about Ryle's visit to his house the previous night to complain about Grifford's activities.

'Did you tell him anything?' the Chief demanded instantly, laying bare his real concern.

'He gave me information,' Devane said sourly.

'You know very well how sensitive this case is,' the Chief said. 'And that we can't afford to have any leaks. Any more leaks,' he added pointedly.

'That's not my problem,' Devane replied. 'My problem is that I have to find out things from the newspapers. And that other people are working on this inquiry without my knowledge.'

The Chief gave him a worried look. 'There are no parallel inquiries,' he said slowly. 'As far as I'm aware.'

'Maybe he's working for the Branch or C3.' Devane named

the sections dealing with political militants and security Intelligence.

The Chief shook his head emphatically, as though he was trying to convince himself as well. 'I'll have a word with his Super, make sure he's got something better to do than poking his nose into other people's business.'

They lapsed into silence, facing each other like weary footballers during a break for injuries. The Chief looked preoccupied and Devane wondered if he really didn't know what Grifford was up to. That was unlikely, he thought. But he couldn't work out what was going on: the almighty panic over Ryle's story seemed to have dissolved as quickly as it had erupted. Someone had changed their mind in a hurry.

'Anyway,' the Chief re-emerged from his thoughts as if he had been wondering about the same thing. 'I really don't think this neutrality business has anything to do with us. It's politics.'

'The dead man was a politician.'

'So?'

'So it's conceivable that politics had something to do with his death.'

'Did it?'

'I don't know.'

'Don't give me that.' The Chief flushed with anger. 'I'm fed up with all this double-talk. We've had all the nonsense about the gun and where has it got us? Nowhere. An open mind is all very well up to a point. Until it becomes an empty mind.'

Devane said nothing and the Chief glared at him for a moment and went back to his chair.

'The point is,' Devane said patiently, 'that this Gantly woman may have been the last person to talk to Clark. And we haven't even interviewed her. Even though we've been aware of her.'

The Chief leaned back and closed his eyes. I knew it from the word go, he thought. These cases are always the same. Always an unholy mess. Messed up by interfering politicians, nosy reporters, nervous superiors, endless theories and sudden lurches in new directions.

'So what am I to do about her?' Devane demanded.

'Whatever you think necessary,' the Chief said without opening his eyes. He sounded tired and defeated. 'You're in charge.'

Devane resisted the temptation to remind the Chief that he had specifically ordered him not to approach Rosie Gantly. Somebody farther up the line had definitely changed their tune, he decided. Clark was being ditched and Rosie was now fair game. And they were still keeping their options open by letting him make the decisions. But that didn't worry him: at least he'd got something clear.

'While we're at it,' the Chief opened his eyes, 'you may as well know that your report is not going to make certain people happy.' He sat up and shoved the photocopies across the desk to the Inspector. 'It doesn't tell them what they want to hear.'

'Accidental death is like innocence,' Devane shrugged. 'Difficult to believe in. And even harder to prove.'

Mike Erlanger dropped the key to the toilet on his secretary's typewriter and crossed to his office where she stood by his desk, holding a phone. She muffled the mouthpiece, grimaced and said, 'Harvey'. He nodded and took the phone.

'What's going on?' Harvey sounded excited.

'Well, it's a dull day in Dublin,' Erlanger replied cautiously, waiting for Harvey to explain what was worrying him. 'I've had an early lunch . . . '

'Cut the crap.' Harvey's voice slurred slightly and Erlanger wondered what he had had for lunch. 'What's with the shares? Why've they taken off?'

Erlanger turned his relief into a professional chuckle that masked his true feelings. 'You want to know if you should sell or hold? Like all the others.'

'I want to know what's going on.'

'Market interest in our enterprise has increased, that's all.'

'Why?'

'Why? What sort of a fool question is that, Harv? Because it's a good investment.'

'Says who?'

'Says the market,' Erlanger shot back. 'What's eating you? You're not thinking of selling, are you?'

'I want to know what's caused all the excitement.'

'The market's like that. You stick to what you're good at and I'll look after things here.'

'I've got my reputation to consider.' Harvey turned peevish.

Erlanger thought an unkind thought about Harvey's reputation, tipped his chair back and swung his feet onto the desk. 'Look on the bright side,' he said, maintaining his determined cheeriness. 'Rich men don't have to worry about their reputations. And you're a hell of a lot better off now than you were a week ago.'

Harvey remained silent for a moment. 'I guess I'm worried that all this is based on the report I gave you,' he said at last.

'It's not.' Erlanger turned decisive. 'The market's a law unto itself. Things develop a momentum. We're on the crest of a wave and it's still building up.' He suddenly regretted the image and changed the subject abruptly. 'How're your protestors? Keeping their heads down, I bet.'

'They've gone quiet,' Harvey admitted grudgingly and changed the subject in turn. 'What's all this controversy about Clark?'

'I told you, that's got nothing to do with us,' Erlanger said sharply and tired of the effort of keeping his voice rosy. 'Nothing whatever. I've got to go, there's another call holding. Keep calm – everything's under control.'

Erlanger dropped the receiver onto its cradle, stared at it and repeated his advice to Harvey to it in a whisper: Keep calm – everything's under control. But everything was far from being under control. Everything might just be getting out of control. He shook his jacket from its hanger and went out to his secretary.

'I guess you're wondering if you should sell your shares too,' he smiled.

'I don't have any shares.' She looked surprised.

'Silly girl.' He wagged a finger. 'I told you to buy, didn't I? If any more of our shareholders call looking for advice, tell them you wouldn't touch those shares with the proverbial bargepole. And that I've gone to an important meeting.'

Outside, it felt like rain and he walked quickly to keep the

damp at bay. He crossed the road to the earthen path alongside
the canal. The trees stood as stiffly as spidery statues along its
length and the still water was the colour of unpolished aluminium, reflecting the dull sky. Cars crawled along behind the
trees, some with their lights on.

Ryle's story had hit him like a fist to the stomach and he had
spent the morning trying to work out the implications. Everything depended, he had decided, on who had given Ryle the
document and, more importantly, why. It could have been
Clark's widow, which could also mean Burke, and it could have
been someone else. But it wasn't meant to have been in widespread circulation. She certainly wasn't supposed to have had
it. And it wasn't supposed to turn up in a goddam newspaper
either, he thought bitterly. Someone was playing a devious
game. But who? And what was the game?

His stomach still felt queasy with the knowledge that, however much he speculated, he just didn't know the answers any
more. And that there was no simple way of finding them
without dangerously exposing himself. Don't panic, he
reminded himself automatically, never do anything rash. Wait
and see.

He walked faster but the disconcerting sense that he was no
longer in control enveloped him like the grey dust of the
daylight.

Eleven

The hollow summons of a recorded gong boomed out over the grounds of Leinster House, its sound muffled by the steady rain. Jim Whelan quickly angled his car into a semi-permitted space as close to the building as he could get and dashed, bare-headed and cursing, through the wet.

Inside, the gong reverberated down the corridors as he gathered his mail from the enquiry desk and took the stairs to the chamber two at a time, dodging around a scattering of visitors on their way to the public gallery. The gong was still summoning deputies to the Dáil sitting as he tipped down a seat on the back row of the Government's benches and sat down, breathing heavily.

The tiers of leather upholstered seats and dark wood dulled the atmosphere in sympathy with the gloom outside and made the chamber feel unused. But it was filling rapidly with sober-suited members and the hum of conversations, heightened by the expectations of a new political week.

Whelan leant down to a colleague on the tier below him, borrowed a green order paper and ran his eyes down the list of questions to be answered. The one about Maurice Clark's death was halfway down the list, tabled by an Opposition deputy with a reputation as a maverick and without the prior knowledge of his party leaders. Whelan handed back the order paper and smoothed his damp hair. He needn't have bothered to rush.

He watched Tommy Lyster march importantly around the circular lobby above the chamber, a clutch of departmental files the colour of dried blood under his arm. Whelan realised that Lyster must be answering questions for the Justice Minister and signalled to him with raised eyebrows.

Lyster slumped down heavily beside him on the top step into the Government benches. 'Great stuff on the radio yesterday,' he whispered conspiratorially. 'Went down very well with the man himself.'

'Yes?' Whelan searched his face anxiously.

Lyster nodded solemnly, as if he was about to do him a favour. 'I was with him at the time. Just what the doctor ordered, he said. Knock this nonsense on the head.' He stood up to let a colleague pass and hunkered down again. 'About your other little problem. If you need any help there we'll have a word with the trouble-maker.'

Whelan smiled at Lyster's use of the plural pronoun, implying that he and the Taoiseach were now a team, ready to leap into joint action at his, Whelan's, request. 'I think he's got the message,' he said confidently.

'Good, good.' Lyster straightened up and sidled cautiously down the steep steps to the second row of Government seats and dumped his files on the ledge before him. He sat down behind them, proud of the symbols of his infrequent authority.

Whelan leaned back with contentment. It had worked, gone like a dream. And now he had confirmation that he had done the right thing. He scanned the public gallery, caged behind protective glass above the chamber, but recognised none of the interested faces peering down. He glanced across to the Opposition deputies gathering in their banked-up tiers across the floor, caught the eye of a constituency opponent and winked at him. He felt on top of the world.

Conversations died down as the Taoiseach led his Cabinet members in single file around the lobby, down the aisles and into their front-row seats. The Ceann Comhairle took his chairman's place and everybody stood and looked solemn while he beseeched God bilingually to guide their deliberations.

Whelan glanced through his mail as the Taoiseach answered questions and easily fielded desultory attempts by the Opposition to take him to task on some minor issues. There was a small exodus from both sides of the House as the Taoiseach finished and left and the Ceann Comhairle called the first question to the Minister for Justice. Lyster rose, flipped open the top folder before him, cleared his throat and read out the answer prepared by his civil servants.

It took half an hour to reach the question about Maurice Clark's death. Lyster opened the file and read: 'As deputies are aware, the body of Deputy Maurice Clark was taken from the sea at Dun Laoghaire on January 15th last. Garda inquiries into the circumstances of his death are continuing and an inquest will be held in due course.'

Lyster closed the file, passed it to one side and reached for the next one as the Ceann Comhairle automatically called the following question. But the Opposition maverick was on his feet, asking if the Minister could tell the House the result of the police inquiries to date.

'It would not be proper to divulge any such information until the gardai have completed their investigations,' Lyster replied primly.

'Can I ask the Minister if foul play has been ruled out?' the Opposition man persisted, couching his question in the indirect formula that was supposed to restrain deputies from hurling personal abuse.

'The gardai are conducting a full and proper inquiry,' Lyster said.

'Can I take it from the Minister's reply that foul play has not been ruled out, and can I ask the Minister who the prime suspects . . . '

'No, you can't take that,' Lyster snapped, his florid face glowering a deeper red.

'And would the Minister tell the House why a member of his party was in possession of an illegal firearm in suspicious . . . '

'Disgraceful,' Whelan howled from the Government backbench and some of his colleagues leapt to Lyster's support with a chorus of shock and outrage. Opposition deputies kept out of it, most of them feeling it was unseemly to question details of Clark's death and silently agreeing that their colleague had gone too far. Lyster maintained a dignified silence, smugly aware that he was on top of the situation.

'Order,' the Ceann Comhairle groaned, privately surprised it had taken so long for the ritual acrimony to surface.

'Is the Minister aware,' the Opposition maverick continued unabashed, 'that there is widespread public concern over this case, and can he give the House a categorical assurance that there will be no cover-up?'

'There will be nothing like that because there is no reason for anything like that,' Lyster retorted, careful not to fall into the booby-trap set up for him by repeating such a loaded phrase as 'cover-up'. 'The gardai are carrying out a full and complete investigation and I am sure that they will leave no stone unturned to find the truth, the whole truth and nothing but the truth. We on this side of the House have complete and total confidence in them.'

Lyster opened the file containing the answer to the next question and began to read but his voice was drowned out by a chorus of cries for the Ceann Comhairle's attention from the Opposition. Four of them, including the Shadow Minister for Justice, were on their feet, prickly with instant indignation. Overwhelmed, Lyster leaned back against the tipped-up edge of his seat and waited.

'Ceann Comhairle, I wish to object,' the Shadow Minister began, 'to the Minister's snide innuendo that we on this side of the House do not have total confidence in the gardai.'

'If the cap fits,' a Government supporter suggested airily.

'A question, deputy,' the Ceann Comhairle chided the Shadow Minister, 'you can only ask a question.'

'Yes, Ceann Comhairle, I'm coming to that, but first I would also like to put on record my disappointment that the Minister for Justice has not seen fit to come into the House and answer these questions himself . . . '

'He's in hiding again,' a voice behind him said.

'Just sent his messenger boy,' another voice taunted Lyster.

'The best messenger boy in the business,' a third laughed. Lyster eyed him from under his lowered forehead and made a mental note to remember him.

'Can I ask the Minister,' the Shadow Minister continued, 'why the garda inquiries are taking so long and when they expect to have them completed?'

Lyster re-opened the file on Clark's death and took a deep breath to soothe his growing irritation. He glanced through the background briefing notes and said, 'That's an operational matter for the gardai and not a matter for the Minister. Who has no responsibility for operational matters.'

'Good man, Tommy,' an Opposition backbencher sneered, 'you can read.'

'Order,' the Ceann Comhairle threatened.

'Why is it taking so long?' the Shadow Minister repeated.

'Procedures,' Lyster replied. 'The deputy is well aware that there are procedures to be followed and that that takes time.' He saw several Opposition members half-rising to their feet and decided, to hell with it, there was only so much a man could take from these gobshites. It was time to go on the offensive. 'In any event, Ceann Comhairle,' he turned towards the chairman, 'I think it's a sad day when some members of this house go out of their way to score political points over the tragic and untimely death of a fellow member of this house.'

'What about the gun?' the Opposition maverick roared.

More cries of 'Shame' came from his own party but Lyster didn't want to be rescued any longer. 'More than sad.' He shot a finger towards the skylight and his voice rose steadily to the steamrolling pitch perfected on hecklers at late-night election meetings in small town squares. 'It's a disgrace, a disgrace that some deputies don't have the simple Christian decency to let one of their colleagues go cold in his grave before turning him into a political football.' A rising tide of snorts and retorts from the Opposition made no impact on him. 'And that they wouldn't for a minute consider the ordinary human feelings of the family left bereaved by this tragic accident and who, in the midst of their grief, are now forced to look on helplessly while the body of their loved one is abused and his reputation tarnished in the interests of nothing more than cynical political opportunism by a crowd of heartless and unfeeling . . . '

Lyster couldn't find a half-respectable word but it was superfluous anyway. Scores of individual Opposition protests had grown into a collective bellow of rage that had finally swamped him. The Ceann Comhairle was on his feet, banging his bell for order and using the extra volume of his microphone to carry his demands that deputies sit down.

The Shadow Minister stood in his place, waiting for silence, and Lyster, poker-faced and breathing heavily, eyed him across the floor. A Dublin deputy at the end of the Opposition benches yelled something at Lyster. 'Feck off, you whinging little gurrier,' the Minister snarled back automatically out of the side of his mouth. His attention remained fixed on the Shadow Minister: he knew he had made a mistake.

One by one the irate members came to heel and silence was more or less restored by a threat from the Ceann Comhairle to adjourn the House.

'Ceann Comhairle,' the Shadow Minister said calmly, 'can I ask the Minister, further to his reply, how he knows that Deputy Clark's unfortunate death was accidental in the light of his earlier statement that garda inquiries are still continuing?'

Lyster knew that he was caught and on his own. His backbenchers had gone as silent as the Opposition and all eyes were on him. If he said it was a slip of the tongue the newspapers would have him denying that Clark's death was an accident. He had to brazen it out. 'Everyone knows it had to be an accident,' he blustered, 'a tragic accident, and it's all the more tragic that some people in this House ...'

'Would the Minister not agree,' the Shadow Minister interrupted sweetly, 'that he is attempting to pre-empt the result of the garda inquiries in spite of his declaration that he has full confidence in them?'

'I'm not pre-empting anything,' Lyster replied sourly.

'Next question,' the Ceann Comhairle came to his aid, 'I'm calling the next question.'

'What was he doing there in the middle of the night?' an Opposition deputy demanded.

'With a loaded gun,' another voice chimed in.

'I could tell the House a thing or two about where you spend your nights,' Lyster shot back at the first questioner. Caught unawares, the Opposition member grinned sheepishly and several Government backbenchers rounded on him with ribald jeers.

'Order,' the Ceann Comhairle moaned. 'Next question.'

'Just one more supplementary,' the Shadow Minister protested. 'In the light of the Minister's contradictory replies ...'

'I'm not responsible for the Minister's replies but I am calling the next question,' the Ceann Comhairle said. 'And if there's any more disorder I'm going to adjourn the House for the remainder of question time.'

Tempers subsided as quickly as they had flared. The Opposition knew it had won a minor victory by goading Lyster into an unsustainable admission and did not want to be held responsible for having the House adjourned in a row over Clark's death. Lyster read out the answer to two more questions but nobody bothered to challenge his replies.

He gathered up the files, slipped out of his row and almost collided with the Taoiseach as he made his way back down to his own seat. 'You were doing fine,' the Taoiseach muttered pointedly as he passed. Whelan gave him a sympathetic glance but the Minister did not notice.

He climbed heavily up to the lobby and walked around the chamber towards the exit to the party rooms. He felt disgusted with himself for having given the bastards an opening in the heat of the moment. But there would be other days. At least he'd put one of the little pipsqueaks in his place.

Seamus Ryle trudged along Nassau Street, his hood up and head bent into the cold wind which bore down unsheltered streets and hurled the rain around corners. He turned into Kildare Street, no longer bothering to avoid the puddles. His feet were wet and the wind wrapped his sodden trousers around his legs.

Leinster House opened up beside him, lit up like a liner in mid-ocean, and he hurried into its blazing lights and wall of heat. Uniformed ushers stood about like ship's officers, watching members ramble by as if they were strolling the decks. The outside world of gloom and rain was far away, distanced by the atmosphere of self-sufficiency and the single-mindedness of people enclosed in a common pursuit.

He hurried down the deeply carpeted corridors to the press gallery and took off his drenched coat. He shook his legs, one after the other, to unwrap the wet trouserlegs of his grey suit. He cursed and got a notebook out of his parka pocket.

'You missed the fun,' a colleague said, looking at him sympathetically. 'Tommy Lyster shot himself in the foot.'

Ryle took a crumpled tie from his jacket pocket and knotted it over the missing top button of his shirt while his colleague told him what had happened. 'Has the special notice question come up yet?' he grunted.

It was due now, the other said. Ryle hurried into the press bench overlooking the Dáil chamber where the Leader of the Opposition was reading out a convoluted question about his story on neutrality and asking the Taoiseach to make a statement on the matter. The chamber had filled up again, appetites whetted by the sparring with Lyster and in anticipation that this might be the main event of the day. The public gallery was still dense with eager faces.

'The report in question has been drawn to my attention,' the Taoiseach began, reading his reply in leisurely tone. 'I wish to state categorically that the document concerned was not prepared on my behalf or at my behest nor have I ever seen it before. The late Deputy Clark had not been requested by me in his capacity as Chairman of the Backbench Committee on Foreign Affairs or in any other capacity to review policy on neutrality. The document, therefore, cannot be said to represent Government policy on this issue.'

He placed a typewritten sheet on the ledge before him and Ryle closed his eyes and felt momentarily dizzy. The word 'forgery' took over his mind. It was a fucking forgery. He opened his eyes and glanced at Whelan and then stared fixedly at the back of the Taoiseach's head below him. His mind raced quickly over his various defences, already justifying himself to Stacy. The fact that Clark had had the documents with him before his death was the significant point. That's what the story had said, not that its contents were necessarily true. Whelan had confirmed Clark's signature but his only source for saying Clark had it was Rosie. And if she had given him a forged document why should he believe her claim that Clark left it with her?

The Taoiseach was still reading from his prepared answer, giving an unexpectedly full account of the development of the neutrality policy. Ryle tried to push his thoughts away and concentrate on what the Taoiseach was saying but he could still feel his heart thumping.

The Taoiseach was still reading in a bored monotone, declaring that the main reason for Ireland's military neutrality was, as it had always been, the continuing British presence in the six counties of Northern Ireland. Ryle's mind was blank by the time the Taoiseach finished and the Opposition Leader rose. Ryle turned to him with the desperate attention of a gambler who has staked all on a trailing horse.

'Would the Taoiseach tell the House,' he asked, 'if membership of NATO is under consideration by the Government?'

'The answer is in the negative,' the Taoiseach replied.

'Has the Government come under pressure from any agency, domestic or foreign, to join NATO?'

'No.'

'Did the Taoiseach ever discuss neutrality with Deputy Clark?'

'No.' The Taoiseach sat down with an air of finality.

A sick feeling had settled into Ryle's stomach. He was really in the shit now. Every answer made matters worse.

The Opposition Leader, however, was only warming up. 'Would the Taoiseach assure the House that the views expressed in the document allegedly in the possession of Deputy Clark when he died do not coincide with his own views on neutrality?'

The Taoiseach got to his feet again with an air of immense patience. 'I have already told the deputy that I was not aware of the contents of that document and therefore it could not be said to have expressed my views.'

'Irrespective of whether the Taoiseach was aware of the document or not, will he assure the House that he does not agree with its contents?'

'Ceann Comhairle,' the Taoiseach sighed and dodged the question again. 'I cannot be expected to give assurances relating to general comments in a document which may be a forgery. And, I should add, that may be the subject of garda inquiries.'

Ryle jotted down a quick note, grasping at straws. What did that mean, he wondered? Why would they have an inquiry into a forgery?

The Opposition Leader seemed to scent an opening. 'Perhaps I could rephrase it, Ceann Comhairle,' he suggested with excessive politeness. 'Does the Taoiseach agree with the conclusion stated in that document that it is time to join NATO in view of factors such as our membership of the European Community?'

'I do not agree with that view.'

'And would the Taoiseach confirm to the House that no change is contemplated in the policy of neutrality?'

'Ceann Comhairle, I have already answered that question.'

'The Taoiseach is mistaken, Ceann Comhairle.' The Opposition Leader smiled benignly at the chairman. 'He has not answered that question. He has ruled out any question of joining NATO: would he also assure us now that he is not considering any change in neutrality.'

'Ceann Comhairle,' the Taoiseach looked to the chairman as if he were an arbitrator who would confirm his reasonableness. 'I have given a very full answer to the deputy's question but perhaps I should remind him of what I said.' He took up the last page of the written answer he had delivered. 'I said "there have been no developments to date which would require reconsideration of current policy". In other words, nothing has changed.'

The Dáil chamber remained quiet with deputies on both sides awaiting the outcome. Something indefinable in the Taoiseach's attitude, perhaps his air of reason or even boredom, stirred all the highly tuned political antennae around him. Two ambitious Opposition backbenchers slid to their feet, ready to leap in with their own questions, but were reseated by a frown from their party's chief whip. Ryle sensed the mood and no longer had any difficulty with his concentration.

'In the light of the Taoiseach's reply.' The Opposition Leader showed he was well aware there might be something to gain from the exchanges. 'Would he give the House a clear and unambiguous assurance that his Government will not, under any circumstance, abandon the policy of neutrality which has stood this state in such good stead?'

'Ceann Comhairle,' the Taoiseach sounded pained. 'How many times do I have to tell the deputy that the document at issue here is a forgery, that it does not represent the Government's views, that I have no reason to believe it represented

Deputy Clark's views, that we are not about to join NATO. That, in short, nothing has changed at this point in time in relation to the policy which has been pursued by successive governments.'

'Then give us an assurance that the Government will not change that policy in any circumstances,' the Opposition Leader retorted.

'I have told you there have been no developments which would require a change of policy.'

'A simple assurance,' the Opposition Leader repeated quickly, hoping to force the pace, 'that there will not be any change.'

'I have given the House a categorical statement that nothing has changed,' the Taoiseach was becoming testy.

'Assure us that it will not change,' the Opposition Leader tried to keep up the momentum.

'Ceann Comhairle, I cannot look into the future and give the deputy the kind of facile commitment he appears to want. Circumstances change and if the circumstances which gave rise to this policy were to change then a new situation would arise which might lead to a re-examination of the present position.'

'I take it from the Taoiseach's reply that Ireland's neutrality is negotiable,' the Opposition Leader said slowly, 'and can I ask him to outline to the House in what circumstances he would be prepared to negotiate an end to it?'

'What'll you sell it for?' an impatient Opposition voice demanded but was silenced immediately by a warning glare from the chief whip.

'Ceann Comhairle,' the Taoiseach said, 'the Opposition appears to be suffering under the delusion that something I have said represents a change in the policy of neutrality. That is not so. Everything I have said here today has been in line with the policy which has been pursued by successive governments including those formed by his own party in the past.'

'The far distant past,' an edgy Government backbencher sneered, drawing a scattering of guffaws and rejoinders about the near future from the Opposition. Ryle cursed them silently and hoped that the Opposition was not going to fall into the trap of allowing itself to be diverted. Just when things were getting interesting.

The Opposition Leader waited until they had subsided. 'Would the Taoiseach tell the House in plain language on what conditions he is prepared to reconsider neutrality?'

'I have set out in considerable detail the factual basis for the policy which has existed since the Second World War and the answer to the deputy's question should be quite clear from that. Indeed, it is quite clear to anyone with even a passing knowledge of the historical perspective.'

'I take it the Taoiseach means that neutrality would be reconsidered if Ireland were re-united.' The Opposition Leader paused. 'If that is what he means, why can't he say it?'

'It has always been the policy of successive Governments that this country should not be used as a base for attacks on Great Britain,' the Taoiseach said carefully. 'Defence arrangements to ensure that that did not happen and to re-assure Britain that it would not happen could be considered in a united, independent Ireland. That has always been Government policy.'

'Is the Taoiseach attempting to trade neutrality for unity at present?' the Opposition Leader demanded.

'There is no question of trading one thing for another as if they were simple items that could be bartered in that fashion,' the Taoiseach snapped with an air of exasperation.

The Ceann Comhairle coughed and suggested that they had spent more than enough time on this matter and they had a lot of other business to get through. Several Government Ministers nodded their approval but the Opposition ignored him.

'Has the Taoiseach raised the interrelated issues of neutrality and re-unification in communications with any other governments?' the Opposition Leader continued.

'The subject matter of diplomatic contacts with foreign governments is confidential,' the Taoiseach said with a hint of weariness.

'It's a straightforward question, Ceann Comhairle,' the Opposition Leader said irritably. 'Can't we have a simple yes or no answer?'

'Such matters must remain confidential,' the Taoiseach repeated. 'As the deputy well knows.'

158

The Leader of the Opposition sat down. There was a moment's pause as deputies digested the implications of what they had just heard and before the chairman had quite realised the exchanges had ended without a raised voice. Opposition deputies flashed tight-eyed looks at each other, like a predatory pack suddenly confirming the scent of a quarry. Behind the Taoiseach, the rows of Government backbenchers sat in stony-faced silence. Jim Whelan stared at the blue carpet on the floor of the chamber and tried to stop himself thinking what everyone else was thinking. It couldn't be, he told himself, it just couldn't be.

In the press gallery Ryle began to breathe again.

Twelve

Ryle hurried through the cramped corridor behind the press gallery but was halted at the top of the main staircase from the Dáil chamber. It was clogged with chattering schoolgirls leaving the public gallery after an utterly confusing hour. Ryle too felt more than a little confused as he waited impatiently to get downstairs.

'What do you think?' A political correspondent stopped beside him.

'I'm not sure,' Ryle admitted. 'You tell me.'

'You were wrong but you were right.' The correspondent summed it up succinctly. 'They're up to something and you've flushed them out.'

'Great,' Ryle said sarcastically. There was no doubting the Taoiseach's emphatic denial of his story but then he had admitted that something *was* happening to neutrality. Not in so many words, but that was the instant and universal interpretation of what he had said.

'We'll all be experts on neutrality before the day's out,' the political correspondent added without enthusiasm as they made their way slowly down the stairs.

At the bottom, the troupe of schoolgirls were led off towards the members' restaurant to be bought soft drinks by a deputy who hoped they would remember his name correctly to their parents. Ryle skirted around them and charged down the corridor towards another exit from the chamber just in time to catch Whelan emerging. He looked suitably glum, Ryle thought.

'You should've listened to me,' Whelan said uneasily.

'I take it you've no objection to my revealing that you identified Clark's signature,' Ryle retorted, 'since you've revealed part of our conversation.'

'You left me no choice.' Whelan glanced along the corridor to check if anyone could hear them. 'I couldn't believe you'd gone ahead and printed that flyer after what I'd told you.'

'But you did identify Clark's signature.'

'You're not going to go into all that now?' Whelan looked alarmed. 'After what the Taoiseach said.'

Ryle realised he had a weapon to wield. 'It depends,' he said, 'I may have to. I've got to protect my neck too.'

Whelan stepped back as the schoolgirls streamed past and trapped him in the conversation. 'What did you make of that?' Ryle nodded back towards the chamber as they stood side by side.

'Never heard such an outright denial of anything in the House,' Whelan said.

'I meant the rest of what he said. That neutrality's negotiable for unity.'

Whelan didn't even want to think about that. At least, not until he'd talked to someone who could reassure him that everybody was wrong. And he certainly didn't want to think about how he should react if they were not. 'He didn't say that,' he suggested blandly.

'Everybody seems to think he did.'

'He was only stating the historical position,' Whelan said. 'Like he said. Nothing has changed.'

'It sounded very different to what you were saying on the radio yesterday,' Ryle insisted. 'Like he doesn't share your devotion to neutrality.'

'You're wrong.' Whelan shook his head. 'I know for a fact he agrees with what I said.' He began to move off behind the schoolgirls. 'You should look into whoever passed off that forgery on you. And why.'

Rosie Gantly heard the gate scratch the concrete path behind her as she rooted in her shoulder bag for her keys. She turned and recognised Inspector Devane but not the other man.

'We'd like a word with you,' Devane said.

Rosie went back to looking for her keys, opened the door and lifted a shopping bag over the threshold. She faced Devane from the open doorway and asked if he was arresting her.

Devane shook his head.

'Do you have a search warrant?'

Devane shook his head again.

'Then I don't have to talk to you.'

Garda Casey began to say something but Devane interrupted him. 'You don't.'

Rosie gripped her bag of shopping and went inside, leaving the door open. They followed her into the living room and waited until she dumped her bags in the kitchen and returned to confront them. She was still wearing her overcoat.

'When was the last time you saw Maurice Clark?' Devane asked.

'Do you want a statement?' She brushed past him to a table.

'That's not necessary.'

Rosie ignored him and took a pad and a sheet of carbon paper from a drawer and began to write standing up. Behind her back Casey raised his eyebrows to Devane. The Inspector lit a cigarette.

When she had finished she thrust the pad at Devane and asked him to sign it. He read the three sentences slowly, signed the bottom of the page and passed it to his assistant.

'Now you can call me as a witness at the inquest,' she said with a hint of a malicious smile.

'It doesn't say why he was in a distressed condition.'

'I don't know why.' She took the pad from the detective, tore off the top two sheets and handed the carbon copy to Devane. He read it through again as if he were seeing it for the first time. It was dated at the top and said: 'Maurice Clark called at my flat about 4 am on the morning he died. He was in a distressed condition. He left after twenty minutes and I did not see him again.'

'Don't you want to know why he died?' Devane flicked some ash into the empty fireplace.

'Do you?' she shot back.

'I do, actually.' Devane settled carefully into a fireside chair as though testing it for comfort. 'I'm always curious about sudden death. Part of my country upbringing, I suppose. I used to marvel when I was young at the way adults passed on every detail of a dead person's last minutes.'

Rosie folded her arms and stared down at him. Casey inspected the posters on the wall.

'But you're a Dubliner,' Devane continued. 'You don't go in for that sort of thing, I suppose.'

'I've got better things to do than discuss quaint rural habits. With you.'

'Who killed him?'

'I don't know. Why don't you ask his political friends?'

Devane nodded. 'They say they don't know either.'

'Then why don't you subject them to your notorious interrogation methods?'

Devane's expression did not change. 'Where did he go when he left here?'

'I don't know.'

'Where do you think he went?'

'He didn't say.'

'What did he say?'

Rosie hesitated and sighed. She told him in brief detail about Clark's last visit.

'A worried man.' Devane shook his head in sympathy. 'What was worrying him so much?'

'I told you, I don't know. I've told you everything.'

'You were late for work that morning.' Devane tossed his cigarette end into the fireplace.

'I slept it out.'

'You're usually a good time-keeper.'

'I'm not usually woken up at four in the morning.'

Devane stood up. 'The documents he is supposed to have left with you? Where are they?'

Rosie gave a short laugh. 'Now we get to the real point. You don't give a fuck why he died. You're only concerned about the trouble he's left behind.'

Devane sighed. 'You've got it the wrong way round.'

'Yeah? Then how come you only arrive here when the political shit hits the fan?'

'I'm here because you're the last person to have seen him alive. As far as I'm aware.'

Rosie turned slightly to see Casey reading something on the table. She reached around him and grabbed a bundle of magazines and pamphlets and shoved them into a drawer.

'He came here at 4 am in a distressed state,' Devane repeated as though to himself. 'Came from a party, more or less directly. But nobody who was at the party thought he was upset when he left there.' He stood in front of her. 'How would you explain that?'

'I don't have to explain it. Or anything else.'

'Maybe he wasn't upset when he arrived? Only when he left?'

Rosie turned away angrily and stood by the door. 'I don't have to take that shit from you,' she said.

'Maybe there was someone else here when he called,' Devane added mildly.

'Get out,' she snapped.

'It's in your interests to help us,' the young detective said. 'If you really were a friend of his.'

'Don't tell me what's in my interest. Out.'

'Or what?' Casey sneered. 'You'll call the police? There's another way we could handle this, you know.' Devane gave him a withering look.

'That's more like it.' Rosie smiled without humour. 'Showing your true colours.'

'Take it easy,' Devane suggested to nobody in particular.

'Out.' Rosie glared at him, stamped out to the hall door and held it open. 'And take your lout with you.'

The policemen walked out. 'We'll be seeing you,' Casey said with as much menace as he could muster. The door slammed behind them. 'Scum,' he muttered as they went down the garden path.

Stacy stood with his shirtsleeves rolled up in the warmth of the news room and with each hand clamped over a telephone mouthpiece as though he were restraining two dogs by their leads. He was talking to his deputy.

'For inside,' he was saying, 'we've got our diplomatic corr doing a background piece on the history of neutrality. He's got another short piece on the international consequences of abandoning it. And there's a substantial piece coming on the military consequences of NATO involvement. Would we have nukes based here, do we become targets, that sort of thing.' He glanced at Ryle approaching and gave him a preoccupied nod. 'Between those, pics or illustrations and the carry-over from the front page, you'd better tell them to allow the best part of a page inside. Right?'

The deputy news editor moved away. Stacy raised one phone to his ear and continued a conversation with someone about coverage of a country court case. Ryle waited and tried to read, upside down, some notes Stacy had sketched on a pad. He couldn't make out anything coherent.

'Well, you've done it.' Stacy dropped the second phone and smiled at him. Ryle looked bemused. 'Stuffed their denials where they hurt most.'

'But the Taoiseach denied it,' Ryle said cautiously, feeling his way. He had the arguments ready to justify his story and had come back to the office expecting to need all of them. But Stacy appeared to be unconcerned.

'What'd you expect him to say?' Stacy shrugged automatically. 'It's a fair cop, Mr Ryle?'

'I've heard enough political denials to know when they are real and when they aren't,' Ryle said, throwing caution to the winds. 'The story wasn't true and he was sure of that.'

Stacy sat down and looked up at him as if he hadn't seen him before. 'What are you trying to tell me? That we abandon the story just as it takes off?'

Ryle shook his head quickly. 'I'm just a little confused. As to why he denied it and then admitted it.'

Stacy got up again, raised a detaining hand towards someone at the other end of the news room. 'It's simple.' He began to circle his desk slowly. 'The Government's negotiating on neutrality, right? Neutrality hasn't been a story here since 1939 or whenever and now it is. Because of your story.'

'But what if my story was wrong?' Ryle asked plaintively.

Stacy shrugged and went away. Ryle watched him go, then picked up an evening paper and wandered over to his desk, feeling bewildered. His story had been comprehensively denied but he was a hero to his news editor. He shook his head and knocked off his damp shoes. A cheery note from the features editor said they were going to run his series on religion next week and could he have the first part ready by Friday. He glanced around nervously, screwed the note into a ball and got down to some serious thinking.

The rain had stopped and the city lay washed and low in the damp air, huddled under a sickly cover of coal smoke and sodium lights. The evening rush hour was over and the streets were almost empty. On the roadway in front of the Department of Justice a group of people walked around silently in a squashed circle with placards in front of their bodies as if to ward off the penetrating cold. Two men held a wide banner declaring 'End Collaboration' and a line of guards, looking cold and bored, stood in front of the building.

Ryle walked slowly along the footpath between guards and the protestors, accepted a leaflet from a young woman and stopped beside a television crew which waited for something to happen. He thrust the leaflet into his pocket unread and surveyed the scene.

Under the yellow lights he could make out the pale faces of a couple of detectives watching from an unmarked Avenger across the road. Police vans were parked farther down the road, their engines running to provide heat for cramped reinforcements.

The reporter he had met at Clark's funeral sidled up to him and stamped his feet. 'What a way to make a living,' he said.

'Us or them?' Ryle asked, scanning the moving lines to find the man he had come to see.

'Us,' the reporter grunted and looked at the guards. 'They're all on overtime. The other lot are doing it for Ireland.'

Ryle saw him, a short, bulky figure, walking alongside a woman with a pushchair and a small child bundled up in a one-piece rain suit. He had a loudhailer slung over his shoulder and was telling the woman an animated story, she was smiling. But for the loudhailer and their surroundings they could have been a couple out for an evening stroll.

'There won't be any aggro here,' the other reporter muttered. 'They haven't got the bodies.'

More demonstrators arrived over the next half hour and more

guards moved, in unobtrusively small groups, to the front of the building. After a time, the man with the loudhailer broke away from the growing picket and came over to the reporters, pulling a sheaf of press releases from his pocket.

'What's the procedure, Billy?' the other reporter asked.

'Marching down to the GPO.' Billy looked speculatively at Ryle.

'What's it all about?' the reporter continued.

'Drawing attention to the cost to the Irish taxpayer of the Free State government's collaboration with the Brits to keep their border in place, a border that the Irish people never asked for and never wanted and that's kept in place by the armed force, torture and repression of British imperialism.' Billy rattled off the statement in the easily outraged accent of Belfast as if he were already rallying the demonstrators with his loudhailer.

Ryle went through the motions of jotting down his comments in order to hide his true purpose from his colleague. 'Millions that should be spent helping the poor, the unemployed and the sick in this so-called state are being squandered to prop up Britain's border,' Billy continued for the sake of their notebooks.

The parade moved off eventually, the protestors spreading across the road in ranks of three to give more bulk to their numbers. A motorcycle garda and a police van with flashing light led them around two sides of St Stephen's Green and down between the shuttered shops of Grafton Street. The few muffled pedestrians on the pavements paid no attention as they chanted 'Out, out, out' to collaborators and 'No, no, no' to extradition.

Ryle hung back to get rid of his unwanted companion and slowly overtook the marchers again as they rounded their way into Westmoreland Street, keeping an eye on Billy. They streamed slowly into O'Connell Street as sluggishly as the River Liffey moved beneath the bridge. A full tide flooded up from the bay, raising the murky water almost to street level.

Billy passed the loudhailer to someone else and Ryle stepped from the pavement and joined him. 'What's the story?' Billy asked.

'Maurice Clark. I gather he may have had some dealings with your lads.'

Billy looked at him in surprise. 'You're shitting me.'

'No. I think he had some dealings with your comrades-in-arms.'

'The army?' Billy said, meaning the IRA, and began to chuckle. 'I don't think they're that hard up they need to recruit Free State windbags.'

They moved up to the General Post Office where a pick-up truck was rigged up with a microphone in front of the building's columns. The crowd gathered around it, swelling out to the traffic island in the centre and blocking one side of the thoroughfare.

'Hang on,' Billy said. 'I've got to get this show on the road.'

He clambered onto the back of the truck and introduced an elderly countryman as their first speaker. The man, gaunt-faced and intense, was clearly unused to addressing street meetings and began a meandering lecture about what the IRA had done to the Black and Tans in West Cork in the 1920s and were doing again to the SAS in the glorious hills of South Armagh.

A handful of wiry city-centre children roamed around the crowd joining in the spattering of applause with enthusiastic screeches. Cars sped down the other side of the street behind a line of guards. The inevitable drunk swayed in front of the platform and let out occasional belches of 'bullshit'. All ignored him.

Ryle stayed put and glanced around the crowd, hoping to see someone else he might know but without any real expectation of success. His contacts with the Provos were sporadic and then mainly at arm's length. He had spent most of the afternoon bemoaning that fact but, if you got too close to them, they began treating you as one of their own and demanding 'favours'. Just like the cops, he thought.

A second speaker roused the crowd with predictions that this would be the year of victory and went on to excoriate the Irish government for its subservience to its British masters. Billy vaulted from the back of the van, one hand on someone's shoulder, and came over to where Ryle waited.

'You're onto a bummer,' he said, 'if you think that Clark was a volunteer.'

'I didn't say that.' Ryle shook his head. 'I'm not saying he was necessarily in the IRA. But he had some dealings with the IRA.'

'What dealings?'

Ryle ignored the direct question. 'What I'd like to do is talk to somebody about it,' he said. 'Somebody who would know for sure.'

'About what?'

He paused while a cheer went up as the speaker poured more invective on quisling politicians. 'I can't tell you at the moment.'

'You're not shooting in the dark, are you?'

'No. I've done a few stories about Clark and they're all right.'

'Neutrality.' Billy nodded thoughtfully and fell silent for a moment. 'If there was anything to this, why should we tell you?'

Ryle shrugged. 'I'm sure you can work out some reasons.'

'It would be a good story, wouldn't it?' Billy asked rhetorically. 'And there are other reporters who take a more progressive attitude towards the national question.'

Ryle said nothing and they stood in silence among the people rambling around the edges of the crowd as the hectoring tones from the loudspeakers washed over them. Ryle gazed past the platform, still vaguely hoping to see someone else who might be able to help him. His attention focused suddenly on a familiar-looking face in profile talking to two men on the far fringe of the demonstration. Rosie. He looked again but the woman had turned away and he could only see the back of her curly head. It was Rosie, he felt sure.

'Okay,' said Billy. 'I'll see what I can do.'

'As soon as you can.' Ryle nodded, trying to keep his eyes on the woman but she and her companions had begun to move. Billy returned to the platform and Ryle straightened up to his full height to keep track of the woman passing beyond the heads in between them. Each time she disappeared he watched one of her companions, a tall long-haired man.

Ryle began to circle around the crowd, keeping the man in view, towards a point where he could intercept them. Billy had begun to address the meeting. The long haired man disappeared from view, re-appeared and disappeared again. He could no longer see the woman at all. Billy was in full flow, haranguing fellow-travellers, coat-trailers and felon-setters. The crowd was packed more tightly at the back and Ryle had to slow down to avoid drawing attention to himself.

Suddenly the man was close by, separated by a few rows of people. The woman was no longer with him.

Ryle looked about but could see no sign of her. He continued on his circuit, moving slowly. Billy was working up to a climax from the platform, condemning the craven collaborationists who delayed the hour of victory and slowed down the march of freedom. But they could never halt the march of the nation, he declared, and the protest ended suddenly in a welter of cheering and clapping. Ryle found himself at the other side of the platform and waited as the crowd dwindled and slowly dissolved. There was no sign of Rosie or the woman who had looked like her.

He gave up as the first cars reclaimed the street and headed back towards his office. Rosie was there, he was thinking. And, what if she was, what difference did that make? It was hardly surprising that she should go to a Sinn Fein demo. It didn't make her any more suspect as a source.

But somehow it did. She had given him a forged document; he had no doubt about that now. Seeing her there had undermined his confidence further. Like the gut-wrenching difference between watching two cars collide and reading the fatal road accident statistics.

Mike Erlanger picked up the phone and his voice turned cold. 'Yes, I remember,' he said. 'You surely don't expect me to forget blackmailers. However incompetent they are.'

Becky, half-listening, switched her attention from the television news bulletin and pressed the remote controller to fade the voices of a group of sombre-faced women giving the usual graphic Belfast account of the latest burst of violence. Wrapped in a rug, she sat in the corner of the couch facing the open fireplace and turned to look over her shoulder at Erlanger.

James Burke hesitated in the face of Erlanger's hostility then plunged on, bolstered by the fact that Yvonne was talking to him again. She had phoned and told him that she was under a lot of pressure but that nothing had changed between them; although she could not see him at the moment. What can I do to help, he had asked. Nothing, she replied. But he had decided to take the initiative anyway.

'There's been a lot of publicity about some papers Maurice Clark had just before he died,' he said. 'You gave them to him.'

'Is this another blackmail attempt?' Erlanger sneered. 'No more competent than the first.'

'I am not trying to blackmail you.' Burke pronounced each word separately.

'You're just telling me this heap of crap because you're my friend. The usual blackmailer's line.'

'I told you before. I know you had something to do with his death and I don't want his . . . Yvonne taking all the blame. It's not fair.'

'And *I* think the fact that you're screwing her probably led Clark to his death. Maybe you even killed him yourself in a fit of passion.'

'Look.' Burke tried to control a surge of impotent anger. 'All I want . . . '

'What does she see in you anyway?' Erlanger broke in with a nasty laugh. 'I'm surprised they haven't arrested you yet. Can't persuade themselves you're capable of enough passion to knock . . . '

Burke slammed down the phone in a fury. Erlanger put down his receiver with a mild curse. He went over to the fireplace and tossed two logs into a spatter of sparks.

'Burke?' Becky asked.

Erlanger nodded. 'Says I gave Clark the material on Ireland's neutrality.'

'What does he want?'

'Sounded like the same as before.' He shrugged. 'I didn't give him a chance to get to the point. If there was one.'

He stared at the flames licking around the logs and she watched him for a moment. 'Don't let him get to you,' she said.

'He pisses me off. He's such a stupid turd.'

'But there's nothing he can do. Is there?'

'After all we've put into this, I'd hate to have it screwed up by a damn fool nut like him.'

He turned and looked at the television where a youth with a jerking automatic rifle was firing unaimed bursts over a barricade in Beirut. They watched while the news reader regained the screen and mouthed something.

'Sit down,' she said and he settled down on the couch. 'What I don't understand,' she added, 'is what they were talking about on the news. As if it was all for real.'

'I don't understand either,' Erlanger agreed. 'There's more going on than meets the eye.' He leaned sideways, rested his head on her lap and swung his legs over the far armrest.

She stroked his face with both hands and he closed his eyes. 'Or maybe it's less,' he sighed. 'It's not easy to tell what's for real in this goddam country.'

Thirteen

Ryle waited on the doorstep with a bottle of wine in a twisted brown bag, an advance appeasement for what could be an awkward meeting. Anyhow, it had been a long day and he could do with a drink himself. Rosie raised her eyebrows appreciatively, took the bottle and led him into her dimly lit living room.

'You just caught me,' she called from the kitchen as she filled two glasses. 'I'm just in and I've got to go out again in a while.'

'Political meeting?' Ryle looked around the room at the posters on the walls and the faded floral wallpaper. A standard lamp cast a mellow glow over the tired grey carpet and two worn armchairs but failed to hide the inevitable seediness of rented accommodation.

'Isn't everything?' She smiled ambiguously as she returned and handed him a glass. She clinked her glass against his. 'I read your report. It was very comprehensive and fair.'

'For the capitalist press.' He smiled warily.

'For the capitalist press.' She nodded warmly and drank to the capitalist press. 'Sit down.' She waved at a chair. 'I have a few minutes.'

He watched her while she knelt down and plugged in an electric heater, unwilling to break the friendly atmosphere. She was wearing corduroy trousers and a green military-style sweater with shoulder and elbow patches.

'I saw you at the Provo demo tonight,' he said casually, willing her to say she wasn't there, to remove the doubt in his mind.

'Wasn't up to much, was it?' She sat down in a frayed armchair.

'Hardly the mobilisation of the masses.' He disguised his disappointment. It still didn't mean anything, he told himself, it was hardly surprising that she was there. He took off his parka and sat down opposite her. The standard lamp was behind her and blurred her facial expressions and the silence lengthened like the shadows. He sighed inwardly and decided to get it over with.

'Have you heard about today's developments?'

'I heard on the news they've admitted it.'

'But the document you gave me was a forgery,' he said.

'I thought we'd been through this before.' She looked at him sharply.

'Yes,' he said and explained cautiously why he was now certain that the document was a forgery.

'I told you I didn't forge it,' she said when he finished. 'And I didn't.'

'Someone did.' Ryle shrugged and let the statement hang between them. She said nothing and Ryle could tell nothing from her shadowed face. 'Obviously,' he went on at last, 'it could be in various people's interests to do it.'

She put her glass down on the floor as if the wine had turned sour. 'You're working with them, aren't you?' she asked, but it was not a question.

'Who?'

'You sent that pig Devane around with his innuendos and his threats. And then you turn up with this' – she waved at the bottle – 'to lure me into a cosy chat. The nasty guy and the nice guy technique. Shit. And I trusted you.'

Ryle shook his head vigorously.

'They're going to pin it on me or someone else. Say we forged it. Another piece of so-called subversion. When the real subversives are busily selling out what little sovereignty and independence this country has.'

'I didn't send him here,' Ryle insisted with growing desperation. 'I don't know anything about it.'

'So how did he know Maurice was here a couple of hours before he died? You were the only person who knew.'

'They worked it out,' Ryle said weakly. He had come to reassure himself that Rosie had played straight with him because he wanted to believe her, for all sorts of reasons. And he had also wanted to find out more from her. But now he was on the defensive and his chances of getting any further help from her seemed to have disappeared. He cursed Grifford silently.

'Look,' he said, 'I was followed here the other night. Without my knowledge. By a detective who says he's tailing me.'

'Thanks,' she said bitterly.

'I didn't know he was following me at the time,' he pleaded. 'Only afterwards when he approached me.'

'And you told him everything.' She raised her chin in an accusatory way.

'I told him nothing. But they probably put two and two together when they saw my story. Devane called at the paper looking for me too.' He finished his drink and held out the empty glass like an appeal. 'You've got to believe me. I didn't set you up. I'm not working with them.'

'You don't believe me.'

'I don't know what to believe.' Ryle stared at her and wished he could see her eyes clearly.

'I've told you the truth,' she sighed and reached for the bottle in a placatory gesture. 'Whether you want to believe it or not.'

Ryle told her quickly that he did believe her and took the proffered bottle and poured himself some wine. Maybe there was hope yet, he thought. She didn't seem all that upset. He asked her about Devane and she shrugged off the policemen's visit like it was a routine matter of little surprise or consequence.

'I don't know how I get caught in the middle of these things,' she said as though talking to herself. 'The shit I've had to take from some of the comrades over Maurice. The snide remarks, the distrust, the sudden silences when I come into the room. And now the pigs trying to make me the patsy for Maurice's bloody friends.' She took a deep drink. 'Christ.'

Ryle watched her stare at the electric heater and imagined that he saw some inkling of what her feelings for Clark had cost her. He wished that Clark's ghost did not keep coming between them but then that was also what had brought them together.

'I'm sorry if I led them to you,' he repeated. 'It was the last thing I wanted.'

She nodded vaguely, either to forgive or to say it didn't matter. He decided quickly that he trusted her and that he would lay all his cards on the table. He badly needed someone to talk over the whole story with. And she seemed to need him for much the same reason. Stacy was no help, preoccupied with the latest twist in the story and uninterested in the question of the forgery. Anyhow, there was nothing to lose.

'What I can't work out,' he began cautiously, 'is why they've made such a point of denying that Maurice's documents were authentic and then admitted that they are up to something with neutrality.'

'They're lying,' Rosie said with the air of someone tired of repeating the obvious.

'But why lie about something while admitting that it's true in substance?' Ryle shook his head and paused. 'I think the denials are true. And I also believe you. Which has to mean Maurice knew it was a forgery too. So why did he put his signature to it and why was he carrying round a pile of forged papers?'

'I don't see that any of that matters very much,' Rosie shrugged, retreating back into her political shell. 'What matters is that they're fucking about with neutrality.'

'It matters to me,' Ryle said. And only to me, it seems, he thought to himself. 'There is another angle to all this,' he added slowly. 'The gun Maurice had was the IRA's.'

'Are you serious?' To his relief, she seemed genuinely surprised, even shocked.

'It had been used in the North.'

'By Maurice?' She sounded incredulous.

'I don't know. Hardly.'

Rosie leaned forward onto her knees to take the wine bottle. She refilled her glass and remained kneeling on the floor looking up into his face as if examining his features for the first time. He was conscious of her scrutiny and her closeness. She shook her head in a silent comment.

'What I'd like to know is how and why he came to have it,' he said.

'Are you sure about this?' He nodded and she shook her head again. 'I find it very hard to believe.'

'Do you have any idea where he would have got it? Who could have given it to him?'

She stared into her glass and didn't reply, immersed in some private thoughts. She got off her knees and sat crosslegged on the floor as if it would help her consider whatever she was thinking. 'Do the cops know about this?' she asked at last without looking at him.

He told her they did.

'And do they know where he got it?' She searched his face.

'I don't know,' he said.

'Shit,' she said and turned back to her glass. She drained it and poured some more wine.

Ryle tried to understand her reaction but couldn't work out what it meant. 'Did he know anybody, any Provos, who could have given it to him?' he repeated.

'Why do you want to know?' She hugged her knees in a protective gesture.

Ryle was taken aback by the question, its answer so obvious that it made him instantly cautious. She looked at him, waiting for a reply, and he said because he was a reporter. 'There may be a perfectly innocent explanation,' he added deviously. 'I don't want to write a story that's going to create a whole lot of conspiracy theories if there's really nothing behind it.'

'I don't think he knew anybody,' she said as if his answer had satisfied her. 'Not anybody of any consequence.'

He picked up her qualification and asked her who Maurice had known.

'There was a guy in college, one of Maurice's students, who was involved with the Provos and got into trouble over an occupation of the administration building. Maurice helped him out, may have saved him from expulsion.'

'Is he still with the Provos?'

'I've no idea,' she said. 'I haven't seen him for years.'

Ryle asked her his name.

She rested her chin on her knees and stared into the heater. Ryle watched the curve of her cheek reddening from the heat and waited.

'Fergal Shercock,' she said at last and leaned her head sideways to look at him. I'm telling you to prove that I haven't lied to you, her look said. 'But I don't think it necessarily means anything.'

'Why did Maurice help him?'

'Because he was one of his students,' she said. 'And he came from the same part of the country. Maurice knew him as a kid.'

The doorbell rang and Ryle cursed silently. Rosie began to get to her feet and he asked her where Maurice had come from and she gave him an address in Tipperary. 'His brother still lives there,' she said.

'I didn't know he had a brother.' Ryle stood up as well.

'They didn't see each other much.'

The doorbell sounded again and she went to answer it. Ryle waited, thinking about this new lead. It wasn't much but it was something. He was more relieved that he had cleared the air with Rosie and that they were still on friendly terms.

Rosie came back with another woman who proclaimed her common political affiliation with patched jeans and a man's bulky sweater. Rosie did not introduce them.

'We've got to run,' she said. She picked up the wine bottle and asked him if he wanted to take it with him.

'You finish it later.'

Ryle sat in his car and watched the two women get into a small van and drive off quickly. He wondered idly if he should follow and then dismissed the idea as ridiculous. He did a three-point turn to get out of the cul-de-sac and by the time he nosed into the traffic on Ranelagh Road there was no sign of the van. So much for my ability to tail somebody, he thought wryly.

Jim Whelan closed the door behind him with excessive care, turned around and bumped into the hall table, jangling the telephone. He glared at it, set down his briefcase and opened the door to the living room. Maura was sitting by a dying coal fire and looked up from a magazine.

'You're drunk,' she frowned in disapproval.

'Not so much pissed as pissed off,' he muttered as he tossed his overcoat onto a chair and opened the drinks cabinet. 'Drink?' He waved a bottle of whiskey in her direction and she shook her head. He poured a large whiskey for himself and settled onto the couch, careful not to spill the drink.

'So, how's life?' he asked.

He looked like an overgrown boy, she thought, and she laughed suddenly. He joined in, drunkenly aware that he was exaggerating his state – he wasn't as drunk as he should be or as he wanted to be. He had given up hours ago trying to probe and pump colleagues for information and to find out what was really happening. There was nothing left to do but laugh.

'Where've you been?' she asked. 'Chasing the alcoholic vote?'

'Worse,' he giggled. 'Been looking into the future. Not a pretty sight.'

'Maybe I'll have a drink after all,' she said and pushed him gently back onto the couch as he made to get up. He stared in a dull, unfocused way at the flickers among the embers while she got herself a small whiskey and topped up the glass with ginger ale.

'D'you think I'm cut out for this business at all?' He moved to the side of the couch as she sat down beside him. 'Seriously now?'

'Seriously now,' she smiled, 'I don't think drink really does much for you.'

'Ha, ha.' He slid down on the cushions and rested his head on the back of the couch, swirling the whiskey before his eyes. The fire beyond it lit up the liquid. 'I had it all worked out. Being very smart. James Whelan TD, the smartest operator in town.' He tried to drink but the whiskey dribbled down his chin and he ran his sleeve over it. 'And now I've landed myself in the shit. The smartest operator in town.'

'Nothing ventured, nothing gained,' she said with a maternal air and the knowledge that she had been right. But it wasn't the moment to remind him that she had advised him not to get involved in the neutrality affair.

'Maurice would've done it right,' he sighed. 'He'd have known how to handle it. He never landed himself in the shit.'

'Oh yes, he did,' she said. 'The ultimate one. He's dead.'

Whelan looked at her sideways and slurred his words. 'I wish you'd liked him. He was a grand fellow.'

'He was up to no good,' she replied smugly, 'and everybody's beginning to realise that now.'

'You're wrong wrong wrong.' He closed his eyes. 'Got him all wrong. Always did.'

He fell silent and she thought for a moment that he had fallen asleep. He opened his eyes again when she tried to ease the glass from his hand and straightened up to drain it.

'Anyway,' he yawned. 'Tomorrow's the day of truth. All will be revealed. All will be all right. All right on the night.'

'Come to bed,' she said and he let her take his glass this time.

Ryle crossed the small car park to the basement, crunching the light dusting of frost that whitened the steps. The cloud had cleared and the sky was illuminated by a sharply etched moon which promised snow. It was almost midnight and he felt tired physically but mentally incredibly alert. Everything was still moving nicely.

He opened the hall door, pressed the time switch that controlled the hall light and stopped in his tracks. Sergeant Peter Grifford was leaning by the door to his bedsitter, arms and legs crossed.

'You took your time,' he grumbled. 'Where's the plonk?'

'What the hell are you doing here?' Ryle demanded, surprise making him sound bad-tempered.

'What a way to greet your mentor,' Grifford said sadly. 'Never mind. We are trained to wait. Not like those slobs you see on TV who can only wait if they've got a takeaway or something to eat. Or if they cover their eyes with a hat brim. We can wait with our eyes open.'

'And see in the dark,' Ryle snorted as he opened the door to the bedsitter.

Grifford followed him in and looked around the brightly lit room with an expression of horror. 'Disgusting.' He dragged the word out to its full length. 'I could arrest you on the spot. For assaulting the senses. Or littering with intent. I'm not surprised your wife threw you out.'

'She didn't,' Ryle said automatically. 'I left.'

He busied himself plugging in a heater and fishing a six-pack of Harp lager from a cluttered cupboard. He was pleased to see Grifford, assuming that he had come here for a reason. The sergeant had never visited him at home before which must mean that there was something big going on.

Grifford turned down the blankets on the unmade bed and selected a spot. 'Somebody needs to take you in hand,' he said as he wrapped his overcoat tightly around him and sat down cautiously.

'How did you get in?' He wondered suddenly how Grifford had known where to find him and remembered the policemen who had called on Breda. Her description was nothing like Grifford, though. 'A little bit of breaking and entering?'

'Your neighbour. Told her I was your legal guardian.' He watched Ryle mangle the caps off two bottles and look around the crowded sink for clean glasses. 'By the neck will be fine, thank you.'

Ryle handed him a bottle, sat down in the armchair and rested his feet on a corner of the coffee table. The remnants of his breakfast were still there, a plate with toasted crumbs and a crust, a cup half full of cold coffee, an open marmalade jar and a small uncovered block of butter. He didn't appear to notice them.

'You should cast an eye next door, if you won't go home,' Grifford suggested. 'She's a grand wholesome girl. Much more suitable than the rebellious Rosie. You'd never know when she'd mistake the saltpetre for the cereal and blow your head off for breakfast.'

'You've got her all wrong,' Ryle yawned.

'Of course, of course.' Grifford nodded his head sagely. 'And does she fancy you too?'

Ryle had been idly wondering about that on his way home and had decided the answer must be yes. Why else did she still talk to him and even give him more information? But am I too ready, too anxious, to believe her, he had wondered. She was either a superb actress or she was telling the truth. He decided again that she was telling the truth.

'Your neighbour fancies you as well,' Grifford added. 'God knows why. But she thinks you have a nice pair of legs.'

'Never knew that before, did you?' Ryle smiled.

'One of the many secrets you've kept from me.'

'Have you been following me again?' Ryle asked to get Grifford onto the story.

The sergeant would not be hurried. 'I've been waiting patiently here for you,' he said in a hurt voice. 'Thought Rosie would boot you straight off the doorstep.'

'No thanks to you she didn't,' Ryle sighed. 'You dropped me in the mire there.'

'But you obviously talked your way out of it.' Grifford smiled. 'Or was she that hard up for a drop of plonk?'

Ryle gave him a snide smile. 'By the way, Inspector Devane sends his regards.'

'Speaking of dropping people in the mire,' Grifford nodded pleasantly.

'Says he hasn't seen you for years.'

'A model for the plotting policeman,' Grifford mused. 'But don't let that fool you. He's a dangerous man, the most dangerous kind of policeman. He believes in right and wrong. Even thinks he can tell them apart.'

'He's in charge of the Clark case, isn't he?'

'Indeed. I've got his report outside in the car. Not very inspired. Nor inspiring.'

'You better bring it in,' Ryle suggested. 'It's not safe out there.'

'And cause a breach of the Official Secrets Act? I'll ignore that attempt to suborn a police officer. This time.' Grifford raised his bottle and took a long drink. 'Besides, there's nothing in it that you don't know.'

'How come he hasn't seen you in years?' Ryle persisted.

'Our paths haven't crossed.'

'So who are you working for?'

'Me?' Grifford managed to look genuinely surprised. 'Who I always work for. The people. The common good. The nation. The forces of light. The same as yourself.'

'You're not working with Devane.'

'That's the incisive deductive ability that caused me to put so much faith in you when this little problem floated to the surface.'

'So who are you reporting to?' Ryle watched him closely.

182

Grifford stared back at him for a moment and then held out his empty bottle. 'How long have we known each other?' Ryle fished another bottle out of the carton and pulled the cap off it. 'Three years or so?' Ryle nodded and got up to hand him the open bottle. 'And have I ever given you a bum steer?'

Ryle shook his head.

'Then don't insist on an answer to that question right now,' Grifford said. 'Or I'll have to lie to you.'

Ryle opened another bottle for himself and abruptly remembered the day of Clark's funeral and the Taoiseach's adviser summoning Grifford away for a private chat. Jesus, he thought happily, he really is in the middle of it all. 'Now you've got me intrigued,' he said.

'I thought that was your normal condition,' Grifford smirked.

Ryle drank some beer and wondered if he should ask him about the Taoiseach's adviser. When it came down to it, he realised, he knew very little about Grifford. Only that he was a great source and had a sense of humour and an anarchic streak. But Ryle had no idea what made him tick. Their relationship was friendly and professional but entirely impersonal. A perfect journalistic arrangement.

'Can I ask you a personal question?' Grifford nodded. 'Why are you still a sergeant?'

'Sergeants are the salt of the earth,' Grifford said. 'And I like sprinkling a little taste onto other people's lives.'

Rye smiled. 'But you could easily be an inspector or a superintendent.'

Grifford shook his head mournfully. 'I never sat the exams.'

'Why not?'

'Because I couldn't retire so early if I was promoted,' he said as if it was obvious. Ryle couldn't make out whether he was joking or telling him to mind his own business. He said nothing.

'Besides,' Grifford added, 'I'm like yourself. I like a little power with minimal responsibility. There's a lot to be said for remaining one of the toiling masses.'

'I don't know about that. I'd opt for the leisured class any day.'

'No, you wouldn't,' Grifford said decisively. 'You'd roll over and die of boredom. You're having the time of your life now, turning a routine inquiry into the death of a harmless back-bencher into a major political crisis. Putting so many cats among the pigeons there's feathers everywhere.'

Ryle smiled slightly to himself and knew that Grifford was right. In spite of all the complexities and uncertainties, it was still great fun to be immersed in a real running story. And to be on top of it all. He mightn't know exactly what was happening but he knew a hell of a lot more about it than any other journalist. And everyone else was now racing to catch up with him.

'You've even singlehandedly launched another police in-quiry,' Grifford added.

'Into what?' he asked, aware that Grifford had turned the conversation back on to impersonal ground.

'Into your famous neutrality documents.'

Ryle straightened up on the edge of the chair and warmed the palms of his hands before the glowing bars of the electric fire. 'But why?' he asked.

'Because the Taoiseach said so. Weren't you in the Dáil?'

Ryle nodded. That line had snagged his attention at the time but he had dismissed it later. It was only the usual knee-jerk reaction to any leak. A little diversion that the Taoiseach hadn't even bothered to pursue himself. 'He only mentioned it vaguely. A throwaway line.'

'Such is a policeman's lot.' Grifford took a slow drink. 'Our lives are ruled and ruined by throwaway lines.'

'You're not doing this inquiry, are you?' Ryle smiled at the prospect.

Grifford shook his head. 'It's at a much more exalted level.' He paused. 'You'd better watch your back.'

'I thought you were doing that.'

'Not anymore. You've become too conspicuous. Don't want to come between the knives and you.'

Ryle shrugged. 'Leak inquiries never get anywhere.'

'This one is serious.' Grifford looked doleful but his voice was grave. 'Why do you think I'm here at this godforsaken hour? Discretion is paramount from now on. You've really stirred it up. Got up some powerful nostrils. You should take it seriously too.'

Ryle stared at him and Grifford looked back and nodded twice. Grifford stood up and enquired doubtfully if he had a toilet. Ryle told him where to go. He sipped his beer and felt the first throbs of a dull headache while he waited and reflected on the warning. Grifford was given to melodrama but this was something else. He couldn't see why the neutrality leak was so important. Especially the leak of a bloody forgery.

'Devane was looking for me already,' he said when Grifford sat down again. 'If that's what you mean.'

Grifford shook his head decisively. 'It's a different ball game now. The stakes have been upped, way above Devane's head.'

Ryle looked at him in confusion.

'You have forced into the open matters that some people preferred to leave in the dark,' Grifford explained carefully, dangling the beer bottle between two fingers. 'They are not amused. Conspiracy theories are running rampant. The fact that you didn't know what you were doing is neither here nor there. Ignorance is not considered to be an excuse.'

Ryle studied him, wondering what the sergeant meant. Is he telling me I'm under suspicion? For what? 'It's true then,' he said. 'They really are selling out neutrality.'

'Leaving aside your new friend's tedious terminology,' Grifford said, 'you have hit the nail on the head.'

'And that's why the Taoiseach went all coy in the Dáil today.'

'Didn't you notice the distinguished visitors' gallery behind him? Bulging with diplomats. British and American. Even the Russkies. He was talking through his back. Through his posterior, if you prefer.'

'What's the deal?'

'Simplicity itself. Like he said, neutrality for unity. We join NATO or whatever and the historic unity of Ireland is restored. It's a nation once again.'

'Jesus Christ,' Ryle muttered. What Grifford said was what everybody had been saying but hearing it from him somehow made it more real. 'How serious is this?'

'I don't know why you're so surprised,' Grifford sighed. 'You were there. The man on the spot.'

'Yes, but it was all so tortured. Politician-speak. Is he actually negotiating? At this moment?'

Ryle shook the last two bottles of lager from their carton. He opened them and passed one over to Grifford.

'It's on the table,' Grifford shrugged. 'The in phrase of the moment. It means they can deny they are involved in negotiations. The proposal just sits there, like that piece of stale bread, and everybody looks at it. And anybody who might be interested says, that's a fascinating piece of bread. Why don't you cut the mould off that corner and we might nibble the other end? And so on. It's called diplomacy, apparently.' He took a long drink and added, 'The problem is that you've turned everybody's attention onto it. Raising all sorts of spectres that don't bear thinking about and manufacturing a domestic political crisis as well. Some excitable backbenchers have got very upset and are threatening to revolt.'

'Whelan?' Ryle smirked.

Grifford nodded. 'Probably feels a bit of an eejit having told the nation that neutrality was the greatest thing since sliced bread. Fresh sliced bread.'

'And somebody thinks I'm involved in all this?' Ryle saw the light.

'Politicians are simple people,' Grifford groaned. 'They see a crisis and you're the one who has manufactured it. So they presume you're doing it for a reason.'

Ryle nodded. 'But I'm not. I'm only a simple hack.'

'Yes, I know that. But they think everybody else thinks and acts the way they do. Deviously.'

Ryle felt tired suddenly: it was all too much for his brain. 'I don't understand anything any more,' he admitted and a thought struck him. 'The IRA connection. That's some spectre. Is that what's agitating them?'

'That's a potential source of some agitation,' Grifford nodded. 'It'd be helpful to have that cleared up, too.'

'That's what I'm after,' Ryle said with determination. That was the best possible story as far as he could see: the fallout over neutrality would be nothing compared to linking Clark, and through him the government, with the Provos. 'Have you worked it out yet?'

Grifford shook his head as if it was not something that interested him very much.

Ryle noted his lack of concern. 'But that's not the main problem worrying everybody, is it?'

Grifford finished his drink, placed the empty bottle on the floor in a neat line alongside the other two and stood up. 'Let's not overburden your brain unnecessarily. Take it one step at a time.'

'Where does the death of Clark fit into all this?' Ryle wanted to know. That was still the bottom line, the event that had set the whole chain of events in motion. And that held the explanation to whatever it was that was going on.

'That,' Grifford grimaced down at him, 'is what the nation is waiting for you to tell it.'

And that's what I'm going to do, he thought as he hauled himself up and walked to the outer door with Grifford. He had a head of steam up on this story now and he was going to get to the bottom of it, keep the competition chasing after him. And the IRA angle still seemed to be the key to it, whatever about Grifford's vague hints.

Grifford stopped on the steps. 'Remember,' he said, 'take care.'

Fourteen

Seamus Ryle drove slowly up the muddy driveway, scanning the fields on either side and examining the buildings ahead of him. A low, two-storey farmhouse in need of whitewashing faced the road and he could see the roof of a rust-coloured barn off to one side. He pulled off the track before it led into the farmyard and parked in front of the house.

A middle-aged woman answered his knock, took him to the corner of the house and shouted to a man at the distant end of a field. The sun was warm but the fields were bleached a pale brownish-green by the winter. A herd of plump black cattle stood as still as the cold air near a wired-off haystack. The woman shivered and invited him into a room lined with glass-fronted displays of Delft ornaments and silver.

'He'll be with you now in a minute,' she said and left him alone. He wondered who she was: she looked too old to be Maurice Clark's sister-in-law and too young to be his mother. His mother couldn't be still alive, he decided, or she'd have been at the funeral. But he hadn't seen Clark's brother there either, hadn't even known of his existence until Rosie told him.

John Clark came in and Ryle realised the woman must be his wife. He was about fifty, a large, balding, heavy-set man with a weathered face; he bore no resemblance to the dead politician. He was wearing worn working clothes and had replaced his boots with a pair of incongruous-looking slippers.

'I've heard about you.' He shook hands with a rough grasp. 'A solicitor friend of mine told me I should get in touch with you. I was up in Dublin the other day and I meant to call you but I didn't get a chance.'

He sounded almost apologetic and Ryle relaxed, knowing that he would have no difficulty getting him to talk. He obviously didn't share the widow's opinion of Ryle or his reports. 'I've been trying to find out how your brother died,' Ryle said.

188

Clark nodded. 'I was up in the Dáil to see the Minister for Justice but they fobbed me off with some fella called Lyster who gave me a right runaround. Treated me like I was some kind of culchie ignoramus.'

Ryle stared at him, open-mouthed at the image of Tommy Lyster playing the role of urban sophisticate. 'What did he say?'

'A long rigmarole about the procedures that had to be followed and how nothing could be rushed and how sorry everybody in the party was and so on. He didn't give me a straight answer to a single question.'

'He said in the Dáil that it was an accident.'

'He told me that too,' Clark nodded. 'Nobody could believe for a minute it was anything else, he said. Maurice hadn't an enemy in the world.'

'Had he?'

'He was a politician, wasn't he?' Clark examined his hands and began to rub at a piece of ingrained dirt on his index finger. 'But I don't know if they kill each other yet. In the North, yes. But not down here. Not yet anyway.'

'What do you think happened to him?'

'I don't know what to think. I went to Dublin to find out what was going on and all I got was a load of bullshit. This friend of mine showed me your articles and told me I should call you if I got nowhere.' He looked expectantly at Ryle.

Ryle took the cue and told him all he knew from the shooting of the dog to the hints that Clark's gun had come through the IRA's hands and that he had left the neutrality document with one of the last people to see him alive.

'A woman?' Clark asked and Ryle nodded. Clark looked like he might smile but the impulse left no more than a fleeting impression on his red face. 'Who?'

'I can't tell you that. For journalistic reasons.' Ryle paused. 'But if you'd like to talk to her I can ask her if she . . . '

Clark shook his head. 'He was always a great lad for the women.'

The door opened and Mrs Clark came in with a tray of neatly arranged cups, a plate of biscuits and another of trimmed triangular sandwiches. Ryle thanked her with feeling as she set it down on a chair and Clark poured the tea. When he had finished Ryle took out the photocopy of the neutrality document, turned up the page with the signature and handed it to Clark. 'Is that your brother's writing?'

John Clark bent over it for a long time. Ryle drank his tea, devoured several sandwiches filled with thickly sliced ham and watched him. He wondered if Clark was reading the whole page – he couldn't see his eyes.

'I don't know,' Clark said at last without raising his head. 'Could be. I just don't know.' He paused. 'I was trying to remember when I saw his signature last. Nor for years, I suppose.' He looked up at Ryle. 'We're not great letter-writers. And Maurice and me were never very close. There's fourteen years between us and I was running the farm when he was still in short trousers. I suppose we were more like uncle and nephew than brothers. That's how he always looked on me anyhow, as an uncle. We were never close.'

'When did you see him last?'

'Must have been about a year ago. At a funeral. Of an uncle, actually.' He picked up a cup and saucer in his large hand and drank some tea. 'Then he contacted me a month ago, out of the blue. Just before Christmas. Phoned me one night, late. Wanted to know if I could lend him some money.'

'How much?' Ryle inquired cautiously.

'He didn't say. Said he had some problems and needed to get his hands on a large amount of cash to get out of an impossible situation. I told him I could get a few thousand together but he said he needed more than that. Said he'd come back to me if he wanted it. That was the last I heard from him.'

'Did he say why he needed it?'

'No. And I didn't ask. I was too surprised to ask, if the truth be told. Too surprised that he should ring me up like that, looking for money. It struck me since that he must have been desperate. He wasn't the kind who liked to be beholden to anyone. And, like I said, we weren't close.'

'You know his widow?' Ryle inquired on the spur of the moment. He did not have any clear idea of what he wanted from Clark and was really going through the formalities of asking about his brother.

'I've met her,' Clark said in a tone that made further discussion of her superfluous.

Ryle picked up the photocopy from the table and folded it back into his coat pocket, the formalities completed. 'Do you know a man called Fergal Shercock?' he asked casually.

'Sure,' Clark replied. 'A bit of a wild lad. I know his family.'

'Does he still live around here?'

Clark shook his head. 'He comes home occasionally. I saw him at mass one Sunday a few weeks ago. Two or three Sundays ago. But he lives in Dublin.'

'You wouldn't happen to know where I could find him? Where he works or anything like that?'

'If he works.' Clark shook his head doubtfully and then remembered something. 'Hold on a minute. I'll ask Pauline. She delivered a parcel to him one time from his mother.'

Ryle poured himself another cup of cooling tea and ate a couple more sandwiches. The Clarks seemed like nice, decent people, he thought idly, the kind of people that it made your day to be able to help. Especially against gobshites like Lyster. An idea struck him as Clark returned.

'You're in luck,' Clark said, handing him a sheet from a copybook with an address written on it. Ryle knew the street slightly, a main route of once fashionable houses on the north side of the city. 'She never throws out anything.'

Ryle folded it carefully and put it into his pocket and got up.

'Won't you stay and have a bite of dinner?'

Ryle thanked him and declined. 'Would you like to say anything on the record about the way things have been going?' he asked. He might as well get a story out of this too, help justify the expenses.

'In the paper, you mean? Say what?'

'That you're not happy with the progress of the inquiry. What you were telling me earlier.'

Clark thought for a moment. 'I asked about the inquest. My friend, the solicitor, told me to ask about that. But he wouldn't give me an answer on that either.'

'Right.' Ryle reached for his notebook. 'You could call on them to clear up the mystery by holding the inquest immediately.'

'Yeah.' Clark brightened up, 'I'd like to give that Lyster fella a root up the arse.'

Tommy Lyster emerged from the back door of the ministers' dining room after an early lunch and stopped in front of the lifts. Either would take him to the Minister for Justice's parliamentary office on the next floor but he decided to stroll back. There was plenty of time.

He checked that one button of his navy suit jacket was closed and set off at a leisurely pace. Lyster loved these corridors for their atmosphere of straightforward politics – not the politics of ideas or major issues but the trading and broking of power in its simplest forms, doing favours for your friends and upsetting your enemies.

The corridors were quiet today. The Dáil was dull with routine matters and real politics was behind closed doors at the parties' weekly meetings. The Government party's meeting had been well attended in anticipation of Jim Whelan causing a row over neutrality. But the chairman had studiously spun out other subjects and nobody tried to force the pace. The meeting was due to resume after lunch.

Lyster gave a sly wink to a party colleague about to enter the members' bar with a defiant air. Everyone knew he had a drink problem and Lyster remembered someone saying that his wife had thrown him out.

'Tommy,' an Opposition deputy boomed as they approached each other down a narrow corridor. 'The crisis meeting's been adjourned, has it?'

'What crisis?' Lyster smirked. 'You don't believe anything you read in the papers, do you?'

The Opposition deputy let out a meaningless guffaw as they passed and he went on his way, his laugh dying like the roar of a passing train. Lyster reached the wide marble staircase to the Dáil chamber and climbed heavily. Halfway up, a serious young Opposition deputy from a neighbouring constituency stopped to tell him about a petty crime problem in his area. Lyster made a point of noting the details in the back of his diary but he had no intention of doing his petitioner any favours. He would pass the query on to his own party's man and let him reap whatever political value there was to be gained.

He continued on through the circular corridor around the back of the Dáil chamber and found his secretary waiting at the door of the Minister's sparse office.

'There are two detectives waiting for you, Minister,' he said with the air of someone bearing startling news. He opened the door and stood back to let Lyster in. 'They say they have an appointment but there's nothing in the diary.'

'Two?' Lyster sat down behind the bare desk. 'Only one has an appointment. Fellow called Devane.'

The secretary nodded uncertainly and showed Inspector Devane in. Lyster shook his hand and motioned to the only other chair as Devane examined the room. It had as much character as any of the interview rooms he had used in police stations. The desk wasn't scratched and scored, the walls had been painted in civil service bland in recent years and there were no bars or metal grilles on the window. But it had the same air of the anonymous public office, home to no one but a functional stop for many, a place with a slightly unsavoury air. Devane wondered, not for the first time since the early-morning phone call to his home summoned him here, whether he or Lyster would be playing the interrogator. And who was going to confess.

His unasked question was answered quickly and predictably. 'This,' Lyster said, setting the ground rules, 'is an unofficial meeting. I'm speaking to you as a member of the public, not as a Minister or even as a member of the Dáil. I thought we should meet here for convenience's sake.' He gave a short laugh. 'My convenience. It mightn't help my political career to be seen coming out of garda stations. And it mightn't look too good for you to be seen with me either. You know what this country's like: everyone always assumes the worst.'

Lyster paused, his introduction completed, and Devane waited with a look of polite interest. 'I've read your report, an excellent document, very thorough. And while I was reading it something occurred to me, something I think you should know. It mightn't amount to anything but I thought I'd better pass it on to you anyway. You can make whatever you like of it. You're the professional.'

He paused again and gave a crooked smile; Devane maintained his façade of mild interest. 'It struck me when I was reading about the party the night before poor Maurice died. I had been invited but I wasn't there, as you probably know. But I got to thinking about Mr Erlanger. And I remembered a conversation I had with him, the day after Maurice's death, I think it was. He offered to sell me some bugs – you know, listening devices and things. And he said something that I thought was a little strange. He said he had a big interest in law and order and that he was especially worried about the subversive threat. That's why he wanted me to buy bugs. For you lads to keep on top of the Provos.'

Devane knew some response was required from him. 'That was it?' he asked.

'Yes.' Lyster nodded. 'I didn't pass much remarks on it myself at the time. I presumed that he was working on some kind of commission or something. It was only afterwards that it occurred to me that it was a bit odd. For a foreigner to be interested in things like that, I mean.'

'What do you think its significance is, sir?' Devane inquired politely.

'I don't know.' Lyster spread his hands and widened his eyes in a much-abused gesture of innocence. 'I just thought it might mean something to you. You fellows are always asking people to come forward with any little snippets of information no matter how small they seem. We never know when the last little piece fills out your whole picture.'

'Would you like to make a formal statement about this conversation with Mr Erlanger?'

'Good God, no.' Lyster looked horrified. 'No, I don't want to make anything much of this. I'm only trying to help with your inquiries. But privately, just between me and you. In both our interests.'

'We'll bear it in mind, sir.' Devane rose and Lyster got to his feet without haste.

'Tell me,' the Minister said with the casual tone of someone about to ask a farmer how much he earned, 'just between ourselves. What do you think happened?'

'My inquiries have not yet reached a conclusion,' Devane said blandly.

'I know that.' Lyster rounded his desk so that he was standing between Devane and the door. 'And I don't want you to think I'm trying to influence you in any way. Nothing could be further from my mind. The papers misquoted me again today about it being an accident. I only said I couldn't imagine it being anything but an accident. Can you?'

'There's no firm evidence one way or the other.'

'Precisely,' Lyster said as if Devane had agreed with him. He suddenly changed direction and got down to the real point behind the meeting. 'I can't quite place your accent, Inspector. You're not a Dublin man, anyway?'

Devane shook his head and told him the county he came from originally. The Minister asked what part and Devane gave him the precise location, knowing that his family background and its political affiliations would be checked out.

'And how long have you been in the Central Detective Unit?'

'Ten years.'

'And you enjoy your work there?'

'Yes, sir,' Devane said evenly.

'Yes,' Lyster mused. 'It's always nice to be at the centre of things.' He looked thoughtful and then stepped aside. 'Anyway, I'd better not take up any more of your valuable time. You're a busy man.'

He took Devane's hand, shook it and held it for a moment. 'We're all counting on you.' He looked directly into the Inspector's eyes. 'It's a difficult task and we appreciate all your hard work, all you've done already.'

Devane walked out, feeling as if he had been mugged verbally and knowing he had been warned. He looked into Lyster's secretary's office and his assistant stood up with a look of anticipation. They walked silently through the corridors to the main entrance.

'Well?' the young detective asked with pent-up curiosity when they got outside.

'A waste of time.' Devane dismissed the conversation. But his mind was working furiously as he got into the passenger seat of their car. Like all his colleagues, he was well attuned to the nods and winks, the carrots and sticks, of politicians. He was in no doubt about what he had been told: clear up this case the right way and soon or suffer the sudden uprooting of a posting to the back of beyond and back into uniform.

That was predictable. What wasn't predictable was why Lyster had told him about Erlanger. There wasn't any point to it. Not that he could see. It was probably just an excuse to get him in there, a transparent cover for the meeting. One should never over-estimate politicians, he thought. At least, he consoled himself, it'll put the wind up the Chief when he finds out I've been seeing the Minister. In secret.

Ryle sniffed, stared into the typewriter and delved through his memory for anything else he should put into his notes. Nothing came to mind and he looked through what he had typed of his conversations with Rosie, Grifford and Clark. Maurice Clark seemed to have had deep financial troubles, according to his brother and to Burke. Was that what he had been talking about when he'd told Rosie he was trapped? It was hardly a reason why anyone would kill him, though, more likely a motive for suicide. Even that seemed unlikely.

There was no obvious connection between that and the IRA gun and the neutrality documents and whatever it was that Grifford had been hinting about so heavily last night. His thoughts were interrupted by a shout from Stacy who had just returned from a long lunch. The news editor was shedding his coat and his jacket and rolling up his sleeves with a fierce burst of energy.

'Where the hell've you been? I tried everywhere. You changed houses and numbers again?'

'Getting a story.' Ryle went over to the news desk. 'In Tipperary.'

'Tipperary?' the news editor shouted in outrage.

'I'm on evenings,' Ryle bridled. 'I'm only supposed to be getting in here now.'

'All right, all right.' Stacy raised a pacifying hand. 'I only wanted to take you to lunch. With an old friend of mine who has a passion for military matters.' He accepted a handful of letters from a messenger boy and tossed them to one side of the news desk. 'Backfire bombers. That's what this is all about.'

'What?'

'Your story. The neutrality business.' He settled into his chair and leaned back comfortably. 'NATO, and particularly the British, are very concerned about Backfire bombers and a sneak attack through Britain's back door. Ireland.' Stacy smiled at him and Ryle realised that the news editor's pleased look was due as much to lunchtime drinks as to satisfaction with the information he had discovered.

'I don't follow. What do these bombers do?' He smirked in turn. 'No, don't tell me.'

Stacy was too eager to explain to notice Ryle's flippancy. 'Russian long-range bombers,' he said, 'based at Murmansk or some such place up on the Arctic circle. They can fly way out into the Atlantic, turn around and come in over Ireland for a sneak attack on Britain from the' – he had to think for a moment – 'west. Through the back door. See?'

Ryle nodded. 'And the back door,' Stacy went on triumphantly, 'is wide open. Unguarded.'

'So there is a reason why NATO might be more interested now in a deal than in the past.'

'Precisely. All hangs together.' Stacy pulled over a scrap of copy paper and scrawled a phone number on it.

'Except for Maurice Clark,' Ryle said. 'I don't see where he fits in at all.'

'Yesterday's story.' Stacy shrugged dismissively and handed him the phone number. 'We've got to keep pushing ahead. Call my man and he'll tell you all about Backfire bombers. He's got loads of stuff on them, magazines and all sorts of things.'

Do I have to go through this every bloody day, Ryle groaned inwardly. 'But I've got a fistful of other angles to follow up today,' he moaned. 'And I don't know anything about military matters.'

'What were you doing in Tipperary?' Stacy suddenly seemed to remember Ryle's journey.

'Talking to Clark's brother.'

'You're following the wrong story.' Stacy wagged a finger.

'I've got him calling for an immediate inquest. On the record. With quotes. Just like you wanted.'

'Forget about Clark. He's dead and buried.'

Ryle began to shift from one foot to the other as he glared down at the news editor. 'His death opened up all this.' He waved at the phone number. 'In case you've forgotten.'

'I hope you're not getting carried away with it.' Stacy looked at him and appeared to change his mind. He picked up the list of reporters and ran his eye down it. 'It's a great pity we never had national service in this country. Would have given you lot some knowledge of defence matters. And some fucking sense of discipline.'

Ryle relaxed. 'And what did you do in the war, Daddy?'

'More to the point,' Stacy retorted, calming down, 'what exactly are you writing today?'

'I just told you.'

'Mickey mouse stuff. Couple of paragraphs.'

Ryle shrugged. 'The guards have begun an inquiry into the forgeries.'

'Wonderful.'

'And I hope to get somewhere with the Provo angle later.'

'I think you're wasting your time,' Stacy said and scanned a list of news headlines. 'Why don't you look into Leinster House and see how your buddy Whelan gets on with neutrality?'

Ryle went back to his desk and took the original neutrality documents from his drawer, remembering Grifford's warning about the garda inquiry into the forgeries. He glanced at Stacy who now seemed to be dozing at the news desk: the news editor would have to hand them over if push came to shove, he decided. He looked around the news room and saw the fashion editor's corner was empty. On the spur of the moment he went over and pulled open her filing cabinet. He stuffed the papers into the middle of a bulging file labelled 'make-up'. The guards were hardly going to search the entire news room: it would take them weeks.

*   *   *

A bunch of reporters hovered around a large leather couch at the end of a corridor, waiting with bad grace and unconcealed impatience. Like unruly undertakers, Ryle thought and he smiled as he walked past the entrance to the members' private bar. A rumble of laughter flowed out as someone opened the door.

'I suppose we can get on with it now that you're here,' a reporter snorted by way of a back-handed compliment to him.

'Sure,' Ryle replied expansively. 'Tell them I've arrived.'

'What do you suppose they're doing up there?' another reporter asked no one in particular.

'Trying to fuck each other out a window,' someone suggested.

'We wouldn't even hear the glass break from here.' The first reporter looked resentfully down another corridor where an usher stood sentry at the stairs leading to the party rooms.

Ryle sidled over to his paper's political correspondent and asked him what was going on. The political correspondent glanced at his watch. 'They've been at it nearly three hours. A lot longer than anyone expected.'

'Any word of what's happening?'

The political correspondent shook his head. 'Either Whelan has a lot more balls than we thought,' he said with the distracted air of somebody already plotting his story, 'or he's got a lot more support than the party leaders thought. Or both.'

Ryle went back past the members' bar to the public bar in search of a phone. He found one on the end of the bar, shoved up against the wall by the elbow of a countryman who was deep in a whispered discussion with two companions. When Ryle asked to get to the phone they looked suspiciously at him, as though he were trying to evict them. He dialled at arm's length and turned towards the wall to try and hear above the noise reverberating around the small room.

To his surprise, Sergeant Peter Grifford answered himself and Ryle asked if they could meet.

'Have you got something?' Grifford demanded in an officious voice.

'Maybe,' Ryle half lied. All he'd really got was a growing

curiosity about whatever it was Grifford had been on the point of telling him when he'd been too tired to appreciate it.

'I'll get back to you,' Grifford said.

The bar seemed to have become more crowded in the previous few minutes and he worked his way out slowly. Grifford's curtness had taken him aback but he put it down to the probability that there was someone with him in the detective unit. His attitude the previous night had been a bit odd, too, he thought. Flippant as ever, apart from his warning, but his heart wasn't in it. He had been going through the motions.

The corridor outside was also full of people and Ryle forgot about Grifford as he hurried back towards the other reporters, surveying the passing faces for some party members who might talk to him.

Tommy Lyster was besieged by three reporters who had slowed but failed to halt him. Ryle joined them, moving slowly backwards in front of the Minister. 'A full and frank exchange of views,' Lyster was saying, 'like all our meetings, gentlemen.'

'But what was the outcome?'

'We are totally united and agreed on policy behind the inspired national leadership of the Taoiseach and the Government.'

'Was there a vote?'

'On what? Not at all. You gentlemen don't understand, don't want to understand. Everyone had their say and we're all united.' He smirked. 'One big happy family.'

One of the reporters muttered 'Jesus' under his breath and they let him go, smiling with delight. A Cabinet Minister, seeing them closing in on him, raised his hands in a gesture of surrender. 'Don't ask me, lads,' he smiled. 'There's a statement on its way. I can't say anything else.' He dodged into the sanctuary of the members' bar.

Ryle looked around for Whelan but there was no sign of him. The crush of people was thinning out and reporters dashed down the corridor to try and catch those who had got away. Several deputies had been cornered and more reporters piled around their colleagues in a loose scrum. The political correspondent parted from a group and Ryle fell into step beside him.

'Very interesting,' he said. 'Nothing's been resolved. They have a real problem.'

'Whelan won't knuckle under?' Ryle asked.

'Not just Whelan. There may be twenty unhappy men. As many more sitting on the fence, waiting to see which way the wind's blowing.'

'Where does that leave everything?'

'All to play for, as usual.' The political correspondent stopped at the opening of another corridor. 'And the other side are now waiting to move a confidence motion. At the right moment.'

The houses loomed large in the dark, set well back from the road behind unkempt lawns and car parks and barely touched by the street lights. Few windows were lit.

Ryle came back down the steps of one house where he had gone to check the number and walked quickly up the road, counting mentally. A line of trees bordered the footpath and threw swaying strands of shadow over the hedges and gardens. A car accelerated up the road; there was nobody in sight.

A small, fourth-floor window glowed dully, the only sign of life in the house, as Ryle walked up to the flaking front door. He squinted at a strip of bells on the wooden pillar but most of the tin name tags were empty or their messages faded beyond recognition. He hesitated a moment and then tried the door. It opened.

He stood on the step, peering into the dark, felt for a light switch and pushed it on. It cast a weak light over a hall that had once been elegant, high-ceilinged and ornate but was now dilapidated. A heavy old table was scattered with overdue electricity and gas bills and a strip of dusty linoleum led to stairs and a passage that curved around towards the back of the building.

Ryle went down the passage and knocked at the first door he came to. It opened almost immediately into a narrow triangle and a man stood there. He was tall and thin with close cropped hair and a gaunt face and his expression indicated that he had been expecting somebody else.

'I'm looking for Fergal Shercock,' Ryle said in a cheerful voice. 'Could you tell me which is his flat?'

'Who are you?'

Ryle told him.

'Do you have any identification?'

Ryle held out his press card, thinking irritably that these types were always the same. They treated everyone else the way they complained that the cops treated them – brusquely and suspiciously. Next, they'd want to frisk him. But at least he'd found the right flat.

The man turned over the card and studied the back and Ryle heard a door swing shut farther down the passage. He glanced into the gloom and there was another man standing there, leaning against the wall. He was short and square and had longish hair parted in the middle and a round face. The two men stood rigid with some unexplained tension and stared back at him.

'What d'you want with him?' the tall man asked. He had an indeterminate accent and his face looked tired and tense.

'He might be able to help me with an article I'm working on,' Ryle said, beginning to wish he could back out of this. Whatever is going on here, I don't want any further part in it. How could I have been so stupid? Thinking I could just casually wander round among a lot of Provos asking if they had given a gun to a Dáil deputy and would they please tell me why. It had seemed like a good idea in the warmth and light of the news room but the news room was a long way from this gloomy and silent house.

'What article?'

'Are you Mr Shercock?'

'What article?' The man's tone carried the underlying certainty of someone used to getting answers to his questions.

'Just a political profile I'm writing,' Ryle said, 'of Maurice Clark.'

The man gave a humourless snort as if Ryle had tried to make a joke. 'What the fuck are you talking about?'

Ryle breathed in deeply to steady his nerve and hoped he sounded merely impatient. 'I'm writing a political profile of a politician called Maurice Clark who died recently. And I thought that Mr Shercock would be, might be able to help me with my research.' Jesus, he thought, that sounds pretty weak. How could I be so stupid?

'How?' the man asked in a slightly bemused tone.

How? Ryle asked himself quickly. 'Because they grew up together. In the same part of the country. I thought he might remember something interesting about Clark from then. Anecdotes or whatever.'

The man looked at him with disbelief. Ryle held his gaze and in the silence he heard a movement inside the room and then a sharp cough. The stairs behind him creaked and he glanced around to his right and saw a third man at the foot of the stairs. A baseball bat swung limply from his hand. Surrounded, Ryle thought immediately and felt a sickly wave wash through his body. Jesus Christ, what have I walked into here?

'Who sent you here?'

The light in the hall went off with a sharp click and Ryle jumped. The tall man's face dissolved into the gloom which was diluted only by the weak or heavily shaded light from the room behind him.

The man was still waiting for an answer. 'I was down in that part of the country,' Ryle said, marshalling his concentration and trying to ignore the men in the shadows on either side of him, 'and somebody said Mr Shercock knew Clark when he was younger and might be able to tell me more about him.'

He resisted an impulse to tell them to forget it and walk away. That would only make things worse. Anyway, he tried to reassure himself, they weren't going to do anything. I'm only a reporter.

'I don't believe any of that horseshit,' the tall man said at last. He glanced at the press card, turned around and went into the room. Ryle waited, pinned in the vague shaft of light from the room and feeling as if he was held in a spotlight. His nose felt blocked and he thought he was running a temperature. There was no sound and he was conscious of his own choked breathing.

The tall man returned and held out the press card to Ryle.

'Whatever you're at, you'd better get the fuck out of here. And don't come back.'

Ryle took the card and turned and walked down the dark passage. He was stopped suddenly by the baseball bat pressing against his stomach and he braced his body and his mind for a blow. The bat didn't move and the light came on suddenly and the bat swung away.

'And don't get any stupid ideas about sending any other visitors round here,' a harsh Northern voice grated by his ear. Ryle didn't look at him and the baseball bat swung up and down before his eyes. He nodded and walked quickly down the hall, concentrating on the faint rosy glow of the outside world coming through the fanlight.

He let the door crash shut behind him and went down the steps, feeling the tension drain from his stomach and his mind. Then the hall door slammed shut a second time and he glanced back to see a man coming down the steps after him. Oh fuck, Ryle thought and the panic swept back over him as he turned onto the footpath, bleakly conscious that the street was deserted and that his car was fifty yards away. He hurried down the road, trying to concentrate on a line of cars stopped at a distant traffic light and willing the red light to turn green and release the cars in his direction.

He didn't look back until he reached his car and the man was still sauntering after him, in no hurry. It's all right, he told himself, it's all right. He's just trying to intimidate me. He started the engine and the traffic lights had changed and he had to wait impatiently while the cars streamed by. He watched the man approach in the wing mirror and waited for an opening in the traffic. The man stopped just behind him and then the road was clear and he sped off.

The traffic lights turned red again and he jolted to a sudden stop and slammed his fist against the steering wheel in anger and frustration at his own reactions. Of all the stupid fucking ridiculous capers. He gripped the wheel fiercely with both hands and told himself that they were only trying to scare him off, to make sure he had gone and didn't send the cops back. And they had succeeded.

The light turned green and an ominous thought struck him. Maybe they had followed to get the number of his car. Which meant they could find out his home address. But it wasn't his address any more. It was Breda's. And Lorraine's. Oh Jesus, he swore aloud.

Fifteen

The sea was the colour and texture of wet concrete and as smooth as a newly laid path. Small waves bunched up and broke on the shore at the last minute and shuffled the shingle with sharp slaps. Inspector Bill Devane trudged down the beach through the yielding stones and stopped short of the water. The morning was damp and hazy and the air smelled of smoke.

He watched a distant freighter move slowly southward, its outline a faint break in the grey backdrop, and he turned once to look at the opaque height of Killiney Hill rising behind him. A dirty haze clung to the treetops and shrouded the obelisk on the summit. Down the beach towards Bray a distant figure held up a stick for a jumping dog and threw it in a high overhand arc. Devane looked out to sea again, lit a cigarette and considered what he should do.

His meeting with Tommy Lyster had not had the hoped-for effect. But he should have expected that. Lyster had used his politician's trick of pretending that he, Devane, had the inside track while all the time playing him off against the Chief. But Devane couldn't see why Lyster had gone to so much trouble. Presumably the Minister was just trying to make sure he had the guards under control and could manipulate their inquiry into Clark's death. Unless there was a lot more to it all than met the eye.

Certainly the Chief seemed to think so, or maybe he was just protecting his career prospects as usual. He had come to Devane's office (which was unusual enough to have put him on his guard). 'I am taking direct, day-to-day control of the Clark case,' he declared with an air of formality, 'and the separate but associated inquiry into the forgery of certain documents.'

Devane looked up at him in surprise and suggested he already was in charge. The Chief shook his head: 'I mean operational control, not arm's length. I'll be directing the in-

206

quiry personally and deciding what we do and don't do and writing the reports. You will continue the investigation into Clark's death for the time being. Another team will look into the other matter.'

Devane waited for an explanation. The silence lengthened and eventually he asked why. 'Because it makes more sense to have both inquiries directed from the one office. Saves time and we have to wrap it up as soon as possible. As I told you before, it's the kind of case where rumours multiply and the waters get more and more muddied with every passing day. Every passing hour.'

'What rumours?' Devane demanded.

'You know what it's like,' the Chief shrugged defensively. 'There is another dimension to all this. It's not just a police matter, it's creating political uncertainty. Instability. It's not in the national interest.'

Bollocks, Devane thought. 'I thought that was no concern of ours,' he said.

'It's a dimension to the problem that cannot be ignored,' the Chief said stiffly.

Politician talk, Devane thought, but restrained himself from saying so. 'I thought the Minister was happy,' he remarked, hoping to unsettle his superior's confidence. 'He seemed to be when I met him yesterday.'

The Chief showed no surprise. 'You should have told me about that beforehand,' he said with an edge of sorrow rather than anger. 'And you got the wrong impression. He is not happy.'

'He told you that?'

The Chief ignored the question. 'We have a job to do,' he said. 'I want a full briefing on what is happening now and what, if anything, remains to be done before we submit a final report.'

Devane sighed and held out a sheet of paper. 'I'm preparing an application for a phone tap.'

'Who?'

'Michael Erlanger.'

'Why?'

'Because of information I have received. Confidential information.' Devane and the Chief stared at each other coldly.

'Information that he is involved in subversive activity?' the Chief asked.

'No.'

'In major criminal activity?'

'He may have had something to do with Clark's death.'

'May.' The Chief took the sheet of paper from him. 'That does not meet the criteria for a telephone intercept. Not major criminal activity.' He tore up the paper.

The sound of the paper tearing merged in Devane's mind with the crash as the smooth water crumpled up and broke again and rolled the stones on the shore. A request to be reassigned would be torn up too. There was no way he'd be let detach himself from this case and be allowed the luxury of watching from the sidelines. No, they wanted him there, nominally in charge but with no control. Just in case anything went wrong and a fall guy was needed. I've been nobbled, he thought.

He shrugged unconsciously and tossed the cigarette end into a receding wave and watched it being dragged away by the undertow. But I'm fucked if I'm going to lie down and be walked over, he decided. At least he had not given the Chief a complete rundown on all the inquiries he had initiated.

Footsteps crunched behind him and Garda Casey joined him, his face as tired as the morning. Devane gave him a quizzical look.

'Nothing.' Casey shook his head. 'Mr Erlanger seems to lead a quiet life. Home by eight last night, lights out at eleven, no visitors, left at eight ten this morning. Chris followed him to his office. He's there now. No sign of anyone else but we assume his wife's in the house.'

They walked up to the dripping, muddy cliff face and climbed the steps to the roadway. Devane stopped at his car and Casey waited for him to get his breath back, wondering if he should commiserate with him about the acquittal of the two men against whom the Inspector had been giving evidence. It was all over the front pages today.

He thought better of it and asked instead about the request for the phone tap.

Devane shook his head. 'Turned down. We're to call this off too.'

'Why?' Casey looked confused.

'Orders.'

'He's been cleared, has he?'

Devane shrugged. 'You're to report back to the Chief and see what he wants you to do. He's taken charge.'

Casey perked up. 'It's coming to a head then, is it?'

Devane raised his eyebrows and sniffed the burnt air.

'I want to talk to you,' James Burke said. 'About something that has a bearing on our previous conversation.'

'I'll be up to you in ten minutes,' Ryle offered with relief. Anything to take his mind off last night's caper was welcome. He had spent the morning trying unsuccessfully to get in touch with various people by phone and had just given up when his own phone had rung.

'No, no.' Burke sounded startled. 'Not here.'

They agreed to meet in a pub full of corners and odd-angled alcoves in Suffolk Street when the lunchtime trade should have slackened off. Ryle got himself a coffee and spread the morning's paper on his desk and read the political correspondent's report on the neutrality affair. Jim Whelan had become the focal point of a group of party dissidents opposed to any change in the policy, it said.

Ryle blew his nose, picked up the phone and tried Sergeant Grifford's two numbers and the Sinn Fein office again. It was better to deal with the Provos through the standard press channels. He had spent a restless night worrying about the three men and their unseen companions and about what he might have stumbled into and what they might do about it. In the silent darkness his imagination had woven numerous possibilities, none of them reassuring, and had left him worn out and exhausted. The cosy inactivity of the morning news room made the whole episode seem more like the farce at the mining site. Except, he reminded himself, that these guys were not farmers with shotguns.

Billy was not available either and on the spur of the moment he called Breda. 'Is everything all right?' he asked.

'Yes,' she said automatically and picked up the concern in his voice. 'Why?'

'No reason,' he replied quickly. He didn't want to infect her with his own paranoia – not that she was prone to that anyway.

'I'm having a birthday party for Lorraine on Sunday. If you'd like to come.'

'Sure,' he said and asked how the child was.

Afterwards, he went and listened to the lunchtime news. There had been a row in the Dáil with the Opposition demanding clarification of the Government's position on neutrality. It had been ruled out of order and the Government had said nothing. A political correspondent commented that the mood of uncertainty and unease among the Government's ranks had not been allayed.

Ryle left before the end of the bulletin to meet Burke who was already in the pub. The accountant was perched uncomfortably on a low stool in a corner and looking as tense and impatient as a truant schoolboy. His eyes darted past Ryle as if he feared a vengeful headmaster might follow ham.

Ryle offered to buy him a drink or another coffee but Burke declined both and fidgeted on the seat while Ryle got himself a pint of Guinness and a sandwich of finely sliced ham.

'So how are things?' Ryle opened the sandwich and tore a wide strip of fat from the meat. He dangled it in the air and dropped it in an ashtray.

'I want it to be clear that what I am going to say to you is off the record,' Burke said as though he were reciting prepared lines. He seemed relieved to have got down to business but he still avoided Ryle's gaze. 'Completely off the record.'

'Yes, sure,' Ryle said automatically.

'And I want to be clear that that means you will not reveal the fact that I have talked to you to anybody. Including your editors.'

'Okay.' Ryle stopped chewing, put down his sandwich and raised his glass thoughtfully. Burke now had his undivided attention.

'That is of the utmost importance,' Burke continued. 'What I am doing is at least unprofessional and possibly unethical.

Naturally, I consider it to be justified in all the circumstances but others may see it differently.'

Ryle waited while Burke sipped the dregs of his coffee and replaced the cup in the saucer, giving it as much attention as he might to the bottom line of a balance sheet.

'You are no doubt aware that shares in Atlantis Mining have shot up in value in the last few days.' Burke glanced up and Ryle nodded, remembering the comments of his financial-page colleague after his report on the uranium meeting. 'It began slowly last week and gathered momentum towards the end of the week, coincidentally after you had written an article about the mine's prospects. The share prices have jumped again this morning to over one eighty. There's a full-scale bull market in them now.'

Burke assumed a professorial tone. 'There are various reasons for this. Erlanger has been talking them up quietly, showing a geologist's report to selected people and so forth. Investors are in the mood for a little excitement in the midst of the present doldrums and there are few exciting prospects on the market these days. To create a good market in the shares, of course, there have to be just enough on offer to keep the price – and the interest – rising. Up to now, in fact, there have been very few Atlantis shares on offer. But that has changed in the past week.'

Burke stopped and looked around. The pub had emptied but for the customers who felt the need to drink right up to the 'holy hour' for which it would shortly close. Ryle took a long drink and tried to keep the details of Burke's crash course in brokerage straight in his mind. Stock markets and financial dealings were a mystery to him.

'What has changed,' Burke said with a deliberation that indicated he was coming to the point, 'is that Erlanger has been selling off his own shares. Not the ones he holds in his own name but those he holds through nominees.'

Burke sat back, unburdened. Ryle felt let down. So what, he thought. 'High finance is not my scene,' he said tentatively. 'What's the significance of this?'

Burke leaned forward and put his hands around his empty

cup as if to encapsulate his information. 'There is an old market saying to the effect that one should sell when directors sell.' He looked up. 'I think it would be of some interest to the people queuing up to put their money into Atlantis Mining to know that the man behind it is taking his money out.'

'But that's not illegal or anything, is it?'

'No. But it raises the question of why he should be taking his money out when everything is said to be going so well.'

'You think it means his mining plans are not going well?' Ryle grappled for a firm line to hold. He felt faintly lightheaded and dabbed at his running nose with a paper napkin.

'Perhaps.'

'What would be the effect of a story appearing in the paper saying Erlanger was selling his shares?' Ryle tried again.

'Who knows? These things sometimes develop a life of their own without regard to logic or reason. Speculators may ignore it or they may drop the shares like hot potatoes.'

Ryle wondered if he was missing something in all this. Burke clearly thought he was telling him information of great importance but he couldn't see its significance. Erlanger was selling shares, making a quick profit – so what? 'Can I ask you,' he said, 'why you are telling me this?'

Burke paused. 'Because I think it should be publicised. Investors have a right to know. In the public interest.'

Ryle took a long drink. He still couldn't see any great point to all this but Burke might prove very useful for other parts of the real story and it didn't cost him anything to play along with him. 'Can I get this information from public records?' he asked.

'No. The share movements are a matter of record, of course. But you cannot find out who the beneficial interests in the nominee companies are.'

'What about the Companies' Office?'

'It will tell you that the directors of these companies are two women. Secretaries in our office, in fact.' Burke paused and looked at him guiltily. 'You can see why I must insist on the utmost confidentiality. I don't handle this account but you can see my dilemma.'

'There must be a piece of paper somewhere to prove that Erlanger is the person behind these companies,' Ryle probed.

'That's completely out of the question,' Burke responded sharply.

A barman came and snatched Burke's empty cup and Ryle's half-eaten sandwich. 'Finish up now, please, gents,' he said as Ryle grabbed his glass and waited for him to move away.

'You mentioned on the phone that this was connected with Maurice Clarke's death?' Ryle prompted.

'It wouldn't surprise me.'

'But what's the connection?'

'I don't know. I told you before that Clark fared badly in his financial dealings with Erlanger.'

Right, Ryle thought, and this could be the reason he was in financial trouble. 'And they had to do with Atlantis?'

'You can take it that Erlanger is not involved in anything else.'

'What happens to Clark's shares in Atlantis now?'

'I presume they go to his widow,' Burke said formally. 'I don't know. Presumably they're tied up until his will is sorted out.'

So the widow might benefit from his death, Ryle thought, if there was anything left over from Clark's debts. But who did he owe the money to? He shook his head: none of it made a lot of sense. And anyway none of this connected with the main story.

'Can you remember anything more about the talk Clark had with Erlanger during the party?'

'I never knew anything about it other than the fact that it took place.' Burke paused and shifted uneasily. 'That's when Erlanger gave him the material on neutrality.'

'What?' Ryle straightened up physically as well as mentally. 'Erlanger gave it to him?'

'So I understand.' Ryle's sudden enthusiasm seemed to make Burke even more nervous. 'At least, he didn't have any documents with him when he arrived there. And he did have them after the party. Or so your newspaper says.'

Holy shit, Ryle thought, his mind racing through a whole series of possibilities. Burke watched him with growing irritation, thinking it was typical of the media: you told them something of importance and they ignored it and got excited about a peripheral matter. The barman called time again and he got to his feet.

Ryle seemed to have forgotten he was there and looked up at him in surprise. 'Could I talk to Yvonne? Would you ask her if she'd see me? Completely off the record.'

'She won't talk to you.'

'Will you ask her?' Ryle rose. 'I really need to have a word with her about this.'

Burke began to move towards the door. 'She will scarcely talk to me since I told her I'd met you.'

Ryle followed him through the pub where several barmen were gathering used glasses and they stopped at the locked exit, waiting for someone to come and let them out. 'Doesn't she want to know why her husband died?'

'Yvonne's a pragmatist,' Burke said with a hint of bitterness. 'She's decided her future's in politics and she's not going to help you or anyone else create trouble for her new friends. Or upset her new career.'

'Somebody's got to her?'

'It wasn't difficult.' The bitterness in his voice was more than a hint now. 'All the people she used to despise ... they've flattered her, given her the full treatment. Even suggested that she could have the cabinet position that was reserved for Clark.'

'But she always had political ambitions, didn't she?' Ryle was intrigued.

'Not in my experience.' Burke paused and gave a short sigh. 'Perhaps I did not see the situation as clearly as I should have.'

The barman appeared, turned a key in the lock and thanked them for coming. On the footpath Ryle stopped in front of Burke. 'It's over,' he said, half-statement and half-question, 'isn't it?'

Burke avoided his eye and turned and walked away purpose-fully. Ryle watched him cross the road into Andrew Street and felt a twinge of sympathy for him. Burke was a natural victim, always just getting the wrong end of the stick, never quite managing to be in the right place at just the right time.

But he had given him something to go on, possibly his best lead yet. No, he revised his opinion, the IRA angle was still the best potential story. But his mind was already racing through the possibilities offered by the fact that Erlanger had given Clark the neutrality document. He glanced at the heavy sky and thought idly, it never rains but it pours.

Rosie walked out of the school gates, buttoning her raincoat and thinking about the teachers' meeting. Bloody parents demanding more extra curricular activities had divided them again between those who saw teaching as a vocation and those who thought it was a job. The nuns versus the workers, she thought, casting some of her lay colleagues into habits. She'd have to check out the union position before they all got landed with extra work to satisfy middle-class obsessions.

She turned left towards the bus stop and a van door swung open into her path. She stepped around it automatically and a Northern voice asked her if she wanted a lift. Rosie glanced at the driver, ready to reject the offer, and recognised Billy.

'Going home?' he asked as she got in. 'Somewhere in Ranelagh?' She nodded a second time.

Billy chattered cheerfully as he drove, inquiring about mutual acquaintances. 'Have you ever considered joining the movement?' he asked casually. 'The vanguard of the real revolution. Getting out of the wankers' outfits.'

'I've thought about it. And decided against.'

'Worried about the armed struggle?' he glanced at her.

'No. I don't think you're real revolutionaries.'

Billy snorted and was about to say something disparaging but contained himself and settled for pulling his class advantage. 'I love you middle-class types,' he smiled, 'teaching us workers about revolution.'

Rosie did not reply and waited to find out what he wanted. 'We want your help,' he said at last.

She glanced at a row of brightly lit shops in Donnybrook. 'Your friend Clark,' Billy slowed and stopped at a traffic light, 'had something belonged to us. We'd like to know where he got it.'

'I don't know.'

'You know what I'm talking about.' It was not a question but a confirmation that he was talking to the right person. He looked at her sideways and she nodded. 'I'm sure you can understand our interest. There's been a breach of security. We need to know who.'

'I didn't know he had it until I read it in the papers,' Rosie said as he turned left at the lights and headed for Ranelagh.

Billy thought about that for a moment. 'The gun's not important,' he said with the air of somebody taking her into his confidence. 'It's the security. If a volunteer is flogging off army material he might be trading other things too.'

'I don't deal in guns,' Rosie replied.

Billy asked where she lived and followed her directions. He parked a little short of her house.

'Maybe one of your comrades was the conduit,' he prompted.

'They wouldn't have given him the time of day.'

'Somebody did.'

'I know nothing about it. That's straight.'

'But you'll check it out for us, won't you?' His tone made it clear that that was an order. 'It's important.'

Rosie looked at him without commitment and Billy thanked her with enthusiasm. 'I'll call you tomorrow.' He waved cheerfully.

She went into the house, tossed her shoulder bag and coat into a chair and watched Billy drive away. She leaned her forehead against the cold window and watched it cloud under her breath. 'Oh Maurice,' she said softly, without recrimination, 'you've really left me in it.' Piggy in the middle.

Tommy Lyster seemed to be asleep. Slumped in the front passenger seat of his official Mercedes, his heavy chin was folded down on his chest and his hands were clasped comfortingly over his stomach. He was breathing steadily and heavily. But his mind was alert, listening idly to the hum of the engine and noting the steady clicking of the indicator as it cruised past other cars. He was thinking about shares.

He had been intrigued ever since his secretary had told him Mike Erlanger had requested a meeting. It had reminded him of his little investment and he had been agonising ever since over whether or not he should sell. After telling his secretary to put Erlanger into the diary for Monday, he had looked up the stock market listings in an evening paper and grinned at the information that Atlantis shares had gone up another eighteen pence. They were over two pounds now and still rising. Should he sell, he wondered, or hold on till he saw Erlanger? If he sold now he would more than double the thousand pounds he had put into them after his last lunch with the American. Not bad for two weeks' work.

Must visit the auntie this weekend, he thought. Take her a present as thanks. Not that she knew anything about the 1,118 shares in her name in Atlantis Mining. Indeed, she didn't know anything much about anything any more. Her mind had slid back into the past and she worried about what to wear to dances and treated him as a boy. Sometimes she asked him to sing for her as she used to long ago. 'Ah now, Auntie,' he'd say with a wink to the smiling nurses, 'I'd only crack the windows.' The nurses thought his attachment to the senile woman was admirable. There was a guaranteed twenty-seven first-preference votes there for him at every election. Give or take a couple depending on how many of the patients were fit enough to be driven to the polling station on the day.

His mind flicked smoothly to politics and he decided it might do no harm to get a couple of key people around to the house tonight. Get them geared up a little; there was only a year to go to the election anyway. And he'd hold onto the shares until he saw Erlanger. Just as in politics, timing was everything.

The driver grunted to himself and Lyster felt the car slow down. He opened his eyes and looked down the beams of the headlights glistening on a straight and empty stretch of wet road. He glanced at the driver who was concentrating on the rear-view mirror and the flashing blue light coming up fast behind caught the corner of his eye.

'What is it?'

'Some of the boys in a big hurry,' the driver said, dividing his attention between the mirror and the windscreen.

The garda patrol car moved out to overtake, its beacon bathing the inside of the Mercedes in blue light. It drew along-side them and Lyster saw a uniformed figure in the passenger seat signalling to them to pull over.

'Do you recognise him?' the driver asked.

'Me,' Lyster said in surprise. 'Don't you know I only pretend to know every guard in the country?'

The driver indicated left, slowed down gradually and pulled onto the hard shoulder. The patrol car eased in in front of them.

'Would you mind putting on your seat belt please, Minister,' the driver said quietly.

Lyster looked at him in amazement but the driver was watching the patrol car which had come to a halt about twenty feet away. Lyster decided not to argue and fumbled with the belt. A young guard stepped out of the patrol car, putting on his peaked cap. He straightened his tunic as he began to walk towards them.

The driver let up the clutch and the tyres dug into loose stones as he steered the Mercedes back onto the road. He changed gears rapidly and the car was racing into third as they shot past the patrol car. Lyster caught a glimpse of its driver, an older man in uniform, mouthing something from a surprised face, and they were gone. Probably obscenities, he thought and muttered one himself.

'Sorry, Minister.' The driver glanced at him. 'Just being cautious.'

Lyster cursed again and undid the seat belt to twist his bulk and look back. The patrol car, its light still flashing, was just moving onto the road. 'You don't think it's a trap?' he looked startled.

The driver overtook a muddied truck. 'It's probably all right,' he said. 'Just that I didn't recognise either of them.'

'Jesus, you don't know every guard in the country, do you?'

'No, Minister. I think it's all right but I just want to be sure.'

They heard a siren wailing behind them and the driver slowed down to a steady fifty miles an hour and waited for the patrol car to catch up

'Where are we anyway?' Lyster asked.

'A couple of miles from Mullingar.'

The patrol car waited behind them while a line of cars coming from the other direction flashed by. It pulled out and came alongside. The passenger window was open and the young guard was leaning out and shouting something to them but it was impossible to hear through the closed window and the siren. Lyster's driver nodded and pulled into the left and the patrol car stopped behind them and killed the siren in mid-whine. In the silence, the driver slid an Uzi sub-machinegun from under his seat, cocked it with a smooth metallic movement and stepped out. He stood beside the open door with the short gun hanging by his leg.

The young guard came towards them, red-faced, without his cap and a little breathless. 'I have an urgent message for the Minister,' he said and went to walk around to Lyster's side of the car. 'This side,' the driver instructed and stepped out of the way. The guard looked at the short sub-machinegun and shot the driver a hostile glare.

'A message for you, Minister.' He leaned through the opened door. 'You're to call that number in Dublin as soon as possible.'

Lyster glanced at a piece of paper and recognised the number of a direct line on his Ministerial desk. 'Thanks, guard,' he said. 'Could we use a phone in Mullingar station?'

'Certainly, sir. We'll direct you in there.'

Lyster nodded and the guard straightened up and was about to say something to the driver but changed his mind. 'Fucking cowboys,' he muttered audibly as he walked away. The driver tucked his gun away, got in and waited for the patrol car to lead the way.

'You've just scared the shite out of me,' Lyster said.

'Sorry, Minister,' the driver repeated. 'It'd be worse if I'd lost you.'

Lyster patted him on the shoulder. 'Not much fear of that,' he chortled. 'Who'd want to kidnap me? Even worse, who'd pay a ransom for me?'

'You can't be too careful these days.'

The station sergeant showed Lyster into the superintendent's office in Mullingar garda station and closed the door behind him. His private secretary answered on the first ring and sounded relieved.

'You're to come back immediately, Minister,' he said.

'What's up?' Lyster grunted sourly at the thought of his weekend being upset.

'The, ah, head man wants you back here for the weekend.'

'Why?'

'This is not a secure line, Minister,' the secretary reminded him primly. 'I don't think we should discuss it.'

'Has there been a jail breakout or what?' Lyster insisted irritably.

'No, Minister. It's more a question of, ah, political problems. You are required at a high-level meeting this evening.'

Lyster replaced the receiver and glowered at it like a thwarted child. Four days in Dublin was enough for anyone in one week. It couldn't be the Clark case, he decided – that was all settled. Probably Whelan and his friends playing with their consciences again. That wouldn't take long to sort out. Lyster picked up the phone with resignation, dialled his home and told his wife to call together a couple of people who he named and put them on stand-by. Just in case.

'What's happening?'

'I'll call you later when I find out,' he promised.

Outside the building, the two uniformed policemen were talking to his driver through the open car window and he could hear the anger in their voices. They fell silent and straightened up as he approached and got into the car.

'Back to town,' he told the driver. 'Some eejit thinks there's a crisis.'

Sixteen

'Don't take your coat off,' Stacy shouted across the news room as Ryle entered, 'unless you've got a shit-hot story to write.'

The news editor looked like an overweight pop star who had just escaped from over-enthusiastic fans: his hair fell over one eye, one side of his shirt had come adrift from his trousers and he was whirling around with manic energy. A sub-editor grabbed Stacy's arm and forced his attention onto a strip of drooping copy-paper. He smoothed it out on the desk and both of them pored over it. Ryle asked a passing reporter what was up.

'No confidence motion in the Government.' The reporter shrugged his lack of interest.

'Right.' Stacy whirled back to him. 'Get up to Leinster House and get any politicians you can find. We need quotes.'

'I told you I don't want to get involved in any of that,' Ryle protested. He had just spent a frustrating hour trying to find Sergeant Peter Grifford but he was not in any of his usual haunts. He needed to talk to him more than ever since Burke's revelation about the documents.

'You *are* involved,' Stacy snapped. 'This is a major story. The government may fall next week. We've a paper to get out.'

Ryle glanced at the news-room clock which showed 7.20. 'There'll be nobody around. The Dáil finished early today, didn't it?'

'Don't argue,' Stacy shouted. 'I want government deputies particularly. Quotes about the neutrality issue. That's the key to it. But anyone will do. I need volume.'

The news-desk phone rang and Stacy picked it up. He pointed Ryle towards the political correspondent who was huddled over another phone, gesticulating with the pen in his free hand. He slid Ryle a handwritten list of government back-benchers. 'But how can you maintain that when we all know

. . .' he said into the phone and underlined Jim Whelan's name on the list. Ryle nodded and his colleague gave him a thumbs up sign.

'And don't disappear,' Stacy called after him as he left. 'Call me every half hour. And I mean that. This is a major story.'

The streets were empty in the lull between the evening rush-hour to the suburbs and the start of the city's night life. Leinster House looked deserted as Ryle walked up Molesworth Street: its large gate was barred shut and the top half of the building was in darkness. Ryle walked in a side gate and an usher opened the door of the reception kiosk to scrutinise his press pass.

'You know the Dáil's up for the week,' he reminded Ryle who didn't need any reminding. There was no arguing with Stacy when he was in one of those frenzies and, besides, there was nothing much he could do until he talked to Grifford about Erlanger.

He crossed the almost empty car park to the main door and stood aside as an Opposition deputy, looking flushed and slightly manic, struggled by him with two large brown boxes. 'Be prepared,' he winked at Ryle over the top of his hoard of postage-paid envelopes.

The central corridor was empty and the top of the stairway leading to the curtained entrance to the Dáil chamber was in darkness. Ryle continued on to the member's restaurant and looked through the glass panel in its door. Most of the lights were off and there was nobody there. He turned back and looked along the side of Government Buildings where ministerial cars parked. The narrow roadway was deserted.

He retraced his steps to the public bar where three small groups were ensconced with the air of travellers on a long and tedious voyage. They all looked up at him as if they had no idea how he had got there. He recognised a reporter from another paper perched at the bar alongside a heavy-set government backbencher and went over beside them. He ordered a glass of Guinness.

'We're just closing,' the barman said.

'At this hour?'

'Ah, give him a drink,' the backbencher ordered in a tone that did not allow for any argument. The barman disappeared behind the partition that cut them off from the members' bar. 'Must be thirsty work, this writing business,' the backbencher said and lifted his pint of beer. Ryle noted the glass of whiskey untouched beside it and smiled at him.

'Very quiet around here this evening,' he replied.

'They've all gone to the country,' the other reporter said and chortled at his double meaning.

'Balls,' the backbencher exclaimed. 'They'll be back next week and the week after and the week after that again. Mark my words, there'll be no election, not for a year at the earliest. And then we'll be back, stronger than ever.'

'Can I quote you on that?' Ryle pulled out a notebook.

'If you want a quote I'll give you a quote.' He replaced the beer with the whiskey and scraped his few strands of hair across his bald head as if he were about to be interviewed for television. 'The people will not stand for this kind of tomfoolery with all the serious problems that are facing the country at this critical juncture in our nation's affairs. The wasting of parliamentary time on a totally irresponsible and pointless exercise is a scandal that shows up what some people think of the taxpayers' money. It's a travesty, a waste of time that could be put to better use for the people of this country.'

Ryle suppressed a tired smile as he wrote. 'Are you going to win it?'

'Of course we're going to win it,' the backbencher's voice rose. 'Haven't we got a two-seat majority? It's a foregone conclusion. A disgraceful waste of time.'

'But what do you think of the neutrality issue?'

'What issue? There's no issue about neutrality or anything else. The party is totally united.' The backbencher drained the whiskey and went back to the beer.

'If you had an air for that you could sing it,' the other reporter muttered. The backbencher gave him a squint-eyed look.

'A lot of your people were worried about it yesterday,' Ryle pointed out. 'You spent a long time discussing it.'

'Why are you fellas always looking for splits?' The backbencher looked at Ryle as if he had a worrying disease. 'There is no split in this party. Over neutrality or anything else. And you'll see that next week if those eejits persist with this non-sense.' He finished his beer and signalled to the barman for another round. 'Anyway, it won't come to a vote at all. Wait and you'll see, they'll withdraw it after the weekend. When the people let them know what they think of their carry-on.'

Ryle excused himself, turning down the backbencher's offer of a drink, and left the bar. 'Who's that long string of shite anyway?' the backbencher asked the other reporter.

Ryle toured the deserted corridors again and settled into a phone box marked 'deputies only'. 'There's nobody around,' he told Stacy. 'Only one backbench nonentity, spouting the usual crap.'

'Put it onto copy,' Stacy replied. 'And call out to Whelan.'

'But I've got some other calls to make,' Ryle moaned. 'Can't you get someone else?'

'No.'

'He's not going to say anything.'

'He's a friend of yours, isn't he?'

'He's still not going to say anything.'

'You don't know that till you ask him. We can't get him on the phone, it's engaged all the time. And call me back in half an hour.' Stacy hung up without putting him through to the copytakers. Ryle cursed him and failed to find the right change for another call. He cursed again with feeling and went up to the empty press gallery to find a direct-dial phone.

Mike Erlanger gazed at his own reflection in the dark of the living-room window as he waited for his call to be put through. 'Mike, how the hell've you been?' The voice boomed over the Atlantic, scarcely subdued by some distant static on the connection.

'Pretty good, Mac.' Erlanger smiled. 'You and your family?'

'Fine, fine. This is extraordinary. Martha and I were talking about you only last night.'

'Yeah?'

'Did you get our Christmas card?'

'No, we've moved.'

'Where the hell are you?'

'Ireland.'

'Ireland?' Mac's voice rose a pitch. 'On vacation again?'

'No such luck. I'm in business over here.'

'Breeding leprechauns?' Mac wheezed at his own wit.

'Not quite, Mac. So what've you been up to?'

'This is extraordinary,' Mac repeated. 'Only last night we were talking about you and the lovely Becky and that time in Florida. Best damn vacation we ever had.'

Erlanger smiled at the memory of Mac spilling over the waistband of his Bermudas and bouncing about with the wide-eyed enthusiasm of a five-year-old at every new sight and sound. They had met casually in a casino and Erlanger had been infected with his exuberance: the two couples had been inseparable for the rest of the holiday.

'We're thinking about flying down there again in a week or two,' Mac was saying. 'It's been some winter here, blizzards every other day, snow up to everywhere. Guess you've seen it on TV. The death toll's up to twenty-eight.'

'They don't get much of that kind of news here.'

'Got their own troubles, right?' Mac sounded understanding. 'Anyway, there we were talking about you last night, reliving the holiday and wondering how you guys were and whatnot and then this morning these two guys turn up at the plant here asking about you.'

Erlanger inhaled sharply as Mac innocently hit on the purpose of his call. He concentrated harder as the volume on the line rose and fell as though it was rolling over the ocean. 'Who were they?'

'Said they were FBI.'

'What?'

'You're not in some kind of trouble, are you, Mike?' Mac wheezed uncertainty.

'No,' Erlanger chuckled with confidence. 'Of course not.'

'Thought for a minute you'd fled the country.'

'What did they want, Mac?' Erlanger shut his eyes to try and catch every nuance.

'Wanted to know how we met, how well I knew you, if we

had any business dealings. I told them about Florida. That's all there is to tell.' Mac paused. 'What's it all about, Mike?'

Erlanger caught the undercurrent of suspicion in his voice. 'Nothing much, Mac,' he laughed. 'Trying to put a bit of business your way, that's all. I did some soft-sell on your surveillance equipment to some government contacts here. They were probably checking out that I did know you.'

'They didn't offer to buy anything.' Mac joked, but his relief was unmistakable. 'Don't mind telling you I was a little concerned.'

'Did you know them?'

'Not these two. They were low-level operatives. But you know how it is with this business. I can't afford to get on the wrong side. I've got to answer their questions.'

'Sure, Mac. You did the right thing.'

'Hey, if I get an order I'll put you down for a sale.'

After he put the phone down Erlanger stood facing the window for a while and drew a circle in the condensation. He rubbed it clean and his reflection came up again, more blurred than when he had begun the conversation.

Ryle heard chimes tinkle inside the house and huddled against the door from the heavy mist gusting down through the street lights. Maura opened the door and made no effort to conceal her antagonism. 'He's not here,' she snapped.

'When will he be back?' Behind her Ryle could see a telephone handset resting beside its cradle on the hall table.

'I have no idea.' She began to close the door.

'Would you tell him I called?'

She had the door almost shut when Whelan's voice said from inside, 'It's all right.' She stamped away from the open door and passed Whelan standing at the entrance to the front room. 'Answer it yourself next time,' she said as she disappeared into the back of the house.

Ryle muttered an apology as he followed Whelan into the room.

'She thinks it's all your fault,' Whelan explained. He was wearing a worn pullover and jeans and seemed surprisingly relaxed. 'And she's probably right.'

'I'm only the messenger,' Ryle muttered awkwardly. 'And I didn't make you go on radio and give that interview.'

Whelan shrugged and took Ryle's coat out to the hallway. The room was warm and Ryle felt his nose clog up. The television was on with the sound turned down and he stared at the pictures of dramatised faces confronting each other. Whelan motioned him to sit down on the couch and retrieved a half glass of whiskey from the floor by his armchair.

'That interview's not the problem,' Whelan said as he went to the sideboard, poured Ryle a whiskey and topped up his own. 'The problem is that I believe what I said.'

Ryle took the whiskey and asked if he wanted to say anything about the confidence motion and how he would vote.

'I'd like to but I can't.' Whelan settled back into his chair. 'The whips have ordered me not to talk to the press.'

'What would you say if you weren't muzzled?'

'Piss off.' Whelan grimaced at him. 'That's it in a nutshell.'

'You're not going to break ranks then?'

Whelan looked at the television which was showing an ad man's idea of a housewife dancing vigorously with a bottle of cleaning fluid. It was followed by a souped-up car speeding through a desert and Ryle wondered why Whelan had invited him into the house. The ads switched to a perfectly photographed pint of frothing beer.

'Do you enjoy what you're doing?' Whelan asked suddenly.

'What do you mean?'

'That's what I mean. Spending your life asking questions.'

'It beats trying to provide answers,' Ryle said glibly and sipped the undiluted whiskey.

'Yes.' Whelan nodded as though he had said something profound. 'I suppose it does.'

They watched the television drama unfold silently for a few moments. 'You are going to break ranks, then.' Ryle turned his question into a statement, confused by Whelan's responses.

'I don't know,' Whelan sighed. 'This is not just off the record. It's way off the record. Not even "it is understood" stuff.' Ryle nodded. 'The merest hint that I've disobeyed the whips and I've had it. They're only looking for any excuse to make an example of me.' Ryle nodded again. 'I don't know what I'm going to do,' Whelan concluded.

'That sounds serious.'

'It's a serious situation,' Whelan said. 'They have put the word out to the Americans that they are interested in a trade-off on unity.'

'Has the Taoiseach admitted that?'

'Not in so many words.' Whelan gulped down a mouthful of whiskey and gave a bleak smile. 'I've got my own sources. It's correct. I've no doubts about that now. None at all. You were right.'

'But what did he tell the party meeting?'

'Very little. Much the same as he said in the Dáil. Times change. It's a pragmatic matter, not a principle. That sort of thing.'

'Could the Government fall over it?'

Whelan shrugged and got up to get the Jameson bottle. 'There are less than half a dozen strongly opposed but at least as many more unhappy. God knows how many will hold out if the going gets rough.'

Whelan filled up their glasses again while Ryle looked at the whiskey nervously, beginning to feel light-headed again. 'Do you think Maurice Clark knew about this plan?' he asked.

'On balance, I don't think so,' Whelan tossed back a large quantity of whiskey. 'That document of yours was a forgery. I'm sure of that too. I'd have got a whiff of it from Maurice if he had known.'

'It's an extraordinary coincidence that he had something like that if he didn't know.'

'I know. I've been trying to work it out but I can't. Unless somebody was playing a very complicated game. But we could speculate about that all night.'

'Like what?' Ryle debated telling him about Erlanger but decided not to. He wanted to be the first to get to him. And not to cock it up this time.

'Like someone wanted it out in the open. To scupper the idea. Or to test the Government's commitment, maybe.'

'I could imagine the British not being wildly enthusiastic,'

Ryle agreed. 'American pressure to do something about unity to get us into NATO would put them in an awkward position.'

'There are endless scenarios like that.' Whelan offered to pour some more whiskey into Ryle's glass but he declined. He couldn't keep up with Whelan's pace. 'It's a waste of time talking about them, though. One of the first lessons I learned in politics. Don't waste energy speculating about maybes. It's shovelling water with a fork.'

He turned up the television's volume as the news came on. The main item was the Opposition motion of no confidence and a brief interview with the Opposition Leader saying that neutrality was too important an issue to be left vague and uncertain and that that was the main reason for his party's action. A Government spokesman said the Cabinet had been having a routine meeting but had not bothered discussing this development. 'Hah.' Ryle snorted his disbelief.

A political correspondent summarised the controversy and concluded that the outcome hinged on a handful of Government backbenchers. Photographs of Whelan and several others flashed up behind his left shoulder as he listed those who were known to be worried about the Government's handling of the issue.

'Great,' Whelan muttered. 'That's just what we need. A proper hit-list.'

'How're you going to make your mind up?' Ryle asked.

'Look into my heart, I suppose.' Whelan quoted a former statesman but without conviction. The bulletin moved to South Armagh where a reporter stood in front of a stretch of white tape across a country lane. In the distance behind him flak-jacketed figures wandered around a jagged hole in the shiny road.

'The fact that I've been misled once already doesn't make it any easier,' Whelan went on. 'After I went on radio about your story I got a congratulatory message from the Taoiseach. Indirectly. And then he went into the Dáil and turned it all on its head.'

'Do you feel strongly enough about neutrality to bring down the Government, though?' Ryle persisted.

'That's all you want to know,' Whelan sighed, 'because that's the story, isn't it? You don't care whether it's about neutrality or headage payments for farmers.' He nodded towards the screen where a farmers' representative looked outraged and sounded aggrieved at the latest alleged assault on their living standards. 'I don't want to bring down the government. I want to protect neutrality.'

The front door chimed and they fell silent, waiting to hear if Maura would answer. After a long pause, she made her way up the hall and they listened to the rumble of a male voice. Whelan kept his eyes fixed on the television while his ears tried to pick up a clue to the caller's identity. The door closed and Maura came in and tossed a long brown envelope into his lap.

'You're being summoned to an emergency meeting of the constituency executive tomorrow night,' she said. She left without looking at Ryle.

Whelan scrutinised his name written with a felt pen on the envelope as if he hoped to find it was addressed to someone else. He tore it open, read the single sheet and handed it over to Ryle. It was blunt and to the point, a single paragraph saying Whelan's presence was required at a special meeting to discuss the present political situation.

'Not requested.' Whelan shook his head. 'Required. Would you say that's going to be a calm discussion about the pros and cons of neutrality?'

'They'll want to know if you're going to bring down the government.'

Whelan nodded a grudging half-agreement. 'It'll be a question of whether or not I will honour my pledge to support the party. Which amounts to the same thing. And half of them will be hoping I won't because they'd like to take over my seat.'

'Will you oblige them?'

Whelan gave a weary laugh. 'The answer is still the same. No matter how many ways you ask the question.'

'It's one of those issues that always come back to the same question,' Ryle said. 'No matter how you try to evade it.'

Whelan shrugged. 'What would you do?'

Ryle finished his second drink. 'It'd depend on how strongly

I felt about neutrality. If I felt it was a major issue, I'd vote against the government if it was selling it out.'

'How many "ifs" is that?' Whelan leaned forward, warming to his theme. 'Suppose you were told privately that they didn't really intend to do anything but were just pretending to for diplomatic reasons.'

'Have they told you that?'

'Don't mind what they've told me,' Whelan said. 'I'm asking the questions.'

'Obviously it would depend whether I believed them.'

'So you wouldn't mind them playing diplomatic games with an issue which you thought was of fundamental importance.'

'I wouldn't like it but it would be different to an actual change of policy.'

Whelan nodded. 'So you say, okay, that's all right with me. And then suppose the game became serious halfway through. Where would you be if you had accepted the early stages on the grounds that they were just a manoeuvre?'

'High and dry.'

'Up shit creek.' Whelan settled back again and they lapsed into silence. There was no easy way out, Whelan thought. I've well and truly snookered myself on this one. The prospect of being a simple ordinary backbencher, towing the party line and looking after mundane constituency concerns, seemed like an attractive idea. A typical piece of rose-coloured nostalgia. He had been there and hadn't much liked it. And it was too late to go back now. He'd wanted to get into the big league and he sure as shit had.

'Who was it liked to say you can't get the toothpaste back into the tube?' he asked Ryle suddenly.

Ryle thought a moment. 'Richard Nixon, I think.'

Whelan let out a sardonic laugh and poured another round of whiskeys and they watched a weatherman point out a high-pressure front coming in from the Atlantic. The weekend would be bright but very cold, he summed up his charts. 'Hot and sticky, more likely,' Whelan mumbled.

'All that hypothetical stuff,' Ryle said. 'It's not hypothetical at all, is it?'

'It is and it isn't. It hasn't been put to me yet but I won't be surprised to hear it over the next few days.'

'And how will you respond?'

'It's all irrelevant.' Whelan threw his hands in the air, almost spilling the remains of his whiskey. 'The real question for politicians is always the same. Not whether to bring down the Government, as you think. But whether to bow before principle or the party. A question of which pressure you give in to.'

'What you need,' Ryle suggested, 'is a principled party compromise.'

Whelan laughed lightly. 'Have you ever felt like resigning over a principle?'

'A principle? In newspapers?'

'Yes. Haven't you ever had qualms of conscience about the editorial line on something?'

Ryle looked at him closely to see if his leg was being pulled but Whelan appeared to be serious. Or at least interested. 'No one takes editorials seriously,' he protested. 'You'd tie your brain in knots if you tried to work out a consistent line in anyone's editorials.'

'I wonder sometimes if you can really be as cynical as you seem.' Whelan's eyes were beginning to look glazed and Ryle realised he was drunk.

'It's hard work. But don't tell me that politics in this country isn't the ultimate in cynicism. The rest of us are only trotting after it.'

'It's not cynical really.' Whelan thought for a moment. 'It's just pragmatic. It's easy to mistake one for the other sometimes.'

'But you're going to change all that next week,' Ryle prompted delicately. 'By making a principled stand.'

'And earn the praise of editorial writers,' Whelan added. 'They love people of principle, don't they?'

'As long as they're not journalists. And then, preferably, when they're dead.' Ryle paused. 'Like Maurice Clark.'

Yes, Whelan sighed inwardly, we love martyrs in this country. But Maurice was no martyr. Or was he? Either way, he was no use as a model any more: he'd never have got himself into this bind.

He turned off the television, poured the remainder of the whiskey into Ryle's glass and went back to the sideboard for a fresh bottle. 'Well, I hope you've got it ready,' he said with his back to Ryle. 'My obituary.'

The group of ministers came down the steps from the Taoiseach's house like company executives emerging replete from a productive lunch. They spread out to their official cars and Tommy Lyster got into his Mercedes with a satisfied grunt. 'The hotel,' he told the driver as the fleet of cars swept by the impassive policeman at the gate and into the quiet suburban streets.

'Did you get a bite to eat?' he asked solicitously.

'Yes, Minister.'

Lyster nodded. 'Great things are happening in our times,' he sighed, like a happy refrain. He rubbed his hands, feeling the warmth of the Taoiseach's brandy and fireside and the more satisfying warmth of being part of the inner circle. The Minister for Justice was going to have a pain in his crabby gut when he returned from his foreign travels, he thought. Do his ulcer no end of harm.

Things were going wonderfully. He was cruising along on the inside track, with a job of major national importance to do. The Taoiseach had made no bones about that, in front of all the others. They were all counting on him. And he knew he could do it, no trouble. Fellas like Whelan and the rest had no real stomach for this stuff.

Lyster drifted into a little reverie about his future prospects but cut it short as a more practical thought struck him.

'D'you know a fella called Peter Grifford?' he asked.

'A D. sergeant in the city,' the driver nodded.

'What sort of a lad is he?'

'I don't know him personally,' the driver said cautiously. 'Only by repute. He's a good detective.'

Lyster noticed his tone and grunted. He lapsed back into his reverie, slotting himself into the stock picture of the next cabinet receiving their seals of office from the President.

*   *   *

Ryle drove back into the city with the exaggerated care of somebody who knows he is drunk. He passed the airport on his right and had difficulty pulling his attention back from its circling beacon. It was almost midnight and the rain had stopped but dull clouds squatted low over the yellow lights of the city like tomorrow's hangover.

The news room was empty but for a scattering of sub-editors and, to Ryle's surprise, Stacy. The news editor had calmed down and sat at his desk surrounded by overflowing waste-paper bins. The tip of the spike by his side was barely visible above its load of discarded documents. The air was heavy with heat and over-use and made Ryle drowsy. He yawned.

'Every half hour, I said.' Stacy glared at him.

'Where were you when I called?' Ryle shot back.

To his surprise his bluff worked and Stacy altered direction. 'What's he going to do?' he demanded.

'I don't know.'

'You spent all night getting pissed with him and you don't know.'

'I don't know,' Ryle repeated.

Stacy closed his eyes, surrendering to the difficulties of a hard-pressed news editor. 'May I ask what you've spent the last four hours discussing.'

'The usual.' Ryle giggled and sat down at his desk. 'The meaning of life. Angels on the heads of pins. That sort of thing.'

Stacy nodded as if that explained everything. 'I don't suppose you got around to actually asking him about his voting intentions.'

'He doesn't know.' Ryle picked up a phone and began dialling.

'Ah.' Stacy perked up and looked at the late-night reporter who was watching the exchange with a happy smile. 'So we do have a story, after all.'

Ryle stopped in mid-dial. 'Off the record,' he said.

'Balls,' Stacy countered and turned to the night reporter. 'We'll slip a par into the city edition.'

'No, you won't,' Ryle shook his head and felt dizzy. 'He wouldn't say anything.'

'Okay. We'll say he wouldn't comment but he is believed to be undecided.'

'We can't say that.' Ryle broke the phone connection with one finger. 'That was off the record. Off off the record.'

'The hell with that,' Stacy retorted, flicking his hair off his forehead like an animal whipping away an irritating fly. 'We're not going to quote him.'

'I told you it was off the record. Totally.'

'Then why did he tell you? You are a reporter, aren't you?'

'He told me as a friend.'

'A friend?'

'Yes. That's why you sent me out to him, wasn't it?'

'I sent you out there to get a fucking story.'

'Yes, but he only talked to me as a friend.'

'Reporters don't have friends,' Stacy snarled. 'Your job is not to satisfy your own curiosity.'

Ryle shook his head but the argument was cut short by a sub-editor who burst through the door with an armful of first editions. He tossed a couple onto the news desk on his way to his own desk where his colleagues gathered around and began dissecting the papers. Stacy glanced down the front page and tapped the lead story. 'A quote from Whelan would make all the difference.'

'Not possible,' Ryle said, dialling again. 'Really, it isn't. Seriously.'

Stacy grunted and the ringing in Ryle's ear was cut short by a curt voice. 'How's my back?' Ryle asked.

'Who is this?' Grifford demanded.

'Me.'

'You must have a wrong number.'

Ryle struggled with his befuddled brain to sort out what game Grifford was playing. He decided to go along with it and identified himself formally, naming the paper as well.

'Before you go any farther,' Grifford cut in coldly. 'I cannot help you. If you are seeking information about police matters you should contact the garda press office.'

'It's closed,' Ryle said feebly.

'It will be open in the morning.'

Ryle put down the phone and cursed his stupidity aloud. Stacy looked up and smirked: 'Still in the dog house?'

How could he have been such a drunken fool? Ryle cringed inwardly. Copies of the early editions of the other dailies were dropped onto the news desk and Ryle joined Stacy to examine them. He felt coldly sober and wanted to forget his own stupidity.

'They don't have anything we haven't,' Ryle said.

'But we have something they haven't. If you'd write it.'

'It would really screw me up,' Ryle pleaded. He didn't want to throw away his relationship with Whelan. Not just after he'd alienated Grifford and got the Provos all excited over something he knew nothing about. 'It's a non-story. If you let this one go I'll get Whelan's decision first. As soon as he makes it.'

'I'll hold you to that,' Stacy threatened and folded a copy of their own paper under his arm. 'And you'd better stop treating this whole story like it's your own personal property. Created for your amusement or something.'

'Okay, okay.' Ryle nodded absently. It seemed a long time since he'd been the hero of the news room for breaking the story. It was a long time, forty-eight hours or so. But he was much more worried about Grifford's attitude than Stacy turning nasty. Grifford was his best chance of wrapping up this whole story and, besides, he might need him for some protection if the goddam IRA decided he knew something he shouldn't.

He left the office and glanced nervously around the deserted street as he got to his car. Suddenly he felt very vulnerable.

Seventeen

Ryle left his bedsitter in a hurry and stopped at the first public phone he saw. He took a deep breath, dialled the number carefully, pressed a button and the coins tumbled into the box. 'Can you talk?' he asked.

'No.' Grifford hung up.

Fuck, Ryle said aloud stepping out of the kiosk and dodging across the road to his car. Had Grifford really gone sour on him, he wondered. Or was he just being cautious? No leak inquiry could be that serious. It had to be something else.

He drove on into the city centre with one eye on his rear-view mirror. No one seemed to follow but it was difficult to tell with the constantly shifting traffic. Impossible to know, if they were using more than one car. He told himself he was being para-noid. And then he told himself again that just because you're paranoid doesn't mean they're not out to get you.

The features editor caught his eye and moved towards him as he walked into the news room. Ryle changed direction rapidly, crossed the room, went out another door and into the men's toilet. At least she can't follow me in here, he thought.

The door crashed behind him again and Stacy stood in the opening. 'Somebody thinks you're trying to avoid her,' he chortled.

Ryle positioned himself before the urinal and grunted.

'She's looking for copy,' Stacy added.

'I can't do it now.'

'Can't you throw something together?' Stacy let the door swing shut.

Ryle shook his head and went over to a washbasin and ran some water. 'I haven't got time. The Clark story's taken a new turn.'

'What?'

'I've found out where Clark got the forged documents. From

an American businessman.' The news editor looked unin-terested. 'And there's something up. All my sources have gone to ground suddenly.'

'But what are you going to do about this?' Stacy held out a sheet of paper. 'The blurb for tomorrow's paper.'

Ryle read it with a sinking feeling. It was headed 'Faith of the Fathers' and announced a major three-part investigation next week into young people's attitudes towards the religion of their forebears. Ryle rubbed his hands dry and scratched his head. It felt painful but last night's dose of whiskey seemed to have killed his incipient cold. At least, he couldn't feel it any more.

'You explain to her,' he pleaded. 'There's nothing I can do.'

'There's a radio ad going with it,' Stacy added.

'You know I've been tied up round the clock on the Clark story,' Ryle said with growing desperation.

Stacy cast his eyes upwards. 'Bloody features.' He turned towards the door and looked back at Ryle. 'Are you going to hide in here all day?'

Ryle emerged a few minutes later and checked the news room. The features editor had gone. 'She's in with the editor,' Stacy said. 'To complain about you. And the guards have been asking him about you too.'

'Shit.'

'They want to interview you. And they want the originals of the Clark material.'

They'd probably questioned Grifford too, Ryle decided. Be-cause he, Ryle, had told Inspector Devane that Grifford was involved. And that would explain why Grifford was cutting him dead. That was it. That must be it. He shut his eyes and tried to remember if he had warned Grifford about his spur of the moment visit to Devane.

'Don't worry,' Stacy reassured him, mistaking his concerns. 'He's agreed to see them on Monday morning. With you.'

'We can't tell them anything.'

'Talk to the lawyer,' Stacy suggested. 'Decide with him what you're going to do.'

'He'll say we have to co-operate,' Ryle groaned. 'We can't give them the documents. It's a matter of principle.'

Stacy gave him a withering look. 'I don't think you should start tossing principles about right now.'

Ryle had a sudden surge of fellow-feeling with Whelan. The features editor came out of the editor's office and walked by without a glance. They watched her go.

'We have no choice about it.' Ryle frowned with determination. 'We can't reveal our sources.'

Stacy opened a drawer and tossed a large envelope onto the desk. 'Then you'd better find a safer place for them.'

Ryle looked at the envelope as if it was a booby trap. Everything seemed to be rebounding on him, tying him up in tighter and tighter knots. The only way out was to get another story, and quickly, he thought. That'd ease some of these pressures.

'Was that meant to be a joke?' Stacy asked. 'Filing them under "make-up"?'

'Why don't you hold onto them?'

'I don't want them. Put them somewhere safe.' Stacy reached for a ringing phone. 'And I don't want to know where.'

Ryle took the envelope back to his desk and phoned Sinn Fein again but Billy wasn't there, so he merely left his name. Erlanger was the only angle open to him. Stacy passed by and threw the word 'Whelan' at him. Ryle nodded absently and drew boxes around Erlanger's name on a sheet of paper as he tried to work out the best approach. Ideally, he should talk to Grifford beforehand but that obviously wasn't an option.

Maybe finance could give him some more background, he thought, and went into their office. A reporter looked up from a glossy company balance sheet which he was studying with the sceptical look of someone examining a discarded bookmaker's ticket.

'Can you tell me anything about Mike Erlanger?' Ryle asked.

'Ah.' The reporter brightened up as if he had been told his horse had won after all. 'Atlantis Mining. Every speculator's favourite American. Why?'

'I hear he's been secretly selling off his own shares.'

'Wouldn't surprise me in the least.'

'I thought there was some rule against that?'

'Insider dealing?' The reporter shook his head. 'Not in this country. That's why it wouldn't surprise me. Behind all the blarney, people like Erlanger love us for our lax ways. No controls on uranium mining, no powerful environmental lobby, no controls on insider deals. All that and government grants as well.'

'Is it worth a story?'

'Sure. If you can stand it up.'

'He's selling off shares held by nominees.'

'You can't stand it up.' The reporter stated a fact. He got up, went to another desk and rummaged through some papers. He held out a letter to Ryle. 'Looks like there's something stirring in the Atlantis woodwork though.'

The letter was headed 'Press Release' but carried no address, name or signature. It was dated two days earlier and said that a number of shareholders in Atlantis Mining were collecting the requisite number of signatures to demand an extraordinary general meeting because they were being kept in the dark about important developments. The people organising the petition were forced to remain anonymous for the present, it concluded, without explanation.

Ryle looked up inquiringly and the financial reporter shrugged. 'Could be anything. More likely a crank than a takeover bid, though.'

The word jolted Ryle who had automatically assumed the letter was James Burke's doing. Was Burke a crank, he asked himself. Not in the usual sense of the loonies who besieged newspaper offices. But he probably came within the bounds of any definition because of his obsession with Erlanger.

'Tell me more about Erlanger,' Ryle urged.

The Chief Superintendent glanced up from his soup, expecting to be contradicted. 'I really do envy you sometimes,' he repeated.

Inspector Bill Devane broke open a bread roll and recognised two other policemen in a conspiratorial huddle over a corner table. This place might as well be a canteen, he thought.

'I'm serious,' the Chief added as though Devane's silence was a challenge. He had taken the Inspector by surprise, suggesting lunch and swamping Devane's suspicion with his own determined cheeriness as they crossed Dame Street, went down a lane and emerged in Essex Street at the fortress-like rear of the Clarence Hotel. Devane still did not know what to make of this burst of forced friendliness.

'You get a change of scenery every day,' the Chief was saying. 'All I ever see is home and the office. Back and forth, like a ping pong ball. And read about what you lads are up to.'

'And what interesting people we meet.' Devane could not resist the temptation.

The Chief ignored or did not notice his tone. 'I do miss it, more than I expected. It's nice to be able to sink your teeth into a case, pursue it from beginning to end, have the satisfaction of a job well done. Instead of dealing with dozens of cases on paper only. But time marches on and we have to change. If we don't go forward we go backwards. We can't stand still for ever.'

Subtlety was not among the Chief's strengths, Devane reminded himself. Least of all when he thought he was being subtle. He waited for him to get to the point.

'You know, when I was a young lad,' the Chief continued his determined discourse, 'playing football was my whole life. I thought there'd be no point to living once I was too old to tog out any more. Seriously. It's a long time now since I've been on a football pitch.' He finished his soup and leaned back. 'Have you ever thought about promotion?'

'Promotion?' Devane looked up suspiciously. Was this the Chief's idea of a sick joke?

'Becoming a superintendent.' The Chief smiled a benefactor's smile. 'More money, responsibility. Being tied to a desk, perhaps. Like me.'

'It's not a very practicable ambition.'

'Why not? You're well qualified. And you're getting a bit long in the tooth for playing football.' The Chief laughed at his own analogy.

Devane gave him a slow smile. 'Do you want me to list the reasons? One, you think I've cocked up the Clark case. Two, no government's going to promote someone who's upset its members. Three . . . '

'Governments change,' the Chief interrupted with a dismissive shrug.

They fell silent as a waitress cleared away the bowls and put down their main courses. Devane stared at the plate as if it might contain some clue to what this was all about.

'I'm beginning to think your friend Peter Grifford has the right idea,' he said. 'Early retirement. Get out while you can still change direction. While there's still some life left.' He helped himself to some mushy cabbage and sliced carrots and passed the dish to the Chief. 'The children are nearly all done for. The last lad's doing his Leaving this year.'

'That's why I wanted to talk to you,' the Chief said confidentially. 'Away from the office. To tell you not to take this Clark case too personally. Not to do anything you might regret later.'

Now we've got to the point, Devane thought. They're worried I'm going to cause them trouble, upset the latest plan, whatever it is. And maybe they're right. 'Your priorities don't make any sense to me,' he sighed. 'When a few sheets of doubtful paper take precedence over a man's death.'

'They're not my priorities.' The Chief reddened slightly, as if he was making an embarrassing admission. Devane was determined to be difficult. 'Those few sheets, as you call them, happen to relate to a matter of major national importance.'

'Politics,' Devane said with unconcealed derision. 'What crime's involved?'

'I don't want to argue.' The Chief made a final attempt to maintain his good humour but merely sounded like a petulant husband. 'God knows, you have no cause for complaint. I've let you pursue every red herring you've dragged up. And it's got us nowhere. We're as wise now about Clark's death as the day he was pulled out of the water.'

Devane took the blunt statement of his failure with stoicism. 'I still don't see what possible crime's involved in those documents.'

The Chief concentrated on his food.

'And I don't understand why we were ordered to keep away from Erlanger,' Devane added, deciding to get everything out in the open. If he was going to be the fall guy, he wasn't going to go down totally ignorant. Or alone.

242

The Chief studiously wiped his plate clean with a crust of bread and looked at Devane. 'There are things that none of us understands fully,' he sighed. 'And that are none of our business.'

They waited in silence, like an estranged couple with nothing more to say. A waitress cleared the table and brought them two coffees. Three other policemen nodded to them as they left the dining room.

'Is this reporter fellow, Ryle, going to give us trouble?' the Chief asked at last.

'How would I know?'

'You've had some dealings with him.'

'I met him once,' Devane said. 'Why don't you ask Grifford?'

The Chief nodded absently and rubbed his eyes as if the light bothered him. 'Yes,' he said grimly, 'Mr Grifford has a lot of questions to answer. But don't you worry about him. You'd be better employed watching your own step.'

Mike Erlanger lay back in his chair with his eyes closed, his hands in his trouser pockets and his feet on the desk. He gave no sign of hearing the outer door to his office open and the mumble of voices as someone spoke to his secretary. She gave a curt knock on his door and came in.

'Another reporter,' she said. 'A Mr Ryle.'

Erlanger opened his eyes and nodded. He was on his feet and coming around the desk with outstretched hand as Ryle entered. 'Good to see you again,' he beamed. 'Still writing about the exploration?'

Ryle took a seat and shook his head. 'I'm interested in a document about neutrality that Maurice Clark had on him shortly before he died.' He had decided to get straight to the issue; there was no point beating round the bush. He had no choice anyway.

Erlanger looked bemused and said politely, 'I've been reading something about it in your paper, haven't I?' He gestured towards a pile of folded newspapers. 'Something about a back-door attack on Britain.'

'I'm interested in how Clark came by that document. I gather he got it in your home.'

Erlanger leaned back slightly and continued to look expectantly at Ryle. 'Sorry,' he said after a moment. 'Was that a question?'

Ryle nodded. 'I'm told he was given it during the party in your house.'

'I'm not sure I follow this.' Erlanger leaned forward. 'You're saying that someone at my party gave Clark a document of some kind?'

'Not someone.' Ryle watched him closely. 'I've been told that you gave it to him.'

Erlanger looked startled. 'I gave it to him? That's ridiculous. Why would I do something like that?'

'You didn't give it to him?' Another story down the drain, he thought.

'No, of course not.' Erlanger frowned, emphasising his denial with a touch of anger. 'Where would I get something like that? I'm a businessman, not a politician.'

'Clark's widow says you gave it to him,' Ryle suggested. 'After you and he had a private talk in an upstairs room.'

'What?' Erlanger sounded even more incredulous and he shook his head. Ryle said nothing and Erlanger stared at him directly for a moment. 'Now I get it.' He nodded slowly. 'This is Burke's doing. Right?' He sighed. 'Sure it is. Part of his vendetta against me.'

Erlanger stood up. 'He's been trying to undermine my company by sending anonymous letters to shareholders and newspapers. I've been plagued by financial reporters asking about boardroom disputes and extraordinary meetings over the past few days. I even assumed that's what you wanted to talk with me about. But this is something else.'

He paused and pulled open the bottom drawer of his filing cabinet and took out a bottle of Bushmills whiskey. 'You like a drink?' Ryle shook his head.

'I appreciate your coming here and checking this out with me. And I can assure you there's no truth in this crazy story. Absolutely none. In fact, if you'd asked me a week ago if Ireland was in NATO I'd have given you the wrong answer.'

He sat down again and looked at the neat whiskey swirling in his glass. 'The bastard's even got me drinking in the afternoon,' he said to himself and grinned a little sheepishly at Ryle. 'I'm going to have to take some action, some legal action, to stop him harassing me. And now trying to involve me in an Irish political controversy.'

'Why would he want to do that?' Ryle asked.

'You know Burke?' Erlanger said. 'He's a turkey. An incompetent fool.' He sipped the drink and went on. 'When I came to Ireland I hired Burke's firm of auditors on someone's recommendation. He was put in charge of my affairs but I wasn't happy with him and made no secret of that. I asked for and got someone else. I guess he was sore and that's why he's playing dirty tricks now.'

'Why weren't you happy with him?'

'This is background, for your own information only. Right?' Ryle nodded. 'At first I thought he was just a nit-picker. He queried everything and tied us up in endless meetings. He was wasting time and that's been proven since. His colleague who took over is a much more efficient guy, gets the job done without the hassle. Then I found out about Burke's affair with Clark's wife and a couple of pieces fell into place. She and I don't get on and I guess that coloured his attitude.'

'What was between you and Clark's wife? Widow.'

'Nothing. Just one of those things where people rub each other up the wrong way. Figuratively speaking.' Erlanger flashed a bleak smile. 'More to do with the state of their marriage probably. And the fact that Clark and I were friendly. Not buddies or anything, just business acquaintances. But any friend of his seemed to be an enemy of hers.'

'Was it to do with money? Maybe she thought you were taking him into deep financial waters.'

'I wasn't. But you might be right about money. It seemed to be a source of argument between them but I never inquired into their marital problems. Clark was a good politician by all accounts but I wouldn't describe him as a financial wizard.'

'By all accounts he was in deep financial trouble.'

'He wouldn't be if he was alive now,' Erlanger said. 'His shares in Atlantis are worth a tidy sum at the moment.'

'How much?'

'I can't say. But it's common knowledge that they've quadrupled in the last couple of weeks. Which is all to Yvonne's benefit.' Erlanger put the glass down on his desk. 'There must be a lesson somewhere in that. One of life's little ironies.'

He shrugged at Ryle. 'That's the whole story. By way of background, since you took the courtesy of checking with me.'

Tommy Lyster strode into the Dáil restaurant and made straight for the table where Whelan sat alone. 'James,' he said expansively and sat down opposite him without waiting for an invitation. 'Mind if I join you?'

A group of Opposition deputies watched from their table at the other side of the room and smiled knowingly. One of them muttered something and Whelan heard the others laugh. He knew what was coming, too, and in an odd way found himself enjoying this new notoriety. But there were better ways of becoming the focus of attention, he reminded himself.

'Just a cup of tea,' Lyster was telling a waitress. 'I've eaten already.' He smiled pleasantly at Whelan. 'I saw you on the box last night. And all over the papers today. You take a good picture.'

Whelan concentrated on levering the bone from a large sole.

'They say there's no such thing as bad publicity,' Lyster went on, 'but there's an exception to every rule.'

'It wasn't my doing.'

'Of course not,' Lyster said soothingly. 'But that sort of publicity doesn't do a man any good at all. Worse than being caught with your trousers down. Worse even than being caught with your hand in the till.'

Whelan looked up at him sharply.

Lyster gave a worried shake of his head. 'Some people are concerned about that little financial scandal you're involved in.'

'I'm not involved in anything. I told you all about it.'

'I know, I know,' Lyster said sadly. 'But it wouldn't do if it was to hit the papers now. You know how these things stick. Like having a lump of dog shit on your shoe. The smell follows you everywhere.'

Whelan laid his knife and fork down on the half-eaten fish and pushed the plate away. 'I took your advice,' he declared patiently. 'I've withdrawn the motion to have the land re-zoned, sorted out the man who was putting pressure on me. Just like you told me.'

'Sure. The good of the party,' Lyster nodded. 'I'm sure he'll see sense. But he's not altogether convinced that you have the good of the party at heart. He said something about people in glasshouses.'

'You were talking to him?' Whelan couldn't hide his suspicion.

Lyster looked hurt. 'I just happened to run into him. He's not very happy with you, I'm afraid. And he's a man with a long family tradition behind him. Whose opinions have to be listened to.'

The waitress put a pot of tea in front of Lyster and the Minister poured it slowly as if it was the most important thing on his mind.

'I hope you pointed out to him that I only did what I had to do,' Whelan said icily.

Lyster nodded vigorously. 'The good of the party comes before him or me. Or you.' Lyster blew on his tea. 'You should put an end to all this speculation.'

'I'm not allowed to say anything in public.'

Lyster waved aside the instruction. 'A dispensation could be arranged. Like eating meat on Fridays in the old days.'

'Depending on what I wanted to say.'

'What would you want to say?' Lyster looked at him wide-eyed. 'Only that you are supporting the government and that suggestions to the contrary are a despicable attempt to smear you personally and damage the party.'

Whelan gave a bleak grin. 'You have it written out already.'

'You can put your own words on it,' Lyster offered with a return smirk. 'There's no point letting this business run amok and ruining the whole weekend for everybody.'

Whelan looked around the almost empty restaurant and watched a man deliver a stack of evening newspapers to the cash desk. An Opposition deputy at the other end of the room caught his eye and gave him a broad wink. Whelan ignored him.

247

'Why doesn't the Taoiseach just put a stop to it?' He turned back to Lyster eagerly. 'Issue a statement saying there's no truth in any of it and that he stands by neutrality.'

'Because he won't play their game. That's why. He won't dignify their bullshit with a response.'

'Balls.'

'There are important principles at stake here,' Lyster said with an unaccustomed solemnity. 'If he gave in to them on this he'd have to spend all his time issuing denials of every cock and bull story.'

Whelan gave him a sceptical look. 'That's balls too and you know it. All he's got to do is say it's not true and the whole thing is defused. The crisis would evaporate.'

Lyster sighed. 'It saddens me, James,' he said, 'to see you throwing away your future over a well-orchestrated conspiracy to discredit the government. You put out your own statement now and let the Taoiseach look after the nation's affairs. I'll clear it for you with the whips.'

'Have a word with him,' Whelan pleaded. He had no doubt that Lyster's appearance was deliberate and that he was acting as the party bosses' messenger boy. Or hatchet man. 'Tell him he could knock the whole thing on the head with one sentence.'

'He won't be dictated to by the media or the Opposition. He's adamant about that.' Lyster opened his hands to show he was willing but helpless. He turned away and summoned the waitress for his bill. 'Anyhow,' he added, 'there are other things at stake here.'

'What?'

Lyster leaned across the table and dropped his voice. 'You're being used, James, by unscrupulous people who don't have the interests of this country at heart. Anti-national forces.'

Whelan sighed. 'All I know is what I see and hear. And what I've heard from the Taoiseach himself indicates that he's prepared to negotiate neutrality away.'

'I'm not suggesting for a minute that you're party to any conspiracy,' Lyster offered. 'I'm just alerting you to what's going on. So you'll be aware of all the facts.' He looked around to make sure there was no one within eavesdropping distance. 'There's a top-level inquiry going on. Top priority.'

'Into what?'

'The whole situation,' Lyster said vaguely, like a man who had already disclosed too much. 'It's very suspicious.'

Whelan knew it would be a waste of time questioning him further. Lyster had run through the whole gamut of friendly concern, political threats and hints of dark manoeuvres. What more can they throw at me, he wondered.

'I still think the best course is for the Taoiseach to end the speculation himself,' he said.

'That's not an option.' Lyster shrugged and stood up. He paused and gave Whelan a pensive smile, as if he was saying goodbye to someone who was emigrating for good. 'Look after yourself, James.'

Ryle stopped and stared at the dark-coloured Renault van with its back windows blacked out. 'You want me to get into the back of that?'

Billy interrupted his studious concentration on the driver's door and looked up. 'What's up with you? Back or front, get in wherever you want.'

'I thought ... ' Ryle began and thought better of it. He waited until the Sinn Fein man opened the passenger door and settled in beside him. The windscreen steamed up instantly from their alcoholic breaths and Billy rubbed at it with one hand while he started the engine.

'Keep an eye out behind.' He nodded towards the wing mirror on Ryle's side. 'Anyone fucks with us there's a weapon under your seat.'

Ryle gave a short laugh and superstitiously dropped his hand under the seat. His fingers brushed against cold metal and ran along a curved surface with holes in it. Jesus Christ, he swore to himself and grappled for the seat belt to help him think as the van lurched forward into the traffic. Christ knew what Billy had under his own seat. What the back of the van might be full of didn't bear thinking about. And Billy was drunk too.

Ryle watched the lights of cars in the mirror, hoping nobody was following him, and that Grifford really had disappeared. He felt coldly sober. They had spent two hours in the pub, waiting for a message which finally came in a phone call for a Mr Hawthorne. Billy took it and returned to the bar all businesslike. Ryle had no idea where he was going or who he was going to meet.

They crossed the Liffey and took the coast road past the park at Fairview and drove towards Clontarf. The traffic was light and there were few pedestrians out in the cold night. Off to their right, the lights of the port were bright and rippled on the water and the red aircraft warning lights blinked on the power-station chimneys.

Billy swung the van inland without warning and accelerated up a tree-lined avenue. He rounded a bend and did a quick U-turn and returned the way they had come at a more sedate speed. There were no other cars in sight. He looked at Ryle and grinned.

'Is this for my benefit?' Ryle grunted. The drink had intensified the sense of defeat that had descended on him after his talk with Erlanger. Back in the office, Stacy had rounded on him and demanded that he get after Whelan or at least do something useful. Billy's call had rescued him but it was probably a temporary respite. He did not feel up to talking to the Provos right now but he had no choice about that either. All his options seemed to be disappearing.

He no longer had any confidence that he could crack this story. He didn't necessarily believe Erlanger but there was nothing he could do about that either. He could only ask the questions and a denial was a denial was a denial. The whole story had wound itself into a ball that bounced back and forth and went nowhere. Like a bloody tennis match at which he was the only spectator, following the ball to the left and then to the right and waiting and hoping for someone to miss a volley. While life went on outside, unconcerned.

I need a break, he thought. In every sense of the word.

Billy stopped at the coast road and steered the van back the way they had come. He began singing in a light voice, 'In Mountjoy jail one Monday morning . . . ' They turned inland before they got back to the city centre, drove fast up a main artery and veered into a maze of housing estates. Ryle soon lost

250

track of where they were as they circled around blocks of similar houses. Nothing followed in the rear-view mirror.

Billy stopped in a quiet street of semi-detached houses. Ryle followed him quickly across the road and around a corner and they squeezed by a parked car in a short driveway. A hall door was opened before them by a woman who said nothing. Billy walked straight through into the kitchen where a dishwasher or washing machine was gushing away. They went out the back door, stepped over the low wall into the next garden, crossed it and went in the back door of the next house.

There were no lights on in the kitchen but Ryle could make out the shadowy bulk of a man standing inside the door. Still trying to adjust to the gloom, someone put a hand on his back and guided him towards the front of the house and into a front room. The door closed behind him and a reading lamp was clicked on by a man sitting in an armchair. He gestured towards the chair opposite him.

'You wanted something?' The man had a neutral accent which matched his demeanour. He was well-dressed in a grey three-piece suit that made him look older than his mid-twenties. His sober tie was pulled loose over an unfastened shirt-button and his eyes were sunken with tiredness. They had the intense look of a troubled priest.

Ryle sat down. 'Maurice Clark. Did he have any links with your people?'

'Links?' The man pondered the word for a moment. 'He was not a member of the Irish Republican Army, if that's what you mean.'

'But did he have any connections, less formal connections, with the IRA?'

'No.' The denial sounded so final that Ryle thought for a moment that the interview was over. 'Clark was a member of the Free State parliament,' the man continued. 'The IRA has a standing order prohibiting members from taking seats in that partitionist parliament.'

'So he couldn't have joined if he'd wanted to?'

'He was not a member. And it's a ridiculous question to ask.'

Ryle shifted awkwardly. 'He had a gun on him when he died. One of your guns.'

'How do you know it was one of ours?'

'That's what the guards think.'

'Are they saying he was a volunteer?'

'No. I've just heard they've traced the gun to the IRA.'

The man stared at a vase of artificial flowers that sat in front of the empty fireplace. 'If he had an army weapon he should not have had it.' He looked up. 'How did they trace it?'

'I've only heard about it at second hand. I don't know the details.'

'I can't check it out without knowing more,' the man said.

'I think it was a pistol,' Ryle replied. 'I don't know the make.'

The man shrugged.

'Did Clark ever have any connections with the Republican movement?' Ryle tried again. 'Before he became a TD.'

The man shook his head. 'He approached one of our people some time ago, asking if negotiations could be started to end the war,' he said wearily.

'Acting as an intermediary for someone?'

'I don't think so. Trying to play the honest broker, so-called. One of many opportunists willing to make their names on the back of the struggle. He was told to tell the Brits to get out of Ireland if he wanted peace.'

'What's your position on neutrality?' Ryle asked, remembering the assumption made by the Fleet Street reporter.

'The current controversy?' the man said. 'It doesn't surprise us. It would only formalise the *de facto* situation. But it exposes how far this puppet state is prepared to go to help the British war machine. The Republican movement's in favour of real neutrality, of course. A free Ireland has no place in the imperialists' club.'

He appeared to lose interest in the subject and stood up. 'Get more details about the gun and I'll see what I can find out.'

Back in the van Billy drove towards the city centre without diversions. 'Are you happy now?' he asked as they waited for a red light to change.

'Not very,' Ryle answered truthfully. The interview had confirmed his pessimism: the two best angles, the only two angles left, had both been shot down within the space of hours.

252

Maybe he could have handled it better, but he doubted it. He believed the IRA man's denial: there seemed no reason for the IRA to deny such a matter if it were true. And it was clear that their only interest was in a trade-off of information that would help them plug a hole in their own organisation. Probably with another hole through the back of someone's head.

'If he couldn't tell you what you wanted to know, nobody can.' Billy revved the engine and shot through the lights an instant before they changed.

'Who is he anyway?'

'Someone who knows everything.'

'He looked like an out-of-work actor trying to play a hard man,' Ryle said irritably.

'You'd better not believe that, friend.' Billy looked at him sharply. 'If anyone nasty turns up at that house it'll be more than our kneecaps are worth. Yours and mine.'

'Don't worry,' Ryle said. 'I'm just pissed off because he killed a good story.'

'And another word of warning while we're at it,' Billy added. 'Don't go blundering about with any more freelance inquiries.'

It was Ryle's turn to look up sharply.

'You'd have been in big trouble, only we knew what you were at.' Billy grinned and shook his head. 'Asking an active service unit for help with a political profile. Jesus.'

He brought the van to a halt alongside the Liffey close to O'Connell Bridge and Ryle opened the door. 'Shercock's not the man, anyway,' Billy said.

'Thanks for your help.' Ryle got out.

'No sweat.' Billy smirked sideways at him. 'Hope you haven't left your fingerprints under the seat.'

Ryle stood beside the low river wall and watched the van disappear down the quays in a cloud of dirty exhaust smoke.

Ryle woke with a start and stopped breathing. He lay with his eyes open and felt his heart thumping. He glanced around involuntarily as his conscious mind told him it was nothing and tried to calm his body. There was nothing to worry about any more. But something had woken him.

253

The yellow street lights from across the car park seeped around the fringes of the curtains and built the shadows into mounds. Nothing moved. Ryle forced his body to unfreeze and he leaned up on one elbow to look around again. There was no movement in the dead silence.

He reached up and pulled back a curtain. The yellow light flooded in, illuminating the room like a badly developed photograph. There was nobody there. A floorboard in the room above snapped sharply and he jumped. He closed his eyes and breathed deeply, trying to still his fear.

His watch showed almost four o'clock and he knelt on the bed and peeped out at the car park. He could see the underside of the nearest car and he stood up for a better look. The cars glistened with frost and there was no sign of life. He shivered.

He stood up and wrapped a blanket around himself. Tiredness covered his face like a grey slime but he knew he wouldn't get back to sleep easily. He yawned and a sneeze caught him in a choking, eye-watering splutter. He cursed and went looking for something to drink.

There was no alcohol left and he sipped from a pint carton of milk. This is crazy, he thought. Paranoia getting out of hand and there's no need for it now. His evening with Billy had stilled those fears, at least. But something had woken him. Just nerves, he decided – he was more strung up than he had realised.

But he still felt vulnerable and exposed and wrapped the blanket tighter. This is fucking ridiculous, he told himself angrily.

He was about to climb back into bed when something under the door caught his eye. He froze again and stared at the little white triangle for a minute, then went towards it cautiously, bent down and pulled in a torn sheet of lined paper. 'Brekkie in Bewleys 9.30,' the message said.

Ryle felt his tired body sag. 'For fuck's sake,' he sighed aloud at the ceiling, in relief and anger and exhaustion.

Eighteen

Ryle's head reverberated with the rattling of china as a waitress banged down a tray on a counter. He stopped, surveyed the room and spotted Sergeant Grifford in a secluded corner, far from the door.

'You're late.' Grifford halted his pursuit of a lightly poached egg with a piece of toast. 'Do you realise the trouble I've had keeping a place for you?'

Ryle watched the yolk dribble back onto Grifford's plate in glutinous strings and felt nauseous. 'You frightened the hell out of me last night,' he said as a fact, without rancour. He was relieved that Grifford was talking to him again but felt unsure of their relationship after the last few days.

'Must be a guilty conscience,' Grifford grunted. He looked as unperturbed as always.

'Look,' Ryle said awkwardly. 'I hope I haven't got you into any difficulties. By telling Devane you were following me.'

Grifford waved away the apology and shoved the triangle of toast into his mouth. Ryle looked away and caught the attention of a passing waitress. He ordered a coffee.

'Anything to eat?' she asked.

'A cherry bun.'

Grifford spluttered and coughed. 'The hard man,' he said when he got his breath back, 'starting the day on a cherry bun.'

Ryle forced his sunken eyes into the semblance of a smile.

'The drink is a terrible thing,' Grifford poured himself another cup of tea. 'Divides families, provokes violence, destroys the liver. And blinds people to the joys of the morning.'

'It wasn't the drink,' Ryle groaned, satisfied that Grifford was back to his usual form. 'It was your middle-of-the-night visit.'

'Right.' Grifford finished his poached egg and turned businesslike. 'What've you been up to?'

'Banging my head against a brick wall.'

'I can see that. You look like you knocked some spots off it.'

The waitress left a coffee and a plate of cherry buns. Ryle split one, licked its sugary coating off his fingers and buttered it.

'How about the gun?' Grifford asked. 'Have the boyos missed it yet?'

'I've got nowhere.'

'Won't your pet rebel tell you?'

'She doesn't know.' Ryle paused and decided he'd better give Grifford something. 'I get the impression they know nothing about it either. But they'd like to know more.'

'I bet they would.' Grifford turned around to summon another pot of tea and slowly scanned the half-full restaurant. 'This is a great country for young men,' he sighed. 'They can play at soldiers, fight their part-time war and go home to their dinner afterwards, safe in the knowledge that nobody's going to shoot them in the back. Most of the time, anyway.'

Ryle waited for him to continue but Grifford did not elaborate. He wasn't quite back to his old form, Ryle decided, more like he'd been at their last meeting. 'I take it the leak inquiry's over,' he said, 'now that you're here.'

Grifford shook his head. 'There's a time and place for everything.' He turned his attention to a salt cellar and twisted it around in slow circles. 'They're otherwise engaged at the moment. Turning over your girlfriend's flat.'

Ryle felt a sick feeling in his stomach. 'Have they arrested her?'

'Not unless she shot through the door. Or beat them up.'

Ryle looked at the milky dregs of his coffee and swallowed the last drops. He wondered whether the documents were still under the mat on the floor of his car: he'd forgotten to look in his hurry to get into town. He'd better do something about them, he decided.

'She really doesn't know anything,' he sighed after a while. 'She had no hand, act or part in forging those things. She's an innocent victim in all this. I'm absolutely certain.'

Grifford nodded absently. 'The conspiracy theorists are

having a field day,' he said in a tired voice. 'The Government's caught in a bind of its own making and has convinced itself that others are being even more devious than it thought it was. It's a common phenomenon. No one's more outraged than the con man who'd been conned.'

'And they think Rosie's conned them?' Ryle asked derisively.

'Someone has. She's an obvious suspect, given her background and associates. And she's the easiest choice. Apart from yourself.'

'How do you mean?'

'The other obvious suspects are, shall we say, less accessible.' Grifford shrugged. The waitress brought his tea and Ryle asked for another coffee. 'Why don't you take a close look at Mr Erlanger?'

'Oh, I have,' Ryle said eagerly and told him about Erlanger's denial that he had given the documents to Clark.

Grifford gave no indication that the information was new to him. 'You should take another look at him,' he suggested mildly.

'He's selling off shares in his company and creaming off a lot of money, I presume.' Ryle sipped at his second coffee. 'The whole story's like a bloody balloon: every time I prod one side, it all bounces out of reach again.'

'A touchingly childish image,' Grifford chortled. 'Have you considered the possibility that he might be other than he seems?'

'Sure. But what?' Ryle could feel the coffee beginning to grind some life back into his brain and he began to butter another cherry bun. 'He seems like a crook. Does that mean he's just a businessman?'

'That he's a spook.'

'A spook.' Ryle stopped buttering.

'A spy.'

'CIA.' Ryle's mind raced back over everything that had happened. 'Holy shit.'

Grifford winced. 'Quite.'

'Of course,' Ryle said to himself and sought confirmation

before his thoughts became totally entangled in tying up the tired old facts with the new information. 'He is a CIA man, is he?'

'How would I know?' Grifford shrugged. 'I'm only . . . '

'Ah, shit,' Ryle burst out in spite of himself. A middle-aged woman at a nearby table gave him a disapproving look.

Grifford raised his palms to him. 'I don't know whether he is or not. Your friend Devane thinks he is. Might be. That's all I know.'

Ryle muttered an apology and sat back for a moment. 'It would make sense of a lot of things,' he said after a few moments.

'It might.'

'Does Devane have any evidence?'

'He's only thinking along the same lines as yourself.' Grifford had adopted the disinterested tone of a teacher who has set a favoured pupil a maths problem and is waiting patiently for him to work it out. 'As far as the circumstantial evidence goes, it fits.'

'It explains why he would have given Clark the document.' Ryle was thinking aloud. 'No, it doesn't. Or does it?' He looked inquiringly at Grifford who gave him a broad smile.

'Now you know why certain other people are in a state of confusion,' he said.

Ryle nodded absently, preoccupied with the effort of thinking coherently and logically. Erlanger was a CIA man. He gave a forged document to Clark and forced him to sign it. Why would he do that? It would only screw up whatever negotiations were going on. As it might already have done.

'I don't get it.' Ryle admitted. 'Why would the CIA want to screw up Ireland's moves to join NATO? They should be all in favour of that, shouldn't they?'

Grifford nodded as if his pupil had justified his faith. 'Maybe that wasn't their intention,' he suggested. 'Anyway, it's not a popular theory. Too upsetting for the national psyche to even consider the possibility that the Americans might be conspiring to keep us out of their military club. Especially when we're prepared to sell our souls to get in.'

'Can't you or Devane check it out?' Ryle inquired impatiently. The trouble with this bloody story was the way every good, solid-looking lead seemed to dissolve into thin air when you tried to pursue it.

'Sure. Phone the American embassy and ask them? Or haul in Erlanger and slap the electrodes on him? And, if he is CIA, the shock to his system would be nothing compared to the shock to our relations with the Americans.'

Ryle nodded. He was beginning to see the official problems involved. *Maybe I shouldn't have stayed so far away from the diplomatic aspects of all this*, he thought. *But no, Clark was still his real target*. Ryle was sure his death was still the best story.

'Why don't you call the Americans yourself and ask them who their local representative is?' Grifford added sweetly. 'You lads don't mind appearing as ignorant as pig shit. You could tell them you have something important for him.'

'A load of uranium.' Ryle smiled and turned serious at the sound of his own voice. 'Shit, that fits too.'

'Good lad.' Grifford smirked. 'You've wrapped it up. I always knew you could do it.'

'Seriously,' Ryle insisted. 'Somebody must know who the resident CIA man is.'

'It's not Erlanger.'

'There could be two of them?'

'There could be a hundred and two of them.'

'Hasn't Devane checked it out?'

'Devane,' Grifford looked doleful, 'is in a bit of a limbo. His popularity's on a par with that of his theories.'

'He's been taken off the case?'

'The headlines are flashing in your eyes again,' Grifford smiled. 'No, he's not off the case. But he's not in control of it any more.'

'What happened?'

'Officially, he didn't go through the proper channels. He asked somebody he knows in the FBI to run Erlanger through the computer.' Grifford laughed. 'Unfortunately for him the answer came back through the official channels which made a number of people very angry. Lowly inspectors are not supposed to take international initiatives without telling anybody.'

'And what was the answer?' Ryle was taut with eagerness to know.

'Nothing.' Grifford raised his shoulders and paused. 'There is no record of a Michael James Erlanger born on whatever date and wherever it was supposed to be. Or so they said.'

Ryle gave a low whistle.

'Precisely,' said Grifford and looked at his watch. 'Which adds up to precisely nothing. But if he is a spook then he knows that we know. Thanks to the plodding policeman.'

He stood up and Ryle looked at him in a panic. 'Wait a minute,' he said, 'I want to talk this through.'

Grifford shook his head. 'Discretion,' he aimed his index finger at him. 'The lads will have realised by now that you're not hiding under Red Rosie's bed after all.'

He walked out quickly.

The phone rang unanswered and Ryle stabbed at a button to retrieve his coins. He went back to his hard plastic seat and stared at the clothes swishing back and forth behind the port-hole of the washing machine. Two stumpy-looking women emptied a drier into black plastic bags and entertained each other with graphic descriptions of their gynaecological problems.

Grifford had certainly opened his eyes to a whole new scenario of diplomatic intrigue that coloured everything and maybe made some kind of sense out of everything. Ryle thought back to Whelan who had raised the possibility that Clark's document had been forged in order to test the government's resolve on the secret neutrality negotations. Could that be it? Then he himself had been manipulated, used as the pawn to publicise it. And that meant that Rosie was also part of it, wittingly or un-wittingly a CIA pawn.

The machine stopped for a moment while the water gurgled away and then took off into a high-speed spin. Was Clark another CIA pawn, willing or unwilling? That would explain why he had had the forged documents extolling the merits of neutrality. And maybe he had changed his mind and Rosie was right in thinking he had left them with her to be leaked in order to scupper the whole neutrality plot. Ryle felt the adrenalin course through his body as the implications of this possibility came home to him. Holy shit, he thought, maybe Clark was killed by the CIA. Or maybe it was the British. If the Americans were in the thick of it, surely the British were even more heavily involved. Because of the North.

Ryle squeezed his heavy eyelids shut and ordered his mind to slow down, to stop speculating. This was a hall of mirrors, reflecting and re-reflecting the same images back and forth and on to infinity. You could spent forever chasing them but all there was at the end of the day was whatever you started out with. A dead dog. And a dead politician.

Outside his bedsitter he hauled the bulging bag of laundry from the rear of the car and looked around quickly. There was nobody about and he reached under the car mat and stuffed the Clark documents into the bag. Once inside, he switched on the electric fire and the water heater and began tidying up, refusing to think any more about the story. On the radio, racing commentaries from the Curragh broke through the background music periodically but he did not listen to the details.

When he finished he tried calling Rosie again but there was still no answer. There had been no answer all afternoon. He had checked with the guards and she wasn't in custody. She'd gone to ground, he supposed.

He tossed the bag of laundry into a cupboard, having retrieved the documents, and sat down with his feet up on the clean table. He had lied to the paper's lawyer about them after the lawyer had said that in his opinion they had no choice but to hand them over to the police.

'But we have to protect our sources,' Ryle had argued.

'There's no privilege of any kind attaching to this case,' the lawyer had sniffed. 'I cannot see any grounds for our refusal to hand over material evidence.'

'Except for the fact that we don't have them any more.'

The lawyer had given him a shrewd look but decided not to question their whereabouts. They could tell him nothing more now and he tore them up methodically, put the pieces into a large saucepan and set them on fire. To hell with them all, he thought. That settles that problem.

Smoke filled the room and he opened the door and the windows and looked out, eyes smarting, wondering what to do next. There was no point calling on Erlanger and asking him if he was a spy. He'd go into his smooth routine again, deny that he was and thank Ryle for his courtesy in checking this ridiculous idea with him.

The smoke cleared and he shivered in the cold air and closed the windows. What he had to do was go and buy Lorraine a present for her birthday party tomorrow. Maybe he should go and see her and Breda now, too. That situation had to be sorted out, one way or another. Were they really going to separate? Or just drift apart? Or drift together again? All he knew was that he couldn't go on living in this dump.

But he didn't know what to say to Breda. It was probably over, he thought. The relationship had gone sour, not dramatically or over any one thing. Slowly and steadily over nothing in particular, everything in general, strangled by two different prescriptions for living.

He suddenly remembered a day several months earlier and the child asking as they passed by a cemetery why all those people were dead. Because they were very old, he said, and she thought about that and said with serene seriousness that she would not have any more birthdays. And now she was looking forward to her party, anticipating fun and presents and the warm achievement of adult congratulations at what a big girl she had become.

A wave of helplessness surged over him, taking him by surprise with its suddenness and intensity. He jumped up and plugged in the kettle and forced his attention on to the radio, unwilling to cope with the emotion. When in doubt, keep moving.

The high-pitched racing commentator brought another set of horses to the finishing post in a thunder of cheering.

The suburban lounge was large and square with a bar running along one side and curving booths of fake leather covering the floor space. It was beginning to fill up with couples claiming the booths and men lining the bar and the barmen were getting busy. Conversations and snatches of casual talk between people who only knew each other in pubs drowned out the piped music.

Ryle sipped at a pint of Harp and glanced at his watch. She's not coming, he decided. Which was hardly a great surprise. He had been more surprised when she had answered the phone and the suspicion in her voice eased when she heard it was him. He had asked her how she was and she had said fine and he'd changed his mind on the spur of the moment and invited her out for a drink.

But she wasn't coming. The only people who wanted to talk to him were the ones who wanted something from him, he thought. Editors, lawyers and guards. Which was some kind of poetic justice, he supposed. He drained his glass and looked around and did not recognise anyone. He held up the glass to the barman for another and decided he might as well stay put. He had nowhere else to go anyway.

'Sorry I'm late.' Rosie stood by his shoulder.

Ryle made more room for the empty stool beside him and she dropped her shoulder bag onto the floor by the bar and took off her coat. She was wearing a long floral dress like the one she had had on the first time he saw her in the school.

'I'd decided you weren't coming,' he said as she sat down.

'A union meeting.' She paused. 'Is this work?'

Ryle shook his head and watched her reaction. She ran her fingers through her curly hair and gave him a fleeting, dark-eyed smile which he interpreted as approval. She wasn't wearing any make-up that he could detect but he noticed a faint scent.

Ryle ordered her a pint of Guinness and asked what the union meeting was about. Then he asked her about teaching and she talked enthusiastically about five-year-olds and how wonderfully free of bullshit they were although you could see it creeping up on them. Then she turned the questions on him and asked him about journalism and he said that it was like working for five-year-olds, the attention span and demands of news editors for instant action and the impossible were just about the same.

She laughed and they talked easily about inconsequential

things and watched the perspiring barmen colliding with each other as the evening wore on and the crowded atmosphere enveloped them in its convivial warmth and noise. Neither mentioned the story and the ghost of Maurice Clark stayed far away as they explored each other's lives without hurry, savouring the unspoken possibilities that lay before them, two weary people seeking a renewed lease of life in each other's newness.

The barmen were beginning to call for last orders when two hands fell on their shoulders and shattered the mellow mood. Rosie stiffened and Ryle cursed silently as Billy pressed his portly bulk between them.

'What a coincidence.' The Sinn Fein man beamed at them with an expression that could have passed for joviality. 'Finding the two of you here together.' He turned to Rosie. 'I wore out my finger calling you earlier.'

'I was out.'

'I can see that now,' Billy smirked, taking pleasure in their obvious discomfort. 'And I thought you might be avoiding me.'

Ryle caught the barman's eye and ordered two last drinks.

'Not for me, thanks,' Billy said pointedly. 'I'm only passing by. I was just intrigued to know which of you is being watched.'

Ryle stared at him and Billy rolled his eyes towards the end of the bar where two men sat side by side in front of two drinks. They were not talking.

'Special Branch,' Billy whispered.

Ryle cursed. 'Are you sure?'

'Course I'm sure.' Billy sounded affronted. 'What intrigues me is whether they're on surveillance duty or protection duty.'

'What do you mean?' Ryle demanded.

Billy dropped his hands from their shoulders. 'Are they keeping an eye on you? Or are they keeping an eye out for you?'

'They're not looking after me,' Ryle said coldly. 'I never saw them before.'

'Maybe they're worried about the company you keep.' Billy shrugged and turned to Rosie. 'Or maybe they're concerned about you?'

Rosie gave him a hostile glare and Billy patted her on the back. 'Not to worry. I must be off. Call me the minute you get a chance.'

Ryle watched him leave, waving at the two detectives as he passed them. They did not appear to notice him.

'Bastard,' Rosie breathed.

'What the hell is he doing here?' Ryle asked rhetorically. There was no answer to that question. And there was no point trying to ignore the wedge of reality Billy had driven between them. There was no escaping this goddam story, he sighed. It seemed to have taken over his whole life.

They drank in silence, each immersed in their own thoughts. In front of them, a barman pulled down a shutter on the pleas of a couple of customers for one last round.

'There's something you could do for me,' she said at last without looking at him.

Ryle heard the reluctance in her tone and waited, automatically adding her to the list of people who wanted something from him. Maybe that's why she came, he thought cynically. No, that's not true: don't let your irritation with that leering fat bastard get out of hand.

'Tell me about the gun Maurice had.' She faced him. 'Where he got it.'

'I don't know,' he said helplessly. He considered telling her about his meeting with the Provo in the housing estate but caution decided him against it. Had she asked him ten minutes earlier he knew he would have told her. But Billy's baleful visit had changed everything. 'I don't have any details about it. It was a pistol or a revolver. That's it.'

Rosie turned back to the bar and finished her drink in silence. The Provos were harassing her about it, Ryle decided. Which was probably his fault because he had told them about it. Everyone who had helped him with this story seemed to have landed in trouble, he realised suddenly. But there was no future in thinking things like that.

Ryle watched the two detectives as he and Rosie left but neither glanced in their direction. 'Do you think they really are cops?' Ryle asked after they had got into his car. He made no move to start the engine and they sat in the cold silence watching the pub doorway until the two men stepped out.

'Probably,' she sighed in a distant voice.

The two men looked around and walked casually down the footpath. Ryle considered going over and demanding to know if they were following him. It might appease his irritation but what else would it do? Caution advised him against a confrontation on the now empty street.

The men went out of sight round a bend and Ryle drove off, checking his rear-view mirror. The road remained empty apart from a speeding taxi which flashed past and disappeared ahead of him.

'I'm sorry,' he glanced at her, 'that all this ... came up again.'

She was huddled into the passenger seat with her arms folded tightly as if for warmth. She nodded slightly but did not look at him. He drove her home in silence.

Mike Erlanger ambled through the crowded room, looking like a caricature of an amiable American. He had an open smile on his face, offered a ready handshake and uttered a 'good to see you again' to everyone he recognised.

He wandered down the hall, examining the bold strokes and strong colours of the paintings which matched the modern furniture. The house was a semi-detached Victorian pile off Leeson Street and the party was into its post-midnight swing. If he hadn't known it already, he reckoned he would have guessed in one that it was the home of an advertising executive.

There were fewer people in the back room. A table of food occupied one wall, looking like it had been hit by a selective hurricane. Erlanger surveyed the half-eaten salads, a congealing stew and dishes of broken desserts.

'Haven't you eaten?' a startled voice said at his shoulder.

'Oh, yes.' He turned to the hostess and expanded his smile. 'I stuffed myself earlier. But this spread's tempting me again.'

'What would you like?' She was in her late thirties and thin to a degree that indicated her horror at her age. 'I've kept some of the main course in the oven for latecomers.'

'No, please don't bother. I'll have some more dessert.'

She picked up a clean bowl and spooned a selection into it with quick movements that were both decisive and distracted.

'Great party,' Erlanger said.

'Cream?'

He shook his head and took the bowl. She introduced him to a heavily made-up woman and slid away. Erlanger and the woman chatted pleasantly and he discovered she was an air hostess on transatlantic flights. They discussed hotels in New York and Boston. In a corner, a couple had an intense, low-voiced argument. The sound of rock music suddenly burst up from the basement.

'Ah, dancing,' the air hostess said brightly.

'Let's go see,' Erlanger suggested.

When he returned Tommy Lyster was bustling into the back room with the hostess offering him food. 'God bless you,' Lyster exclaimed. 'I'm starving.' Erlanger gave him a genial nod and passed on to the front room.

Becky was in a group listening to a chubby man who used an unlit cigar like a stage prop and was in the middle of a innuendo-laden tale about the pleasures of doing business in Bangkok. Erlanger joined the audience but his attention was focused on James Burke who was talking to two people at the other side of the room. He stared at him until Burke caught his eye. Burke looked away quickly.

The businessman finished his story and one of the women said, 'Now tell us what you really got up to there, Gerry.' Everybody laughed and Erlanger moved away and warmly greeted one of the others in Burke's group. He turned to Burke and raised his voice. 'Isn't the grieving widow with you?' he asked.

Burke blushed and a couple of people nearby sniggered, delighted that the party was creating some gossip for absent friends. 'Give her my sympathy, won't you?' Erlanger added and wandered away with his innocent smile.

Tommy Lyster was standing alone, giving his plate of steaming food his full attention. 'I needed this,' he said as Erlanger joined him. 'You can't beat the hot dinner.'

'Haven't you been eating regularly?' Erlanger smiled.

'I have, I have. But my appetite has improved. Exercise, you know.'

'You're a sportsman?' Erlanger said dubiously.

'I love a bit of sport,' Lyster laughed. 'Have you ever been coursing?' Erlanger shook his head. 'I used to love it, kept a couple of dogs myself. It's not fashionable any more, of course. Some people seem to think it's not natural for dogs to chase hares. But you can't argue with nature, I always say.'

'I guess not.' Erlanger was bemused.

'Nature will take its course,' Lyster nodded. 'Bloody and all as it might be.' He forked some more food into his mouth.

'How was the coursing?'

'I wasn't there today. Busy on a different sort of exercise. Chasing a different class of a hare, you might say.' Lyster gave him the benefit of an evil smile. 'Anyway, how are things with you? Business proceeding nicely?'

'Very nicely.'

'Any fear of the bubble bursting?'

'No,' Erlanger said decisively. 'Uranium is a hard substance. It takes a lot to burst it.'

'And causes a bit of a bang when it does.' Lyster shook with laughter.

'That only happens in highly controlled situations.' Erlanger smiled back to conceal his mild irriation. Another investor looking for information, the third of the evening so far. At least Lyster made no pretence of disguising his financial interest beneath a spurious concern for the state of the world's natural resources.

'So, you think a body should stay calm and hang on.'

'Well now, Minister, I wouldn't venture to give investment advice to an astute man like yourself.' Erlanger raised his shoulders. 'You know how these things are.'

Lyster didn't bother trying to look like a man who knew how things were. 'Sure, I'm only a simple country politician,' he said. 'I wouldn't know anything about high finance.'

'I don't think I'd bet on that. If I were a betting man.'

'You wanted to see me?' Lyster wiped his plate with a crust of garlic bread.

Erlanger nodded vaguely, 'It was only a minor matter. I'm sure you don't want to be bothered with it now, at a social occasion.'

'Fire ahead.'

'Well.' Erlanger glanced around uneasily. 'It's a little embarrassing really. I called your office on the spur of the moment after I'd heard some upsetting news. It doesn't seem very important any more.' He paused as Lyster put down his plate. 'Somebody's putting about a rumour that I had a hand in this political controversy you've got going at the moment. I just wanted to assure you I hadn't. In case these rumours were given any credibility. In official circles.'

'Ah,' Lyster sighed, 'it's a terrible country for rumours.'

'I over-reacted,' Erlanger confessed. Out of the corner of his eye he noticed Burke pass by the open door towards the stairs. 'Particularly at the suggestion that it was all tied up with Maurice Clark's death. You'll appreciate, I'm sure, that it doesn't help business confidence to be linked to something like that. Even though, as you know, my only connection was the fact that Maurice was at my home the night before he died.'

'And who's putting about these rumours?'

'I have my suspicions but I don't think it would be proper for me to say. I don't have any hard evidence.'

'There's always busybodies at work,' Lyster said as if imparting a special insight. Sell, he decided, first thing Monday morning.

'I'm beginning to appreciate that fact.'

Lyster clapped him gently on the shoulder. 'Well, you can put your mind at rest. The inquiries into young Clark's death have finished. It was an accident. Pure and simple.'

'That's a relief. Tragic, of course, but a relief to know there was nothing more to it.'

'That's between ourselves for the moment.' Lyster gave him an elaborate wink. 'There'll be an announcement in a couple of days. When all this neutrality nonsense has been sorted out.'

'I really appreciate your telling me,' said Erlanger earnestly. 'And I hope nobody thinks I've been meddling in your politics. As a guest in your country I wouldn't want . . . '

'Not at all,' Lyster cut him short. 'Not a word about it. We've got no shortage of meddlers of our own. Fellas who think they know all about politics and can make capital out of an unfortunate tragedy. They'll get their answer next week.'

'It's all under control?'

'It is,' Lyster said happily. 'There'll be no hiccups.'

'Glad to hear it. I've no axe to grind, of course. But you can never tell how the markets will react to uncertainty. Any upsets now could be unhelpful as we go into the crucial phase of raising the production money.'

'There's many a slip 'twixt cup and lip.' Lyster drained his glass of wine. 'Do they have any real drink here, do you think?'

Erlanger pointed him towards the table of drinks and excused himself. He went upstairs and waited outside the bathroom door. Surprise flashed across Burke's face when he emerged, then turned to annoyance. 'That was a terrible thing to say,' he blurted.

'It was, wasn't it?' Erlanger smiled without humour and blocked his way. 'Gives you an idea of what it feels like, eh?'

Burke looked around Erlanger uneasily but did not meet his stare. He could barely see over Erlanger's shoulder.

'At least I said it to your face,' Erlanger added as if he was explaining the benefits of a bad business decision. 'Not behind your back.'

'Excuse me,' Burke muttered.

'I think we should have a little talk.' Erlanger did not move. 'Face to face. In one of those rooms.' He pointed behind Burke towards the bedrooms.

'I have nothing to . . . '

Erlanger put his hand on Burke's chest and pushed him backwards. Burke almost fell but recovered his balance and tried to catch his breath. 'Move,' Erlanger snarled, turning him around and pushing him down the unlit hallway and through the first doorway. The street lights showed a narrow room with a single bed and a mirrored dressing table. Erlanger stood with his back to the door and waited for Burke to turn towards him. Burke's face was in shadow.

'My lawyer tells me that the most effective action would be to report you to your professional body,' Erlanger said quietly. 'Or we could expose you with a public court injunction. I'm not so sure. Where I come from there's only one way of dealing with vermin.'

Burke said nothing but his breathing was heavy. The sound of conversation came muffled from downstairs and accentuated the stillness in the room.

'If you've got something to say about me, say it now,' Erlanger demanded.

'Let me out of here.' Burke tried to keep his voice even but was unable to contain a nervous croak. Erlanger's face looked ghostly in the yellow half-light, adding menace to his unclear shape.

'I take it you have nothing to say.'

'You have assaulted me and you are detaining me against my will.' Burke steadied down.

'If you don't have anything to say to me, don't have anything to say *about* me either. Say it now or don't do it behind my back again. And don't call me with any more threats.'

They stood in silence, merging into the unmoving shadows. The lights of a passing car swept across the room, freezing them in position like a photographic flash. A rumble of laughter came from downstairs.

Erlanger stepped aside and swung the door open with his foot. The sounds of the socialising increased. Burke looked at the open doorway and the dim hall beyond. He moved towards it.

Erlanger caught the lapels of his jacket and stretched Burke up on his toes. 'I take it we understand each other,' he whispered. 'Unless you want your lady friend to be widowed twice.'

Erlanger released him as Burke felt a surge of panic and began to struggle. He half-ran down the landing to the stairs. Erlanger went to the bathroom and washed his hands. He examined his face in the mirror while he dried them slowly. Crude, he thought grimly, but effective.

Becky was standing in the hall with Lyster and another man. They fell silent and watched Erlanger come down the stairs with his amiable smile back in place. 'Mike,' she said in a worried half-question half-comment as he approached them.

'Honey.' He smiled at her and put his arm around her shoulder. 'Should we be getting home?'

'The night's young,' Lyster said with enthusiasm. 'I was just telling your lovely wife about coursing but she doesn't seem to share our view that nature's best left to its own devices. Has its own ways of dealing with busybodies and meddlers.' He gave Erlanger a knowing wink. 'Maybe you'd be able to convince her that nature sometimes has to be cruel to be kind.'

Outside, Burke leaned the palm of his hand on the frozen roof of his car as he tried to get the key into the lock. His mind was jumbled with worry and wonder at how he had ever become involved with these kind of people. He felt a strong urge to get back to simple, inanimate figures, to a world where things added up or did not and there was none of this emotionalism. All he had ever wanted was to be a good accountant. They could keep their world of deaths and threats and back-stabbing and betrayal. Erlanger and that obnoxious Minister could go to hell. And take Yvonne with them.

He got the door open and slumped into the driver's seat. The windscreen was opaque with frost. With a curse and a half-sob he fumbled around the back seat for an old newspaper to scrub it away.

Nineteen

The congregation flooded into the sunlight and filled the cold air with the banging of car doors and engines starting up. Jim Whelan was among the last out and he queued at a newspaper stall, aware of the added attention of his constituents. Several people said hello to him and one man ostentatiously shook his hand and wished him luck. Whelan recognised him as a member of the Opposition party and scowled in silence.

He bought copies of all the papers, noticed a narrow picture of himself on the front page of one and folded the lot into a thick wad.

'That's a grand church you have here.' Tommy Lyster fell into step beside him. 'I love these old-style ones, don't you? They feel like real churches, not little cattle marts. God forgive me, but that's what the new ones always remind me of.'

Whelan did not acknowledge his presence and nodded to a group of men outside a pub, waiting for its doors to open. 'How are ye, men?' Lyster said automatically and continued his monologue.

'You could be here this time next week, canvassing in the cold. Handing out leaflets and roaring through your loudspeaker. If you have any leaflets. Or a loudspeaker. You take those things for granted when you have a party behind you. There's always somebody to look after them. But it's a different kettle of fish being an independent.'

'Why don't you shag off,' Whelan snapped under his breath.

'And where'll you find an organisation in a week?' Lyster went on, unperturbed. 'And the money to get a campaign together? Nobody's going to follow you into the wilderness. That's as clear as the nose on your face from the meeting the other night. You'll be on your own. All on your ownio.'

Whelan stopped to let a line of cars pass and crossed the road, walking more quickly. Lyster kept pace. 'The public are not impressed by independents, especially not with fellas who renege on their solemn oath to back a party. The Irish people have always had strong feelings about turncoats. Everyone will be out to do you. You won't have a friend in the world.'

They turned into the housing estate where Whelan lived and he saw Lyster's official Mercedes in the distance, parked outside his house.

'It's a lonely road being an independent,' Lyster said as if the empty street before them proved his point. 'A lonely road. That leads nowhere.'

Whelan stopped and eyed him. 'I'm going to phone the Taoiseach right now,' he said slowly, 'and tell him there is no way I'll vote with the party if I see your face around here again between now and Tuesday.'

Lyster looked at him dolefully. 'You're only a young lad, James, and I'm just spelling out the facts of life for you. I've seen bigger men than you go out in a blaze of glory with great plans and disappear from sight. Without a trace. Men who were very powerful.'

'I know what you're doing.' Whelan began to walk again. 'You're trying to intimidate me.'

'I'm trying to get you to face reality.' Lyster adopted a pained tone. 'You were the one who came to me looking for advice when the boot was on the other foot.'

'Advice is one thing. This is intimidation.'

'It's for your own good, James.' Whelan paused to catch his breath. 'You young lads think you know it all. Think you can upset the whole applecart because of your conscience or something. Think you know what party policy is or should be. Well, you don't. Party policy is what the party says it is.'

'Very democratic,' Whelan sneered.

'Yes, it is. You've had your say like everybody else and you've been out-voted. That's it.'

'And what if the party is wrong? Going against all its traditions and selling out its own heritage? There are some things more important than the party.'

'That's where you are wrong, James,' Lyster retorted emphatically. 'No one person is more important than the party.

The party made you and you either accept its policy or you get out. It's as simple as that. And if you want to get out you do it properly. Wait till the next selection convention and stand down. And in the meantime you keep your mouth shut and honour your solemn pledge.'

They stopped outside Whelan's gate. 'I'll make up my own mind,' Whelan said, 'without your advice.'

'One last word,' Lyster insisted. 'Keep the phone off the hook and have a quiet day with the family. Talk to nobody and think hard about your future.'

Whelan glared at him and walked up his garden path.

'By the way,' Lyster called after him, 'you can complain to the Taoiseach about me in the morning. He wants you in his office at eight. Sharp.'

Whelan went into the house without a backward glance and Lyster got into his car and rubbed his hands.

Seamus Ryle sat slumped before a typewriter with his eyes closed and half an ear tuned to the radio. The voices droned on, a succession of politicians pronouncing their predictable views on the crisis facing the government. All the usual posturing, he thought, as he opened his eyes briefly to add the name of the latest speaker to his typed list.

He stretched himself after a while, got a coffee and waited impatiently for the news magazine programme to end and for someone to come into the news room and relieve him. He had worked out two possible ways of getting at Erlanger and was in a hurry to test his theories. Both were long shots, neither ideal or even likely. But they were all he had and they were better than sitting around listening to this rubbish and, even worse, having to transcribe chunks of it later.

Another reporter arrived at last and Ryle told her he had to go out urgently to follow an angle on the neutrality story. He left the news room before she had time to argue and raced up to the library. He waited impatiently for a picture of Erlanger, then hurried to his car and sped to Dun Laoghaire.

It had come to him in the middle of another sleepless night. The woman who owned the dog had not identified Clark as its killer. Maybe that was because the gunman was Erlanger, not Clark. And maybe she would recognise Erlanger. It was a very long shot but it was worth a try. If he could only place Erlanger on the pier at the same time it would be a major breakthrough.

The pier was almost deserted, awaiting its afternoon strollers, and the sea was a brilliant blue when he stopped outside Ethel Barnes' house. The hill of Howth was etched sharply against the deepening blue of the sky and the still air was cold. He rang the bell at the basement flat and took the photograph from his pocket to study it while he waited. It was a standard, carefully lit publicity-style shot that gave Erlanger a sort of halo and made him look younger and less interesting than he really was. There was no answer. He rang again and waited a while and then went up the steps to the main door and tried the bells there.

An old woman answered finally and told him Miss Barnes wasn't at home, she had gone away. Where, he asked and the woman looked at him nervously; he left her his name to allay her suspicion rather than in any hope that Ethel Barnes would ever get the message.

One down, he thought as he turned the car and drove inland through Stillorgan and into the suburban sprawl of Dundrum. He was soon lost in a maze of greying semi-detached houses on roads that twisted and curved into loops and dead-ends. He stopped twice to ask the way and finally found the road he wanted, but the houses seemed to have been numbered by someone picking figures out of a hat. On a hunch, he stopped near a black Mercedes with a man sitting behind the wheel and found the house.

A young man opened the door and took his name when he asked for Mrs Clark. He swung the door almost closed and went away. Ryle heard heavy footsteps approaching down the hall and the door was jerked open by Tommy Lyster, red-faced and furious. 'You have a brass neck,' he thundered. 'Get out of here before I wring it for you.'

Ryle stood his ground, surprised but not taken aback by Lyster's appearance. 'I want to check a story I'm writing with Mrs Clark.'

'You're checking nothing. You're trespassing on private property and you'd better get off it before I have you thrown off it.'

'Then I'll have to say she was unavailable for comment,' Ryle said reasonably, turning dogged in the face of Lyster's fury. 'It'd only take a minute.'

'Say what you like. Just fuck off out of here.'

'Okay,' Ryle shrugged, 'but if the Taoiseach accuses us tomorrow of . . . '

Lyster slammed the door and Ryle walked down the garden path, thinking that was interesting. Lyster certainly wasn't there for Sunday lunch. He smiled at the Minister's driver who watched him without expression and sat in his car for a minute to show he was in no hurry to carry out Lyster's instructions. Two down, he thought, but the exchange with Lyster had cheered him up. At least he hadn't let the bastard get away with anything. But he hadn't got anything either.

He reversed into someone's drive and gave Lyster's driver a friendly wave as he headed back towards the city. He could call on Erlanger but that would be a waste of time, too. Besides, he'd feel a right twit asking Erlanger if he was a spy. Fuck them, he thought suddenly, why not write a story quoting Erlanger denying that he had given Clark the document. And get the widow into it, unavailable for comment. Yes, he grinned, a real shit-stirrer. It was playing dirty but it would be interesting to see what it shook out of the woodwork.

He stopped at a traffic light in Ranelagh and thought of Rosie. Last night had turned into a disaster but that was neither his or her doing. Why not call and see her now, maybe pick up where they had left off after Billy's appearance? Now that he had a story to write there was no need to hurry back, he'd only get landed with all that political garbage. The light turned green and he changed direction.

Rosie's hall door was open and he heard the sound of voices inside. He hesitated and wondered if the guards were going through her place again. But then a woman laughed and he pressed the bell.

Rosie came into the hallway, stopped in surprise and burst

out laughing. 'That was quick.' She gave him a quick kiss on the cheek. 'I'm really impressed.'

Ryle smiled at her uncertainly, speechless at the warmth of her welcome. She was a totally different person to the glum companion he had driven home last night.

'I just called you,' she said. 'To tell you about our demo.'

Her living room was crowded with a dozen or more people bustling about. A woman was on the phone giving the message to another newspaper while a man beside her stapled a sheet of cardboard to a stick. Another woman was dividing up bundles of leaflets while a third was busy with a thick felt marker. 'Stop the sell out', Ryle read over her shoulder.

'We're always ahead of the news,' he said to Rosie. The woman on the phone gave the address of the government party's office slowly as if someone was writing it down.

'I bet the pigs will be there ahead of us too,' Rosie said without concern. 'Proving that they listen to my phone.'

'I hear they've been here in person too,' he said tentatively.

She nodded absently and handed him a leaflet. 'Have you got your car?'

They set off in two cars and a van. Rosie sat beside Ryle and two men hunched in the back with a bundle of placards across their knees. Nobody said anything. So much for my journalistic independence, Ryle thought ruefully. This is going to look great to the tail. He glanced in the mirror automatically but decided he didn't care.

He coasted to a halt at the end of a street of Georgian houses and killed the engine. The street held the peculiarly sabbatical peace of a business area on a Sunday and there was nobody to be seen. A handful of cars were parked along its length and the weakening winter sun touched the small windows of the top floors along one side.

'They mustn't have been listening in after all,' Ryle said.

'This is a peaceful protest,' one of the men growled. They left their placards on the back seat and sauntered casually towards the party headquarters.

'Did I say something wrong?' Ryle inquired.

'George doesn't like flippancy.'

'Pity about George,' Ryle replied. They watched the two men climb the steps to the party headquarters and linger for moment. Ryle couldn't see what they were doing but presumed they were trying the door.

'This,' Rosie said with a little selfconscious laugh, 'is a sort of memorial service for Maurice. Even though the silly bugger would argue that there was a better way of doing things if he was here.'

The two men came back towards them but stopped to talk to their colleagues as the other car and van arrived.

'Is that wise?' Ryle asked, thinking with a twinge of jealousy that Clark had come between them again. He reminded himself of her kiss on his cheek and decided it didn't matter: maybe this was her way of finally burying Clark. 'Seeing as the cops may be trying to pin the forgery on you.'

She gave him a crooked smile. 'Maurice planted them on me. I can only assume he wanted me to make use of them. Which is what I'm doing.'

Ryle studied her profile, trying to follow her reasoning. She looked ahead, a contented smile on her face. The two men returned to the car and opened the rear doors to get their equipment. One of them shook his head to Rosie.

They waited for her and Ryle got out too. Several cars swept up and people began to pile out of them beyond the party headquarters. One of the men said something to Rosie. 'Shit,' she muttered and her expression turned grim.

'What is it?' Ryle asked as he walked with her.

'Provos,' she said.

A blue police van cruised by and deposited a handful of guards who took up positions on the steps of the building.

'Is this bad?' Ryle asked bemused.

She shook her head, seemingly distracted by the developing scene, and gave no explanation for her obvious concern. They reached the protesters, now parading up and down silently and Rosie joined them. Ryle dropped back to preserve his neutrality and another police van slid into the kerb about twenty yards away and kept its engine running.

Ryle leaned against the railings of a neighbouring house and watched the ritual settle into its preordained pattern. Everyone slipped into their roles as easily as production-line workers carrying out frequently practised tasks. The demonstrators and the police and the media stamped their feet against the cold and chatted idly in their respective groups like mourners awaiting a funeral service. Which is what it is, Ryle thought, the strangest memorial service I've ever seen.

A television crew turned on their lights to push back the dusk and the demonstrators shouted a few slogans for their sound man. The twilight settled in suddenly when they doused their lamps and then the street lights came on.

Ryle watched Rosie lead a chant against NATO and wondered idly what she saw in him. Was he just someone neutral she could talk to? About Clark, in particular. That was okay with him, for the moment, at least. But there seemed to be more to it than that.

He checked his watch and decided he'd better get back to the office. He waited until he caught her eye, smiled a goodbye and moved his frozen limbs.

He was approaching his car when the reporter he had left in the office came up the road in a hurry. 'Ah, Jesus,' she exclaimed. 'Why didn't you say you were doing this?'

'I didn't know. I just happened on it by accident.'

'The way you took off I thought you were after a really important story.'

'I was,' he insisted. 'I'll give you a lift back.'

'Will you do this too? I've been landed with all the political stuff off the radio.'

'Sure,' Ryle said soothingly and opened the car door. There was a sudden crash of breaking glass and voices raised in anger. He whirled around to see a couple of men standing in the middle of the road and hurling something at the building. One bent down, a light flickered and he threw it with full force towards the first floor windows. The petrol bomb exploded in a splash of flame against the wall. The police surged forward to escape the blazing spatters and collided with the main line of demonstrators. The two groups merged into a shouting and scuffling mêlée.

Ryle and his colleague ran back towards them, passing the television cameraman who was cursing in a loud and continuous stream of profanities at the sound man who had got his wires tangled on their open car boot.

The men in the centre of the road hurled two more petrol bombs and then fled up the street as a couple of guards broke from the struggling crowd and gave chase. Ryle saw them clamber into a waiting car which took off at speed around a corner. It was all planned, he thought superfluously. The Provos. That was why Rosie was upset at their arrival: she knew they were going to cause trouble. A corner of his mind noted with satisfaction that he now knew for certain that she wasn't a Provo stooge.

Garda reinforcements from the second van waded into the group, batons drawn and swiping at agile protesters who fenced back with their placard poles. They hauled two demonstrators back to their van, warding off darting attempts to free their captives. A man lay huddled on the ground, rolled into a ball with his arms over his head and surrounded by policemen. One of them kicked him viciously in the thigh.

Ryle tried to get in close without becoming embroiled in the dozens of individual fights, looking for Rosie. He saw her through a gap in the crowd, standing with her back to the guards and screaming at somebody to stop. He moved towards her as the urgent tones of a fire engine's siren rose and fell and came closer.

A guard pushed her from behind and she retaliated with a backward slam of her elbow into his stomach. He doubled up and one of his colleagues grabbed her around the neck, pulled her off-balance and dragged her backwards. Two other guards grabbed her arms, hauled her clear of the mob and ran her backwards up the road to their van. Ryle saw her face contorted with fury as she screamed and kicked and twisted in vain. The van door closed on her.

Mike Erlanger let the curtain fall back into place and turned from the window. 'Let's go out to eat,' he said.

'Is that wise?' Becky looked up from her fireside chair.

'We've got to eat.'

'There's some food here. We can put something together.'

Erlanger shook his head. 'We're not under siege. Not yet.'

'But we haven't got a reservation.'

'Come on.' He clapped his hands. 'You don't want to leave the fire. Someone'll take us in in Dalkey.'

Becky looked doubtful but straightened up on the edge of the armchair and went back to their earlier conversation. 'But the Minister said they had finished their inquiries and you aren't involved.'

'Would you trust the lovely Lyster?' he asked rhetorically. 'He's the kind of guy has trouble telling himself the truth.'

'What do you think it means?'

'Someone's been checking up on me,' he shrugged, 'which could be good or bad. Could be some investment analysts about to put some bucks our way. The shares are bound to have attracted some attention abroad.'

She looked sceptical, knowing that he was trying to put the best interpretation on events for her sake. 'But Mac said they looked like feds.'

'What do the feds look like any more? Probably means they were someone else, trying to look like feds. He said he didn't recognise them. Anyhow, he wouldn't know. He's only a businessman.'

Becky still looked doubtful.

'Let's go,' he said. He bent down and put his arms around her and lifted her up lightly. 'And cheer up. We're just going out to eat. It's not the last goddam supper.'

Breda looked at him dully and he thought for a moment she wasn't going to let him in.

'I got caught in a riot,' Ryle apologised. He had written a quick report on the minor riot as soon as he got back to the office. But the deputy news editor, angry at Ryle's earlier disappearance, had asserted his authority and demanded that he also do his story on Erlanger immediately.

'She's asleep.' Breda turned away and went into the living room. She was wearing a full-length dressing-gown and Ryle looked at his watch and swore. He hadn't realised it was that late.

He stepped into the hall and took the wrapped present from the plastic shopping bag. He looked into the living room where Breda sat in front of the television, watching someone crooning a love song, and went into the kitchen. Mounds of used plates covered a counter alongside a barely-touched cake and bowls of half-eaten jelly and melting ice cream. Torn party hats were scattered on the table and a balloon rested lightly on the cooker. He took a fistful of potato crisps from a bowl and crunched them.

Ryle climbed the stairs to the child's bedroom and stepped around a neat collection of new toys. Lorraine lay with her arms stretched in total surrender to sleep, breathing easily, her body barely raising a hump in the bedclothes. One foot stuck out and he looked at the perfect little toes that he had nervously and hurriedly counted the night she was born. He eased it back under the quilt.

He took a birthday card from his pocket and laid it with the present at the end of the bed. 'Sorry,' he said quietly and kissed her round cheek.

Breda was still in front of the television and Ryle sat on the edge of the other chair and watched a singer and his host reciting their well-rehearsed exchanges with a professionalism that passed for spontaneity. This wouldn't have happened, he thought guiltily, if he hadn't been so eager to see Rosie and hadn't got caught up in the demonstration. He dismissed the awkward thought as soon as it formed.

'I really am sorry,' he said. 'I tried to get away earlier.'

'It doesn't matter.' She kept her eyes fixed on the screen.

'Did it go all right? Did she have a good time?'

'It was fine.' She sounded as drained as she looked.

'I had every intention.'

'She didn't notice anyway.'

'You don't have to rub it in,' he said testily. 'I feel bad enough about it already.'

'It's been a long day.'

'For me too.'

'I could have done with some help.' She looked at him and her face was grey and tired, enlivened only by the flash of hostility in her eyes.

'I had every intention. I told you.'

'I know.' She turned back to the television. 'Work.'

He rested his chin on his chest and closed his eyes. Canned laughter underlined the inanity of a television comedian's jokes. 'I have to get back,' he said and began to get up.

'I don't want you coming here any more.'

He froze, bent double, and stared at her. She had her eyes riveted to the television and he sank back into the chair.

'You can see Lorraine on Saturdays,' she said in an even, decided voice. 'Collect her and take her away for the afternoon. From two to six.'

'Where?' he demanded, bewildered.

'Wherever.' She glanced at him involuntarily, surprised at his question. 'To your flat.'

'I couldn't take her there,' he exclaimed. 'It's a dump.'

She went back to the television and he rested his head in his hands and stared at the carpet. His brain seemed to have stopped functioning and he felt numb. Too many things were happening at the same time. I can't cope, he thought with a surge of self-pity, everything's crowding in at the same time.

'All right,' she said with the air of a negotiator falling back to a pre-determined position, 'you can see her here alone. I'll go out.'

'Can't we talk about this some other time,' he burst out with sudden desperation.

'There's nothing to talk about.'

'I just can't concentrate at the moment,' he pleaded. 'I'm supposed to be back in the office.'

She looked at him with a touch of disdain. 'I have my life to lead, too,' she said. 'And I don't want you hanging about any more. You decided to leave and now I want you to leave me alone.'

They stared at each other like two shoppers squaring up for an argument over who had been first to a special bargain. Then he saw the hurt behind her eyes and recognised the tip of the pain he had caused her and he backed off. 'Okay,' he said softly, 'okay.' He felt hollow.

Inspector Devane jerked awake on the first ring of the telephone and stared at the flickering television. He squeezed his eyes and opened them again and looked at his watch. His wife gave him an enquiring glance and he shook his head.

She went to answer the phone and he listened to her explain that he was visiting relatives and would not be home until very late.

'You're to check with the office when you come home,' she said when she returned. 'No matter what time it is.'

'Says who?' he grunted.

'A message from the Chief.'

'Was that him?' he asked suspiciously.

'No. I didn't catch his name. He said it was a message for you from the Chief. Very important.'

Devane cursed under his breath. That young pup Casey got the wind up and has gone and told someone about the plan, he thought. He checked his watch again. Well, he'd know for sure in an hour or so. When, and if, Casey turned up.

'I never got it,' he said.

'Are you going to be late back?' she asked.

'I'll be back tomorrow. At the earliest.' And I'll either be suspended or a hero, he thought as he closed his eyes and folded his arms over his stomach. He still had a trick or two up his sleeve.

'Did you get Whelan?' the deputy news editor called as Ryle stormed into the news room.

'I wasn't looking for him,' Ryle retorted.

'Then where were you?'

'On my tea break.'

'Stacy said you'd have an exclusive interview with Whelan.' The deputy news editor stood in front of him with his hands on his hips. 'It's on the news list.'

'Tough shit,' Ryle snapped. 'I'm not going to write the whole fucking paper.' A couple of other people raised their heads and stared at his heightened voice.

'But we've left space for it,' the deputy news editor said warily, taken aback by his aggression. 'It's down for the front page.'

Ryle took off his parka and threw it on his desk. 'I've already done you two substantial stories. One an exclusive.'

'I don't know about that one.' The deputy news editor followed him.

'Neutrality's the flavour of the week and it's an exclusive new angle to it. You don't think that's a story?'

'It's with the editor at the moment.' The deputy news editor shrugged. 'But the story everyone wants is what Whelan's going to do. Four other waverers have put out statements saying they're happy with government policy. It's down to Whelan now.'

Ryle rounded on him. 'My story is going in, isn't it?'

'I don't see much point to it,' the deputy news editor said defensively. 'I mean we can't go running stories about people denying things nobody's ever accused them of.'

'What's Stacy's number?' Ryle demanded and dialled standing up as it was called out to him. He was damned if he was going to explain anything to the deputy news editor.

'Get this prick off my back,' he snapped at Stacy.

'What's the matter?' Stacy asked calmly.

Ryle raised his voice to make sure the deputy news editor heard. 'I'm tired, hungry and fed up being fucked about by cretins who wouldn't recognise a news story if they fell over it.'

'Calm down,' Stacy snapped back. 'What are you talking about?'

Ryle slid onto his chair and told him that some guards thought Erlanger was a CIA agent and gave Stacy a run-through of the story he had written to try and flush out some more information. 'And the editor's going to kill it now.'

'And what about Whelan?' Stacy asked.

'I can't find him,' Ryle lied.

'Keep trying. The others had better not have him in the morning. For your sake.'

'Look,' Ryle snarled, 'I've just written one exclusive, covered a bloody riot and missed my daughter's birthday because of this gobshite here.'

'All right, all right,' Stacy soothed him. 'Put me onto him.'

Ryle transferred the call and dialled Whelan's number. It was engaged and he dialled it again and again, slamming the dial around and around until his finger hurt. He knew it wouldn't answer but he had to do something and any action was better than thinking.

The deputy news editor sidled over to him with a sheaf of photographs. 'Why didn't you explain it to me?' he asked in a hurt tone.

Ryle shrugged. He was beyond trying to explain anything to anyone any more.

'Would you have a look at these?' The deputy news editor dropped the pictures in front of him. 'See if anyone in them was arrested.'

Ryle stared at them and recognised Rosie between the backs of two policemen as she was dragged away. Her face was contorted and blurred and became more indistinct the longer he looked at it. In his mind's eye, he saw Breda again and felt the anguish behind her controlled anger. Christ. How come I never saw it before, he thought. Until now when it's too late.

'Four have been charged and will be in court in the morning,' the deputy news editor was saying. 'That's why we need to know which ones. We can't use their pictures.'

Ryle glanced at him as if he was speaking an obscure language. 'I don't know,' he said.

'I suppose we'd better not use any of them,' the deputy news editor said as he gathered them up. 'Better safe than sorry.'

Ryle went back to dialling Whelan's number automatically and tried to drag himself out of his despondency by forcing his attention back to the story. Why did everything always have to happen at once? The guards were after him; Whelan was keeping the whole country in suspense; Erlanger was an enigma; and Clark's death was as much a mystery now as it ever was.

The deputy news editor called to him a second time and held up a phone. Breda, Ryle thought illogically as he hauled himself out of his chair but he knew it wouldn't be – that was all over, the formalities that he had been putting off completed. It was finished, like it had been for a long time, he reminded himself. The thought did not make him feel any better.

He took the phone and the deputy news editor said 'Jonathan' with a look that presumed he was a friend. Ryle almost put the phone down again but the anti-nuclear campaigner was already talking in an enthusiastic voice.

'Interesting little development here I thought you should know about. Friend of mine with access to a geiger counter brought it down for the weekend and we took it out to the Atlantis site and ran it over everything, the drills and the mud from the bore-holes and so on. It registered nothing. Nothing more than normal levels, that is.'

Wonderful, Ryle thought cynically. Stop the presses. 'So you've got nothing to worry about,' he said, making it sound like a criticism.

'Appears that way,' Jonathan burbled. 'My friend believes there is nothing there at all. No uranium.'

Ryle thanked him perfunctorily and hung up. It took him a moment to absorb the information. Of course, he thought, that's perfectly bloody obvious. I should have known that all along. The mine was only a blind, Erlanger's cover to insinuate his way into the political and financial establishment. But his cover had taken on a life of its own and the whole thing had gotten out of hand. And now half the establishment was speculating like crazy over an empty hole in the ground.

Ryle gave a tired laugh. Burke had been right all along: he had Erlanger taped even if he didn't know exactly what it was that he knew. And Clark? Had Clark found out too? Was that why he died? At the hands of the CIA?

'Your story's going on page one,' the deputy news editor looked at him uneasily.

Ryle dashed back to his desk with a sense of purpose and rooted among his notes unitl he found an old message giving him Jonathan's number.

'Is that sidekick of Erlanger's still around?' he asked him.

'Harvey? Yes.'

'Where'll you be in the morning? I'd like to come down and have another look around.'

'Bring a flak jacket this time,' Jonathan laughed and gave him directions to his home.

Ryle rested his forehead on the telephone. Now he really had something hard with which to flush out Erlanger and get to the real story. I am going to do it, he told himself. I'm going to get to the bottom of this story. And bring something to a successful conclusion.

Twenty

Ryle turned cautiously on the frozen footpath and passed two young women with pinched faces who were looking up at the barred windows in the side wall of the Bridewell garda station. One held a small child by the hand and tried to quieten an infant whining in a rickety pushchair. The other yelled, 'I can't hear you, Robbo.' A muffled voice came back, indecipherable beneath the crying. 'Can't you shut him up?' the woman complained to her companion.

Ryle went the other way towards the district court building and walked quickly under the shelter of a canopy to the last courtroom. It had a very high ceiling and stout wooden furniture and was packed with policemen at the front and young women and old people at the back. He sat into the narrow press box and Billy squeezed in beside him.

'What are you doing here?' Ryle demanded in surprise.

'The same as yourself,' Billy smiled.

'This is the press box.'

'Aye. I'm reporting it. Aren't you?'

The court clerk ordered silence as Ryle was about to ask him why the Provos had disrupted the demo and got Rosie arrested. The judge took his seat and scowled at everyone. He looked grey and impatient and even more displeased than everyone else to have to be there.

The crowd shifted and changed continuously against a low hum of whispered conversations as officialdom shuffled through a dozen or so cases of minor pub brawls, loitering with intent, and shoplifting, the usual Monday morning detritus.

Rosie and the three others were called just as Ryle began to worry that they would not appear until the afternoon. She emerged first from the stairwell leading to the cells underneath, looking pale and indifferent. Ryle recognised one of the others as one of the men to whom he had given a lift to the demonstration. They sat on the hard bench which served as the dock.

An intense-looking solicitor said he represented them and he wished to draw the court's attention to a gross abuse of power by the gardai. The judge glowered at him through hooded eyelids.

'One of my clients, Justice,' the solicitor hurried on, 'has been subjected to interrogation about an entirely separate matter while in custody, a matter of certain political documents which . . . '

'That is not a matter for this court,' the judge stopped him.

'I submit that it is, Justice. She was subjected to a grossly improper procedure after being charged and while waiting to appear before this court . . . '

'It is not.' The judge's tone brooked no argument and the solicitor gave in.

A succession of policemen gave evidence of arresting each of the four. They all admitted to the defending solicitor that the accused were not the ones who had begun the disturbance. The judge quickly fined each of them for breaching the peace and the next case was called. It had taken less than fifteen minutes.

Ryle nodded to Billy who let him out of the press box and watched him push his way through the crowded doorway after Rosie. Ryle caught up with her and the others near the gate and they all stopped when he called to her. She turned towards him with a cold glare.

'Why don't you leave me alone?' she said before he had time to say anything.

'What happened?' he asked.

'Just fuck off.' She walked away.

One of her companions stood for a moment and stared at Ryle as if memorising his features but Ryle scarcely noticed him. Then he hurried after Rosie and put a protective arm around her shoulder. He glanced back at Ryle as they went out the gate.

'The course of true love,' Billy moaned at Ryle's shoulder, 'never runs smooth.'

Aw, shit, Ryle thought as he stared at the empty gate.

'Our mutual friend is waiting for you to come back to him,' Billy dropped his voice. 'He says you were to find out something for him.'

'He's mistaken.' To hell with that, Ryle thought, that was a dead end. They knew nothing more about it than he did.

He made up his mind quickly and hurried back into the building and down a narrow stairway to the cramped press room. An elderly reporter looked up from his newspaper at the intrusion. Ryle phoned the paper's lawyer and told his secretary he was sick and would not be able to make their appointment with the gardai this morning.

'Tell him as well that the documents involved have been accidentally destroyed,' he added.

She repeated the message and Ryle raced out. The elderly reporter raised his eyes and went back to his paper.

The traffic moved in slow motion. Cars glided along gingerly, well-spaced as their drivers grappled with the unaccustomed problems of icy roads. On the radio a telephone caller spluttered in indignation at the failure of the city corporation to sand the roads when everybody knew it had been freezing hard the night before. Thousands of people were having a hard time getting to work, the presenter agreed.

Ryle hit the steering wheel with the palm of his hands and cursed aloud with frustration. Then he held his breath and resisted the temptation to hit the brakes as the back of a double-decker bus began to weave and waltz about the hill thirty yards ahead of him. The driver regained control and Ryle followed, keeping his distance.

I should call Stacy too, he thought. But he'd only order me back. Wait till I get there, present him with a *fait accompli*. If I ever get there. And what the hell is up with Rosie? What have I done to her? He cursed aloud again. At everything.

The journey took more than three hours and Ryle arrived exhausted outside Jonathan's house. The countryside was iced white and the morning sun was already beginning to sink back into the distant south, defeated.

'Bad journey,' Jonathan greeted him and gave him a cup of coffee.

Jonathan had nothing more to tell him but he went back over what had happened in greater detail. 'My friend is certain,' he said, 'there should have been some trace of extra radiation. I don't mind telling you that that's why he brought down the geiger counter. We were hoping to use the readings to launch another phase of the campaign locally. Concentrate minds with hard facts.'

Ryle waited until he finished before he got to the real reason for his visit and asked him about Erlanger's associate. Harvey drank a lot, according to the local gossip, but did not socialise much. He left with directions to Harvey's house and drove cautiously along a myriad of minor roads where the few cars to pass previously could be counted by their tracks in the frost.

The River Shannon was a deep and placid blue and in full flood, hardly moving. Ryle watched its unbroken surface and plotted his questions as he waited for an answer at Harvey's hall door.

'What is it now?' a tiny woman with an accent as flat as the Midlands demanded. 'Haven't you let him go yet?'

'I'm sorry.' Ryle tried to think quickly. 'You must have me mixed up with someone else. I'm a, ah, an acquaintance of Mr Erlanger.'

'Oh, Mr Erlanger,' she said and Ryle wasn't sure whether she thought he was Erlanger. 'I've been trying to phone all morning. He said to phone Mr Erlanger and tell him what had happened but the bloody phone won't work. I've got the number in Dublin but there isn't a peek out of it.'

'What happened?' Ryle realised her agitation was not normal and his own pulse quickened with anticipation.

'They took him to the barracks.' She began to calm down and folded her arms in conversational style now that she had someone to hear her news. 'At eight o'clock this morning. Two carloads of them arrived and took him away. A couple of them stayed behind and said they were going to search the place but I said they would not. Show me your search warrant, I said and they huffed and puffed a bit but they went on their way.'

Fantastic, Ryle thought, and had difficulty maintaining his look of deadpan concern while she went on. 'Anyhow, I said, what did they want to search a person's house for over a drunken-driving case which is not to say that he was drunk when they stopped him. What's the country coming to, I said to them, if people are going to be treated like criminals for taking a drink too many? It'd be much more in their line to be out catching drug pushers and bank robbers and the like.'

'They arrested him for drunken driving?' Ryle was getting confused and suddenly saw the story shrinking beyond his grasp yet again.

'I know,' she nodded, mistaking the disappointment in his voice for disbelief. 'That's what I said to them. What's the country coming to at all if they're carrying on like that over a couple of drinks. It's not as if we don't have enough crime for them to be occupied full time. Only last week . . . '

'Where did they take him?' Ryle interrupted. 'Which barracks?'

'The little place they have back in the village there.' She pointed down river. 'It's only a hut really.'

Ryle thanked her and told her he'd better go and see what was happening.

'What'll I do now?' She stepped out of the door as he backed away. 'There's no need for me to keep trying Mr Erlanger now, is there?'

'It might be no harm,' he said evasively.

'And I'll tell him you've gone down to the barracks. What'd you say your name was?'

Ryle told her his surname and said he'd get on to Mr Erlanger as soon as he could. He slid down the steep driveway and caught the iron scrolled top of the gate to stop himself from falling. He drove off in a hurry, no longer caring about the state of the roads. The story was breaking open at last.

The garda station was more than a hut but not a lot more. It had the temporary look of a prefabricated construction but was merely modern and probably supposed to last. Ryle found a space in its tiny car park and noted happily that there were many more cars than there should be. Most of them were unmarked.

A young garda opened a frosted glass hatch in the tiny entrance hall and scrutinised his press card carefully.

'I can't make any comment,' he said as he handed back the card at last.

'He is still here though?'

'You'll have to talk to the superintendent.'

'Okay. Can I see him?'

'He's not here.'

Ryle nodded knowingly and tried a shot in the dark. 'Inspector Devane?'

'He's busy.'

It really is breaking open, Ryle thought in disbelief. 'Would you ask him if he could have a word with me? Please?'

'I can't interrupt him. He's in conference.'

'When he comes out. I'll wait.' He saw the refusal coming and added, 'Outside.'

Ryle resisted a sudden temptation to let out a whoop of delight as he returned to his car. He reversed and turned it around until he could see the station entrance and settled down to wait. All night if necessary, he told himself triumphantly. All the forty-eight hours they could hold Harvey for under the Offences Against the State Act. But that didn't bear thinking about too deeply. Stacy would go berserk. Stacy. He couldn't call him now, couldn't move until he found out what was going on. He was going to get to the bottom of this damn story if it was the last thing he ever did.

Nothing moved. Country noises broke the silence. Some cattle were lowing in a field nearby, waiting to be fed. A couple of cars droned by and the noise lingered and receded slowly in the crisp air. A new moon hung in the dark-blue sky, ready to take over even before the sun had finally given up. There was no sign of life behind the blinded windows of the station.

The cold seeped into him, dampening his enthusiasm, and he got out and walked about the car park, flailing his chest with his arms to get his circulation going. Two uniformed guards emerged and got into a marked patrol car and drove away. They ignored him. He got back into his car and turned on the engine for heat.

Daylight had given way to a blue-lit night when a man stepped into the doorway of the station and stood there. Ryle squinted to see better but could not make out his features. A match flared and the man lit a cigarette. Ryle killed the engine and was about to get out when the figure came towards him and opened the passenger door.

Inspector Devane gathered his blue raincoat about himself, got in and exhaled a cloud of acrid smoke. 'What are you doing here?' he demanded brusquely.

Ryle looked at him and couldn't think of a suitable answer.

'I want your co-operation,' Devane went on. 'Things are at a delicate stage. Publicity would not be helpful at the moment.'

'That's okay. Anything I do won't appear until tomorrow morning.'

Devane shook his head, rejecting Ryle's perception of the time-scale involved. 'Your report this morning didn't help,' he grumbled. 'Who told you to write that stuff about Erlanger?'

'Nobody.' Ryle blurted in surprise. Devane had an unnerving ability to put him on the defensive, make him feel shifty and guilty.

'When did you talk to Erlanger?'

'Friday. And the week before.'

'And that's all he said? What you have in the paper?'

'About the documents, yes.' Ryle sighed and told himself to regain the initiative. But Devane had him at a disadvantage. He seemed to think Ryle knew what was going on, and yet he didn't, at least not in any detail.

'I'll fill you in on everything,' Devane offered, as though he was reading Ryle's mind, 'if you hold off for a couple of days.'

Ryle rested his elbows on the steering wheel and clutched his head in his hands. 'I don't think I can do that,' he said mournfully. 'This story is obviously about to break. I can't hang back and be scooped by someone else.'

'You won't be.'

'You can't guarantee that, can you?'

Devane rolled down his window and tossed out his cigarette end. 'I'll talk to your editor if you like. Explain the situation to him.'

Fuck it, Ryle thought bitterly. The story's within my grasp now and I'm not going to let it bounce away again.

'Look,' he said. 'I don't want to screw up whatever you're doing. I don't even know exactly what you're doing. All I know is that you're the man investigating Clark's death and that you've arrested Erlanger's site manager or whatever he is. And there's obviously a connection between these facts. I honestly don't see how publicising these facts would screw you up.'

He paused to give Devane an opportunity to explain but the Inspector said nothing. 'You're worried about Erlanger, right?'

Devane grunted.

'I presume you've taken steps on that front,' Ryle said. 'Anyway, Harvey's housekeeper is busily telling everybody what's happened and trying to phone Erlanger to tell him about Harvey's arrest.'

'He hasn't been arrested.'

'What's he doing in there?'

'Helping with inquiries.'

'Into what?'

Devane shook his head. They fell silent for a moment.

'I'm sorry,' Ryle said. 'But I don't see how a straightforward story tomorrow morning is going to cause you any difficulties. I really don't. Is it because of Erlanger? Because he's CIA?' Ryle watched for his reaction but Devane gave nothing away. 'Is Harvey CIA too?' he asked.

Devane shook his head but the gesture wasn't meant as a negative; it was more like an animal shaking away an irritating itch. 'What makes you think that?'

Ryle shrugged. 'It would make sense. Some sort of sense,' he amended.

'I can't help you,' Devane said. 'Only on the condition I mentioned.'

They looked at each other for a moment before Devane nodded a curt goodbye and got out of the car. Ryle watched him return to the station. Something wasn't quite right, he thought. But he still had the makings of a hell of a story. He had to get to Erlanger, hit him with all the questions.

He looked at his watch and saw with dismay that it was nearly six o'clock. Stacy would have a bloody fit and the longer he left it the worse it would be.

He drove off to find a telephone and parked outside the kiosk he had used on the night of Erlanger's meeting. It felt like a long time ago, a lot longer than ten days or so. He honed the story into a short dramatic narrative and braced himself for Stacy's wrath while he waited to be put through.

'Where the fuck are you?' Stacy roared. 'What's all this about being sick and destroying documents?'

Ryle told him where he was.

'Christ almighty,' Stacy moaned. 'Will you ever grow up?'

Ryle launched quickly into his dramatised account of what was happening.

Stacy listened in spite of himself for a moment before interrupting. 'You are in deep trouble,' he said. 'Can you get that into your head?'

'I had to do it,' Ryle pleaded. 'I had a good tip-off at the last minute. The story's breaking.'

'The editor's furious. The guards are talking about the wilful destruction of evidence and charges and arrest warrants. And as far as the editor's concerned they can have you.' Stacy gave an exasperated groan and went silent. 'Why didn't you call me? I've spent the whole fucking day making excuses for you. Without even knowing where you were.'

'I should have. I know. I'm sorry.' Ryle tried to sound suitably penitent even though he was too excited to feel it.

'And we still have a bloody paper to get out,' Stacy said. 'I want the interview with Whelan.'

Not this shit again, Ryle groaned inwardly. 'But Erlanger's the real story. I've got to get to him as soon . . . '

'Don't argue,' Stacy roared down the phone. 'I want Whelan by eight o'clock. We have to have him tonight.'

'It'll take me hours to get back. The roads . . . '

'Have it here by eight.' Stacy slammed down the phone.

Ryle stepped out of the kiosk and the cold air failed to cool his indignation. He should just shag off and get pissed. Let the guards come and arrest him. Let Stacy be scooped on the Whelan story. Fuck the lot of them.

But he knew he couldn't give up now that something was happening at last. He cursed Stacy for his refusal to see the real story, that Erlanger was the key to everything. By tomorrow Stacy would be pleading with him to follow up the Clark story when the shit really hit the fan.

The main roads had been emptied by warnings of another heavy frost. Ryle split his concentration between driving and working out the story in his head. With what he had right now he could kick off with an intro saying that Harvey was helping gardaí with their inquiries into the death of Maurice Clark two weeks ago. Give some details about him and his whereabouts, bring in Erlanger as his boss and a couple of pars from today's story about the documents. Then thicken the plot by winding up with anti-nuclear groups being relieved to find no increase in radioactivity in the mining area. Maybe call Jonathan again and get a few quotes on the record.

But what he really needed was to get to Erlanger before he knew what was happening. Put the CIA question to him. Even a denial would do nicely at this stage. And the phoney uranium mine. He glanced at his watch.

His eyes ached with exhaustion by the time he arrived at Whelan's house and checked his watch again. A quick in and out and he might make it to Erlanger. As long as Whelan was home. Please God, he prayed as he approached the house. Maura opened the door and turned her head away and called, 'are you in, Jim?'

Ryle almost hugged her with relief.

Whelan's sunken eyes stared out from the living room. He seemed to have shrunk within himself, the skin on his face hanging down in limp folds.

'Jesus, you look like I feel,' Ryle said. Whelan sank back into his chair and gave him a dull stare. You've been through the wringer.'

Whelan nodded absently. 'I told you. I can't talk to you.'

'You've made up your mind?' Ryle perched himself on the edge of the couch, still wearing his coat.

'They only want the slightest excuse. I told you the whips have ordered no interviews.'

'But they've all been talking,' Ryle retorted and cursed inwardly. The last thing he needed was a protracted session here. Yet he had to get something or Stacy really would throw him to the wolves. 'Today's paper is full of statements from your colleagues getting onside. Anyhow,' he added, 'declaring your intentions can't be a bigger sin than voting against the government.'

Whelan did not reply and Ryle realised suddenly the implications of what he had just said. Whelan wouldn't be worried about publicity if he was going to buck the party line. 'You're going to support the government.' He made it a statement.

'What choice do I have?' Whelan stirred like someone waking from a deep sleep. 'I'm a full-time politician. I can't do anything else. I have to make a living. I've got a mortgage. Children to feed.' He paused and looked earnestly at Ryle. 'You know how it is.'

Ryle said nothing and Whelan turned away and sighed. 'I want to stay in politics,' he said quietly, almost a whisper. 'It's my life.'

'Have you told them?'

He shook his head. 'There's a party meeting in the morning. They can sweat it out till then.' A touch of spirit enlivened his voice.

'What about your comments on the radio last week? That neutrality was not for sale and all that.'

'What about them?' Whelan said defiantly.

'You're going to be asked about them. Have them played back at you.'

'A lot can happen in a week.'

'That's going to sound pretty feeble.'

'I know a lot more now than I did then. About neutrality and everything else.' An edge of bitterness sharpened his voice. 'It's only a tactic anyway, this offer to negotiate neutrality.'

'Who told you that?' Whelan did not answer and Ryle continued, 'We talked about that. Remember? If they told you it was a tactic and locked you into the policy then you couldn't object.'

'All politics is tactics.'

'You've really been through the wringer,' Ryle said with feeling.

'I seem to remember we also talked about you giving up your career on a point of principle.' Whelan stared at him. 'And you thought the very idea was a joke.'

'How did they change your mind?'

'Did I change my mind?' Whelan asked rhetorically and sighed. 'The carrot and the stick. The Taoiseach offered the carrot and everyone else wielded the stick. He told me I had a great political future and it grieved him to see it thrown away over a simple misunderstanding. Other than that it's been all threats and abuse.'

He picked up a file from the floor beside his chair and tossed it onto the coffee table in front of Ryle. A couple of sheets fell out and Ryle recognised some telegram forms. He picked up a sheet torn from a copybook and covered in a disturbed scrawl which offered to pray for the repose of Whelan's soul. A black-edged mass card was pinned to the back. 'Jesus.' Ryle muttered.

'I stayed with my sister last night but this stuff began coming through her letterbox too,' Whelan said. 'One of the kids came home from school today and asked me if I was in the IRA. He doesn't even know what the IRA is but another child taunted him about me fighting against the government.' Whelan stretched an up-turned palm towards Ryle as though it held proof of something as well as a supplication.

Ryle shook his head in astonishment. 'And you want to remain part of all that?'

'It's my life.' Whelan shrugged. He took another sheet of paper from the floor and tossed it onto the table. Ryle read the printed address of the Taoiseach's office and Whelan told him the person it was addressed to was the chairman of his constituency executive.

It said Deputy Whelan would not be ratified as a candidate again by the national executive and instructed the constituency to select a replacement. It ended with an appeal to the constituency to work hard to prevent the election of any independents in their area. Independents distorted and undermined the stability of the political system. It was signed by the Taoiseach. Ryle noticed there was no date on the letter.

'Has this been sent?' he asked.

'Not yet.'

'I'd love to take this stuff away and quote the lot of it.' Ryle waved a hand over the coffee table.

'You can't quote anything.'

'But I'll write a story saying you're going to vote with the government. It is believed and all that sort of stuff.'

Whelan gave no indication that he had heard him. Ryle stood up and, in the hallway, Whelan said, 'Do you know that ad for the hospitals sweepstakes? "If you're not in, you can't win", something like that?'

Ryle nodded.

'That says it all,' Whelan said. 'I have no choice.'

Ryle shivered as he got into the car, not just from the cold. Whelan looked and sounded a broken man, like a vagrant seeking support for his self-justification while endlessly recounting the origins of his misfortune. He turned off the heater and opened his window as he felt his eyelids grow heavy and his mind begin to wander.

'Have you got it?' Stacy put his hands on his hips as Ryle tottered into the news room, half frozen and exhausted.

'He won't go on the record,' Ryle said and Stacy cursed explosively, 'but he's not going to break ranks.'

'Right.' Stacy leapt into action and yelled to the chief sub-editor that they'd re-jig the lead story to say the government would survive with Whelan's support and they could still make the first edition. A sub-editor careered off to the case room to prepare for the change.

'Why's he changed his mind?' Stacy turned back to Ryle and fed two sheets of paper and a carbon into a typewriter.

'Pressure.' Ryle shrugged. 'He's wrecked.'

Stacy sat down. 'We'll put a new top onto the pol corr's story and weave it into that.' He began typing.

Ryle headed for the door. 'Where the hell are you going?' Stacy yelled without looking up.

'Erlanger. I've got to get to him before the story breaks.'

'What story? This?' Stacy pointed at his typewriter.

'The story I told you about on the phone.'

'How's it going to break if you haven't written it yet?' Stacy said. 'There's a deadline, you know.'

Ryle cursed and came back slowly.

'Give me a quote on Whelan's change of heart.'

'No quotes. I told you,' Ryle said, looking over Stacy's shoulder. 'And make that "government sources", not "family sources".'

Stacy paused but scrolled the paper back and made the change. 'We've got to explain why,' he insisted. 'We've dug out his quotes from last week.'

'You'll think of something,' Ryle said and went to the coffee machine, realising he hadn't eaten all day. He looked around for a copy boy and pleaded with him to get him a pub sandwich.

'I've got it,' Stacy said, holding up a sheaf of copy paper. 'He had a half-hour meeting with the Taoiseach this morning.' He began typing quickly. 'Get the top of this stuff back from the subs,' he ordered without looking up.

Ryle did as he was told, dropped the material beside Stacy and went to his own desk. He stared at the blank page and tried to remember the story about Harvey that he had sketched out in his head. It came back to him in disjointed bits that no longer seemed to hang together as smoothly and neatly as they had when they were just in his mind.

Stacy thrust his typewritten sheet in front of him. 'Okay?' he demanded. Ryle read it and nodded. Stacy went into a huddle with the chief sub. He returned at a leisurely pace and looked over Ryle's shoulder at what he was writing.

'The garda press office says there's no connection,' he said.

Ryle stopped typing in mid-word and let his arms drop to his side. 'You asked them?' he said angrily. 'What'd you do that for?'

'It's standard procedure in this news room to check things out,' Stacy said icily.

'I don't believe this.'

'Don't you start throwing the head with me,' Stacy warned slowly. 'I've had it up to here with you.'

'But this is an exclusive story.' Ryle stood up. 'And they'll tell everyone.'

'They denied it.'

'Balls. It's true. I was there.'

'Your judgement on this story has become suspect. You've let yourself get carried away. Become too involved for some reason.'

'For fuck's sake,' Ryle howled. 'Why'd you take my word on Whelan then?'

Stacy glared at him, then went back to the news desk and got a copy of another story and handed it to him. The couple of paragraphs said garda inquiries into Maurice Clark's death were almost complete and quoted their press office as saying that a full report would be presented to the Minister for Justice on his return tomorrow from an official trip abroad.

'Balls,' Ryle repeated and crumpled the paper into a ball. 'That is absolute balls. This case is about to break wide open and this is the story. And it's a much bigger story than all the political bullshit.' He ripped the sheet out of his own typewriter.

Stacy looked at him closely and then took the paper. 'Finish it,' he said, 'and we'll talk about it. And eat your sandwich.'

Ryle chewed at the slice of unyielding beef and pounded out the rest of the story. 'You'll be making one hell of a mistake if you spike this.' He handed Stacy the completed report. He sat on the edge of the news desk and began telling him everything that had happened

'All right, all right,' Stacy interrupted. 'Will you let me read the goddam story?'

Ryle withdrew to his desk and picked up the phone in a reflex action. He flicked through his contact book and looked at Erlanger's number while he drained his coffee. No, he decided. This wasn't a situation for a phone call. It was almost midnight but it mightn't be too late for a visit. He leafed forward through the notebook and dialled Rosie's number instead.

A male voice answered and Ryle hesitated and asked for Rosie. The voice demanded to know who was calling and Ryle gave his name. 'Fuck off,' the voice growled a repeat of Rosie's last message and the phone went dead. Ryle let the receiver drop slowly onto its cradle and stared down the length of the empty news room

Stacy came back, showed him the top copy of the other story

then jammed it onto a spike. 'Okay?' He clapped him lightly on the shoulder. 'Go and get some sleep. And phone me in the morning before you come in and we'll try and sort out the other problems.'

Ryle felt less tired now and less like going home to his gloomy bedsitter. He called a good night to Stacy, got back into his car and drove southward to Killiney. A light powdering of snow lay cleanly on the city, smoothing its gap-toothed face like the balm of a new morning.

Maybe Stacy was right, he thought, maybe I have become too involved in this story. Maybe everyone in this story is too involved. Maybe it's just a too-involved story. He shrugged. He simply wanted to bring something to a conclusion. For once.

He drove cautiously up the narrow, humpbacked roads towards Erlanger's house and caught its nameplate in the side glare of his headlights. The heavy metal gate was closed. He parked a little further on and walked back. Beyond the gate a gravel driveway twisted away to the right but he could see the house from one side. It was dark.

A small cloud of snow drifted down from a tree as a breeze off the sea caught it. The snow on the driveway was unmarked and there was no sign of life. Ryle turned away.

Snow began to drift down lazily as he drove home.

Twenty-one

The car skidded to a halt in the driveway and Inspector Bill Devane slammed the door and raced into the house. The snow was beginning to cling to the lawn, smudging the concrete path. He half-noted the faint outline of footprints already leading to his door but he didn't wait to think about them.

He kicked the hall door shut behind him, picked up the phone and dialled. It rang out with the peculiarly empty tone of a phone that is not going to be answered but he still held onto it absently, wondering where he could round up some bodies without going into headquarters. The heat in the house made his eyelids heavy and he rubbed them with his spare hand.

When he opened them again his wife was standing in the door to the living room, looking tense. She nodded silently towards the room behind her and he put the phone down and brushed past her. Garda Casey was getting to his feet, wiping biscuit crumbs from his lips and taking care not to overturn a coffee table. A half cup of tea wobbled as he lifted the table aside.

'Good,' Devane nodded, too preoccupied to wonder at his presence. 'I was just calling you. We've got to get a couple of lads together. Immediately.'

Casey coughed apologetically. 'The Chief wants to see you now. Sir.'

'No time for that.' Devane glanced around the scene of domesticity as if he had stumbled into someone else's living room. 'We've got a job to do.'

'He's waiting in the office,' Casey persisted, willing Devane to understand. 'He was very insistent.'

'Not now.' Devane checked his watch which showed it was almost one o'clock.

The young detective took a deep breath. 'He said I'm to arrest you . . . '

'What?' Devane glowered at him.

'If you don't come immediately,' Casey stuttered and reddened, 'I am to arrest you. That's an order. I mean, he gave me that order. As an order.'

'Fucking eejit.' Devane stared through him.

'I'm sorry.' Casey spread his hands plaintively. 'What am I supposed to do?'

'Okay, okay,' Devane sighed. 'We'll get it over with now.'

His wife looked from one to the other and asked Devane if he wanted a cup of tea or something but he walked past her and was gone again. Casey grabbed his overcoat, thanked her for the tea and sped out after the Inspector. He drove and made a single attempt to explain his dilemma but Devane cut him short with a grunt and kept his eyes closed. They drew up silently in the narrow street at the back of Dublin Castle.

'Gather up as many men as you can,' Devane ordered. 'And draw out firearms for them.'

The hotel bar had been shuttered and dark for hours but the group of politicians still clung to a corner of the lounge like survivors to a raft. Tommy Lyster squatted in the middle of them, overflowing a tight armchair and revelling in the unmistakable deference of his cronies towards his new role as the man who really knew what was going on. The table was cluttered with empty glasses and smoke hung thickly in the light from a standard lamp.

Another rumble of ribald laughter rolled around as the backbenchers tried to outdo each other in scatological comments about members of the Opposition front bench. 'Do you think, does he have a conscience, too?' one of them wheezed and the laughter rumbled again at the reference to their earlier conversation about Whelan and their dissident colleagues.

Lyster chortled happily and dug into his back pocket for a fistful of notes as the elderly night porter balanced a tray of drinks on the corner of the table. 'There's a man over there wants to see you, Mr Lyster,' he said.

Lyster squinted through the darkness to the door and saw his secretary peering uncertainly into the gloom. 'Duty calls, Tommy,' one of his cronies sniggered reverentially.

'Don't worry, I'll be back in time for your round.' Lyster provoked another drunken laugh and pulled himself to his feet.

His secretary stepped back into the lobby as though he feared Lyster's anger. 'There's a problem, Minister,' he said quickly and handed him a copy of Ryle's newspaper. Lyster cast a furious eye over the report of Harvey's arrest and then caught sight of the lead story saying Whelan would support the Government. He scanned it with a satisfied snort and turned back to the other story.

'What the fuck do they think they're doing?' he demanded.

The secretary gestured vaguely. 'I don't know, Minister. The Commissioner says he's only just heard about it.'

'Doesn't he know he's under orders not to go near the Americans?'

'Yes, Minister. But he says that nobody ordered this man's arrest. It was an inspector acting on his own initiative.'

'Jesus Christ,' Lyster exploded. 'He's the Commissioner, isn't he? He's supposed to be in charge of the bloody outfit.'

His secretary nodded his wholehearted agreement and plunged on. 'He says they may have to do something about it. Now that it's in the papers.'

'He may have to do something about it,' Lyster parroted sarcastically and sank into an armchair. He took up the paper and read through Ryle's story again, realising its full implications this time. 'Like what?'

'Question Mr Erlanger.'

Too bloody right, Lyster thought, seeing his shares and his profit blowing like litter down a gutter. A thousand quid down the drain. I'd like an hour in a quiet room with that smooth shit myself. 'Well, what are they waiting for?' he snapped 'Why don't they pull him and beat the truth out of him?'

His secretary looked nonplussed at the Minister's vehement attitude towards law and order and decided he was drunk. Hoped he was drunk. 'But they're under orders not to approach him,' he said patiently, 'because of the, ah, possible diplomatic ramifications.'

Lyster gave him a sour look. 'So they do remember their orders, do they?' He had only himself to blame: hadn't he decided to sell his Atlantis shares first thing this morning? It had slipped his mind in all the political hustle of making sure there'd be no problems with tomorrow's meeting. That bastard Whelan, he thought, it's all his fault. He's cost me a thousand quid. I'd like to get *him* into a quiet room for an hour, too. Him and his fucking conscience.

His secretary coughed. 'Shall I tell him to go ahead then, Minister?'

Lyster squeezed his eyes into slits. So that's what they were up to – passing the buck. 'He wants me to make the decision for him, does he? Now that he's made a balls of it.'

'Well, no, Minister. I don't know.' His secretary sighed, inwardly angry at being used as the messenger by his superiors. 'All he said was that he thought the Government should be appraised of the situation. In the light of the possible wider considerations for the national interest.'

Lyster glanced at him and decided he would go far in the civil service. The national interest, indeed. He gripped the sides of the armchair and got to his feet. 'All right,' he said with as much authority as he could muster. 'The Government is appraised.'

His secretary thanked him and left quickly while Lyster made his way up to his bedroom. He took his time, in no hurry to make the phone call and wake the Taoiseach. He's going to chew the balls off me, he thought matter-of-factly. Better now than in the morning. The junior Minister for Justice wasn't going to be left holding this buck either.

The door opened and closed with a sharp slap, like the first clap of thunder after a calm.

Inspector Devane lay back in a hard wooden chair with his heavy chin on his chest, drifting on the edge of sleep and feeling the base of his spine ache. It had been an hour, maybe more, since he had been brusquely banished to the vacant office and ordered not to move. He took his time opening his eyes.

'Mr Devane.' The Chief stood between the two desks that cramped the tiny office and surveyed him like a suspect. He had countermanded Devane's order to his assistant and disappeared back to the round of frantic phone calls that had interrupted his evening of therapeutic carpentry four hours earlier. He still wore a worn sports jacket, faded trousers and an open-necked shirt and seemed to have shed some of his authority with his uniform.

'What exactly were you planning to do with this private army you were trying to recruit?' he barked

'Round up some suspects.' Devane eyed him appraisingly. He had been told about Ryle's story and knew that things could hardly be worse. But he was ready for whatever might be thrown at him.

'Names?'

'Everybody who can help us get to the bottom of this case.'

The Chief gave a snort, circled the other desk slowly and settled onto a chair. 'And does that include some of our duly elected leaders?' His voice oozed sarcasm and he lifted a pile of files to one side to clear his view. 'The entire cabinet, perhaps?'

Devane gave him a scathing look. 'We're wasting time,' he said. 'We've got to pull in Erlanger, Burke, Gantly and Clark's widow.'

The Chief swore. 'Are you out of your mind?'

'There's no time to lose.' Devane pulled himself painfully upright on the chair, prepared to argue his case, but the Chief cut him short.

'Just what the fuck do you think you're doing?' he demanded. 'So far today you've disobeyed orders. Made a false arrest. Tried to give orders to some culchie superintendent. Involved your subordinates in an unauthorised operation. Just what are you up to, Inspector?'

'Trying to find out why Clark died,' Devane snapped. 'And every minute we waste here's making that more difficult. We've got to move fast.'

The Chief slammed the desk with his open palm. 'You don't seem to appreciate the situation you're in. You arrested a man under the Offences Against the State Act, questioned him for ten hours and then ordered,' his voice rose as if he were trying to deal with a recalcitrant child, 'ordered, if you don't mind, a superintendent whose territory you'd invaded to hold him for forty-eight hours. All in contravention of specific orders. And without any legal justification.'

Devane frowned impatiently at his superior's refusal to address the main issue but he had to go along with him. 'Nobody told me Harvey was off limits. Nobody.'

'On what grounds did you arrest him? What's the scheduled offence you suspected him of?'

Devane shrugged, aware that the Chief had picked on the one question on which he was vulnerable. He should have had a suspicion that Harvey was involved in some kind of terrorist-related crime, however tenuous, to justify his use of the holding powers of the law. He knew he could think up something but he couldn't be bothered right now: this was all irrelevant.

'What is it?' the Chief repeated and answered his own question. 'There isn't one. He can sue you for false arrest. Abusing your powers. And if he does, you're on your own. You had no right.'

'Oh, for Christ's sake,' Devane shouted back, 'we've got evidence of a crime now and you're trying to stop me doing anything about it.'

'What crime?' the Chief retorted derisively.

'Fraud.'

'Fraud?'

'Yes, it's a crime.'

'But it's not a scheduled offence,' the Chief said doggedly. 'And now you want to race around in the middle of the night arresting people for fraud? You want to arrest Clark's widow for fraud?' His voice rose with disbelief and anger at the idea.

'I want Erlanger.' Devane sprang to his feet and rounded his desk with his hands out to halt the Chief who was also rising from his chair. 'And I've got him for fraud. For starters.'

'You're out of your mind. You were given a direct order not to approach him. So you set about circumventing that and manufacturing . . . '

'Oh come on,' Devane shouted. 'Don't you understand anything? Erlanger's not a businessman, whatever he is. We know it. The whole country knows it. It's in the fucking newspapers. We've got him on fraud and he's involved in Clark's death. And you're still trying to protect him. Why?'

'People have rights,' the Chief snarled. 'Innocent until proved guilty. And we have our orders.'

'Fuck the politicians.' Devane leaned on the Chief's desk, his lugubrious face hardened into an implacable mould. 'What do you think they're going to say when the shit hits the fan and everybody wants to know why we let Erlanger get away? Blame us. You and me. The bumbling gardai. Fucked it up again.'

'This is a disciplined force,' the Chief said icily. 'We obey orders and nobody under my command is going to rum amok on some private vendetta.'

'A vendetta?' Devane straightened up and shook his head in disbelief, seeing suddenly how he was going to be thrown to the wolves. 'What vendetta? I'm only doing my job. The job you should be doing instead of political arse-licking and looking after your pension.' The Chief's chair crashed to the floor as he leapt to his feet and Devane's voice rose. 'You know I'm right. You'd have done the same in the old days. Acting as a policeman first and not been worried about ... '

'That's enough,' the Chief warned, red with fury.

'I used to admire you,' Devane careered on, disgust dripping from his voice. 'You were a good cop. You wouldn't have put up with this shit. You ... '

'Get out of here,' the Chief roared. 'You're suspended. Pending disciplinary charges.'

'Bollocks.' Devane threw his hands up in an explosive retort.

The door opened and Sergeant Peter Grifford walked in, looking as fresh as if he were arriving for work after a good night's sleep. He glanced from one man to the other, at the Chief poised furiously across his desk, his tight face glowing, and at the defiant glower from Devane's strained features. 'Evening all,' he muttered doubtfully.

Devane swore and stepped back from the combat.

'Don't you know what doors are for,' the Chief shouted.

'Oh, sorry.' Grifford rapped sharply on the door behind him.

The Chief turned and set his chair back onto its legs and sank tiredly onto it. Devane lit a cigarette and exhaled noisily at a dark window. Snowflakes drifted haphazardly in the street light outside. Grifford looked unconcerned, he took a wad of newspapers from under his arm and left them gently on the desk.

'What are you doing here?' The Chief eyed the papers suspiciously.

'Volunteering, sir,' Grifford smiled and gave him a mock military salute with one finger. 'Happened to be passing and heard you needed some assistance.'

Devane guffawed sarcastically and Grifford turned to him. 'I heard you need some bodies for a raiding party. Thought I should offer my services.'

'And I thought I just heard a cuckoo,' Devane snarled back. 'Why don't you go back to hauling drunks out of gutters?'

Grifford tut-tutted. 'Birds in their little nests,' he said softly as he turned back to the Chief. 'So. Are we taking on the might of the CIA?'

The Chief was staring blankly at the unopened newspapers, in some kind of reverie. Devane, on the other hand, stepped back from the window and appeared to come back to life

'We have no alternative,' he said decisively to the Chief, realising that Grifford's appearance gave him a powerful new card. He didn't know or care why but it was clear that the Chief thought so too.

'Look,' he said slowly to the Chief. 'There really is no alternative. We've got to act immediately. We've no choice.'

There was another knock at the door and a head peered in and told the Chief there was a call for him. He marched out of the room, leaving the door ajar.

Grifford caught Devane's eye and gave him a broad wink. 'Sorry if I interrupted your little tête-à-tête.'

Devane felt his shoulders sag and made no effort to straighten them. He stood in front of Grifford like a crouching boxer. 'What the fuck are you playing at?'

'Now, now,' Grifford said soothingly.

'This is all your doing.' Devane poked a finger into the chest of Grifford's tweed overcoat as if he was testing his defences. 'Acting the bollocks as usual. Sending your tame journalist down the country after me. What game are you playing?'

'You've got it all wrong again,' Grifford sighed. 'I didn't send him after you. How could I have known you were about to take the law into your own hands?'

Devane jammed his finger into Grifford's chest again and then appeared to give up. He turned back to the window thinking, What was the point. You couldn't get anywhere with a smart ass like Grifford. Anyway, he hadn't the energy to try. He felt empty after his row with the Chief. I went too far, he sighed to himself: I shouldn't have attacked him personally.

The Chief pushed open the door. 'Inspector,' he said formally, 'you are to detain Mr Erlanger for questioning.'

Devane stared at him, trying to find a conciliatory combination of words to ease his victory. The Chief looked sunken and he felt a sudden twinge of sympathy for him: he had only been trying to carry out orders in a game where the rules were set by morons and charlatans and kept changing.

'Oh good.' Grifford rubbed his hands together. 'My journey hasn't been in vain.'

'You're not coming,' Devane barked.

'Take him.' The Chief went to his chair and lowered himself cautiously, like an old man. 'And get the fuck out of my sight.'

They set off through the dead city in three unmarked cars. The snow had stopped falling again but it had already wrapped the unmarked streets in its cocoon, filling the night air with a luminous white and deadening the sound of their passage. Casey drove the first car and Devane sat beside him with Grifford lounging in the back. Nobody said anything.

The driver slowed cautiously at a red light in Ballsbridge beside the round American embassy which sat in the snow like a giant Christmas cake. Grifford began singing 'The Star-Spangled Banner' softly and the sound of his voice seemed to arouse Devane. He told the driver gruffly to go on.

'Sorry,' Casey sighed.

'And stop fucking apologising,' Devane added irritably. He checked his watch again and saw it was after three. Time seemed to be moving both quickly and slowly. 'What do you want with Erlanger?' he asked Grifford without turning.

Grifford abandoned the anthem. 'To act out my fantasies.'

Devane sighed at the curving white of the tree-lined Merrion Road before them. 'Yes,' Grifford added, 'always wanted to surround the CIA. Get them out in the open with their hands up. See the whites of their eyes.'

'Ask a gobshite a question and you get a gobshite's answer,' Devane said to himself, aloud.

'Can I use the loudhailer when we get there?' Grifford inquired innocently and cupped his hands into a megaphone. 'This is the Garda Siochana. Throw your poison darts and mind-manipulators into the pristine snow and come out like a man.'

'He's not CIA.'

'He's not?'

'He's a con man.'

'But it was your theory. You persuaded that cat to fly among the pigeons.'

Devane grunted. 'As far as I'm concerned right now, he's just a con man.'

'Ah,' Grifford sighed with disappointment. 'Then they won't send in the Marines if we arrest him.' Our masters can sleep easily.'

'I've got him on one criminal offence,' Devane said grimly. 'And I'll prise the rest out of him.'

Grifford smiled to himself and felt a sudden empathy for Erlanger. If he fell into Devane's hands when the Inspector was in this mood he could find himself confessing to every unsolved crime in last year's files.

Casey wound cautiously down the snow-covered hill into Blackrock village and Devane urged him again to hurry up. 'You're not going to skid in this mush,' he added. The car speeded up a little and they took the coast road for Dun Laoghaire.

'Of course, fear of the Marines is not really what has been keeping our masters awake at nights,' Grifford said mildly and Devane turned around to look at him. 'There's something you should know.' Grifford nodded. 'That not even the dear old Chief knows. The real reason why Erlanger was declared out of bounds.'

'What?'

'But you didn't hear it from me. And our young friend here didn't hear it at all.'

'Cut the shit.'

Grifford looked hurt and fell silent. 'Tell me if you're going to tell me,' Devane mumbled, as near to an apology as he could bring himself to make. He was fed up to the back teeth with games and particularly with policemen who played them.

'They're afraid Erlanger will start talking in public,' Grifford said. 'About a matter that might shock the plain voters of Ireland.'

'What?' Devane tried to curb his impatience. 'Some of them are tied up in the fraud?'

'No. A sex scandal.'

Devane groaned. That was all they needed.

On their left the high lights of the car-ferry terminal shone down on its car park, deserted but for a couple of container trailers. They passed the submerged railway station and the ferry terminal building and the pier curling inwards to enclose the icy sea where Clark had died. The water was grey and its movement almost imperceptible. They did not notice.

'The morning after his party,' Grifford was saying, 'Erlanger found a couple of guests who had neglected to go home. Made themselves at home in his house instead. Curled up snug and warm in one of his spare bedrooms. A Minister and a woman who could have been his daughter. Except she was not a relation of his at all. If you follow my drift.'

'And Erlanger threatened exposure.' Devane nodded to himself.

'Erlanger was a perfect gentleman. Made coffee and offered to call a taxi for the lady if she wanted to leave. The Minister wouldn't wait, wouldn't even give her a lift. Said he had urgent business to attend to. Of a cabinet nature.'

Devane swore. 'And we're all in this mess because of a Minister's prick.'

Casey choked on a sudden giggle and quickly concentrated on the narrow hill-road climbing up to Killiney. Houses disappeared into the hillside as they went up, isolated behind their high walls and curving driveways and the shelter of well-matured trees.

'Pride,' Grifford suggested. 'Pride is the word you want. The young lady was somewhat displeased with one thing or another and was giving Erlanger a graphic account of the Minister's prowess, or lack thereof, as he fled.'

Devane signalled the driver to stop before they turned into Erlanger's road and checked that the other cars were behind.

'Certain people have nightmares about him popping up on the television news if you as much as say "boo" to him,' Grifford continued. 'Which is why they are even now kneeling by their connubial beds praying that you don't find him.'

James Burke woke suddenly and stared into the bedroom gloom. The doorbell rang again, a long peal of electronic tones rising and falling. Yvonne, he thought immediately. She's back.

He was still moping like a lovelorn teenager, alternating between self-pity at her callous discarding of him and the aching loss of her absence. She hadn't been far from his mind in the past week, even if his thoughts were becoming less and less affectionate. She was dominating his life, undermining his work, destroying his concentration. He couldn't seem to shake her off. And now she was back.

He grabbed a dressing-gown and hurried down the stairs in the half-light and reached for the front door. A sudden sense of caution broke into his semi-conscious mind as he opened the door but it was too late. Two large men stood on the doorstep.

'James Burke,' one said and Burke nodded helplessly. 'Police.'

'What?' he mumbled, mind racing.

'Just a few questions,' the detective said, firmly shouldering the door open.

'What?' Burke retreated a step. Oh no, his mind screamed in panic, she's set me up. They're going to pin it on me. Murder. The bitch.

'We'd like you to come down to the station with us. Help us with our inquiries.'

'Inquiries?' he repeated, horror flooding down into his stomach and making him feel physically ill.

The detective nodded politely, in control. 'Into the activities of Michael J. Erlanger.'

Erlanger. Burke was suddenly overwhelmed with relief. They only wanted information about Erlanger. 'Certainly,' he said, more than happy to help. 'Anything I can tell you. Anything.'

Inspector Devane had divided his group into three and two teams split off to work their way through the enclosed gardens on either side and around the back of Erlanger's house. Casey sat in the car with instructions to block the driveway when they were all in position. Devane and Grifford and another detective waited at the back of their car beneath the high pebbledashed wall in front of the house. The only sound was the sighing of disturbed snow through branches when an occasional breath of wind touched the trees.

Security lights around the house next door flashed on suddenly with all the impact of a loud crash as one of the teams tripped a sensor. Light flooded through the trees and created an illuminated mosaic of branches. A dog barked. Devane cursed, jumped on the boot of the car and clambered over the wall. He dropped into the grove of evergreen trees beside Erlanger's driveway and Grifford and the other detective followed. Other dogs in the neighbourhood took up the alert, spurring each other on to a frenzy of barking.

Devane crouched down to look through the tree trunks at the house, bulking large and dark on its snowy hilltop. It remained a silent centre amid the lights to their left and the howling dogs. They ran quickly through the grove, bent double to dodge the low branches, and up to the side of the house. In the distance a police siren was growing stronger.

Devane swore again and told the detective to get onto Control and order all cars away from the area. The detective mumbled quietly into his radio and Devane and Grifford ran across to the hall door. The Inspector glanced back through the closed gate and saw his car in position. He nodded to Grifford who pressed the bell.

Devane gave him a scathing look, pulled out his Smith and Wesson revolver and hammered its butt on the door. Bang, bang, bang.

The noise reverberated through the house and bounced back to them. In unison the dogs stopped barking in order to identify this new intrusion. In the sudden silence they heard a car engine and a single shot cracked through the night.

Grifford was already running down the drive, ploughing up the soft snow. Devane shouted to the other detective to watch the house and set off after him. They burst through the gate, their car was already revving up and they fell into it.

'What is it?' Devane panted at Casey who was spinning the wheels through the mushy snow.

'A car,' Casey said excitedly, gaunt-faced with tension and concentration. 'I tried to stop him but he kept on going. Nearly ran me down.'

Devane pulled out the radio microphone and called for help from anyone in the area. 'What kind of car?' he demanded as they sped up the narrow road, bounced over a low rise and went down a long slope.

'White saloon. I don't know what. Fucker nearly killed me.'

Devane repeated the skimpy detail into the radio and opened his window to clamp a flashing blue beacon to the roof. 'Was it Erlanger? Did you see him?' He flicked on a siren.

'One man. I didn't get a good look.'

They sloughed around a corner and saw the tail-lights of a car disappear around a bend at the end of the straight. 'Faster,' Devane yelled and they accelerated down the road, leaving a trail of fluttering snow. They rounded the bend into a series of twisting turns and suddenly they were almost upon the other car.

Devane tried to get a bearing on a mental map of where they were and shouted into the radio for anyone available to block the Vico Road. The other driver, as if he had heard, swung to take a sharp fork to the right which would bring him away from the Vico Road and into a tight corkscrew down to the bottom of the hill and the seashore. His car slewed to the left and there was a rending, screeching howl as the passenger side hit a wall and ground its way along it.

Casey did not attempt to take the fork and they skidded to a halt fifty yards on, then the three of them were out and chasing back up the hill. The driver's door was open and the man was careering down the steep hill towards the sea, running awkwardly through a restraining snow drift. He disappeared around a bend with Casey, gun in hand, gaining on him and Devane falling farther and farther behind.

The man lost his footing suddenly, toppled forward and Casey was on him with his revolver jammed into the back of his neck. 'Spread your hands where I can see them,' he shouted between breaths. 'Slowly.'

The man eased his empty hands into view and Casey put his foot under his shoulder and turned him onto his back. He lay breathing heavily, a sheen of sweat and melted snow on his frightened face, his hands spread out limply. He looked up at Casey and at Grifford and they all breathed large clouds into the crisp air.

'Who are you?' Casey demanded.

'The abominable snowman,' Grifford sighed.

The man looked past them and began to cower backwards when he saw Devane approach. The Inspector towered over him. 'What are you doing here?' It would have been a roar if he had recovered enough breath.

'They let me go.' He slid backwards and the detective stopped him with his shoe.

'Where is he?' Devane demanded with menace. 'Where's Erlanger?'

'I don't know,' Harvey stuttered. 'I told you all I know. I swear.'

'You were to meet him at the house.'

'No, no.'

'And if he wasn't there, where were you to see him? What was the plan?'

'There's no plan.' Harvey gathered himself up on his elbows. 'I swear. I don't know where he is. I was going to his house because I couldn't think where else. I mean I want to find him too. He's left me in the shit, no money, nothing.'

Harvey stared at Devane, ignoring the others, and they stood in a silent group, feeling the cold seep into their bodies. 'Can I get up?' Harvey asked plaintively.

320

'Why didn't you stop?' Casey demanded.

'I didn't, I didn't know who you were.'

'You nearly killed me,' Casey said and thrust his gun forward in an unconscious threat. Harvey shrank back.

Devane cursed at no one in particular. Harvey sat up slowly, now watching Casey, and held his head in his hands. 'I think I might have hurt my head,' he moaned. 'I knocked it back there.'

Grifford coughed politely. 'It appears, gentlemen, that we are chasing our tails.'

Devane turned and walked back up the hill.

Twenty-two

The banging pulled Seamus Ryle out of his sleep and he stumbled to the door. It crashed in against him as soon as he released the catch and he staggered backwards as two armed men rushed past him. A third grabbed his shoulder and flicked on the overhead light with his spare hand. Ryle blinked in the brightness and stood in his shirt, trying to comprehend what was happening.

'Where is she?' the man shook him. 'Where's Rosie Gantly?'

One detective pulled open the door to the built-in wardrobe and cast a cursory look inside. They lowered their guns and seemed to overwhelm the small room with their presence.

'Who're you?' Ryle croaked.

'Police. Where is she?' The third man rubbed his shin where he had collided with the low coffee table, unable to scale down his initial charge to fit the room's dimensions.

'How the fuck would I know?'

They walked out as quickly as they had entered and Ryle stepped into the hall and threw up both his hands in two-fingered farewells to their backs. He looked at his watch and saw it was after seven. 'And thanks for the wake-up,' he muttered.

He rooted through his laundry bag for clean jeans and a shirt and shook them vigorously in a vain attempt to obliterate their creases. He pulled them on, then stopped for a moment and breathed deeply. His hands were trembling.

Goddam Rosie, he thought as he tied his shoes and slipped into his leather jacket. As if it wasn't enough having her turn nasty.

The street lights were still on and the first cars were cruising cautiously towards the city, churning the snow into grey slush. Ryle drove in the opposite direction and steered a wide berth around a lorry full of men scattering shovels of sand on the road.

He followed the Bray road as far as Loughlinstown, and turned left to climb up the dark heights of Killiney.

The wheels spun on the last stretch and the car slid back down the shoulder of the hill. He gave up after a second attempt and let it run backwards onto the narrow grass verge. He trudged over the hill, the cold catching his breath, and the bay brightened slightly below him. A fresh fall of snow lay on Erlanger's driveway and had smoothed away the night's activities. It crunched under his feet in the stillness.

The bell jangled inside and he watched the sky diluting into grey above the horizon. He rang a second time, more insistently but without any expectation of an answer. The door swung slowly open.

Sergeant Peter Grifford stood before him with his shirt-sleeves rolled up and wearing a plastic apron with a dazzling yellow sunflower on it. Ryle stared at the flower, speechless.

'You have the right to remain silent,' Grifford said in a tired sing-song, 'anything you say will be taken down in writing and will be given in evidence.'

Ryle cursed.

'He says "fuck",' Grifford noted. 'Which, Your Honour, when added to "all" adequately sums up the extent of his knowledge. And current usefulness.'

'He's gone,' Ryle said and cursed himself silently for not calling on Erlanger two days earlier. It was too late: he had missed one hell of a scoop.

'Your ability to grasp the obvious never ceases to amaze.'

Ryle sighed, the tension drained away and was replaced by tiredness. The sunflower danced before him as he yawned. 'Why are you wearing that?'

'This is a stake-out,' Grifford replied in a hurt voice.

'And you're disguised as the butler.' Ryle gave a dry chuckle.

'I am here to arrest the first person who comes through this door. Which happens to be you.'

Ryle held out his wrists to him. 'Why not? It might as well be you.'

Grifford winked. 'I think you could do with a little breakfast.'

'We can't go on meeting like this.' Ryle gave a bitter laugh.

He stepped into the unlit hallway and could make out the form of a central staircase rising at its end and dividing in two as it swept up to the next floor. A detective lounged against a wall in the shadows beside a half-moon table. As his eyes adjusted to the gloom, Ryle saw an Uzi sub-machinegun lying on it, looking as harmless as a discarded child's toy.

Grifford stood on the doorstep inhaling the morning air. 'So much for the stake-out.' He pointed towards Ryle's footprints.

'Are you expecting him back?'

'You never know.'

'Maybe he'll think it was the milkman.'

'The milkman who stayed to breakfast.' Grifford shut the door and shivered. 'They turned the heat off. Shows a mean and methodical mind. Proof of criminal intent.'

Grifford led him across the hall and down narrow stairs to the basement. Ryle noticed other men in several of the rooms they passed. 'There's no cherry buns, I'm afraid,' Grifford added, 'but they thoughtfully left some rashers and eggs. In the hopes of pleading mitigation I suppose.'

The lights were on in the kitchen, gleaming on wood-panelled cupboards and modern equipment. An electric fan heater whirred and blew hot air in the centre of the floor. Ryle smelled and heard the bacon sizzling under an electric grill.

'How long've you been here?'

'All my life,' Grifford grunted and looked at him solicitously. 'Put on the kettle and we'll have a cup of tea.'

Ryle filled the kettle and switched it on while Grifford got out a pan and broke a couple of eggs into it. He hummed a lively piece of Irish dance music and seemed thoroughly at home. 'The cutlery's in there.' He pointed to a drawer and Ryle got out a couple of knives and forks and set the table.

He sat at the table and watched Grifford. 'Thanks for the wake-up call,' he said. Grifford looked at him quizzically and Ryle told him about the raid.

'Not my doing,' Grifford said. 'But if you will lie down with lionesses . . . '

'I think the lioness has moved on,' Ryle said, partly to

324

himself. 'Or whatever it is they do.' It had probably been doomed from the start, he thought, overwhelmed by the circumstances that had created it. It was only a matter of convenience anyway, he told himself, but a sense of loss undermined his conviction.

Rosie was gone from his life and he might as well accept the fact. Her rejection outside the court had had a determined finality. Only yesterday, he remembered, not even twenty-four hours ago but it already seemed to have receded into the distant past. It was probably as well: he didn't relish regular early-morning visits from large men.

Grifford slid the eggs onto two plates and picked the slices of bacon from under the grill with kitchen tongs. 'You do like fried eggs, don't you?'

Ryle nodded helplessly and they settled down to eat. Grifford flicked on a radio as the pips sounded at eight o'clock and a news reader declared that the Government faced its toughest test to date in a confidence motion in the Dáil today.

'A historic occasion,' Grifford muttered.

'Balls,' Ryle retorted, 'it's all plain sailing for them. No problem.'

'You know this for a fact?' Grifford looked up, interested.

Ryle nodded.

'That's good.' He turned back to his food, without explaining whether he approved of the Government's survival or Ryle's certainty.

The news reader went on to record the death of a part-time policeman in the North who had been shot in the back in an ambush on his farm a week earlier. Industrialists were calling for wage restraint and electricity workers were meeting to decide on a strike. Another car bomb had gone off in Beirut, NATO ministers were meeting in Brussels and the garda press office would not comment on reports that a man was helping with inquiries into Maurice Clark's death.

'Hah,' Ryle snorted happily. 'They've changed their tune.'

'That little story, as you persist in calling these things, caused me some difficulty.'

'Why?' Ryle asked in surprise. 'It had nothing to do with you.'

'How true. It must be the only thing you've found out for yourself.' Grifford poured more tea. 'But your friend Devane holds me responsible.'

'Serves you right. You should have told me.'

'I didn't know,' Grifford protested as if admitting to a serious defect. 'You can testify to my innocence when he comes back.'

'I don't think he'll be too happy to see me,' Ryle said warily.

'What would he care?' Grifford shook his head. 'There are others, though, who'd be only too happy to throw the book at you. Breaking and entering, stealing rashers to the value of seventy-eight pence, wasting police time and interfering with the scene of a crime.' He smiled brightly. 'For openers.'

And that was only the police, Ryle thought. It was nothing compared to the troubles he faced in the office today, explaining why he had stood up the editor and the lawyer yesterday. At least he had Stacy back on his side. But a good story would help to divert them. An interview with Erlanger would have done it: his disappearance might be okay for starters but he needed more.

Ryle finished his breakfast and sat back, comfortably warm for the first time since he had dragged himself out of bed. He felt surprisingly relaxed and he smiled at the unreality of the scene. Sitting in Erlanger's house, surrounded by armed men, calmly having breakfast. But there was obviously no hurry.

'Don't worry,' Grifford said soothingly. 'Those lads should be running for cover today. I doubt if they'll be along to view the scene of their shambles. And Devane's laughing.'

'He is?'

'Metaphorically speaking, of course. The only man to emerge with his reputation intact. A man of perspicacity and deductive brilliance. Thwarted by desk-bound imbeciles. A hero of the force, from inspectors down, that is. The higher ranks can't touch him without making him a martyred hero. For the moment.'

'Because he rumbled Erlanger?'

Grifford nodded. 'Had him under surveillance last week but was ordered to desist. Then he was all set to take unilateral action at the weekend by questioning Erlanger himself but was thwarted again.'

'And that's why he went after Harvey?'

Grifford nodded again and offered him more tea. Ryle shook his head and he poured a cup for himself.

'And he did that without authority?' Ryle added.

'Without anyone's knowledge. Which is not quite the same thing.' Grifford sipped his tea thoughtfully. 'I told you he was a dangerous type of policeman. Even if he is the hero of the moment.'

'So who told him to leave Erlanger alone? And why?' Things are looking up, thought Ryle, the guards actually let Erlanger slip through their fingers.

'One of his betters. Who thought he knew better.' Grifford looked up at him. 'But actually he knew fuck all. Like yourself.'

'But who wanted Erlanger to get away?' Ryle asked eagerly. 'And why?'

'I explained all that to you. The powers that be were wary of moving in on him. In case he was what he seemed to be.'

A detective walked in carrying a two-way radio with the volume turned down to a muted mumble. Ryle fell silent and Grifford offered the detective a cup of tea. He drank it standing up and Grifford asked if there were any developments.

The detective gave Ryle a cold look before replying. 'The BMW at Shannon is confirmed. It was his. Leased by him.'

'Anything upstairs?' Grifford asked.

'Not a thing. You wouldn't think anybody had been living here at all.'

'A light traveller,' Grifford nodded as though the idea was of deep significance.

The detective finished his tea and went out.

'He's gone west. Back to America,' Ryle stated. The detail was building up nicely, getting better and better.

'West or east. And never the twain shall meet. I doubt if we'll meet him again anyway.'

'I have a theory about Erlanger,' Ryle said. 'That *he* might have shot the dog, not Clark.'

Grifford shook his head decisively. 'No. He has an alibi. He was here at the time.'

'Who's the alibi? His wife?'

'And others.' Grifford raised his eyebrows in an impish smile. 'Including one of our lads.'

'What was he doing here?' Ryle's voice rose with sudden interest.

'It's a delicate matter.' Grifford went coy. 'Not of any relevance to our inquiries. And a state secret. An official secret of the most important kind.'

'Ah, come on.'

'Well.' Grifford dragged out the word. 'Only on condition that you never breathe a word of this to anyone. This could shake the foundations of the state if the revolutionaries got to hear of it.'

'There's no fear of that. Not any more.'

Grifford nodded as if satisfied and told him about the Minister and his sexual exploits. Ryle visualised the scene and let out a barking laugh. 'I'd love to have been a fly on the wall there.'

'We suspect the Minister might have been misleading us,' Grifford concluded with a serious face, 'about the Cabinet business which dragged him away in such a hurry.'

'I love it,' Ryle chortled. 'Who was it?'

'An upstanding leader of the community.'

'Obviously. But which one?'

'Not one who leaps readily to mind.'

'Ah come on,' Ryle pleaded. 'You can't leave me in suspense now.'

'As the actress said to the bishop.'

'She's an actress?'

'And the Minister's a bishop. I can't tell you any more. It's an official secret. And I'm relying on you not to repeat it.'

'These things never remain secret,' Ryle protested. 'Not for long.'

'You'd be surprised.' Grifford shook his head. 'Never mind the common belief that you can't hide anything in this town.'

'But Erlanger knows about it. The guards know. Everybody who was at the party probably knows.'

'They don't.' Grifford said seriously. 'That was the other reason Devane and his hounds were called off Erlanger. Certain people were terrified he'd spill the beans to the likes of you if he was hassled.'

Ryle cursed himself again for having sat on the story and not approached Erlanger after his last breakfast with Grifford. What a story he could have got. He ran his mind's eye over the members of the cabinet sitting in a half circle on the Dáil's front bench. He could visualise a couple in Grifford's story but he thought about the least likely ones. The effort stretched his imagination beyond its early-morning capabilities.

'You're being sadistic,' he groaned at Grifford.

The sergeant shook his head again. 'It really is a closely guarded secret. And I'm only telling you because you look like you need a little light relief. After all your labours. Besides,' he added, 'we've got away from the point. I was merely explaining why your theory about Erlanger doesn't stand up.'

'Does this Minister feature in the statements on the Clark case?' Ryle asked as the germ of an idea took hold.

'Don't waste your time even wondering,' Grifford told him impatiently. He got up, gathered the plates and piled them into the sink. He turned on a tap and tossed a dishcloth to Ryle.

'What about Harvey?' Ryle asked.

'One of life's losers. Always landing in the shit and never knowing how he got there.'

'But he must have known there was no uranium down there.'

'Harvey sees everything through a glass darkly,' Grifford shrugged. 'Apparently he'd have trouble telling a fried egg from a lump of uranium. But he's very perceptive at divining different brands of alcohol. Become a connoisseur of Irish whiskies in a remarkably short time.'

Ryle accepted another wet plate from him and asked if Erlanger really was a CIA man.

Grifford shrugged. 'Maybe the owner of this lot will find out. He's very upset about a little matter of outstanding rent. Not to mention the absence of the three months' notice required by the lease.'

'That doesn't sound like the CIA. Leaving a lot of debts.'

'Maybe they're strapped for cash,' Grifford grunted. 'Manipulating the world must be a costly business.'

'Rented house, leased car,' Ryle mused. 'I presume the office was rented too.'

'We're waiting for someone to show there. Someone other than you,' Grifford added warningly. 'And he had overdraft facilities, used to the full, in three banks. At least.'

'That's hardly the mark of the CIA,' Ryle repeated more emphatically.

'You know for a fact that's not their modus operandi, do you?' Grifford turned from the sink.

'He was flogging off his shares, too. Raking in money while paying out nothing.'

'On paper,' Grifford nodded, 'although he wouldn't have got all the cash from his share sales yet. Not until the end of the account period, I'm told.'

'It still doesn't sound like the CIA.'

'Unless they want you to think it couldn't be them.' Grifford handed him their two cups.

Ryle considered that for a moment: we're back to the hall of mirrors again, he thought. It was pointless trying to work out those kinds of probabilities. At least he could write about them now that Erlanger was officially a fugitive. In fact, all in all he had a nice juicy story. It was going to need space, a long piece inside with a front page wrap-up of the main points.

Grifford dried his hands and Ryle stacked the dry crockery on the counter.

'So what happened to Clark?' he asked.

'Ah, the bottom line.' Grifford untied the apron and folded it carefully. He retrieved his suit jacket from the back of a chair and rested himself against the counter. 'Suicide, probably. Accident, maybe.'

'There is a difference.'

'Great minds have agonised about that. Did he repent after he jumped? In the moment before he went under for the last time? He couldn't swim. Did you know that?'

'But why kill himself?' Ryle sat down at the table.

Grifford went to the window and gazed at a spray of sunshine glancing shyly through the trees on the summit of the hill. 'Why was he standing on Dun Laoghaire pier with a gun in his hand at that ungodly hour of the morning? Unless he was thinking of killing somebody? And there was nobody there for him to consider killing except himself. Until the woman wandered by with her dog. And he didn't kill her. He killed the dog. And he can't have had any real motive for killing the dog.'

He seemed lost in his thoughts for a moment, then moved away and went to turn out the lights. A grainy daylight settled into the room.

'He was in deep trouble, financially. Bankrupt in all but name. Waiting for someone to push him over the edge. Erlanger, for one, could have done it. Clark owed him twenty grand for shares he couldn't afford. You know, of course, that Dáil deputies can't remain Dáil deputies if they're declared bankrupts.'

Ryle nodded. 'But those shares are worth a lot now. He could have sold them and cleared that debt.'

'That's happened since he died. And that was only one of his debts.' Grifford began to pace a slow circle around the room and Ryle shifted in his chair to follow him.

'His plans were in a shambles. He was speculating in all the riskiest shares to make enough money to set himself up comfortably in politics. In a hurry to do it before he became a minister when such ventures would be more difficult. Then the money-making schemes went wrong and became a threat to his political career. A vicious circle, you might say. Shooting the dog put the lid on it. Maybe he was only contemplating suicide until then but there was no turning back after that. He was ruined anyway. Who'd vote for a dog-killer? So he just stepped over the edge. Of the pier.' Grifford paused. 'And he needn't have done it. If only he'd waited . . . ' He stopped and gave Ryle a questioning look.

'So he was susceptible to blackmail,' Ryle said, thinking of the forged neutrality documents and trying to knit everything into a seamless narrative. 'Even if he found out about Erlanger's mining scam.'

'Especially if he found out.' Grifford continued his circle of the room. 'Either way, Erlanger put the screws on him, forced him to sign the neutrality document and began to control him politically. Which,' he raised a finger in the air, 'leaves only one question. Erlanger's motivation.'

Ryle nodded in anticipation.

'Was he out to make money? Or wield political influence? Could hardly be both. The CIA undoubtedly favours private enterprise but surely not among its own operatives. But it's some coincidence that he should play around with the neutrality issue just at the precise moment when the Government was turning its gargantuan brain to it too.'

Grifford stopped and spread his hands in a gesture which said that was it, the question was unanswered.

'I thought you didn't believe in coincidences?' Ryle said, a hint of accusation reflecting his disappointment. It would have been nice to have everything neatly wrapped up, to be able to say as a fact that Erlanger was an American spy. He'd have to make do with suspicions, it seemed.

Grifford shrugged. 'One must learn to live with loose ends.'

'And the gun?' Ryle added. 'Where did he get that?'

'God knows. Not from the lads. Not officially anyway.'

Ryle nodded. That had been obvious from the IRA man's reaction.

'They ship them in by the container-load,' Grifford sighed. 'Maybe it fell off the back of a lorry.'

'Can I use this?' Ryle went towards a wall phone.

'I wouldn't advise it. I don't want to have to explain how we came by transcripts of your breathless prose.'

Ryle nodded his understanding and turned to another question that had been playing on his mind. 'Just for my own information,' he said. 'What exactly is your role in all this?'

'Another loose end,' Grifford said brightly.

'You mean you don't know?' Ryle smiled.

'Very droll,' Grifford drawled and sat on the edge of the table with his arms folded. 'A certain important person asked me to keep an eye on developments. In case the normal reporting procedures failed to keep him fully informed.'

Ryle nodded with satisfaction: it was as he had thought. 'You mean you were working for the Taoiseach?'

'Weren't you?'

Ryle shook his head impatiently. 'But why?'

'We're old friends. Of a sort,' Grifford muttered as though he was embarrassed. 'In the land of the cute whores, the cutest whore is king.'

'Did he know you were tipping me off?' Ryle was intrigued.

'Of course not.' Grifford said with indignation and straightened up suddenly as if he was late for a pressing appointment elsewhere. 'It's all been a most salutary experience. I've discovered I'm not cut out to be a cute whore, after all. Very upsetting at my age.'

'I don't know what you thought I could do,' Ryle said, mystified.

Grifford shrugged. 'It's all a shambles. Another victory for the cock-up theory of history. Leaving a trail of shattered reputations. Except for you, of course. You've done nicely.'

'I don't know about that,' Ryle said dubiously although privately he agreed. He thought about Rosie trapped by obscure machinations, about Whelan wrestling with his conscience and Burke battered by events. Even Erlanger didn't seem to have got away with much, if money was his object. And Clark had killed himself unnecessarily. It was a shambles.

'You and Devane.' Grifford shook his head in wonderment. 'Maybe he is right. Play it straight and to hell with being too smart for your own good. That's the moral of the story. Tedious but true.'

Ryle left another trail of footprints on the way out and glanced back at the house as he closed the gate. It was the first time he had seen it in daylight, a large, square, solid mansion standing deserted in the crisp sunshine. The warning notice caught his eye as he turned away. He wondered idly what Erlanger had done with the dog.

Ryle whistled happily as he drove back into the city. The sun was shining, he felt on top of the world – he had a rattling good yarn about Erlanger, Clark and incompetent policemen. It had almost everything he could ask for: spies, diplomatic and political chicanery, police cock-ups, financial skulduggery. Even sex, but that was another story.

He had all day to tell it and there would be lots of space too. The political rubbish would be out of the way by the afternoon and a decent story would be needed. It would solve his problems in the office. And the guards who had wanted to interview him would be too busy scurrying for cover to bother any more.

He switched on the radio and amused himself with the story he couldn't write. Sex alibi for minister in murder mystery. A senior Cabinet minister has been cleared of involvement in the mysterious death of a party colleague because he was having sex with an actress at the time. That would do nicely as an opening par, he thought. Not too sensational, in keeping with the paper's style, but getting the mixture right: sex and violence.

The editor wouldn't like it, of course. He didn't like the word 'mystery' and he wasn't wild about mentions of sex either. Pity, he thought. But he still had a cracking good yarn about Erlanger. Another three-letter word beginning with 's'. Sex-crazed minister gives spy alibi. That was it.

He groaned contentedly as a reporter on the radio gave a breathless description of deputies arriving for the Dáil debate. 'What's happening right now?' the studio anchorman demanded. Right now, the reporter said, all attention is focused on a meeting of the Government party which began just over half an hour ago. Nobody knows how long it will take but we should have a clear indication afterwards of the outcome of the Dáil vote.

Prepare yourself for an anti-climax, Ryle advised him mentally. The anchorman said they would go back to Leinster House if there were any further developments before the end of the programme and moved on to another item. Don't they ever read the bloody papers, Ryle wondered.

What the hell, he decided, he might as well go into Leinster House too. He was not due into the office for a couple of hours and he had to phone Stacy first anyway. There was no point going in too early, while they were still preoccupied with this garbage. Better wait until the bubble had burst and they were desperate again for a real story.

He stopped to buy the morning papers and scanned the others. They had all played safe with predictable lead stories under equally predictable 'day of decision' headlines. His paper was the only one to declare that the Government would survive.

He showed his pass to the usher at the gate of Leinster House and noticed the crowd gathered around the main entrance. Television arc lights lit up the shadowed front of the building and he could see cameras held high but not who they were aimed at. The tight knot around the door loosened as he approached and a couple of people came towards him. A running photographer slipped on the ice and fell heavily with his camera held safely aloft.

Ryle felt a twinge of nervous uncertainty: there was a bit too much excitement in the air for an anti-climax. He saw Whelan emerge from the side of the crowd and a couple of people followed him but he shook them off with a wave of his bowed head. Ryle veered towards him, anxious to tell him about Erlanger's flit and that Maurice Clark had probably killed himself.

The words dissolved away unspoken: Whelan was as grey as the trodden snow and looked as if he was in shock.

'What is it?' Ryle asked. 'What's happened?'

Whelan glanced up at the urgency in his voice. His eyes seemed to have receded further into his head and his face was drawn tight. He stared at Ryle.

'What's happened?' Ryle demanded.

'An election,' Whelan said hoarsely. 'There's an election.'

Ryle's mind raced in confusion. 'What?' he shouted.

'He's called an election.' Whelan sounded distant, as if he was talking about something far removed from himself.

'You changed your mind,' Ryle accused him angrily. His paper's lead story flashed before his mind in a sickening reminder of what they had written. Oh Jesus.

Whelan shook his head and took a deep breath. 'We had a roll-call vote and every single person said yes, we all support the Government. Then he just announced he was going to the Park to ask the President to dissolve the Dáil.'

'Shit!' Ryle gave vent to his feeling of personal betrayal. 'What did he do that for? He'd have won the fucking vote.'

'He didn't say. He just wished us luck and left.'

But it doesn't make any sense, Ryle thought, trying to force back the unpalatable reality with impotent logic. He stared blankly at the photographers and broadcasters accosting more people emerging from the building. They had broken up into groups now that the first wave of excitement had flowed over.

'The letter,' Whelan sighed. 'He's sent it.'

Ryle swung his stare back, he had almost forgotten Whelan was there. What letter? What's he talking about, he thought irritably, more concerned with his own problems.

'I'm finished,' Whelan said flatly.

Jesus, the letter, Ryle remembered, snapping out of his self-pity. The letter from the Taoiseach telling Whelan's constituency chairman not to re-nominate him as the party's candidate. 'But why?'

'In the interests of party discipline,' Whelan recited like a refrain, a refrain that was already cut indelibly into his psyche.

'Can't you appeal or something?' Ryle searched his dead eyes.

Whelan shook his head. There was no appeal. He'd pleaded with the party secretary who'd given him the message. The Taoiseach was adamant, the secretary said, in the interests of party discipline. There could be no reprieve, no leniency, no exceptions for people who broke ranks. In the interests of party discipline. He was being sacrificed, a lesson to everyone else.

'I'm finished,' he gave a helpless shrug and wandered over to his car.

Ryle felt he should say something, offer sympathy perhaps. He went to follow him but nothing adequate came to mind and he turned back towards the building again. Poor fucker, he thought. At least I've still got a hell of a good story.

Whelan sat with his hands on the steering wheel, staring ahead with unseeing eyes. Finished, his mind said in a numb repetition. Finished. Two of his party colleagues passed by, their faces flushed, voices high with excitement, and averted their gazes.

The corridors were still seething. Politicians, secretaries, ushers and reporters dashed about, merged into instant groups to exchange animated comments and dissolved again. 'Is there a press conference?' a harassed reporter shouted to Ryle. Two opposing politicians clapped each other on the back like team members at the end rather than the beginning of a game.

Tommy Lyster came down a narrow corridor at the head of a tight wedge of other barrel-shaped men, their faces fired by fierce grins. Ryle was forced back against the wall out of their way and Lyster bared his teeth and gave an animal-like grunt. 'You'll get all the answers you want now, boy,' he roared as he passed. One of his backers shoved an elbow hard against him. Ryle gasped.

'Pity about your seat,' Lyster smirked to an Opposition deputy who had also stepped aside. 'Sure you're all right for the pension, anyway.'

Lyster's supporters guffawed and were gone. 'Bastards.' The Opposition deputy squinted after them and looked at Ryle without seeing him. 'We'll see about that.'

In the cramped press gallery the adrenalin was crackling between the walls like static electricity. 'Three o'clock,' someone shouted, 'press conference at three.' Another voice replied, 'That's not definite.' Ryle pushed his way through a loose crush to a free phone.

'Hold on,' Stacy snapped and Ryle heard him argue with somebody about getting a reporter up to the President's residence in Phoenix Park. 'Can you get up to the Park quick?' Stacy demanded.

'No, I . . . '

'I hope you've got a copy of today's lead in front of you,' Stacy snarled.

'Now hold on,' Ryle bristled, determined that he was not going to accept any blame. 'My information was right. Whelan climbed down. The story was right.'

'Who gives a fuck about the story? Read the intro.'

Ryle didn't need to: he could still see it as clearly as a bad dream with its confident pronouncement that the threat of an early election had disappeared last night with the decision of Jim Whelan to support the government in today's vote.

'You wrote it, not me,' Ryle sighed but Stacy was talking to someone else again.

'Where are you?' The news editor returned.

'Leinster House.'

'Any interviews?'

'No, I just happened to be passing.' Ryle's sarcasm was lost on Stacy who was now on another phone telling someone to forget what he was at and get back to the news room. Ryle felt tired again; his leisurely breakfast in Erlanger's house already seemed as distant as an event in a previous life.

'Listen to me for a minute,' he pleaded when Stacy came back. 'I've got a great story. Erlanger's skipped the country and I've got enough to do a long piece on the whole saga. A great tale of . . . '

'Finance is doing that,' Stacy butted in impatiently.

Ryle wasn't sure for a moment if Stacy was talking to him or had gone off on another tangent. 'What?' he said to be sure.

'Aren't you listening to me? I said finance is doing all that stuff.'

'What the fuck have they got to do with it?' Ryle's voice climbed into a wail of protest and anger. Nobody around him paid any attention.

Stacy dropped the receiver yet again and Ryle waited with growing agitation. What the hell was he talking about? He didn't seem to have understood. Around him reporters were dictating stories to evening papers, agencies and radio stations. Words like 'snap', 'shock', 'surprise' and 'stunned' were hurled down phones like so many echoes. Ryle was too preoccupied to notice.

'Finance is doing that,' Stacy repeated. 'There's been a run on Atlantis shares and the stock exchange has suspended trading. It's turned into a financial scandal.'

Ryle did not know what to say. 'Anything you've got on Erlanger, pass it on to them,' Stacy added in a distracted tone.

'Like fuck I will,' Ryle howled. 'This is my story and I'm going to do it. It's not a financial story. He's a CIA man and the cops have fucked the whole thing up and Clark . . . '

'I don't have time for all that now,' Stacy interrupted.

'I want to write this story, finish the thing off.'

'It's finished. We're into a whole new situation, we're into an election campaign.'

'Jesus, the world doesn't stop because of that.'

'No, but everything starts from here. The rest is history.'

'Are you telling me not to write this?'

Stacy sighed and finally gave him his undivided attention. 'Look, you've done a good job. And we'll run a piece tomorrow about how we, how you, broke the whole neutrality business and the Atlantis shares scandal and the whole lead up to the election. But you need a break. Go home, come back refreshed on Monday and I'll slot you into the election team.'

'Stuff the election team.'

'Listen,' Stacy said patiently. 'You've gone over the top on this story, run yourself into the ground. I told you last night you need a break. Take it. We'll tidy up the bits and pieces.'

'There's more than a few bits and pieces,' Ryle began but Stacy had left the receiver down on his desk again. Ryle looked around the room wearily as he waited. Most of the others had finished filing their stories or had handed over to colleagues with more batches of quotes. All were busy.

Except me, he thought bitterly. I've got a great story and nobody wants to know. He looked at his watch; a couple of minutes after noon. He wondered what to do. Go down to the news room and argue it out with Stacy and get thrown into the election hysteria. Or go back out to Erlanger's, see if Grifford was still there and free for lunch. And talk some more about the story.

He hung on, hearing the frenzy of the news room from a long way off, and his anger faded slowly. Deep down, he knew Stacy was probably right. The election had changed everything. The story had moved away. And you had to move with it or get left behind. That was part of the price you paid for the illusion journalism gave you of being close to events.

He'd got as near to the bottom of the Clark mystery as anybody could have. As near as anyone ever would. And at the heart of it was another mystery about Erlanger. But nobody would ever tie up all the loose ends. That was the nature of these things. More bits and pieces might emerge about Clark, about his life, which was, to Ryle, every bit as mysterious as how he had ended up the way he did. But the story was as dead as Clark himself and no more relevant to tomorrow's news. It would settle down into a minor footnote, the known facts wrapped into a smooth re-telling to prove whatever point the teller wanted.

The room was beginning to empty. Through the phone he could still hear the distant sounds of the frantic news room, the ringing phones and snatches of fevered conversations. Eventually a louder voice asked if anyone was using this phone. Ryle said nothing and he heard the receiver being picked up and dropped onto its cradle. The line went dead.

They were going to run a story saying he had caused all this. Which wasn't really true. He knew that but they didn't and he'd end up with a moment of glory halfway down page five. But he'd only scratched the surface.

He walked down corridors which were settling back into their placid routine. The hysteria had dissipated like a tidal wave that has swept by, leaving those behind in stagnant pools analysing its impact. He felt washed up, a piece of flotsam thrown aside by the onrush of events.

He had wanted to get stuck into a story, revive his journalistic career. And he had done it, had enjoyed every minute of the pursuit, the exhilaration of piecing together something that someone else didn't want you to know, the notoriety among his colleagues, the sense of forcing events, the illusion of power. But he had got in too deep, sacrificed everything to getting the story and left no room for real life. He had moved beyond the point of no return with Breda and Lorraine. His tentative relationship with Rosie was inextricably bound up with the story and just as dead. He had nothing to hold on to. He had pinned too much on too little.

Ryle went out into the remaining sunshine, his hands jammed into the pockets of his jacket, and walked slowly down a narrow path cleared in the snow. Outside the gate, he turned left onto Kildare Street but stopped after a few yards as the realisation sank in. He stared at a poster by the gate of the National Museum advertising an exhibition of ancient artifacts but without actually seeing it.

He had nothing to do. Nowhere to go.

Twenty-three

The man stepped out onto the iron balcony and gazed out over the masts of the marina and the harbour to the sea beyond. The morning sun had not yet burned away the light fog which turned opaque in the distance. The air was cool but there was a promise of warmth to come.

He tightened the cord of his dressing-gown and turned his attention to the promenade, waiting for the woman to appear. When she came she had her head lowered over the newspaper. He watched her turn in towards the hotel and willed her to look up. She went on reading.

When she entered the room he said, 'That must be interesting.' She said nothing but handed him the *International Herald Tribune* and he recognised the faint frown of worry around her eyes. He told her the coffee was fresh and nodded towards the tray on the bedside table.

The paper was folded at the story he wanted and he read the compacted agency report without haste. Ireland's Prime Minister accused unidentified foreign agencies of 'tampering' with his country's military neutrality at the launch of his re-election campaign Wednesday, it began.

'They think you're an Intelligence agent.' She sipped her coffee at his elbow.

'Good,' he smiled.

'Is it?' She looked doubtful.

'Sure it is.'

'What about the real agents? They won't be so pleased.'

'They've got more to worry about than the paranoia of some two-bit politician.' He went on reading.

'They've called in Interpol,' she added.

'Going through the motions.' He folded the paper, stuffed it into his pocket and turned to face her. 'Don't go jumpy on me now.' He looked at her calmly. 'There's nothing to worry about.'

'I hope you're right.' She still looked troubled.

'Forget about it,' he said quietly. 'It's over.'

'I don't think I have your nerve,' she said. 'For this way of life.'

'Next thing you'll want to get married,' he joked. 'In a church.'

'And what name will we use this time?' she said tightly, finishing her coffee and taking the cup inside. He looked thoughtfully after her for a moment, then rested his palms on the railing and gazed out to sea again.

'It says his death was an accident,' she said when she came back, as if that were a consolation.

'They're very deferential towards the dead,' he shrugged. 'Don't like admitting suicides. Some religious reasons, I guess.'

'I don't understand why he did it.'

'Maybe we pushed him too hard.' He sounded uninterested and she shivered slightly. He glanced at her. 'But he left us no option. Remember that. He chose to play it like that. We just beat him at his own game.'

She did not say anything and he put his hands on her shoulders, lightly but firmly. 'He brought it on himself. We didn't make him kill himself.' He shook his head sadly. 'I hate blackmail. It's so crude.'

She looked into his eyes, switching her serious gaze from one to the other as if she was comparing their colours. He recognised her gesture but did not understand her concern.

'Listen,' he said quietly. 'He was a cheap blackmailer. You and I know that. Whatever other people think. My one regret,' he sighed, 'apart from the money, is that I couldn't expose him for what he really was.'

She turned away and he watched her and told himself she'd get over it, it was a hangover from the tension of the last few days. He looked out along her line of vision and imagined he could see the fog lightening on the milky sea.

'It's an amazing little country,' he said with a touch of nostalgia. 'So calm on the surface and seething underneath. Like a pool of piranhas. Cast a crumb on the water and they start tearing each other apart. I was beginning to enjoy it. Once I got to know my way around the undercurrents.'

She shivered again and he suggested they go in.

'Can't we go a little further south?' she pleaded.

'Sure.' He put an arm around her shoulder and led her inside. 'We'll get to the sun.'